After some indeterminate period of time—maybe a half hour, maybe more—the throbbing beat of the ancient wheezebox downstairs thumped-ran down to a stop.

Without that heartbeat, the expectant hush inside the red-painted building turned painful.

When Lara pushed herself up on her sharp-starved elbows, stealing back into her body bit by bit from the faraway place where not much could hurt her, the first rounds took out two of the watchtowers, splashing concrete, broken glass, slivers of red-hot metal, and rags of guardflesh down into Suicide Alley along the electrified fence.

The Federals—and Swann's Riders—had arrived.

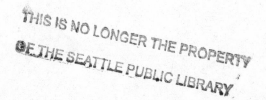

By Lilith Saintcrow

Cormorant Run

GALLOW AND RAGGED

Trailer Park Fae

Roadside Magic

Wasteland King

BANNON AND CLARE

The Iron Wyrm Affair

The Red Plague Affair

The Ripper Affair

DANTE VALENTINE NOVELS

Working for the Devil

Dead Man Rising

The Devil's Right Hand

Saint City Sinners

To Hell and Back

Dante Valentine (omnibus)

JILL KISMET NOVELS

Night Shift

Hunter's Prayer

Redemption Alley

Flesh Circus

Heaven's Spite

Angel Town

Jill Kismet (omnibus)

ROMANCES OF ARQUITAINE

The Hedgewitch Queen

The Bandit King

AFTERWAR

LILITH SAINTCROW

www.orbitbooks.net

Copyright © 2018 by Lilith Saintcrow
Excerpt from *84K* copyright © 2018 by Claire North
Excerpt from *Cormorant Run* copyright © 2017 by Lilith Saintcrow

Author photograph by Daron Gildrow
Cover design by Lauren Panepinto
Cover illustration by Kirbi Fagan
Cover copyright © 2018 by Hachette Book Group, Inc.

Orbit
Hachette Book Group
1290 Avenue of the Americas
New York, NY 10104
orbitbooks.net

First Edition: May 2018

Orbit is an imprint of Hachette Book Group.
The Orbit name and logo are trademarks of Little, Brown Book Group Limited.

The publisher is not responsible for websites (or their content) that are not owned by the publisher.

The Hachette Speakers Bureau provides a wide range of authors for speaking events. To find out more, go to www.hachettespeakersbureau.com or call (866) 376-6591.

Library of Congress Cataloging-in-Publication Data

Names: Saintcrow, Lilith, author.
Title: Afterwar / Lilith Saintcrow.
Description: First edition. | New York : Orbit, 2018.
Identifiers: LCCN 2017044125| ISBN 9780316558242 (softcover) | ISBN 9780316558273 (ebook (open))
Subjects: LCSH: Regression (Civilization)—Fiction. | Genetic engineering—Fiction. | BISAC: FICTION / Science Fiction / Adventure. | FICTION / Science Fiction / Space Opera. | FICTION / Alternative History. | GSAFD: Science fiction. | Dystopias.
Classification: LCC PS3619.A3984 A69 2018 | DDC 813/.6—dc23
LC record available at https://lccn.loc.gov/2017044125

ISBNs: 978-0-316-55824-2 (trade paperback), 978-0-316-55827-3 (ebook)

Printed in the United States of America

LSC-C

10 9 8 7 6 5 4 3 2 1

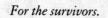

For the survivors.

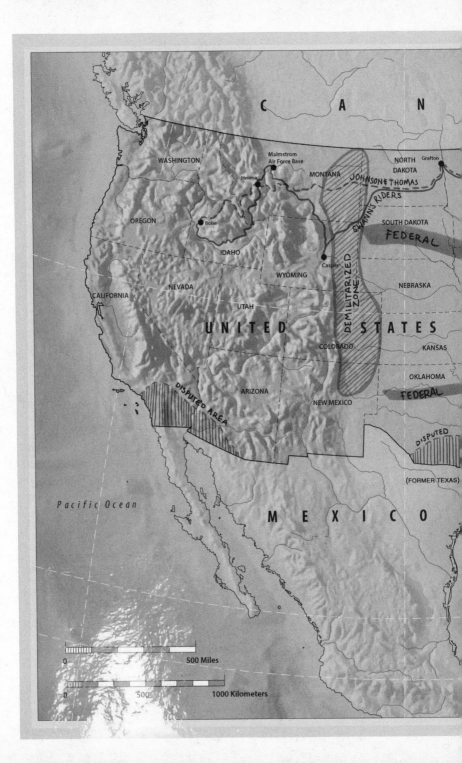

...solitudinem faciunt, pacem appellant.

—Tacitus

PART ONE

DIES IRAE

CHAPTER ONE

DETAILS LATER

February 21, '98

The last day in hell ran with cold, stinking rain. A gunmetal-gray sky opened up its sluices, mortars and bigger artillery shook the wooded horizon-hills at 0900, and roll call in the central plaza—down to two thousand scarecrows and change, the dregs of Reklamation Kamp Gloria—took only two and a half hours. Pale smears peered from the red-painted kamp brothel windows, disappearing whenever the Kommandant's oil-slick head and unsettling light blue gaze turned in their direction. Stolid and heavy in his natty black uniform, Kommandant Major General Porter stood on a heavy platform; the raw edges of its boards, once pale and sticky with sap, were now the same shade as the lowering sky. The skeletons in dun, once-orange dungarees stood unsteadily under a triple pounding—first the Kommandant's words crackling over the PA, then the thick curtains of rain, and last the rolling thunder in the hills.

Not just partisans, some whispered, their lips unmoving. Convicts and kampogs learned quickly how to pass along bites of news or speculation, despite the contact regulations—worth a flogging if you were caught talking, a worse flogging if more than two kampogs were "gathering."

Nope, not just partisans. Federals.

Feral rumors, breeding swiftly, ran between the thin-walled Quonsets, bobbing over the reeking, sucking mud like balls of ignes fatui down in the swampy work sites, drifting into the empty stone rectangle of the quarry, flashing like sparks off the sicksticks the uniforms and jar captains carried. Raiders, Federals, knights riding dragons—who cared? Hope wasn't a substitute for a scrap of moldy potato or a filched, crumbling cube of protein paste.

On the second floor of the joyhouse, in a room with dingy pinkish walls, cheap thin viscose curtains twitched a little, and the narrow bed underneath them shuddered as he finished. The bedspread had been freshly laundered, and the white, sharp smell of harsh soap and dead electrical heat from the industrial dryers filled Lara's empty skull. It was a darkness full of small things—a glimpse of the dusty silk flowers in the tiny vase on the nightstand, a twinge from her discarded body, the burn of slick soylon fabric against her cheek, the indistinct mutter of the PA as Kommandant Porter, the God of Gloria, spoke. Someone would later tell her the Kommandant, his hair swept back and his mirror-shined boots splattered with that thick, gluey mud, had made a speech about how the shivering pogs had paid their debt to society and were to be taken to a Re-Edukation Kamp. Porter audibly hoped they would remember the struggle and sacrifice the uniforms had suffered to remake them—brown immies, any-color degenerates, white politicals since the brown ones were shot, traitors all—into productive members of the Great United States of America First.

It didn't matter. Nothing mattered then but getting through the next sixty seconds. Lara heard all sorts of details later, without meaning to. Right now, though, she lay flattened and breathless under the weight on her back, life and hope and air squeezed out.

"I love you," the Kaptain whispered in her left ear, hot sour breath against her dark hair. It had grown back, first in the sorting shed and now here, though the ends were brittle and fraying. She was lucky to be in the pink room; the plywood stalls downstairs could see as many as six, seven an hour between first roll call at 0500 to midnight, no breaks, no lunch. Up here in the rooms named for colors, though, there were special clients. A special diet too, more calories than the average kampog, especially a twenty-niner, could dream of. Exemption from even "light" labor in the sorting sheds.

Some of the uniformed guards, or the jar kaptains—the highest class of kampog, because why force a uniform to work in the stinking jar-barracks, where you lay three or four to a shelf-bed—brought "presents." Tiny containers of scent, either liquid or paste, not enough to get drunk on. Lipstick—it was edible, more welcome than the damn cologne. They often brought food, the best present of all. Cigarettes to trade. Some of the girls here drank the colorless, eye-watering liquor the uniforms were rationed, instead of trading it away for more substantial calories.

It let you forget, and that was worth a great deal. A few minutes of release from the tension was so seductive. The poison dulled you, though, and dull didn't last long here. Soaking in bathtub booze was a good way to drown.

"I love you," the Kaptain repeated, the hiss of a zipper closing under his words. The mattress had finished its song of joyless stabbing, and it barely indented under her slight, lonely weight. "I've organized a car, and gas. A good coat. I'll come back and get you." He bent over to arrange her, pushing her shoulder so she had to move, wanting her to look at him.

Rolled over on her back, Lara gazed at the ceiling, the damp trickle between her legs aching only a little. More raw lumber. Paint was a luxury—the red on the brothel's outside was left over from something else. The only other painted building was the Kommandant's House on the outskirts, with its white clapboard walls and picket fence. Lara had even seen the high-haired, floral-dressed wife once or twice, sitting on the porch with a glossy magazine back when the war was going well. Some kampogs used to work in the house or the garden, but that stopped when the siege of Denver was broken. Even the Kommandant's family had to go back to the cities, retreating eastward.

The Kaptain was blond, his bloodshot blue eyes showing his worry over the war. He was her special client, and his status meant she didn't have others. Black wool uniform with the special red piping, the silver Patriot Akademy ring on his left third finger mimicking a wedding band, the back and sides of his head shaved but the top longer. He'd begun growing it out a little while ago.

When the war turned.

He examined her while he buttoned his outer jacket, settling his cuffs, made sure he was zipped up completely. A hurried visit, for him. How many hours had she spent in this room, blessedly alone, and how many with him talking at her, unloading his worries, his thoughts, words dripping over every surface, trying to work their way in? Most of her energy went toward being impervious, locked up inside her skull. Building and maintaining walls for the steel bearings rolling inside her, so their noise could drown out everything else.

"I'll be right back." The Kaptain bent over the bed again, and his lips pressed against her cheek. There was almost no pad of fatty tissue over her teeth—still strong, they hadn't rotted out yet. Childhood fluoride had done her a good turn, and with McCall's crew there had been pine needles. Berries. Ration bars with orange flavor and minerals all in one nasty, grainy mouthful.

She was lucky, really, and how fucked-up was it that she knew? The question was a waste of energy. Here, you couldn't afford to ask. Every effort was channeled into one thing only.

Survival.

"I love you," he whispered yet again. Maybe he needed to convince himself, after all this time. His breath made a scorch circle, a red-hot iron pressed against shrinking flesh. Branded, like the Christian Courts were so fond of decreeing. *B* for "bandit" or *P* for "partisan," or the ever-popular *A* for "scarlet woman," because "adulterer" could possibly be the man, and you couldn't blame *him*.

The Kaptain slammed the door on his way out. Yelled something down the hall—an order, maybe. Quick, hard bootsteps, scurrying back and forth. Looked like he was clearing the top floor. The girls up here might be grateful for the respite, unless they were waiting for a special to bring them something. If they were, they'd assume Lara had pissed the Kaptain off somehow, or something. They didn't quite dare to band together against her—it wasn't worth the risk—but the top-floor joyhouse girls were pariahs even among kampogs, and she was a pariah even among *them*.

Exclusivity, like luck, was suspect.

I'll take care of you, he'd promised. *Wait for me.* Like she had any sort of choice. So Lara just lay there until he went away, his presence leaching slowly out of the small, overdone, dark little room. Nobody wanted bright lights in a joyhouse. A lot of the specials may have even honestly believed the girls in here were glad to see them, glad to be somehow saved.

As if anyone here didn't know it only took one wrong move, one glance, or even nothing at all, and into the killing bottles you went.

It didn't matter. She drifted, letting her ears fill with the high weird cotton-wool sound that meant she was *outside* her skin. Just turned a few inches, so she could look at whatever was happening to her body without feeling.

After some indeterminate period of time—maybe a half hour, maybe more—the throbbing beat of the ancient wheezebox downstairs thumped-ran down to a stop. Without that heartbeat, the expectant hush inside the red-painted building turned painful.

When Lara pushed herself up on her sharp-starved elbows, stealing back into her body bit by bit from the faraway place where not much could hurt her, the first rounds took out two of the watchtowers, splashing concrete, broken glass, slivers of red-hot metal, and rags of guardflesh down into Suicide Alley along the electrified fence.

The Federals—and Swann's Riders—had arrived.

CHAPTER TWO

REGRET

It took longer than Adjutant Kommandant Kaptain Eugene Thomas liked to finish his arrangements for a retreat, mostly because Kommandant Major General Porter, unwilling to delegate *or* make a goddamn decision, kept Thomas for a good half hour, going on about paperwork. Maybe Porter never thought the Federals would have the unmitigated gall to actually interfere with his little slice of republic cleansing, or maybe the old man had cracked under the pressure. He was certainly sweating enough. There were dark patches under the kommandant's arms, sopping wet, and his flushed forehead was an oil slick under the crap melting out of his dyed-black hair.

At last, though, Gene saluted and was released with a packet of "sensitive documents" to take east, flimsies and digital keys rustling and clacking inside a tan leather pouch. The stairs outside Porter's office were choked with guards, but no officers—Gene's fellow shoulderstraps would know better than to possibly be sent on some bullshit detail while the degenerates were already so close. If Gene hadn't been such a believer in prudently covering his own ass at all times, he would have already collected her from the pink room and would be speeding past the gate in a shiny black kerro, watching the girl's face as she opened the box and the fur coat, vital and black and soft as a cloud, rippled under her chewed fingertips. Even her habit of nibbling at her nails was enchanting.

She'd be grateful for the coat and the escape—she would *have* to be. He'd finally see her smile.

The Kaptain accepted the salutes of the black-clad guards still unfortunate enough to be on duty with a single, frosty nod as he passed, keeping his step firm and unhurried in shining, scraped-clean boots. The ancient yellow lino in the hall of the admin building squeaked a little under his soles; there were no kampogs in striped headscarves or faded dungarees working at streaks of tracked-in mud with their inadequate brushes. One or two of the guards enjoyed smearing the worst filth they could find down the hall and kicking pogs while they scrambled to clean it, but Porter frowned on that.

The smell alone was unhealthy. Just because the pogs lived in shit didn't mean the soldiers, being a higher class of creature, should get it on their toes.

Soldiers. Gene's upper lip twitched as he lengthened his stride. As if any of these assholes had ever seen *real* combat. Kamps were supposed to be cushy jobs, good chances for advancement once your loyalty and capacity were proven. An endpoint like this meant hazard pay and extra alcohol rations, both useful things. So what if combat troops looked down on them, or if his fellow shoulderstraps were a collection of paper pushers and rear-echelon weekend warriors? *He* was probably the only true patriot in the lot.

A thumping impact made the entire admin building shudder just as he reached the side door, and he took the stairs outside two at a time. Mortars. At the *fence*. The degenerates weren't in the hills anymore. They were moving fast, just like the hordes descending upon Rome back in the day. That rather changed things—he had to get back to the joyhouse and collect the girl—

Another *wump*. Something smashed past the fence, and a high whistling drone screeched across Gloria before the admin building shuddered again, hit from the opposite side. There was an instant of heat in Gene's left calf, a flash of annoyance as the world forgot what it was supposed to do and heaved underneath him. Then the world turned over like an egg flipped on a griddle, and after a weightless moment he hit gravel with a crunch. It was a minor wound, all things considered, but the guard he'd paid and left with strict orders to watch the kerro dragged his superior to the now-dusty, low-slung black vehicle. Before Gene could shake the ringing from his ears, he'd been tossed in the back like a sack of processed starch lumps, and the guard—a weedy, pimple-faced youth who had less than twelve hours to live, though neither of them knew it yet—was already accelerating on the wide macadamized road out of Gloria.

Instead of watching the girl with her wide, empty eyes and pretty cupid's-bow mouth and full underlip, Gene had to work shrapnel free of his own leg and grind his teeth, improvising a pressure bandage as the kerro bumped and jolted. The wheelless vehicle wasn't meant for gliding at high speed, its undercells humming and sparking as chips of pressed rock jolted free under the repeller field.

Driving that way would have gotten the kid a reprimand two weeks ago. Now, though, Gene just dug under the seat for a bottle of amber Scotch—the good stuff, imported, he'd been looking forward to seeing her reaction when he produced it—and didn't bother to glance out the back bubble, wasting a bit of the stinging, expensive liquid to disinfect the cut.

One small Rome had fallen, but the rest of the empire would endure. Or at least, Kaptain Thomas hoped it would. He settled in the cushioned back seat, easing his wounded leg, and took a healthy hit from the bottle.

If he drank enough, he might even be able to forget her—and the pink room—for a little while.

CHAPTER THREE

LAST BLOODY HOURS

It was the third camp they'd...what was the word?

Found? Bombed? Liberated?

Each was worse than the last. At least by this time both raiders and regular infantry knew mostly what to expect, and CentCom was moving up supplies—electrolyte drinks, gruel, medics with clean needles, sanitation engineers. The filth was indescribable, and the skeletal campogs could perforate their tissue-thin stomach walls gorging on ready rations. You could kill just by performing the oldest of human kindnesses, sharing your calories.

The shitholes were *all* bad, even the showplace camps closer to the more densely populated sectors. But Reklamation Kamp Gloria, lost in swampy pinewoods, was...Christ. It was the first Reklamation site, the one where the Central Federal Army found the bath bays, their glassy sides holding deep, shimmering caustic unfluid capable of swallowing flesh, bones, even tooth enamel when a mild electrical current was passed through. That current did double duty, shocking those who tried to cling to the sides, too. If a victim managed by some freak of fate or chance to hang on to a simulacrum of consciousness in the killing bottle, the chute poured them dazed and convulsing into the bays, and they were eaten away in short order. The side products—saponified fat, traces of gold or other valuable metals and minerals from bones, the magchips in left arms, or old-style fillings—were skimmed off and shipped away.

The Quonsets were emptier than at the last camps they'd come across, because Gloria, sunk in the marshland, wasn't really a work site. Though it had a quarry and workshops, the rail spur only led *in*; the side products were trucked out in boxes. Literally and figuratively, Gloria was the end of the line.

The Army InfoSecs managed to capture about 60 percent of the records before the digital worms could finish their work. The black-jacket, red-piped Patriot administrators and officers were gone, probably got away right as the Federals arrived. All the Special Group motherfuckers, the hardcore Patriot believers in the Leader and the Flag, were long gone too, probably because the advance had finally sped up since Swann's Riders knew the terrain. And fuck if it wasn't that asshole General Leavy who busted the *other* asshole General Specter, who wouldn't fucking listen to the raiders because they were outside the chain of command.

With Leavy in charge things started to steamroller, what with a raider or two in every damn company telling them what to look out for and how to avoid getting their asses blown off by booby trap, guerrilla action, or rear guards grown brutal after four years of Insurrection Kontrol.

Chuck Dogg, a helmet clamped over his 'fro, was the first of Swann's through the gates, tagging along with the army grunts hopping to secure the damn place. Chuck was, in fact, with the platoon that found the goddamn bath bays, and sometimes Zampana said he was never really right again after that. He just stood for a while, watching the harsh overhead lighting ripple on the placid, green-glowing surface. It was him and Hank Simmons—Simmons the Reaper, that big blond bootstrap bastard—who rounded up what they could of the uniformed fuckers captured in Gloria's corners and tossed six of them in the bays before they were stopped. It took Swann himself, striding in with his boots almost striking sparks and that goddamn vermin-ridden hat clamped firmly on his shaved head, to get the Dogg to stand down.

Raiders believed in eye for eye, tooth for tooth. You had to, running behind the lines and sabotaging installations or gathering intel. CentCom called them "irregulars," and the Firsters called them "partisans" or "traitors," but they were *raiders*, and the name meant vengeance.

It also meant no quarter.

The InfoSec squad got an eyeful of the prisoner rolls, and one of them grabbed Simmons—who was almost skunkfucking drunk by then, but still ambulatory through some freak of his big old Norwegian constitution—as smoky dusk hung over the swamp, to tell him there had been twenty-eight raiders sent to the camp. Easy to tell who had been a raider: they were the prisoners with a thick band of lase scar tissue across the left wrist, which meant they had to be magtatted instead of chipped.

There was no use wasting a chip on an enemy of the state.

Twenty-six of the raider prisoners had gone right to the baths upon arrival. One died right after liberation, his emaciated body found in the mud of the central plaza, where he'd fallen in the middle of the Kommandant's speech and hadn't been hauled away yet by his jar fellows.

The last remaining raider prisoner was in the two-story building slapped with blistering red paint, transferred there after a stint in the sorting shed where the belongings of each prisoner who hadn't already been processed through another camp were searched, stacked, fumigated, baled for transport, and taken back into the heartland to be distributed to America First party members.

No name and no citizen file, which meant she hadn't broken under any torture and given them any information that would find her in the old gov databases. Just a half-wormed prisoner number—QIP-x834xx16x— and a single note in the locator field: *Remanded to Joy Duty rm 6, Kpt E. Thomas.*

Joy Duty. That was what they called the brothel.

When Simmons found Room Six at the end of the second-floor hall, he also found a hollow-cheeked, painfully thin but not skeletal prisoner— they had better rations in the red house, just like the prisoners forced to work the bath bays did—in a paper-thin viscose slip, sitting primly on a pink soylon bedspread and staring vacantly at the wall. The pink dress she was supposed to wear to match the room had been torn into strips, and she stared at the Reaper for ten very long seconds. Some of the dress's pink soylon was wrapped around her bloody right fist, a rough and non-absorbent but very capable bandage.

Below, some of the brothel's inhabitants were screaming at random intervals. They couldn't help it—they would stop in the middle of drinking or shell-shocked wandering and begin to shake, and a long cry would ribbon up and out, accumulated terror whistling through vocal cracks. The sound of smashing glass from the bar, which had supplied the uniforms and some of the more favored jar captains, had just petered out; even drinking to blackout didn't stop the random cries of the newly liberated.

A couple MPs at the door earned a lot of heat for keeping even the frontline officers out of the red building, but orders were direct, thorough, repeated, and unequivocal from General Leavy, who might have been an asshole but was not a man who thought troops deserved a little fun whenever or wherever there were cunts—especially brutalized ones—hanging out to dry.

How Simmons got past the MPs was a mystery even to him. Maybe because he was a raider, and they weren't known for rape. Or maybe because he was too drunk to even contemplate getting his pecker swabbed, which was, even for that blond bastard, very drunk *indeed*.

Simmons blear-blinked, trying very hard to focus, his rifle poking over his shoulder and his breath enough to kill a cactus at fifteen paces. He took in the room, the faded silk flowers in a tiny scrap-glass vase on the nightstand, the sliver of mirror over a washbasin—even that sliver was splintered; someone had driven a fist into it, to judge from the bloody mark in the middle of the breakage. She stared at him, the dark-haired woman in the cheap slip, and even through the liquor he saw glaring bruises on her skinny arms. Around her ankles, too.

Her pupils shrank a little, her dark eyes focused, and she coughed, a painful, racking sound. "Lara Nelson," she said, in a cracked, reedy whisper. "Senior medic, Third Band, McCall's Harpies."

Big, pale-headed Simmons stood there, filling up the door, and tried to think of a reply. Any reply.

"Lara Nelson," she repeated. "Medic. Third Band. McCall's Harpies.

Captured March twenty-second." Her face crumpled slightly, smoothed. "Year…ninety…ninety-six?"

Simmons finally found his voice. "It's '98. At ease, soldier." It came out crisp instead of slurred. Even a raider couldn't drink enough to get away from the fucking war. You could pour down engine degreaser until you went blind, it didn't fucking matter.

"Ninety…" Her chin worked a little, her mouth trying to open, closing, turning into a thin line. Simmons watched it, and of all the situations in the goddamn Second Civil, he would later say that was the second worst. *Here's this girl, and she's been…Christ, man. They even had kids in that goddamn house, we found an eleven-year-old boy from Indiana in the stalls downstairs, and here this girl was, repeating "McCall's Harpies. McCall's Harpies." And I couldn't fucking tell her McCall was dead at fucking Memphis.*

Memphis, that graveyard of raiders. Of *course* she knew McCall was dead; she'd been captured during the ill-fated uprising. The one the Federals were supposed to push in and relieve the pressure on, supposed to coordinate with. The one they hadn't helped a tit's worth with, because cooperating with irregulars wasn't part of CentCom's strategy back in '96.

Simmons ended up taking off his rancid camo field jacket—a veteran of both the Casper and Third Cheyenne battles, where Swann's Riders had run supplies for the Federals and bloodied themselves taking out rails and quite a few bunkers—and wrapping it around her shoulders. He picked her up—she weighed less than his kid brother—and carried her out of the red house, straight to Swann.

Who didn't want to fucking *debrief* her, and double didn't want any more goddamn problems…but he poured himself another shot of colorless engine cleaner, downed it, and told Dogg to get the new medic some fucking clothes and whatever kit could be scrounged. There were bales of civilian clothes in the sorting shed, but the girl refused to go in there, so it was Zampana who eyeballed her sizes and went in with Dogg, both of them nauseous at the sheer amount of clothing. Plenty of it had been shipped from other camps to be sorted and packaged here, but still, it was hard to look at all the jackets, shirts, skirts, jeans, and the small mountain of unsorted shoes and not see the bodies tumbling from the gas-filled killing bottles into the placid-looking, caustic bays.

The front elements left Gloria the next morning in a stinking rain that would swell the rivers and make the next set of engagements miserable slogs through sucking mud that sometimes swallowed shells or mortars whole. Swann's folk left too, and the new medic went with them, big-eyed and clutching two first aid kits Dogg had managed to find. The raiders also drew extra ration bars and stole cans of condensed calories from the camp supplies to soak the bars in, and Zampana got her hands on a Firster sidearm for the medic, too.

For a Christer, Zampana was all-fucking-right.

The frontliners were supposed to leave all prisoners in Gloria for critical care, processing, and medivac, but goddamn if Swann's crew was going to abandon another raider in that fucking place. It was probably a mercy, since the second-wave troops weren't kept on as tight a leash as Leavy's boys, as witnessed in DC later that summer.

That was how Lara Nelson, later christened Spooky, joined Swann's Riders in the last bloody hours of America's Second Civil War.

CHAPTER FOUR

GOOD FOLK

Lara woke with a jolt as the hybrid kerro-petroleum truck bounced over something a little too high, the undercarriage scraping, and dropped onto pavement at last. Her hands tried to fly up, ready to protect her head. She was wedged so tightly in a breathing, rattling dark, she thought she was in the jar barracks again, or, God forbid, in a closed cattle car shuttling between kamps. It smelled in here, but not of shit and death. No, instead it was kerro fumes, the oily dry dirtsmell of soldiers, and someone who had found a can of beans somewhere and taken them down a little too fast, with the end result escaping air perfumed by gut flora and fauna.

Across from her, someone else was awake. It was a tall 'fro-headed raider, a lean ebon-black man with grenades hanging across his chest. "Here." He rummaged in his pack as the truck smack-bumped over potholes. "You was at Memphis?"

Lara nodded. She dredged his name out of memory—Chuck. He was Chuck. The big blond man sleeping among the boots on the truck bed—Simmons—was snoring almost loud enough to drown the engine noise; Lara was packed between a squat Hispanic woman with a black kerchief neckband on one side and a skinny, cornrowed first sergeant on the other. The sergeant, her eyes half closed, moved her lips as if she was praying; the Hispanic woman was almost asleep herself and doing the same. Christers, both of them, but one was a raider and the other was a Federal, and that was safe enough. Lara hadn't missed how these two bracketed her so she wouldn't have to squeeze against a man inside the truck's deep, malodorous dark.

It was a damn sight better than the railway car to Gloria, that was for sure. Still, the jolting motion was uncomfortably familiar.

Chuck found what he was digging for. The whites of his eyes gleamed; he proffered something small and fabric wrapped, jamming his boot toe against Simmons's beefy shoulder to brace himself as he leaned across the middle space.

The blond man's snoring didn't even pause.

Chuck's package was a celluloid box of old-fashioned smokes wrapped in a black bandanna, and Lara regarded his hand for a moment, her gaze stuttering to his face to gauge the cost of this gift.

"I got plenty," Chuck said. "And you're one of Swann's now. The guy in the stupid hat, he's our kaptain."

Good enough. Lara accepted it, and her quick, bony fingers took care of folding the bandanna. It wasn't too fresh, but it was cleaner than her hair, and when she knotted it around her head like a kampog her throat threatened to close up completely. Her stomach was warm, a tiny fist clutched tight around a lump of ration crumbles, and even though she was ravenous, the Hispanic woman—Zampana—had her on strict, small amounts.

Lara didn't mind. The last thing she needed was the running shits while they were on the advance, or any other gut problems.

Slow and steady, chica, was Zampana's advice as she patted Lara's skinny shoulder gently. *You with us now.* And oh, God, wasn't that good to hear.

She coughed twice before she could speak, nodding to show she understood. "Swann." Shaven headed and smelling like a distillery, the kaptain was up front with the driver. That hat of his was a weird, furry bundle that had maybe once been wool; it was impossible to tell what shape it had been. A bedraggled red feather depended from its striped approximation of a band, and it looked like the kaptain slept in it. For all that, Swann's eyes were bright and direct, and his crew were good folk.

When you were a raider, *good folk* could mean anything from "knows their ass from a hole in the ground" to "won't give you up if the Firsters come knocking."

Both were rare, and the overlapping space in the middle even rarer.

"Yes ma'am." Chuck nodded. "You was with McCall, right? Harpies? You know a kid named DeShawn?"

Lara turned the smokes over. It was a half-full pack of Camels, stuffed with nicotine, not the new smokes they called candies. Old-school, old-fashioned, good enough to buy a week's worth of food if you had a contact on the kitchen staff. You would have to be careful not to let your contact get greedy, ration them out by ones and have a good place to hide the balance. Everything that could be stolen would be, unless you were smart, fast, and vicious.

Regular criminals got the kitchen and sorting sheds, the light labor. The twenty-niners—resisters, deniers, and partisans, politicals by default—could barely dream of such easy positions. It was hard labor for *them*, and summary judgments—a few grams of lead, as the saying went, right in the back of the neck. Jar kaptains, responsible for keeping their entire barracks in check, were "regular" criminals too. They ended up brutal if they hadn't been before, effective, and terrified of losing their privileges.

There'd been one good jar-kee in Gloria, and he'd been shot for it.

For the first month at Gloria, Lara had been on rock detail, until the day she almost made a break for the electrified fence. She'd straightened, dropping her wheelbarrow handles, and maybe she would have made the run if the black-jacketed Kaptain hadn't been passing, in his high-shine boots and red-piped uniform, staring at her while her head filled up with colorless fumes. A couple hours later she'd been shoved through the warehouse doors and told to find something to wear before getting to work.

Sorting Duty meant you could filch trade items from the possessions of pogs going straight into the baths. It was a plum position, one politicals couldn't aspire to, and she hadn't really understood her luck until two weeks afterward when the Joy Duty kombers came to fetch her. Those two weeks had been a nightmare of fearing someone would find out she was a political and send her back to the death hole of the quarry, or she'd be bottled and dumped in the baths…

It took a few moments to wrench herself back to the present, and the man across from her. He'd asked her a question. *DeShawn.*

"Last name?" Her throat was dry; she had to scrape the words out.

"Williams." His mouth set itself, sculpted lips thinning as his nostrils flared. Bracing himself for the worst.

There was a lot of worst going around.

She nodded, finding the face in memory. Thin Willie, they'd called him. "He was Second Band," she croaked, trying to enunciate over the noise. Lara tapped at her left shoulder, almost crushing the carton of smokes in her fist. "Missing front right tooth. Had a star here." Where the hot tag had been taken out of his shoulder when he escaped from the plantation in Florida. Those star-shaped scars were a death sentence if you were caught in Firster territory, either by summary or by remand to the nearest plantation for a hanging, if you were lucky.

The unlucky were put on shit details and worked to death, after forty lashes.

Lara watched Chuck's face go through relief into unwilling hope, and settle itself near expecting the worst again. The man's rifle, poking up between his knees, was a good place for him to rest his hands, and by the set of his knuckles, he was squeezing like he wished he had a Firster throat in his palms.

"That's him." Chuck didn't ask anything else.

You learned not to. You learned to just wait.

She shook her head. Her skull was full of emptiness, a high drilling buzz, and the bandanna made her invisible again, just another kampog. "Alive last I saw. Two weeks before Memphis when Second Band peeled off to get into position." Another two weeks of feverish activity, running messages, scavenging for supplies; Forster and Goggles taken the day before the attack; the sick thump in her stomach when the Firsters found her medical station. The screams of the wounded, the Firsters going bed to bed putting a bullet in the head of everyone incapable of walking.

A doctor was supposed to protect her patients.

Chuck absorbed the news. There was nothing else she could say. The chances of Thin Willie still being alive were…not good. The squat, spit-frothing screamer initially in charge of the Memphis prisoners had made it clear what anyone who didn't Put America First could expect from his henchmen. Partisans were the lowest form of traitors, worse even than violators of the Clean Blood Act.

What was that screamer's name? Galb, that was it—she'd glimpsed his breast tag. That bastard was on her list. Whenever she thought about a time after the war, if she didn't end up in a shallow grave or a bath bay, she went over the list and thought of what she would do to each of them.

Every single one.

Lara leaned forward, gingerly offering the smokes back. Chuck shook his head. His own black bandanna was knotted around his temples and looked far too tight to be comfortable.

"Keep 'em," he said.

Lara held still for a little bit, in case he changed his mind. Finally, though, she settled back, her hips wedged firmly against the seat. She watched Chuck's face, his eyelids drifting down to half-mast, until the fact that she had really left Gloria began to sink in and she fell into the deathly half doze that passed for sleep in the kamps.

When the truck stopped, she wanted to be ready.

CHAPTER FIVE

TOTAL WAR

March 30, '98

A chilly early-spring evening starred itself with blares of bright white, the spotlights stabbing skyward in defiance of any electricity rationing. Antique helicopters and the newer cell-bottomed sleds burred and buzzed overhead, the crowd raising their fists each time the throbbing mechanical heartbeat crested. On the steps of the Lincoln Memorial—the abolitionist's statue inside draped with sackcloth and ritually spat at during schoolchild visits—the lectern was empty, but ranged on either side were the luminaries. There were the generals at the bottom of the stairs, in black uniforms except for Kallbrunner, who wore the old blues. Nobody paid much attention to him, anyway; the Marines were a faded branch, dishonored by the Parris Island Plot in '93 and superseded by the Patriots. Kallbrunner was a frail, broken scarecrow, generally under house arrest but dusted off and brought out for the occasion.

Which meant something special was going to happen.

The huge LED screens, on gleeson cells like the sleds, floated serenely before the pillars. They rose slightly and sank in increments as loudspeakers blared "The Star-Spangled Banner" over and over, its hum a constant reminder. Each time it began again, the crowd would dutifully tense, and each time the chorus swelled, their voices rose with it.

When it cut off abruptly and the beginning bars of "America First" rose, brassy and full of electric guitar shred, the crowd pushed forward against phalanxes of black-clad Patriots with their tricorne dress hats. The Patriots faced the People, just like at every rally, but the other floating screens at the back of the crowd made sure they didn't miss a single image, a single movement of the damp, mobile mouth of First President Mc-Coombs.

But where was the great man? The first verse finished and the second began, everyone doing their best to remember the words. Just mouthing it wasn't acceptable—it was too easy for a seagull-size T-drone humming by to capture your expression or the fact that your vocal profile was missing. The drones could also see if your right arm, fist raised high in the Amer-ica First Salute the historians and traitors had never liked, wavered too much.

You could be fined for insufficient patriotism, if you were lucky. If you were unlucky, well, the kamps still had room.

They *always* had room.

The second chorus, with its bloody imagery and jerky, impatient rhymes, ended. It was not at all usual for the great man to make his crowd wait this long, but there were disturbing rumors about the war. Maybe that was what this rally was about? Nobody really knew—only that it was, as usual, obligatory to attend.

The bridge blared from the speakers, then a swelling roar went through the crowd, front to back. The screens blipped, darkened, and the live feed came up, zooming in on a familiar, heavy-jowled face, its cheeks apricot from dermaspray, with goggle-circles—bright white above, puffy and bruise-colored below—around small, dark, glowing eyes. His thick black hair gleamed as he pursed his shiny lips, and the generals ranged behind him all politely clapped.

Except Kallbrunner. The old man stood straight and stick-thin, his thumbs precisely arranged at his trouser seams.

On the steps below the lectern, facing outward, stood the glittering court. Platinum-dyed Mrs. McCoombs, her broad corn-fed Kansas face set with Botox, her cat-slanted eyes heavily ringed with brown liner, smiled vacuously. McCoombs's sleek dark-haired daughter Vanessa, trim in a Young Patriot uniform since she was that organization's titular head, smiled blankly. Instead of her vanished, rumored-to-be-a-globalist husband Jack, Swastika Stevie the Secretary of State stood next to her, round and rumpled with pitted cheeks, his cold-coffee gaze moving in predatory arcs over the backs of the black uniforms, rarely rising to take in the crowd packed on either side of the long, rippling reflecting pool. There was the porky head of the Patriots and the New Justice Department, squeezed into an acre of black broadcloth and gleaming medals, shifting from one overloaded, black-booted foot to the other. The powerful used to be grouped alongside McCoombs when he spoke, but since the battle of Second Cheyenne, they were relegated to a space not quite spectator but definitely not shared.

"Amerika!" McCoombs raised his arms, his small hands spread wide. The famous pinkie ring with its pink diamond glittered sharply, and his wedding band on the other hand squeezed its host finger unmercifully. *"Amerika, can you hear me?"*

The crowd heard. Baying, they waved their right hands furiously overhead. Any sign of less than total excitement would be logged. The small silver oblong drones zipped and zagged in an algorithmic pattern, meant to catch the most raw data for facial-recognition-and-analysis feeds.

Even now, the great man said, some people didn't believe in Amerika, best of all countries. There were people who doubted Amerika would win the war, people who doubted how huge and great Amerika would be. A nasal weight filled the words. The bobbing tone, added to the habit of putting a fruity weight on any vowel—especially an *ooh* sound—turned it into classic leaderspeak. At least, that's what the pundits had named it back before the Press Responsibility Initiative had made it worth a spell in a reedukation kamp to do so.

The actor who had played McCoombs in several comedy skits late at night during the Last Election had disappeared first.

Even now, McCoombs said, licking his lips between words, the Federal degenerates were committing atrocities in the West, slaughtering Patriots. The traitors and their immie bastards were fighting dirty against the Firster armies, and McCoombs had to do something he didn't want to. He wanted to ask them first, though, because he was *their* President.

A hysterical cry rippled through the crowd. The Patriots stood stone-faced, arms linked to make them a human fence, chests proudly forward. "U-S-A!" the citizens chanted. "U-S-A! U-S-A!"

McCoombs let the frenzy rise, smiling in his peculiar way, his eyes almost lost under his eyebrows and his cheeks bunching at the top. When he'd had enough, he raised his hands, a gentle, fatherly motion, and his glare-pale palms quieted them. When the noise had died somewhat, he leaned into the microphone, gripping both sides of the simple wooden lectern he affected to favor, with its huge round shield—the Stars and Bars the liberals had tried to steal, with a stooping eagle over it—glinting on lase-etched metal.

He told them what he wanted, and they erupted. Screaming, spittle flying, they didn't even notice the drones had retreated to a safe distance, scanning with bouncers instead of risking delicate lenses in the crush and press of a mob. Seen from above, rosettes of violence bloomed—shoving matches, jostling, a ring of anger around an unlucky, too-brown face that could possibly have been an immie spy or sympathizer. The sirens wouldn't start until later, when the crowd spread out across DC and the nightly news leapt from one city to another, blatting over loudspeakers, televisions in every home flicking to the state channel or turning on as the override signal was broadcast.

There would be no more Federal prisoners taken. The entire economy, at last, was to be geared for war. There was to be no quarter given to immies, to sympathizers, to Federals, to anyone who lifted a *finger* against God's greatest nation.

Kallbrunner the Marine, his hands tense at his sides, gazed over the bobbing heads and raised fists. He did not move, and his mouth was a thin line as the generals around him chanted with the crowd. The leader of Amerika First, the president of a shrinking number of semi-united states, nodded along.

Boots stamping, fists flying, somehow the crowd also found time to weep and to chant, over and over, the two words McCoombs had poured, almost lovingly, into his microphone.

"Total war. Total war. TOTAL WAR."

A week and a half later, DC was bombed for the first time.

CHAPTER SIX

INCOMING

April 12, '98

"Incoming!"

The first mortar hit came over the pine-clad ridge—a local counterattack, maybe, or some jackshit diehard Firster commanding officer deciding to go out with a bang. The raiders hit the ground first, as usual, because you were either quick to eat dirt or you died, running behind the lines. Shrapnel whickered, peppering the canopy, and more mortars pop-thumped.

Zampana yelled for backup, but Lara was already running toward her, bent double and scurrying between explosions of turf on either side. No helmet, not even a hat since her bandanna was knotted around her left arm now, just her filthy dark curly hair flopping as she dove for Pana, who was ministering to a couple regular grunts. One of them was gurgling on his own blood, a hand clapped to his throat—the shrapnel had sliced clean through both carotid internal and external on that side, and antiseptic foam didn't do shit with spraying wounds. Welling, sure, all right, but spraying dispersed the proteins too damn quick. Chunks of white vertebrae showed in the wound, cervicals sheared and shattered, adding to the whole mess.

Lara snatched a knotted blue do-rag from the grunt's beefy arm, doubled it, and slapped it over the wound, pushing on the other side of the throat as well while she glanced at the second injured asshole. Her scrawny, dirty fingers clamped with surprising strength, and the first man's consciousness would flee quickly; there was no saving him. The second grunt only had a splinter of flung metal through his lower leg; Zampana already had it removed and the antiseptic foam setting. Heavy black braids crisscrossing over Pana's head were dewed with blood; sweat grimed her forehead. She nodded when her gaze met Lara's.

Black card. Dead where he fell, goddammit. Get his tag.

No words were needed. Raiders knew what death looked like, and Lara had already done what she could to make it painless. More explosions. Someone was screaming for their mother, a high-pitched cry mixing with the blood and the shit and the massive noises. In a few moments that *other* smell would roll through the thicket of young pines and damp, smoke-belching firs, a brassy reek you couldn't pin down, but you knew if you'd spent any time on the front lines. Death delivered en masse, maybe souls exuding a compound as they left all at once.

It was always the same, whenever the dying started. Mama and that smell, death and Mommy.

Lara snapped the bottom third of the Category 1's—combat casualty, already gone, don't bother—tag off, her fingertips slipping in blood. Zampana made one of her Christer signs, supposed to help a person leave the body or something, but Lara just pointed with two fingers at the leg wound and then at their six, toward the rear. *Get him to the med station. I'll go up.* In another moment she was gone, not waiting for Zampana's nod, dodging through smoke and ground-shattering impacts, heading for another cry of "Medic! Medic!"

Light support had already been called in. The shimmer-shaking of armored sleds, drifting on their gleeson cells and pushing aside treetops, filled bones and back teeth with a weird whining; you had to keep your mouth partly open so the change in pressure didn't fuck up your eardrums, just like the artillery jungoes on their own slippery, straining, jury-rigged gleesons.

Plazma shots flashed through rising smoke. The sleds began to toss cannos onto the other side of the ridge, using the canopy as a screen, shells locking onto heat signatures and biometric nags. The familiar crisscross popping of the cannos rose, and Lara skidded on her knees into a shallow declivity holding another small squad. Their sarge had taken a hit—mushroom cartridge, a chunk torn out of his left side, but it didn't smell like the bowel was cut. Lara's right hand plunged into her mud-crusted bag, her left peeling back uniform and pushing aside the man's canteen, probably nothing drinkable left in there. Two of the squad were one-knee, rifles up as they covered both sides; their comms man was screaming into his handset; small-arms fire popped and pocked around them. A fallen tree, wet from the rains and sending up foul-smelling steam from a shell hit, sheltered most of them, and Lara's head turtled between her shoulders as she found the soyplas tube she wanted by feel and tore its top edge off with her teeth. This motherfucker was lucky—blood stippled his paper-white face, she got the ragged edges of what could have been a nasty gut wound together, smearing the plasco-norpirene as it filled in, crackle-dried, and shrank. You needed a light touch to get plasco to cover everything without bunching up.

*"Sonuva*bitch!" the sarge howled, but Lara already had the pop-pack of antibiotic in her left hand and smacked it over the wound with just enough force to get it to seal and discharge, but not enough to rupture the edges of the plasco bandage. The man howled and thrashed against the grunt holding his arms—it must have hurt like a bitch, especially since they were short on painkillers—and sagged, his face going pale gray, a weird smoky tint under his stubble.

Shock. So she grabbed his map bag strap and got a good handful of his ammo rope too, hauled him up, glanced at the scared, big-eyed Federal Army kid pinioning his commanding officer's arms, and slapped the sarge briskly, twice.

That brought him back, and the plasco-norpirene finished setting, turning milky white. She already had her last trauma tag out and was scribbling on it with a grease pencil filched from a med station two days ago. "You!" She pointed at the kid holding him down. "Get him back to the aid station!"

That meant the striper on her left was squad command now. She glanced at *that* big piece of Federal muscle, who jerked his chin at the

kid and began to curse the few men who were now his problem back together. When the sleds stopped pouring on the cannos, it would be these
guys sweeping the wreckage over the ridgetop, and if there was anything
resembling resistance, well, she'd deal with those casualties when they
happened. Right now her job was to keep moving, patching up whoever
could be returned to the firing line or dragged back to the aid station.

Firing on the left. More mortars and cannos landing, throwing up
plumes of dirt, shrapnel singing and slicing. There were no longer separate
incidents, just flashes—bloody, unshaven faces; another squad commander
with her lower half blown off, still trying to push herself upright, not understanding she was done. Broken legs, a dislocated shoulder Lara set with
a quick crunching sound, a swallow of burning-icy liquor from a corporal's flask while they cowered in another shell hole, the world shaking and
shuddering and throwing up clods of dirt all around them. Screaming for
mother or sweetheart or God knew who, the wet gray slithering of intestines and the sudden word passed down the comm channels that *there
are goddamn mines, get those fucking engineers strapped in now!*

Through the smoke she glimpsed a familiar shape—a flicker of a bald,
egg-pale head usually covered by a rancid, battered hat. She dove for
cover inside a moss-grown, abandoned concrete culvert, coming to rest
right next to Swann's lanky length. The raider captain's eyes were half
closed; he plugged his other ear as he listened through his comm handset.
He spared Lara a single nod. She realized her entire right side was a bar
of pain and her lungs were full of heaviness. Her breath came in heaves,
and she was, as usual, mildly surprised *she* wasn't bleeding, too.

Going up the interstate would have been easier instead of slogging
through the bands of wastewood, but the Firsters had sleds too. Not
nearly as many as the Federals, though. The goddamn Patriots were running out of all sorts of things. DC was still sieged, but plenty of the
Northeast had just been waiting to get rid of the Firsters and were taking
to the streets now that there looked like a chance of the Federals reaching
the Atlantic somewhere, anywhere. Most of the grunts rolled their eyes
and said, *Once we take DC we can leave the fucking South alone. Build that
fucking wall the Firsters was always on about.*

They had a point.

Swann bellowed into his handset again; Lara laced her fingers over her head and crouched, pressing her back against the culvert's damp wall. Her too-big boots sloshed in sulfur-smelling groundwater, she ached all over, and her clothes could probably stand up without her in them.

Nobody in range was screaming *medic*. And since she'd happened across Swann alone, she had to stay attached to him just in case. Simmons and Zampana were out on the field, Chuck Dogg was back at CP, the rest of them were attached to different companies, and the explosions around them reached a crescendo.

Lara shut her eyes.

Then, all of a sudden, the artillery stopped, replaced by *pop*s and *ping*s of rifles. Swann was still yelling into the handset, giving coordinates and cussing out whoever was on the other end for good measure. It was Prinky, the lazy-lidded, foul-mouthed, sniper-sharp motherfucker, and Swann was swearing because redheaded Prink had just told him it wasn't a local counterattack but a whole mess of trouble up over the damn ridge.

Swann's piercing hazel gaze rested on Lara, just the way it would have on a chair or a gun or a table. She peered through her lashes every few seconds, checking to see if he had an order for her, but each time he just shook his head slightly, his stubbled jaw set and his hat looking even sorrier than usual because it had been shot right off his damn head in the ruckus, clamped back on once the shelling quit. He was a lucky-ass fucker, and liked to say Napoleon would have made him a general.

That little French fuck liked lucky bastards, and you're looking at one.

"All right, you sonofabitch. Look for me on the other fucking side." He toggled the chopswitch and let out a long breath; Lara let go of her head and rocked on her haunches a little. He stuffed the waterproof map back into its case, clamped his hat more firmly on his shaven head, and nodded at her. "Get your iron out, medic. We're going over the top."

Well, that's not so bad. She nodded, chin dipping sharply, and her hand found the sidearm Zampana had stolen for her. There was no shortage of clips, not since they'd found the ammo dump. The Firsters, pulling back in a hurry, hadn't even wired it to blow, though there had been one or two hairy moments in the barn, the engineers freezing and anyone with any sense doing the same. It wasn't until after that particular engagement that the booby traps started to get serious, the engineers requisitioning raider sweepers to pool experience once the shooting stopped. It was a far cry from Federals turning their noses up at irregulars, that was for damn sure. And medics were always welcome.

Right now, though, the hill had to be taken. Lara was raider first and medic a distant second.

"We got 'em on the run now," Swann said, more prayer than fact. But he whistled, a short sharp note, and all she had to do was keep up with him as they bolted, both hunched even though the mortars and cannos had stopped, up the slope.

CHAPTER SEVEN

SKINNY-ASS IMPOSSIBLE

April 15, '98

There were still bodies on the gallows, swaying gently under a smoke-choked breeze. "Jesus Christ," Simmons said, rubbing a hand over his stiff blond buzz cut. "How do they have anyone left, they keep this shit up?"

"Indoctrination." Zampana's broad face, set with disgust, had turned ashen. "No birth control." Her hands were fists, skinned knuckles glaring. "Incentivize that Quiverfull shit."

"That was rhetorical, Pana." But Chuck said it quietly. You never wanted to fuck up another raider's way of coping, and Zampana's was to lecture. She was the one who had remarked that morning that it was tax day, at least on the Federal side of the line.

Charred, shattered wooden frames marched side by side down a long, dusty central street. The roll-call square was packed dirt, and the entire place smelled like sap and roasted pork. Along the south edge of the camp, just outside an electrified fence, was a long hand-dug trench, the dirt mound over it exhaling an evil stench of gasoline and rot. You'd think after Gloria few soldiers would ever be nauseous again, but you'd be wrong. Even the older grunts were tossing their cookies on this one. By unspoken agreement, you went back to the truck when you needed a few minutes to get the smell out of your nose. Even the diesel fume in the back of an un-altered or hybrid truck was better than the aroma of…cooking meat.

It smelled just like a cookout.

The new medic stood with her head down, rocking back on her heels every once in a while as Swann gazed at the only unburned structure. Painted white and standing prissily apart from the shattered barracks, the administration building even had boxes holding leafy green plants under its largely unbroken windows. A bristling cellular tower jutted from its roof, and its front door was thrown open. Charlie Company's Bravo squad had just cleared it, with Prink in their midst checking for booby traps. The worms were already running inside the ancient mainframe this camp held, and the data recovery boys from CentCom were a few hours behind the leading edge. There would be precious little way of figuring out who had died here unless some of the other kamps in this one's network could be captured with data intact.

Prink was doing his best to slow the worms down, but it was a thankless task with the old, overworked laptop he'd managed to scrounge. The thing didn't even have a thumbprint port, for God's sake.

A hastily painted sign leaned against the gallows. TRAITORS, it shouted in large white block letters. One of the hanging bodies wore a Patriot's winter uniform, black wool, red-and-white piping. The faces weren't too swollen yet—winter still had its grip on the Missouri pinewoods. The guard's small, hard potbelly looked pregnant next to the skin-and-bones rags of prisoners in their tattered orange coveralls. One of the prisoners was hooded. The other two stared, dead gazes moving across the roll-call square somberly, with all the time in the world.

So many of the dead lay with their eyes open. They couldn't look away either.

Lara's head jerked up. What little color had come back into her thin cheeks drained away. She staggered sideways and elbowed Swann hard enough a *huff* escaped his lungs. "What the fu—" he began, but she took off, pelting toward the white clapboard house.

"*Get out!*" she yelled. "*Get out now! NOW!*"

She hit the front steps—painted green, muddied by the platoon's tracking back and forth—with a clatter of her scavenged, too-big boots, and threw herself inside.

Simmons had dropped to one knee, his rifle tracking; Zampana's sidearm was out; and most of Charlie Company began cussing and scrambling, grabbing weapons and looking for the cause of the disturbance.

Not eight seconds later, Prink catapulted out of the house and flew off the front steps, landing so hard he almost lost a tooth in the dusty gravel. Behind him came the new medic, and while she was airborne there was a breathless *wump* as a timed shell tucked in a rusting file cabinet moored in the damp cellar—there were two inches of standing water down there, and the cabinet had looked unassuming enough—exploded.

Lara landed on redheaded Prinky, glass shattering and wood turning to deadly splinters where it hadn't vaporized. The shock wave rolled over both of them, pushed the hanging bodies into fresh, gentle motion. The gallows creaked and moaned, but didn't break—quality construction. The gallows' steps were mined too, as Prinky found later when his ears had stopped ringing.

Simmons was the first there, grabbing the back of the medic's too-big camo coat and picking her up just like a suitcase. Zampana, hard on his heels, got Prinky by his belt and, truth be told, a handful of his hair, since he wouldn't cut the coppery mop, and hauled him back toward the truck, his heels cutting long furrows in gravel and dust.

Miraculously, neither of them were dead, just temporarily deafened. Charlie Company's captain, Brian Crunche—his real actual no-foolin' name—escaped a Swann-size bollocking only because Prinky was already swearing at himself up one side and down the other for assuming the rusted file cabinet wasn't backtrapped and just checking its front. Wisely, everyone else kept their mouths shut except to congratulate him on his escape, and to ask if the new medic was okay.

I still ain't sure what happened, Prinky told Swann that night, once they'd made it back to the temporary base at the edge of the scar cut in the pinewoods. There was even a shower courtesy of the antique, underfunded Parks and Rec Division and a highway ribboning through, a rest stop plus parking lot of Great Historical Interest. Now, of course, it was full of Federals in canvas camo and a few more of Swann's Riders—Sal the Greek, Lazy Eye, and Minjae had been attached to Thirtieth Battalion and were glad as fuck to see their own folk again. *Allasudden she comes in, grabs me by my scruff—how can a skinny-ass girl like that pick me up and throw me? It ain't natural.*

Swann merely grunted and clapped him on the shoulder, telling Prinky he was a lucky fuck and that he'd seen all sorts of skinny asses do the impossible under fire. And when Lara showed up damp from the cold showers, shivering but much cleaner, space was made for her at the Riders' fire pit. Zampana handed her a hot MRE, and Prinky, still rubbing at his ears, asked her for a smoke.

She gave him a battered Camel, from another pack scrounged somewhere by Chuck Dogg.

"Thanks, Spooky Girl," Prink said, and the name stuck.

CHAPTER EIGHT

LIGHT IT UP

The advance bogged down after that, a thaw coming in and softening the ground. Mud, mud, more mud, and nobody complained when CentCom held them static for a while. They dug in where the glop wasn't too bad, fortified what they could of the park's buildings, and avoided what they took to calling "the burning camp" unless they absolutely had to patrol it. The persistent grumbling of artillery to the south- and northeast, accompanied by flashes, was just loud enough to remind you to be grateful you'd been pulled back, and sorry for the poor sonsabitches who were up to their asses in mud, blood, and shells now. There was even mail for the Federals, and the news that Villarosa had taken Waco and hung that bastard Governor Gabranch was greeted with cheers and the breaking out of much engine degreaser. Nobody liked losing chunks of Texas to Mexico, but given what the Lone Star State had inflicted on the rest of America, there were some who called it justice. Besides, nobody needed the oil much anymore. Kerros and gleeson tech had taken care of it, and some said McCoombs's first mistake was deciding he could middle-finger the petro lobby in the middle of the war.

They may have been dying dinosaurs, but they were dying, well-connected, *rich* dinosaurs.

It took a war to get people to care about the goddamn news, Swann remarked sourly, but nobody paid much attention. It was the raiders who went out on recon, slogging through the sludge and finding nothing but deer, feral dogs, porcupines, and two more mass graves, each a mile and a half from the still-smoking prison camp.

Not a single one of Swann's complained, because it was left to the Federals to haul the bodies out of the torched barracks and bury them properly, not to mention dealing with the other stinking, bubbling pits. The corpses on the gallows were cut down, buried, and spoken over after the mines were disabled.

Except for the guard. That black-clad body they left swinging. Even the crows and buzzards wouldn't touch *that* motherfucker.

Sal the Greek, squat and handsome, even figured out a way to jury-rig some heat, so the showers in the cement-walled rest stop were tepid instead of freezing. If the Federals weren't glad of Swann's crew before, they were now, and even more so when Chuck and Minjae brought back a gutted deer or two. Fifth Medical showed up with the mail, and when they left, Lara and Zampana both had full medic kits instead of just odds and ends.

Captain Crunche got orders the day after Fifth Medical left. "Son of a *bitch*," he said, wrinkling his long Gallic nose. He looked perpetually sleepless, rings under his muddy brown eyes and his mouth bitter even while he smiled. "They're pushing on DC." The command tent, its sides open to get air to move through and dry everything out, made a flapping, disconsolate noise. "But we don't get none of that."

Swann scratched under his hat band, accepting the scrap of hotpaper. "It's the river for us, then. Fan-fucking-tastic."

"At least we can get *across* Ole Miss." Lieutenant Azer, her blonde buzzcut glinting in the sun through the tent flap, didn't sound like that was a reason for optimism. "Tell me we're getting our battery back."

"They're already on the bank, waiting for our happy asses." Crunche, if it was possible, sounded even more doleful.

"I hate the fucking South." Swann glared at the hotpaper before passing it to Azer, who read it with her eyebrows drawn together, her scraped knuckles a little swollen. She'd just broken up a fight between two squads that morning, an altercation fueled by too much hot-still booze and not enough work to keep the men busy. Everyone was getting antsy, even those with enough sense to be happy for the rest and semirelaxation.

Crunche rolled his head and his shoulders, dispelling a persistent ache. "Yeah, well. You get three guesses where we're going after the Miss."

A silence full of rustling and the faraway groan of artillery brimmed over. Azer crumpled the hotpaper, closing it in her fist. Body heat would activate the rest of the coating; sweat would help turn it into an unintelligible mess of paper fibers. You could tell an experienced officer by what they did with flimsies. There were stories of some noncoms who ate the particularly sensitive ones.

Needless to say, the result was often constipation. But really, that was a perennial risk, and motherfuckers with a few stripes or straps were likely to be cranky even if they escaped such a fate.

Crunche was really a decent sort. "It's Memphis," he said finally, scratching alongside his blurred, bulbous nose. "I understand if your folk don't want to."

Swann appeared to think this over. His thumbs hooked in his belt, his eyes narrowed, and his right boot pressing its toe into the ground just a little, then easing up, he stared at the map table and the comms bench beyond it. An oscillating pattern on the secondary screen showed there was no incoming, and the hunched back of the comms operator was bisected by the line of a map bag that probably held a photograph or two of loved ones. The operator, her shoulders curved forward and the headphones giving her giant ears, couldn't hear a damn thing.

Still…

"Memphis," Swann said heavily. His chin dipped a little, and the brim of that verminous hat of his flopped a little in the freshening breeze. "Be a pleasure to see that sonofabitchin' place shot to shit."

"Well, we're gonna light it up." Azer had no respect for a sentimental moment, which was why she was Crunche's second-in-command. "We head out at 0500 tomorrow."

Swann actually unbent enough to clap Crunche on the shoulder, a light, glancing blow that nonetheless left a two-week bruise on the good captain's deltoid. "Memphis or bust," he said, and furthermore snapped

Crunche a salute before turning on his heel and striding away. At least he waited until he was a good ten paces from the tent to bellow for Zampana, which made everyone in the damn bivouac pretty much guess something was afoot and their rest behind the lines was goddamn well over.

CHAPTER NINE

TIGHTJAW

April 14, '98

Kaptain Gene Thomas shoved his back against crumbling oily dirt, his breathing hard and fast, his ribs aching. They wouldn't stop coming. The degenerates now had sleds, gleesons for their heavy armaments, and working supply lines. A horde of soulless animals busily chewing at the legs of what used to be America. Time and again, orders came down to hold "at all costs" and to make a "last stand" that would throw the enemy back. Which was just about as possible as stopping a tornado in its tracks, or changing the path of a hurricane.

The screaming hordes had *supplies*. They had an abundance of weaponry and support. It wasn't like Gloria, where they knew their place, firmly under the boot. Someone had made a mistake, had not crushed the snake of rebellion when the West seceded six months after the Last Election. Now the tide was past the West Virginia border. Rumors flew from shell-hole to cover about what they did when they caught Patriots, or even just regular citizens in good standing.

"Bastards," the soldier next to Gene said. "Fucking immie bastards."

There was no quivering kampog to shine Gene's boots, and the rations were, in a word, complete shit. Cannos began to pop over on the right flank, and the soldiers hunched, as if a hole in the mud and a heavy helmet could save you. Gene's belly griped from the tan water that passed for coffee and the sawdust crumbs they called biscuits. Somewhere behind the lines, some motherfucker was organizing himself a nice cozy nest with real coffee and actual bread, of course, and if they'd been able to halt for any amount of time Gene could have done some arranging of his own. Instead, he'd been pressed into a scratch company after the kerro broke down and the jug-eared orderly vanished into a heavy ground fog peppered with booms and flashes. Anyone in a uniform was expected to fight, and his rifle had been wrested from the still-warm corpse of a double im—an immigrant impressed into military service, used for mine clearing.

The double ims were supposed to get secondary citizen status, *after* the war; Gene shuddered at the thought. It was probably a gentle misdirection to get them to fight, since immies were crafty, cowardly little bastards.

His silver ring was tucked in his boot and if things went badly, he'd have to ditch it. He'd even have to pretend he was only a low-ranking soldier. There was no Federal mercy for officers, less for Patriots.

On the bright side, if somehow they managed to beat back the hordes and make the homeland safe again, he could claim he'd been on fire with real patriotism, burning to join up with the military instead of cooling his heels in a kamp, and parlay that into a good position afterward. The bright side was better than the likely, but at least he was still able to think ahead. Plan. Survive.

For the moment.

Sometimes, between the rumbling of artillery and the pops and pings of smaller fire, he wondered how *she* was faring. The degenerates had probably swept through the camp, raping everything they could find. The thought sent a fierce, scorching hatred through him, and each time it did he gripped his rifle afresh, determined to kill at least *some* of them.

It could have been so perfect. He'd been organizing at Gloria, quietly since Kommandant Porter was a diehard Three Percenter and the rules were very strict. A few careful bribes, one or two files electronically burned, and he could have arranged to take the girl somewhere, ideally the moment his transfer came through. It had been very close—an office job, a pretty, compliant, utterly grateful wife who knew her damn place, and a reasonably lavish lifestyle.

Then the degenerates started winning at First Cheyenne and the Dakotas Offensive, the transfer freeze went through, and all his plans were knocked awry. Perhaps he should have simply left her there and transferred out, but where would he find another woman with the right looks and the kamp habit of compliance? A partisan past just meant she'd been led astray, as women often were.

Besides, he didn't want another one. Access, in this case, did not breed contempt.

The artillery quieted. Gene squinted over the top of the shallow hole scratched in oily Virginia mud, eyeing a line of woods probably very much as his distant great-great-more-greats-granddaddy—a bona fide certified First Civil War veteran, registered and everything—had a long time ago. Waiting for the Yankees had turned into waiting for the immies and degenerates. Different century, same fucking thing.

Gene squeezed his rifle, lifted it, and exhaled sharply. Each one he killed should have been for America, first, last, and always. Instead, they would be for *her*, because the thought of even one of those filthy brutes touching the skin he had fondled, sticking himself in that purity, owning that little piece of warmth Gene had reserved solely for himself…

Shapes in the fog. Whistles blew urgently. "Stay down, stay down!" Admonitions not to waste ammo. The soldier next to Gene grinned, both of his top front teeth knocked out and the hole bloody from tight-jaw gnashing. "Jus' let 'em get close enough," the young man said. "Jus' let 'em."

Gene braced himself. The shadows grew clearer, more definite.

He couldn't imagine dying, but he knew very well how to kill.

✳

CHAPTER TEN

PAINT

May 1, '98

Chuck dipped his fingers into the tin bowl. They came out smeared with thick, oily, vivid red. "Fuckin' Memphis, man." He pushed Sal the Greek's helmet strap back a bit, and drew his fingers along Sal's cheekbone. The paint smeared, caught on stubble, and stuck. Sal, his mouth slack and his eyes half closed under a shelf of oily black curls, just stared straight ahead. What he was thinking of, nobody could tell, except maybe Swann.

Sal had been with the bald man from the beginning, or at least, longer than anyone else. Even Pana.

"You were there." Lazy Eye, blinking madly, hunched down next to the fire. "What was it like?"

Lara, now called Spooky or Spookster or sometimes even, with rough good nature, the Spook, held out both her skinny hands, warming them or watching the fire's leaping shadows against their backs. Her chin dipped, and she stared at her fingers while both hands shook, muscles in her forearms twitching. "Like that," she said, and clenched them into fists. Her face had filled out a little more, her high cheekbones no longer sharp-gaunt. Her dark curly hair stuck up anyhow, and Chuck had tied bits of it with red thread unraveled from a cotton bandanna, just like his own woolly locks. *Ain't gonna dread up,* he said, *but keeps it out of yo' face.*

"I heard they scalped the raiders they caught." Lazy Eye shuddered.

His wrists were too big for his camo jacket, his fingers too thin. He was put together from nonmatching parts, every piece of him either too delicate or too thick, an uneasy conglomeration. Even his teeth were different sizes, a crowded picket fence. He crouched, rocking back and forth a little, hugging his knees, and his face twitched, cheek muscle jerking under skin.

"Didn't see that. Hung a few; sent the rest of us to kamps." The paint on Spooky's left cheek itched a little as it dried. A steely weird smell of four in the morning filtered through the pine trees, and whenever the breeze veered eastward, a hint of that sickening barbecue reek drifted through the rest stop campsite again. Bits of paper from the explosion at the clapboard house still tiptoed around the burned camp's charred remains.

Any casualties the timed shell could have caused were incidental to destroying the goddamn evidence. Typical.

"I hate those bastards." Lazy Eye kept rocking. He was next in line for the paint. "My aunt Connie was in Florida. We barely got out." His left eye wandered sideways, caught on Lara's nose, came back. "Visiting, you know. They took her at a checkpoint. 'Cause of her last name. Jewish."

"Everyone hates those bastards." Sal held very still, his lips barely moving. "My mom, she was an antiwar protester. She told us what was gonna happen if McCoombs got reelection. We all laughed at her, you know. She was a hippie."

"Peace and love." Chuck's soft words were almost lost in the susurration as the Federals all started to stir at once, purposeful movement spreading from the command tent. "I hear the trucks are crossing the river with us, and we go straight south to Memphis."

"Maybe they'll fucking bomb it, since we got an air force again." Sal closed his eyes, his Adam's apple moving as he swallowed. "Finish up, man. I want some more coffee."

"Done." Chuck took his fingers away, surveying his work with a satisfied air. "Bring back some for the rest of us. You're up next, Lazy, my man."

By the time Sal came back with more of the thick black caffeine mud the Federals had for coffee, they were doing equipment checks. Spooky was still trembling, her cheeks pale except for two high round spots of unpainted red, high up. The whites of her eyes showed more than they should, but nobody mentioned it.

Swann appeared at 0445, clean-shaven and grim. Zampana arrived with Prink and a hungover Simmons in tow. The latter, his blond head freshly shaved as well, crouched next to Lara and held out his hands for the bowl of paint. Chuck handed it over.

"Listen up," Swann said. There was a new turkey feather tucked in his hat band—legend said he ate the old decorations, but nobody had ever seen him do it. Nobody had ever seen him throw them away, either. "Y'all ever heard of Elvis Presley?"

A chorus of *yessir*s and a few nods. Zampana snorted. "I told you, everyone's heard of him. What kind of Americans you think we are, old man?"

"Melt-pot ones." Swann grinned, but it didn't reach his eyes. His big shoulders were tense. "We made it this far, and we're heading to Graceland. We ain't quite front row; we'll be cleaning up with Crunche. But this is *Memphis*."

"Raider's graveyard," Lazy Eye supplied, not very helpfully. Nobody paid any attention, and he glanced nervously at Lara.

"I don't want to lose a single one of you. So I'm telling you now, take it easy." Swann fixed Simmons with a steady look. "No heroics on this run, we're support *only*."

The big blond guy dipped his fingers in the bowl of paint. One stripe down the outside of the right side of his face. Two, this one coming down his forehead, skipping his eye, starting again on his cheekbone and slicing down. Then a third, parallel, touching the side of his many-times-squashed boxer's nose. He finished the third line, then pushed his coat aside to dab his fingers high on the left side of his bared chest, right over his heart. Curly, wiry golden-brown chest hair glinted in the firelight, a solid mat of fur.

"What's that one for?" Lazy Eye wanted to know. Zampana smacked him on the back of the head, lightly.

"Cut it out, kid." Gold glittered at her ears, jewelry a Federal would get busted for during inspection.

A raider wore whatever the hell she pleased as long as she could fight. And as long as he knew when to keep his fucking mouth shut. Painting up was private.

Still, Lazy was just a kid. A nervous child whose eyes took on a flat hateful shine when there was killing to be done.

Simmons still didn't say a word. The silence stretched out, full of rustling, coughing, the sounds of tents being loaded and fires hissing as they were extinguished. It was almost time to move. Finally, the Reaper passed the paint bowl to Zampana, who dipped her first and second fingers, drawing them down from her bottom lip to give herself fangs. Dots under her eyes completed her usual look.

Finally, Swann shook his head. The new turkey feather bobbed. "All right. Gimme the bowl, then we're out of here. Lazy, your ass is on fire duty, and you'll be digging privy ditches if you don't keep that mouth of yours in line."

"Yessir," Lazy mumbled. "Sorry, Simms."

"No problem." Simmons unfolded, looming over the fire. Zampana and Swann exchanged a worried glance, but the big man just turned halfway, looking over the Federal camp. The rest of them finished equipment checks, and Spooky Lara hitched her pack higher on her back, held her hipbag open and gazed at the contents as if she expected them to have changed in the last ten minutes. Her shoulders quivered, and those hectic red spots on her cheeks glared like the paint stripes.

The breeze picked up, dawn pushing air across the world from the east. The days were getting longer; the thaw had deepened. So had the mud, but they'd be on actual roads now. Winter's back was well broken, and the Mississippi might even flood this year.

"You want some more?" Swann offered the bowl to Spooky, who shook her head.

"Not yet," she said, then swallowed hard, as if the words stuck. Swann studied her for a moment, letting her change her mind if she was going to.

She didn't, and he nodded curtly, accepting. Chuck took the bowl and set off to wash it out before they left.

Simmons stepped close to Spooky, who dropped the flap of her hipbag and tilted her head back, staring up at him. Her face settled into dull rage and resignation at the consciousness of a male too far in her personal space.

"Hey. I'll tell you." He pointed to his face. "My sisters, and my brother." Then his closed fist struck over his heart, and the red paint, rapid drying but not yet set, smeared in his chest hair and on the inside of his coat. "This one, for the camps." He held her gaze for a long moment, then turned sharply and set off for the waiting trucks. One of the truck engines woke, then another, and their roaring was deep and jarring as the first jolt of caffeine hitting a sleepy soldier.

Spooky watched him go. The hiss of Lazy Eye putting out the fire in its concrete park pit was lost in the general, disciplined noise.

CHAPTER ELEVEN

MEMPHIS

The Mississippi had swollen, but not much. It carried a glitter and gleam on its broad, lazy, tea-colored back.

Memphis was aflame.

Disposable drones dropped zappers first, electromagnetic pulses taking out lights and frying small electronics. Spotters in the cell towers were crispy-crittered, the packed hospitals suddenly went dark, and the streets were silent for one long eerie second before anthill activity started, people finally understanding that something worse than potshot artillery was coming.

What remained of the Second Southern Patriot Army, in full retreat, had failed to make it any farther. They crammed into the city along with refugees streaming eastward and the Firsters who couldn't get official permission to leave. Which was pretty much all of them, since the Firster party chiefs got out before the roads jammed up, and without them to sign off on any action, the rest of the organization was paralyzed.

State's rights, the Firster articles of faith said. *Petty fiefdoms* was more like it, *jealously guarded.*

Just before dawn, the Federal columns heading for Memphis got the order to stop. Traffic snarled and soldiers began cursing, logistics people holding their heads. The roads in the opposite direction filled suddenly

with Federal vehicles—heavy artillery, engineer squads, and the like—
pulling back in good order. Yelled questions across the meridian or the
yellow line got no answer except that orders were to get the hell back.

The Federal Army paused, a giant fist hovering over a fly.

The delay meant Memphis refugees and civilians were cramming the
bridges and roads out of town in every vaguely southerly or eastern direction instead of cowering in holes that might shelter them. Word spread
quickly that the Feds were retreating, and rumors inside the city were full
of wonder-weapons, something happening in New York, an end to the
war? A miracle?

As soon as the Federals were pulled sufficiently back, K-jets boomed
overhead, and the Feds caught their breath. The planes came in waves,
darkening the sky, but only the last fringe dropped their payloads on
dark, seething Memphis.

And what they dropped were burners.

The previous night, while Swann's Riders had been sleeping—or, in
Simmons's case, drinking to blackout to get some rest—the siege of DC
had reached its inevitable conclusion, and the fighting surging toward
the White House shattered even McCoombs's last illusions of winning
the war. His cabinet had fled, even the diehard Confederate Yells who'd
sworn to hold DC until death. The biggest bastard on the heap was determined, however, to go out in style, or in what passed for it in his lexicon.
McCoombs still had a few airfields and launch codes, and he chose the
city he hated most, the city he'd started out in, the city that had be-
trayed him with resistance almost all through his tenure. After a decade
of Firster governance, including four-plus years of civil war, New York
was a shadow of what it used to be, but when McCoombs knew all was
lost, he decided to take the biggest apple of all with him.

Then, while the sound of tanks echoed on the sandbag- and obstacle-
choked lawn of 1600 Pennsylvania, when the rifle fire and yells of infantry
were audible, the Firster President for Life retreated to the Oval Office
and bit a capsule he'd been told would provide him a painless death.

For whatever reason, it didn't. But that was too late for New York.
The Firsters had been busy with all sorts of toys during their twelve-year

reign, and the worst of them detonated just north of the middle of Manhattan.

Nobody afterward could pin down just who among the Federal generals gave the orders to blow the South's capitals and trade centers off the map. Every plane the Federals had capable of carrying burners, from K-jet to antique Thunderbolt, was loaded up, and that had to take a while. Some suspected a Great Burn had been planned on both sides, and New York was just the prelude to McCoombs's version. Insanity on one side matching insanity on the other, or the Federals had decided that two civil wars were one too many and in order to build a better country, maybe they had to level a few stubborn patches.

All of which meant Swann's Riders sat on or leaned against a gray-and-green hybrid Umvee, watching Memphis burn at a safe distance. Lazy Eye chewed on a long stalk of hay grass he'd found somewhere, while Simmons stared unblinking at the spectacle. Zampana's lips moved, silent prayers or a stream of invectives; you couldn't be sure. Sal and Prink passed a bottle of found bourbon back and forth. Swann held his hat in both large hands and worked at its brim, his long face thoughtful; Chuck Dogg let out a soft tuneless whistle every once in a while, when the burners found a patch of congenial fuel and sent gouts of greasy blue-white skyward. Those flames ate everything, even the top layers of concrete, but it was the firestorm they created, stealing oxygen and roasting everything within radius, that accounted for most of the casualties.

You could maybe escape—*maybe*—if you had a deep enough hole and a source of air while the firestorm lasted. Or if you were lucky enough to get to a body of water big enough not to evaporate, and prayed. Once the burners went down, there wasn't a lot left.

After the first two hours the flames turned orange and yellow, shading into a paleness at their bottoms. Billows of grease-black smoke lifted in an almost perfect column since the dawn breeze had died. Federal soldiers climbed whatever they could to get a good view from Highway 51, and when the planes circled back and dropped another payload the joking stopped, replaced by an awed silence. When the mess on the roads leading back cleared, the orders came down to move out again, north and east to Jackson, which had escaped burning only because the Federals needed somewhere to rest their troops.

The historians called it the Battle of Memphis, as distinct from the raiders' Memphis Uprising. The surrender was signed a little afterward, so the same historians called it the end of the war.

CHAPTER TWELVE

HISTORY

They lied.

CHAPTER THIRTEEN

FAST AND CAUTIOUS

A thin trickle of blood smeared on Spooky's top lip. She didn't notice, staring out the truck's window. Today she had shotgun, Swann was driving, and they crept along the freeway at a respectable idle, following a long line of similar trucks carrying infantry. Charging the kerros or fueling the hybrid engines wasn't a problem—supplies had moved up, and the whole army was shifting off of petroleum. There was even going to be a field kitchen tonight, someone had said. The prospect of hot food, no matter what quality, cheered everyone immensely.

"Horses, sometimes," Swann said. His hat lay on the seat between them, a sodden, shapeless mass. The turkey feather was a little bedraggled now, dispirited at not seeing combat. "But you've got to feed those fuckers. You know the Second World War was fulla horses?"

Spooky made a soft, noncommittal sound, chewing on yet another ration bar. They tasted like glued-together sawdust, but they were *food*. Zampana was monitoring her intake, and so far, Lara hadn't come down with the runs or the bricks. It was a goddamn miracle, and she was past the most dangerous part. The human body was a downright phenomenon, as Sal often remarked.

All the same, she wouldn't have minded a chocolate bar. Or a grilled-cheese sandwich. Some kampogs dreamed of elaborate, table-groaning feasts, but all *she* wanted was grilled cheese and a glass of milk. Not skim, either. Full-fat. Cold from the fridge, and the cheese full of fat too, the butter—not margarine—crispy and soaking into the bread…

"Had to use 'em to haul the artillery. Bunch of dead horses in the Second World War. And bicycles. You see the pictures of them on bicycles. The Russians in Berlin were stealin' watches and bicycles." Swann's hazel eyes were narrowed. His window was rolled down precisely a quarter, and the cool air coming in was a blessing. This particular truck couldn't shut the heating fan off or the lights would stop working.

Raiders were used to crappy equipment. It was better than no equipment at all—most of the time, anyway.

Spooky made another soft sound, just to show she was listening. Swann glanced at her. "You're leakin'."

"Huh?" She blinked, rubbed at her lip. Blood smeared. "Oh *shit*."

"That a regular thing?" He dug in his coat, finally finding a scrap of black bandanna wrapped around a wad of something crusty. "This is all I got."

"It's fine." She took it, didn't even make a face at what it probably contained, and pressed it under her nose. "Happens sometimes. Since Baylock."

"Baylock?" He kept his eyes on the road. It was easier for people to talk about bad shit when you weren't looking at them. If prewar road trips didn't teach you that, everything after the West Coast Secession did.

Spooky's voice was muffled, quiet. "First kamp I was in."

"They had you somewheres else before that shithole?"

"Yeah." She shuddered, a quick, suppressed movement. "Transit kamps, mostly. People going through to different places. Was in the glass-block for a while."

"Huh." A question lay just under that single word, but he wasn't going to press it.

"Hospital. Experiments." She scrubbed angrily at the blood, tilting her head back a little, carefully holding the ration bar away on her right side, between her and the door. Like she was afraid someone would snatch it. "They went through and sorted us. Raiders, mostly—they had everyone with magtat or scar instead of chip go through selektions first off. First we thought it might not be so bad, because hospitals had to have better food, right? They told us they were quarantining us. Poking, prodding, taking blood, scraping." She turned her head, not quite looking at him. From this angle her nose was a little too big, and her mouth a little too small. "Is it still going?"

The blood had slowed, already clotting.

"It's stopped." Swann went back to eyes-front, staring at the bumper of the transport in front of them. One of the Federals—a private with a bandage on his neck and close-cropped brown hair—was pissing off the tailgate, but politely, aiming the flow to the side instead of trying to hit the hood of the truck behind him. "Still some in your nose."

"Yeah." She balled the cloth up in her fist, took another bite of the ration bar. "Turns out they just wanted us patched up before they started. All the Memphis casualties got care. Some civilians, but I never talked to any of them."

"So mostly just captured raiders?"

"Uh-huh. They kept measuring us and poking and swabbing. They even weighed your shit, when they were feeding you enough to make any. Hooked a bunch of us up to EEGs, ECGs, everything. Gave us injections. All sorts of crazy shit. Electroshock." Another bite, this one chewed hard and fast. "Then people started dying."

"Fuck."

"You wouldn't…" She shook her head gingerly, as if expecting her nose to go again. "I was about to say you wouldn't believe what they did. But I'm guessing you might."

"Rumors. Light me up a smoke?"

"As a medical officer, I would be glad to."

His mouth curved upward, fleetingly, before settling back in its usual line. "Good girl."

"They did…things. Grafting. Spinal taps. One guy…I can't even…" Her hand shook, but she got the smoke lit. Medics got half an officer's ration of old-fashioned, but they were saying the candies were going to become standard and the nicotine fiends would have to be weaned. "Saw

a guy try to peel his own face off, while they stood around taking notes."
She took a drag and passed him the cancer-stick, gingerly, doing her best
not to touch his skin. "I don't like thinking about it."

"Fair enough." Swann took a long, long drag. It burned all the way
down, and the familiar nicotine haze eased his nerves. Nonsmokers were
goddamn rare in combat, and the little paper-wrapped sticks were cur-
rency, besides. "I got a question."

"Yeah?" Bracing herself, the medic shifted a little farther toward the
door.

"The admin building. In the burning camp. How'd you know?"

A long, ticking silence. "I could say I guessed." She made another tiny,
restless movement.

Swann didn't seem to notice. He just tapped his ash out the window,
like a gentleman. "Yeah, well, war does that. You get to where you *know*.
Like an animal."

"Yeah." Lara didn't relax, but she did bring the ration bar back up and
take another nibble.

No brake lights flashed ahead, but the column slowed. Commanders
were getting sleds and kerros, but for the foot soldiers, it was old-style
guzzlers and hybrids. At least the engines were mostly fitted for kerrogel
now, and more kits were coming up all the time. Now that the goddamn
war was winding down, every supply problem from the last six-seven
years was getting solved in a hurry.

"We had a runner—Franco. Slippery little piece of shit, but he could
get through any terrain and always knew where north was. He said could
smell the fucking Firsters." Swann measured the steering wheel between
his blunt fingers.

"Did they catch him?" Runners generally didn't last that long, even if
they were fast and cautious. You couldn't really be both all the time.

"Nah. Gangrene. Last winter. Christmas '97, now that was fucking
grim."

She made another sound of agreement. They went a quarter of a mile,
and things were beginning to speed up a bit. Someone was probably up
front untangling things, or the road had widened.

"How'd you get out of that camp?" Swann finally asked. "Baylock."

"Drones bombed it. Don't know why." She shifted in the seat a little. Along with the diesel fumes and colorless reek of kerrogel, a fresh green scent of rain slid through the window. "Went through two transit kamps, got selected out each time." The medic carefully folded the ration wrapper around the uneaten portion and stowed the bar in a pocket. "Then it was Gloria."

"Those sonsabitches." Swann cleared his throat, preparing to spit, and rolled down his window.

Spooky made another of those agreeing sounds and closed her eyes. She rested her head against the window, the engine's vibration cradling her brain inside its bony home. Dried blood crackled inside her nostrils, but that didn't matter. She clutched her medic satchel, even as her eyelids fluttered a little and her lips moved, and after a while Swann, craving another cigarette but unwilling to wake a tired soldier, settled both hands more firmly on the wheel and tried to avoid the potholes.

CHAPTER FOURTEEN

UNCONDITIONAL

May 7, '98

Outside a miraculously still-intact hotel in downtown Jackson, Tennessee, cries rang through the smoky streets spattered by sporadic gunfire as night rose. Some of the suburbs had been shelled to pieces, but Firster resistance had pretty much collapsed all the way through the city, so the power, while weak, was still on. That meant hot water, and frontline troops grabbing the best billets they could find.

"Hey! Hey guys!" Lazy Eye poked his head in the door, blinking through the fug of cigarette smoke, both old-fashioned and candy. As usual, when he was excited, his mouth pulled to the side and thickened his drawl past molasses into full-on gleeson dip. "Lissen up! They's a nowcast!"

"Shut the *door*," Simmons snarled, glaring at the cards in his big chapped hands. A brand-new, buff-colored ten-gallon hat was clamped firmly on his gold-stubbled head, and his shirt was open all the way to the waist.

Zampana, directly across from him, grinned around the monstrous Cuban cigar stuck in her mobile, red-painted mouth. A silk tie—*real* silk, and shaken free of glass from a Firster Party Selekt Store's windows blown in by shells or simply shattered by other frontline troops—was knotted loosely around her freshly scrubbed throat. A strong scent of expensive hotel shampoo hung on her long, dripping black hair.

The shower was running behind one door, and through another, Swann could be heard cursing at a pair of boots he'd snatched from a broken store window as well. They should have been the right size, and were good leather…but somehow, they didn't fit, and several open bottles of champagne floating around probably didn't help. Sal was already snoring on one almost-wrecked hotel bed, and Prink eyed his own cards, occasionally glancing at Chuck, whose luck at poker was rivaled only by his capacity to swear at someone else's.

"Naw, man, y'wanna *listen*!" Lazy banged the door shut on his way in, causing a brief interruption to Sal's fruity, gassy snoring. "Surrendah!"

"Oh, for heavensake, kid." Zampana rolled her eyes. "You are too goddamn young to be this drunk."

"'M *serious*." He banged across the room, tracking heavy red mud on the salmon-colored carpet, skidding to a halt in front of the flatscreen. "CentComm sennout a hotpaper. Crunche tol' me come tell Swann." He hopped from one foot to the other, jabbing at the flatscreen.

"Don't you dare turn that fucker on," Simmons snarled. A bottle of amber Scotch—good stuff, imported, grabbed from a Firster supply dump on the edge of town before word came down the troops were offleash for at least thirty-six hours—sat at his elbow, half empty. He'd shown no inclination to leave the billet to get into trouble, but that could change in an instant. The whole city was breathless in the space between conquering army and martial law, Federals roaming in gleeful bands and civilians burrowing into whatever cellar they could find.

In the bathroom, the shower turned off, and the curtain rattled on its plastic rings, clicking like dry little bones.

Lazy Eye finally managed to punch the right button. The flatscreen woke, its blank blind eye turning luminescent; a blaring screech of *oh beautiful for spacious skies* jolted Sal up out of his slumber and halted Swann's steady swearing. The bathroom door squeaked, and the new medic, her dark hair plastered to her head and a snow-white, fluffy towel clutched to her skinny chest, stared out with wide, terrified dark eyes.

Zampana laid her cards facedown, puffing the cigar once, decisively. "This better be good, Lazy, or I'm letting Reaper kick yo' ass."

"God *damn* it." Simmons surged up, bumping the table, and Minjae let out an exasperated bark as her ashtray danced.

Crackling silence. Spooky pulled the towel tighter, and they all stared at the flatscreen. Lazy's mouth was slightly open and he looked pleased; Simmons dropped back down in his chair with a thud; Minjae stood slowly, as if her muscles ached. Swann appeared in the connecting door, his eyes narrowed, and the Greek blinked away congealed sleep, pushing himself up on his elbows.

"…a special bulletin." The screen wavered, a rippling American flag—the *Federal* flag, the Stars and Stripes, not the star-bar rag the Firsters had forced everyone to fly—filling its immensity. "Citizens, prepare for a special bulletin."

The flag faded, and a burst of static cleared to show something extraordinary. A thin, nervous-looking old man in a moth-eaten blue uniform, his white hat laid at his elbow and his gray hair neatly buzz-cut, sat at a makeshift desk under glaring lights. He read from a sheaf of papers, and the news filtered slowly into the room like a heavy, colorless gas. *Surrender.* That magical word. *Unconditional,* another magical word.

The scratchy, thin voice reading out the document was familiar to Swann, who breathed, "Holy *fuck,* it's Kallbrunner."

"Who?" Lazy wanted to know, too young to remember the Parris Island Plot, but nobody answered.

A cease-fire was declared. Civilians were to remain in their homes, and all Firster forces were to lay down their arms. The 'cast droned on, and Lara went back into the bathroom to get dressed. When she opened the door again, in a medic's uniform two sizes too big, tightly belted and rolled up, the black bandanna knotted around her upper arm again, Kallbrunner was just coming to the end of the legalese.

A long, scratchy pause. Simmons tipped his head back, his throat working convulsively. Swann leaned in the doorway, his jaw working too, his head down, his shoulders bowed. Zampana's lips moved soundlessly around the cigar; she crossed herself repeatedly, quickly, her hands almost blurring. Minjae grabbed her own upper arms, hugging herself, the holster under her left armpit well-worn and visible. Prink had his eyes closed, but his hands worked at each other, the stump of his left pinkie twitching spasmodically.

"To those who have destroyed the peace of our nation, I have only one thing to add." Kallbrunner took a breath, and Swann inhaled with him. So did Spooky, and Zampana's lips stilled. "You will be found, wherever you hide. And you will be brought to justice." A soft sound of paper shuffling, a slight cough. *"God bless America!"*

The flag came back, its ripple pausing before continuing on loop, and the music started up again. Sal the Greek swung his legs off the bed, sat up rubbing at his crusted eyes like a kid on Christmas morning, not quite sure he was really awake. Minjae's cheeks were wet, and so were Swann's.

Simmons picked up his bourbon, set it back down untasted.

Then, the big blond bastard let out a whoop, throwing his cards in the air. Zampana sagged in her chair, her hand twitching for a sidearm before pulling back quick as a snake. She shook her wet hair, and her expression—a contortion of the lips, a roll of her dark eyes, her nose wrinkling—was similar to that of a woman in labor just after the head was free and the crisis mostly past. Prink tossed his cards down too, before throwing his fists in the air, a soccer fan's salute.

Spooky simply stood, straight and pale, staring at the flatscreen. A muscle in her cheek twitched once, twice. That was all.

Chuck Dogg, still sitting with his cards in hand, stared at the table's surface, now frosted with cigarette ash and spotted with damp patches from Zampana's hair or Prink's nervous fingertip jabbing. He didn't move until Simmons clapped him on the shoulder and demanded, in no uncertain terms, that Chuck go along for some celebrating.

The rest of that night and the following day were a blur to most of Swann's Riders, but everyone agreed it was full of broken glass. Mirrors, windows, anything that could shatter did.

And Zampana, less drunk than the rest of them, remembered Spooky's white, set face, and how the new medic had bloody knuckles the next morning.

CHAPTER FIFTEEN

MAGCHIP

May 9, '98

The end of America, and Kaptain Eugene Thomas was stuck in a shitty little shack with a bunch of mouth-breathing dregs, the bandage on his head sticky and warm with blood. Of course the stupid fucks held their mouths slightly open—concussions from artillery shook the farmhouse, drifts of dirt or plaster falling from the ceiling. They cowered, all equal in the face of terror, blond blue-eyed Sorenson with his pants full of crap and the reek of it assaulting Gene's nose.

That was something not covered in the Patriot schools, how a man could casually shit himself when the shooting started. All the heroic movies and the music videos with soldiers staring manfully into the fray didn't show it. They didn't show a man holding a double handful of his own guts blown out by shrapnel either, or the tumble of bodies from a killing bottle into the bays. Like sticky spaghetti sliding out of a pot.

Gene's legs ached from trying to push him backward into the concrete of the basement wall. Another good hit or two would bring the whole thing down, and good luck scrabbling out of the rubble.

The knife was rusty, but it pierced his skin. He worked it back and forth, ignoring the other Patriots' screams as another shock wave jolted the building on its foundation. The inside of the left forearm, where a small nubbin held cargo that could kill him after the surrender.

He wasn't like the other fools in here. Anyone with half a brain could see the Federals had won. When they did, they would process anyone lucky enough to survive surrendering, and he wasn't idiot enough to think anyone with a Patriot's record would be left alone, no sir. "The wheat and the chaff," he muttered, while working the blade into the pale underside of his arm. Red blood welled.

She had a rectangle of scar tissue on her forearm, where a lase had cut her magchip free. The goddamn rebels were well supplied. She wouldn't say how she'd been seduced into joining them—not that he'd asked. Not that he could remember, anyway. Somehow her file had been corrupted, only the vitals remaining—name, age, height, weight. He didn't even know where she'd gone to school. All he knew was seeing her straighten that one sunny day in Gloria, and reading the determination in her thin shoulders. Those huge, starving eyes, somewhere between hazel and green, and—

The tiny chip corner pushed up on a welling of blood. Good clean Amerikan claret. Gene dropped the knife and worked at the sliver of metal with his filthy fingertips. He'd probably get tetanus or gangrene and save the degenerates the trouble of killing him.

Another hit, close to the already half-shattered farmhouse they were all hiding in. The reverberations died away just as he got the chip free. He squeezed it between dirty fingernails, bending the sliver back and forth, ignoring the pain in his arm. Had he cut too deep? Christ, if it got infected, he'd be in trouble.

The silence jerked his chin up. They'd stopped lobbing shells. The Patriot major nominally in charge of this ragged band stared apathetically at the wall, his tricorne hat cockeyed and his uniform coat flopping loosely at one torn sleeve. He had a ragged, filthy bandage low on his left forearm, too.

Probably wasn't a combat wound.

Gene picked up the knife, wiping it uselessly on his dirty trousers, and one of the other soldiers—Polk, a jug-eared kid who reminded Gene of his vanished Gloria Kamp orderly—whimpered. Flat-footed old men and kids barely out of grammar school—the government was scraping the bottom of the barrel. How had it come to this?

It didn't matter. Thomas braced himself against the wall, dropping the broken magchip. He ground it under the flopping heel of his boot, once mirror-shiny and polished by a kampog twice a day. Amerika had gone mad. The degenerates had won. No use in pretending.

The Federals didn't throw a grenade down to clear the farmhouse basement only because they'd already shot Sorenson, who edged out waving a scrap of material that was nowhere near white.

The surrender was well under way.

CHAPTER SIXTEEN

BACK HOME

May 15, '98

Two weeks after Memphis, Crunche received the turn-in-your-guns order he was supposed to enforce on all raiders under his command. They were to take enlistment in the regular army and join the chain of command for realsies, now that the fighting was supposed to be over. There was to be no more raiding, no more sabotage, no more derailments or lightning runs against Firster installations. The surrender had been signed by the rump of McCoombs's cowering cabinet, most of them caught trying to get over the border into Canada.

It was probably best that they didn't make it; ever since the Ontario Five trial, public feeling in the Great White North had precluded any fraternal hand-holding with McCoombs's "presidency." Everything had to get back to normal now, with the Federal government moving back home in dribs and drabs. Part of that normal was making sure the oddballs who'd developed a taste for sabotage, bombing, terrifying Firster watch posts and breaking Firster stockades were tucked neatly away.

Oh, sure, they were heroes in wartime. But this, suddenly, was *peace*.

"So." Swann pulled his lips in, bit at them as if he had to stop a curse or two from escaping. He read the order again, nice and slow. "So, we don't join up as buckytail privates, you arrest us?"

Crunche, his bloodshot eyes blinking, leaned hipshot against the wheel bulge of a retrofitted Umvee while he rummaged in his pocket for a fresh cigar. "Well, that's the *spirit* of the damn thing, but not the *letter*, my man. Occupation duties, it says. Discretion on the part of the immediate commander."

"Huh." The single syllable held a world's worth of disdain.

"It's a shitty order," Crunche agreed, chewing at the end of the brown-wrapped tobacco tube. He never lit them; he just masticated. "*Officially* it ain't arrived yet. I ain't thumbed it, Azer hasn't been able to find me." His right eyelid drooped a fraction, his version of a wink. "Figured I owed you that much, at least."

"Mmhm." A noncommittal sound.

Azer stood about six feet away in the shelter of a comms tent, studying a table of maps with apparent unconcern.

"We lost that truck over there in the pileup on the highway, too." Crunche scratched at his cheek. "Just now catching up on paperwork for everything we left on the way."

The army-green truck in question sat, in plain sight, with half of Lazy Eye vanished under its hood. The boy was a mouth, but he was also good with engines and retrofitting. His gray, much-worn rag of a T-shirt rode up a little; ropy, vivid, healed welts peeked out. The seamed scars on his back—the reason he rarely took his shirt off and stayed filthy rather than shower with everyone else—were from Public Atonement in the small town he'd grown up in, the Firsters believing in that *spare the rod, spoil the child* thing, and someone had accused him of being an atheist.

The kid had survived thirty lashes, which was damn near miraculous. Lazy hummed as he banged on something deep in the engine's guts. "...that, you sonofawhore," he finished, slithering backward and hopping lithely to the ground. "Yep, that'll do it."

"How long we got?" Swann asked.

Crunche bit down on the cigar end again. "I won't thumb the order 'til sundown."

"Well, I ain't making any promises." The raider nodded thoughtfully. "Be a goddamn shame to miss that next poker game."

"Not for me, you bastard." Crunche owed Swann fifteen smokes and a pile of credits.

Swann offered his hand. "You're a good egg, Crunche."

"You too." They shook, and Crunche ambled away, studiously avoiding looking at Zampana or Simmons, who were occupied with roasting a couple rabbits over a fire instead of waiting for the line around the field kitchen. Zampana caught sight of Swann, elbowed Simmons, and they both leapt to their feet. Lazy Eye hunched his skinny shoulders, and when Spooky wheeled out from under the truck, chewing on a ration bar, her face grimed with motor oil and dirt, she froze, catching the tension.

By now, even she knew that look.

They gathered around the truck, instinctively close to shelter while Swann laid it out for them. Simmons leaned against the quarter panel, smoking meditatively, his eyes half closed. "Occupation duty," he quoted, and shook his head. "Babysitting."

"Not necessarily," Zampana weighed in. "Could mean hunting Firsters."

"Now that'd be something I'd like." Prink exhaled sharply. "Minjae? What's our chances?"

"Mathematically?" Minjae rubbed at her close-cropped black hair, her round face shining with sweat. Her hips shifted slightly under her trousers, deceptively soft. She was all packed muscle underneath. "Sign on, get pension. Good bet."

"Pension." Simmons blew out a long cloud of smoke. "Never thought I'd live that long."

All eyes turned to Chuck Dogg, who looked fixedly at the ground. "I dunno." He took his time thinking, and they waited patiently. "I ain't too keen on taking orders from no come-latelies."

Swann nodded, his lean face expressionless.

Zampana made a restless movement, her palms pressed together as if she were praying. "They could break us up, too?"

Dogg nodded, his collection of small, red-tied braids bouncing a little. "Crunche wouldn't. But above him, who knows?"

"Unless he's gonna rank me in to where I can keep y'all together." Swann rubbed under his hat band with one finger, scratching hard and thinking harder. "Can tell him we want to hunt those fuckers down."

"You think he'd agree?" Lazy piped up, eagerly. His eye rolled a little, his cheek twitching.

"To which one?" Zampana elbowed him, a gentle nudge.

He leaned into the contact, the regular half of his mouth pulling up in a smile. "Both. Either." The kid sobered, folded his arms. "I ain't got my thirty yet."

Simmons settled more firmly against the truck, rubbing his big chapped hands together. "What are you gonna do if you get 'em?"

"Start on another." Lazy's face squinched up, restrained from a *Well, duh* by Zampana's warning glance.

"Might run out of Firsters." Sal coughed a little, hunching and cupping the brief flame of a lighter, inhaling from an old-fashioned. That caused a general movement among the others, and for a little while, the smokers smoked in silence, while Zampana, Lazy, and Lara simply stood thoughtfully.

Swann smoked almost down to the stubby filter before turning his head to gaze at the new medic, a line between his fiercely furred eyebrows. "Well?"

Her mouth had turned to a thin colorless downward curve. "Reservists?" Her nostrils flared as the last sibilant of the word slanted up, a tentative slide common among camp veterans.

"Ha, good idea." Minjae fieldstripped her smoke with a sigh. "Hunt the bastards one weekend a month."

"Be all you can be," Chuck cracked.

When the laughter died down and the last smoke had been fieldstripped under boots broken in by hard use, Swann straightened, settling his hat the way he did before giving important information. "Anyone who wants to go home, that truck's the ticket. Sundown's when I have to answer."

Chuck shook his head, digging one bootheel into the half gravel, half mud. "Shit, man, anyone got anywhere to go back to?"

Spooky shrugged. Zampana whitened. Simmons did too, his blue eyes lighting with a suspicious, familiar glow.

But it was Lazy who said what they were all thinking. "This is home now." He rubbed at his forehead with the back of one grimy hand.

Crunche had some pull with Division, and he used it to get Swann in as a captain. He wasn't so sure about keeping them all together even if they did sign on, but fortunately, a brass head at CentCom had a brainstorm right in his uniform trousers. Getting conscripts back into the peacetime economy was the overriding concern; the regular army had its hands full with other cleanup, including certification—the only way for a card-carrying Firster to rejoin society after the surrender—and the pool of raider manpower was tailor-made and motivated to pursue another task.

That was how the Blue Companies were formed; they were mostly squad-sized and nobody knew quite where the name came from, but it stuck. Their mission was simple: to find the jar kaptains, the officers, and the black-clad Patriots who staffed the kamps, from the simple work or Re-Edukation stockades to the killing grounds. Not to mention the petty Party functionaries who submerged once it was clear the Federals would win.

Ideally, the Blues were to bring them in for televised trials, so the world would see America regain its favored moral high ground.

CHAPTER SEVENTEEN

REALITY

It didn't quite work out that way.

CHAPTER EIGHTEEN

PAPERHEAD

May 19, '98

Inside a commandeered Clarkesford elementary school, Swann's Riders stood in a tightly bunched group, scrubbed and sullen. A pen scratched, and the lean, close-shaven, long-nosed man behind the principal's desk wore rank stripes and the supercilious air of a longtime paper pusher. A pair of steel-rimmed glasses glittered on the desktop, usually perched in the little divots on the officer's nose. "You were with the division that liberated Reklamation Kamp Gloria, correct?"

Spooky, her hands dangling limp at her sides, her medic's uniform still too large but now well laundered, tensed.

Slightly in front of her, Swann nodded, took his time inhaling to answer. "Ayuh, we were."

"You have three females in your squad, then?" The bureaucrat, that long nose reddened by a nip or two from the bottle in his desk drawer, blinked blearily at the group of indifferently uniformed raiders. Simmons had point-blank refused to change his coat, Zampana's long hair was against army regulations, and Lazy's faded, bloodshot eyes half hid under their lids while his left cheek twitched and danced madly. "Cis, I mean?"

"Ayuh." Swann's shoulders had set. He didn't like how this was going. What the fuck did it matter? Women got the shit beaten out of them just the same as men did, in the woods behind the lines, or in a pissant town when a neighbor talked, or in a city when they were caught out after curfew.

They died just the same, too. Holding double handfuls of their own guts. Vanished into the basements of the Party Police. Hanged in the square. Rotted with gangrene since the raiders didn't have enough antibiotics. Shot, shelled, stabbed, strafed, and more.

"And they all three were with you before Gloria?" The pen pusher looked up, blinking blearily.

Swann had a split second to decide how to handle it. This wasn't a briefing or a called-to-carpet; it was more like a fishing expedition. Swann's bunch were just about to draw supplies from the quartermaster, but this asshole had some paperwork he just *had* to fill out. "Ayuh." Maybe he should have said *Yessir*, but a raider didn't give respect until you'd *earned* it, by God.

"There was a female raider in the…let's see." The bureaucrat's mouth turned down, sucking on something sour as he shuffled through the stacks on his desk, thin hot-type paper and pop stencils, frangible and probably already fading. They'd have been scanned in, though. "Joy Duty, they called it. The camp brothel."

"There was." Swann figured he was committed now, might as well go the whole way. "Died just after." Everyone knew raiders didn't last long in camps. Not unless they were lucky, or tougher than usual.

Of course, the new medic had gone through a couple, right? There were news reports beginning to filter through now. One word in particular perked Swann's ears mightily.

Baylock. It was accompanied by other whispered words. *Experiments. Medical. Genetic.* And, last and most thought-provoking, *mutations.*

"That's a shame." The bureaucrat gazed at Zampana, at Minjae, at Lara. All three of them stood stolid and silent. With the exception of Zampana's raised eyebrow, they were stone-faced as well. "Did you bury her?"

"Wasn't time." Swann's back teeth began to ache, a sure sign of trouble. "Figgered rear echelon would. Why?"

The crag-faced man blinked. "Routine check, that's all." But he studied the new medic more intently now. "Vitals were lost in the worming; we thought maybe you'd have a couple clues. We could notify next of kin."

And that was why the summons had called for *all* of Swann's group? The newly made captain took a hold of his temper, as his mother would have said. Lord, but it was irritating when a man behind a desk assumed you were stupid. "Welp. Anyone got clues for the man? That raider, what was her name?"

"Never said," Simmons piped up. "Died right outside the camp gates."

"Dysentery," Zampana drawled, with the particular Hispanic accent she reserved for prying idiots. She'd once gotten waved through a road-block, pretending to be an immie indentured too stupid to understand much English, brazening out with a shivering Mickle and Prink hidden between wooden boxes holding bags of manure in the back of the truck. Her fake ID had left streaks of ink on her sweating fingers, but they'd let her through, the dogs uneasy but none of the Firster block-guards wanting to get into the back of a vehicle that smelled that awful.

Mick was shot two weeks after that, during the run on the pharmacy in Fredericksville. Gutshot *and* lung shot, and Zampana had been the one there holding his hand after she used some of the precious stolen morphine to ease him out.

The bureaucrat stared at Spooky. She lifted her chin a little and stared back, her dark eyes lightening to between hazel and green. Swann wanted to elbow her, but he stood, rigid, nailed in place. The clock wired to the wall next to the door ticked, keeping a steady marching heartbeat. Chopping up time into little pieces, like breaking up a ration bar for a toothless child. A few female raiders had given birth in the wilderness. Everyone had pitched in with extra rations to keep them producing breast milk, even though a baby's cry was a goddamn danger with sniffers and drones over the woods.

Sixteen ticks. Twenty. Thirty. Chuck Dogg shifted uneasily on Spooky's other side.

Spooky Lara's lips moved, slightly. There was very little resemblance to the Gloria scarecrow in the thin soylon slip remaining, now that her face had filled out a bit. Swann, his peripheral vision trained as only a raider's could be, almost turned his head as if he heard her. It was just a slight exhale, but the moment it finished, the bureaucrat wadded up the papers on his desk. He selected a couple more of the original flimsies, then held them up.

Swann stepped forward and accepted them. His palms were a little moist. He couldn't quite pin down why, but he had the heebie-jeebies, as if a streetsweep was just about to start, Patriots and their guns herding a compliant crowd for ID checking.

Selection, they called it. The word had a darker meaning in the camps.

"See these get destroyed." The bureaucrat's tone had gone flat as a flimsy. "That will be all, my friend. Pleasure to speak to you."

Swann nodded. He did an about-face, and Zampana was already moving for the door. So was Simmons, who didn't look troubled in the least. Lazy Eye had a perplexed air, but thankfully kept his mouth shut; Sal and Prink exchanged significant glances. Minjae, expressionless, held the door.

Spooky kept staring at the bureaucrat, holding eye contact. The thin line between them snapped, and she glanced guiltily at Swann. He shook his head a little, making a shooing motion, and she preceded him meekly out into the old-style nylon-carpeted hall that smelled of dust, markers, and the chalky, dry-oily smell of kids cooped up for long periods of time. A few pictures of McCoombs's black-haired, sneering smile had been ripped from the walls and trampled, but other than that, everything was in good order.

Swann stopped at the end of the hall. He glanced at the papers, and a strange rippling sensation went through the bottom of his stomach. The medic, her dark curly hair pulled back under her black kerchief and her cheeks dead white, stopped too. Simmons halted to their left, Zampana saying something to him in a low fierce tone, and Lazy bounced onto his toes, full of questions but not daring to spill a single one. The left-hand hall was full of uniforms and a bustle of soft activity; the right led past a trophy case and posters telling kids to look both ways before crossing the street, to be respectful and love America and to wash their hands, before finally ending at glass double doors, miraculously unshattered by the shelling.

The suburbs generally had it better than anywhere else, as usual. That was where most of McCoombs's support had come from. Houses made of margarine, and margarine souls, too. Mass-produced, fake, and full of grease.

"That was weird," Minjae said, a little louder than she had to.

Sal grunted. "Paperhead." But he eyed Lara, and glanced quickly at Swann, gauging the other man's reaction.

Swann held the wad of flimsies out. Some of them were a little thicker than standard, probably originals. His hand didn't shake, and later, he wondered why. "Here."

Wonder of wonders, he even sounded natural.

Spooky took them. A bright bead of blood had started under her left nostril; she wiped gingerly at it. "Thank you." Two pale, almost whispered little words. "I…Thank you."

"We stick together." Swann pitched it just a little louder than he had to, just like Minjae. "Ain't that right?"

She nodded. So did Prink. Minjae subsided, and Simmons shrugged. The big blond bastard wasn't the one Swann was most concerned about, since he was not precisely untroubled by complex thoughts but profoundly uncaring if he judged they didn't pose a threat to his cohort.

Not for the first time, and definitely not for the last, Swann thought the Reaper would have made a bang-up Patriot if the Firsters hadn't done…what they did to his family.

"We gonna get supplied?" Chuck Dogg said, and Swann's worries eased significantly. Chuck's opinion carried more weight than his own, really.

"Let's move out," Swann replied, and didn't move until Spooky did. Just to make sure she knew she was included in the damn order.

She put her head down, folding the papers with her thin, nail-bitten, capable hands, and meekly followed.

CHAPTER NINETEEN

WHAT SURRENDER MEANS

"I've been thinking." Minjae laced her hands behind her head. "Haven't you?"

"Hard to stop." Zampana bent over her boots, working the polish in with swift, sure circles. An unfinished Patriot Kommunity Kourt had been commandeered for the troops, and the big shiny gym was partitioned down the middle. Camp cots and footlockers stood in neat rows, and it was drafty but not cold. You didn't have to sleep with your head wrapped in whatever blanket you could scrounge up, or huddle in a heap. After so long living rough, it was almost uncomfortable to be back inside. Even the hotel billet in Jackson hadn't exactly made either of them feel easy. "Let me guess. San Francisco."

"What, so I could swim to class? Nah, man. Portland."

"Rains all the time. And riots."

"Should be a nice change. You think they mean it?"

"Mean what?" Zampana could tell where this was heading, but she preferred things methodical. Which was partly why she and Minjae got along so well all the time. Well, *most* of the time.

While Min appreciated systematic thinking, she didn't have much patience for deliberate obtuseness. "New GI bill."

That was the rumor. "They better mean it." Zampana kept polishing.

These were fine, really, but she preferred her old boots, even if the tread on them had worn completely off. Better for forest work. "Could end up a doctor."

"Huh. What does sniping get me?" Minjae's eyes half closed, and the high hard small slopes of her breasts pointed up aggressively. She watched her own boot toes tick-tocking back and forth on an internal rhythm, and rubbed the back of her head against her hands, producing a sandpaper whisper from short, thick black stubble.

"Fifty before hanging." Zampana scooped up more polish.

"Not funny."

"Mh." The rag had to be very wet, but not dripping. Another round of buffing and she'd have a respectable shine, but just once, she was going for a mirror gloss. Just because.

Just to see if she could.

"Where's Spooky?" Minjae closed her eyes. Her shoulders loosened. "Man, that's some goddamn weird shit, ennit."

Zampana weighed the nickname one last time. It was pretty apposite, with the way the new girl stood around, quiet and bug-eyed. Not to mention this morning, and the incident in the burning camp. Her grandmother would call the girl *bruja*, and make the sign of the evil eye. Like jaguars, those with the touch were to be respected, propitiated, feared—and burned if they became malignant. "Prink taking her and Lazy to get ident. Swann got Crunche to cosign on an affidavit or something."

"Huh. Maybe I should get one." The way Minjae was lounging, you could barely tell there was a knife under her pillow. The boots were a dead giveaway, though. A raider learned to sleep in her footwear, along with where *not* to wash her goddamn Div-cup in the woods. Finding a place to dump old blood was harder than you'd think, and who wanted to cram a pollution-dirty cup up her hoo-haw?

Not Emiliana Inez Compaña del Torres, now Zampana for her grandmother, that was for damn sure.

The edge of Minjae's T-shirt rode up. You could just see the top of the bar-like scar peeking over the edge of her uniform trousers, her belt loosened but not completely and her skivvies the dirty-gray army issue that were itchy as fuck to begin with, but wore like iron and eventually matted down and turned buttery.

There was the same horizontal scar on Zampana's abdomen. Glimpsing it on Min made her exhale a bit, and she turned it into blowing across the shoe polish like she thought it would help it dry, or something.

Minjae settled her hips more comfortably. If she were really looking to nap, she would have already been asleep. Something was bothering her. "Pana?"

"Spit it out, *chica*."

"You think he's really gonna die?"

So that was it. "Who?"

"*Him.*"

Oh. She meant *him*. The Great Big Fucktard, the First among Firsters, the Caudillo of DC. "The 'cast said critical condition." They said McCoombs had bitten a glass pill full of something, they didn't know what. Acid, some rumors hinted, ate half his face off. Or poison, said some others, but it hadn't worked on the malignant fuck. "Maybe he just too mean to die."

"Then what? You really think the war's over?"

"That's what surrender means."

"I dunno. I've been thinking."

"I could tell."

Minjae's peculiar chuffing sound of true amusement pulled her chiseled lips taut. Her shirt came up a little more, showing the smooth edges of the scar. Rectangular edges crisp, shiny thickened skin where they'd pressed the contact pad and held it for ninety excruciating seconds.

Zampana's own abdomen twinged a little. It was the last time she'd cried, standing on the public zapbus back in the immie section, her hand flat against the raw, throbbing, deep burn from the targeted waves and the knowledge that her *abuela* had been right, she would never have children. The old woman had a touch of the touch herself, goddammit. It hadn't saved her, or her grandchild.

If she kept thinking about it, she'd end up thinking about the fence, and that was something Pana saved for nightfall and nightmares.

There was no shortage of the latter.

Min began running down the list of what bothered her. As usual, it was logistics. "How are they gonna get all these people home? How are they gonna pick up all the fuckin' *shells*, man? Everything burned down."

"Means more for everyone left." Zampana shook her head like a horse tossing its mane, her heavy braids securely pinned. Playing hide-and-seek with Firster patrols out in the Panhandle had been one thing; the woods had been a welcome change. Places to hide that weren't RVs on empty roads, fewer rattlers, but more chance of stumbling across a patrol. Then it was time for knife work, for quick thinking and the sudden whisper of blood spurting, a hand clamped over the mouth.

The desert had its dangers, too. Once, she and Prink had found a trio of "militia" snoring in their camo sleeping bags around a sullen ember gleam of a sagebrush fire.

The three, with high-powered rifles, freeze-dried rations, and beer bellies, never knew what hit them. Served them right, too, out without a guard in the middle of the desert, thinking white skin made them immune in the wastelands where the coyotes, fourfoot or biped, prowled. Their patches—oh, the militias had all sorts of freelancers, all sorts of weekend warriors—were still tucked in Prink's go-bag, bloodstained and stiff. The rations had been welcome, their rifles and ammo put to good use, but after that Prink had been sullen and gray lipped for a while.

They was fat, he said once. *I don't trust me no fat man.*

"Yeah, well, more of what? Bombed-up shit?" Minjae's upper lip curled a little. "No, my girl, we're in for some fucked-up times."

"You mean worse than Kansas? Bitch, I tell you, *nothing* worse than Kansas."

Minjae's shudder was adequate proof Zampana had carried her point. "Okay, fine. I just wanna go to school."

"Good. You're smart enough. And the West Coast didn't get much boom-boom after '95." You learned not to fuck with someone's dreams. The only raider Zampana thought had no plan for the future, even a hazy one, was Simmons, but the principle still held. "You kickin' out?"

"Soon as they put that GI bill in writing, mothafucka." Minjae found this funny, and laughed. So did Zampana, until their chuckles faded and Min's breathing evened out. She dropped off in the middle of the clamor and bustle, trusting Zampana to keep an eye on the other soldiers even though they were girls—chatting, smoking candies, repairing uniforms or gear, reading, bullshitting, playing cards, sleeping, all the disorderly discipline that was human beings grouped up.

One human was a saint, two were friends, you got three and two of them would make a group to freeze the other one out. A cave in the woods was probably the better bet.

Zampana polished, and while she did, she thought. She wasn't as quick as Minjae, she knew that, but she got there on her own. She had a sneaking suspicion the other woman was right. Fucked-up times were indeed ahead.

Whether or not they would be worse than the war was the bigger question, and one she suspected nobody had an answer for.

CHAPTER TWENTY

FOUR HANDS, FOUR FEET, TWO HEARTS

The new rectangular fluoro-magtat, set above the curved rectangle of scar tissue on her left wrist, itched a little. Spooky sat in a kommunity kourt's bathroom cubicle, the door locked and her body wedged uncomfortably sideways. Soldiers came in, pissed or unloaded their bowels, ran the water, bitched, smoked in defiance of posted signs, ran the hand dryer. Everyone was quickly taking electricity for granted again, at least in this little slice of the army. Old-style fluorescent tubes buzzed, HVAC hummed, water ran. It was as noisy as the woods, but it didn't smell nearly as fresh.

She stared at the magtat. According to it, she wasn't Lara Nelson anymore. She was Anna Gray, born miles away from her actual self, on a day two days removed from her actual birthday, in Memphis.

Anna was easy to remember. It rhymed with…

Spooky shuddered. Her shoulder, hard against the partition between this cubicle and the next, ground into thin metal. It would bruise. Her head felt strange, stuffed with clouds. The dried blood in one of her nostrils was a minor irritant.

It was getting easier.

Many of the flimsies had probably been copied, but a lot of the papers were originals. She'd scanned them before tearing each into tiny pieces, flushing every once in a while when a wad accumulated in the toilet bowl. There was only one she bothered to keep, and it was a partial, not even *her* file, nothing to do with her paper or digital ghost in the Firsters' kamp system.

No, instead of any bread crumbs that could lead to her, this flimsy was a partial officer list from Gloria. The names were familiar, each followed by a number and a registered address for citizen voting. Not that casting a vote changed anything, since after the second-to-last election in '90 there was McCoombs and only McCoombs on the only Firster ballot they made a show of counting. Everything else was appointments, all the way down to school boards.

Those addresses, though, showed where the bastards would likely return. Who wouldn't want to crawl back to whatever they'd had, after all the mud and the blood and the hunger? Home, that fantastical place. Soldiers talked about it, and so did the Firsters.

His name was on the list. *Eugene Thomas.* She shuddered again.

Swann didn't ask any questions. He didn't have to. There were probably plenty of raiders who didn't want to keep their names, who had named themselves for the dead, or who were dead as she was.

No. Not me. Her. The body on the gallows, swaying gently. That yellow-and-blue floral dress, the one she knew so well because it was *hers*. The legs, so like her own. Bare feet with the second and third toes the same length as the first, just like hers. Dark curly hair hanging matted as the head lolled, and her neck ached because it was stretched so savagely.

Had she suffered? Had the cervicals fractured cleanly?

Go to the crossroads, she'd said, nose to nose in their shared bed. Lara's face, identical in every respect, down to the striations in their irises and the delicate shape under the middle of the bottom lip. Lara and Hannah, Hannah and Lara, their own private language shared from the womb, Larahannah and Hannahlara.

There'll be a man there. Pretend you're me. You have to.

She hadn't asked a single question. The man—one of his eyelids drooping—hadn't said a word either, just motioned her into the back of a pickup. By the time she knew what was happening she was miles from home, in the company of a band of raiders who seemed to know her sister, and who expected her to help them with Lara's medical knowledge.

✦

Be me, Lara had whispered.

Well, now she was. She was Hannah-now-Lara now pretending to be Anna Gray, and her head felt strange.

They shared everything, from the walnut tree in back of the big white house to the secret language, from the love of fresh tomatoes to outright hatred of cilantro. Their plates had to be exactly the same; they would trade spoonfuls of peas until it was all equal. Their clothes were the same size, the same colors, and in school they had often switched classes.

It was no use. She couldn't find the right angle to put her head at. If she could, maybe Lara would step into her body and they could share again.

The only way to get that angle was with a ligature and a swift drop. But then, Lara wouldn't be able to come back, and she didn't know if she could go to whatever soft, dark place her sister, her *self*, rested. The uncertainty kept her heart squeezing away like the dumb beast it was, missing its paired transmitter. Just blinking a signal from the middle of her body, in a wavelength there used to be a constant reply on.

The big white house was a charred mess now; no doubt the kudzu had claimed it, and the walnut tree was most likely chopped down. Their mother had died giving birth; their father, a benign gruff stranger, died in their first year of college. Had Lara started helping the raiders then? Had she been part of the campus revolts?

Now she couldn't even remember Hannah's major. What had she been studying? Did it matter?

The shock treatments at Baylock hadn't helped. Leather in her mouth, the smell of ozone, Lara's ghostly face bending over hers. *Go away,* her twin sister said. *I'll make it hurt less.* Then the needles, and the sickness. High fever, the white-coated monsters leaning over her, tossing cryptic terms back and forth. Lara told her what each long medical word meant, just like Lara knew how to set a bone or deal with a combat wound. Everything blurred, and sometimes Hannah wasn't sure...

Not Hannah. Lara. Now Anna.

What was the point?

I love you, Lara whispered. *You have to go. Be me.*

Before, there were four hands, four feet, two hearts making a whole. Now there was only her. During the Uprising, all through Baylock, through the transit kamps and the long nightmare of Gloria, it had been Lara suffering, Lara in pain.

It was Lara *he* said he loved, while he did those things to her. He hadn't let her die on the electrified fence. No, he'd pulled her out of the quarry and done those things to her, over and over. Sometimes there were the restraints, her body inert on the bed while he grunted and heaved.

"Anna," Spooky whispered. "Anna Gray."

The fog inside her skull slowly receded. Anna Gray, from a place that didn't exist anymore. A ghost like all the others.

"Anna Gray." Her voice firmed, took shape, was no longer a cricket-reedy breath. "Swann's Riders, Crunche Company."

Now she knew what she had to do. She folded the paper carefully, tucking it inside her new uniform jacket, and wiped at her nose with trembling fingers, dried blood mixed with snot forming crusty nuggets. Next time it probably wouldn't bleed. Her neck and shoulders ached, but that was all right.

Everything was all right, really. Now that she had the last goal in sight.

CHAPTER TWENTY-ONE

ATTENDED PERSONALLY

May 21, '98

Some things were best attended to personally. Like arranging for one's own safety.

The degenerates' excuse for a kamp was soft, but that didn't make it any less humiliating. No roll calls, simply a morning shuffle past medical staff before breakfast, and those with missing magchips were quarantined. The cots were too soft for true patriots, and there were *showers*. Actual showers, with hot water. The food was hot too, even if much of it was beans or bean-derived. Several times, Gene overheard someone remark that if they'd known captivity would be like this, they would have surrendered sooner.

Such sentiments were not expressed loudly, but they were still too common for his taste. He'd often thought the Three Percenters were exaggerating when they crowed that only a few among the master race would resist, but it looked like they'd been masters too, of fucking understatement.

All in all, though, it wasn't so bad. Gene had ditched his silver Akademy ring, though it hurt to do so. He kept his story simple, switching middle and last names and adding a *-son*, admitting he'd dug his magchip out because he was an officer, but regular Southern Army instead of Patriot Korps. *I was afraid,* he said, and the questioners seemed to accept it as a given.

And what questioners! *Cunts*, for God's sake, two of them, both looking white but obviously immie sympathizers. Blood traitors, then, both of them. Neither of them taking even the least amount of care with their appearance, so probably raging dykes, too. Or both fucking the black man in the old but well-maintained Marine dress blues who headed the troika, too. The rumors were that the other "certification boards" were similarly staffed by the unfit, polluted, and traitorous. Gene bowed his head each time, searching for just what they wanted him to say, aiming for a thoughtful, repentant expression. Yes, he'd believed in McCoombs—the man brought jobs back, and pride. No, he hadn't been lucky enough to get into the Patriot Korps, and he was thankful for it now. No, he hadn't gone to any special schools. He'd joined up at the beginning of the war, flush with patriotism.

It wasn't a bad set of lies, he told himself. Believable, admitting a little cupidity and wrongheadedness, but altogether normal. You heard the same story everywhere in the camp. Whether it was universally, objectively *true* or not, well, who cared? The war was over. The mud underfoot had warmed up, civilian clothes were rationed out. Probably from the central warehouses Gloria and other kamps had baled and sent excess to. The thought that he was wearing a degenerate's jeans and fatigue jacket was bleakly amusing.

He had four meetings with the troika, which was standard. His story didn't change, except in small, reasonable ways. Interrogation was an art, and these degenerates were too blunt to dissect *him*. He was just a fish in a crowded pond, nothing exceptional, a pasty face in a crowd of similarly badly shaven men.

It irked him. He'd excelled all through school and officer training—only the best went into the Patriots, at least until the third year of the war. After that, the manpower crunch had loosened the requirements considerably.

In the prisoner canteen, he ate slowly, spooning up canned peaches, watching the harsh fall of aggressive sunshine outside the open double doors. Flies gathered, waved away from plates and trays with loose swatting hands. The mud of a wet spring was drying and thirty soldiers had been certified out of the kamp just yesterday, including a few taken prisoner along with Gene. Things were looking up.

Or so he thought, until his neck began to itch. There, on the unquarantined side of the canteen, was a familiar face. Chalky now, and loose jowled because the bland, overcooked diet here perhaps did not agree with him, Kommandant Major General Porter turtled his graying head between his soft, shrinking shoulders and stared at his erstwhile subordinate with beady, thoughtful dark eyes.

Gene made no sign of recognizing the man. His chest turned leaden, though. Fingering another Patriot, especially one involved in Gloria, would no doubt get someone preferential treatment. He and Porter had both cut their teeth in Chicago, in the basements of police stations—hunting conspirators, immies, and those who didn't fit into the vast body politic that was Amerika First. You got to know how the world worked.

The degenerates were a disease, and Gene always thought of himself as a humble white blood cell, doing dirty work to keep the rest of society whole. He had to survive, to keep the rest of the structure healthy. It wasn't hubris if you understood you were just a small part of a complex system, right?

That night, accompanied by the blatting of crickets, he slipped through the quarantine barracks, past a degenerate soldier nodding in the alcove near the door—and at Gloria, he would have had that bastard striped for sleeping on duty—and along the side of the barnlike building. Moving across the clear ground toward the east barracks was the tricky part; it took him a long time to work around the edge, keeping to the shadows. He did have one piece of luck—the guard here had stepped away to piss against the side of the building.

Inside, it was just the same as the other barracks—snoring, farting, a mass of humanity on makeshift cots or in camp-issued sleeping bags. They weren't packed together like the jars in Gloria, where the beds were pasteboard shelves on either side of the Quonsets, wide and indifferently supported. Only a few had collapsed, but each time, the mess was cleaned up quickly.

Gene decided not to think about that. Everything went more smoothly if you just enforced that one simple decision inside your own skull. Follow your orders, arrange and organize what you could, and move forward. Progress didn't wait for the lame, the lazy, or the immies.

This was the most personal way to erase a problem. The only thing closer and more satisfying was to sink your thumbs into the windpipe, but that was too inefficiently intimate. Much better to use your forearm across the throat, putting pressure on the carotids. The only trouble was a struggle tipping a cheap cot over, but Porter, newly arrived, had only a bag and a mat. Fortunately, Porter also slept on his back, his snoring oddly harmonic to his neighbor's.

Gene squatted over his former commander, feet on either side of the man's hips. He leaned forward, his knees coming down to rest as his body weight pitched directly over his forearm. The Kommandant barely woke up, his arms flailing fruitlessly, but the lack of oxygen robbed him of strength soon enough.

He was, after all, an old man with black dye leaching out of his hair. And he was soft.

There was very little change in the soughing sea of sleep-breathing around him. Just yesterday another prisoner had been stabbed in the showers, blood running across grimed tiles. No man had admitted to seeing a thing, and the shiv wasn't found.

It took an eternity to do something right, Gene reflected, the twitching body under him losing its battle. The stink of the sphincters loosening took him back to Gloria, and to the desperate urge to shut some of the filth and the stench away. He concentrated instead on the pink room, the curve of a skinny woman's hip, her dark eyes lightening every once in a while to hazel. The shape of her lips, crushed under his. He'd brought her perfume—not the cheap, alcohol scent but imported, French, in a fluted glass bottle, full of raindrops and musk.

Gene Thomas, now Gene Robertson according to Federal paperwork and close to being certified, pressed down a little harder to finish the job thoroughly. And smiled.

PART TWO

SIC TRANSIT

CHAPTER TWENTY-TWO

INTERVIEW

July 6, '98

Simmons grinned, wide and toothy. He slapped the back of the subject's head, lightly, and stared at his own reflection in the flyspecked one-way mirror. On the other side, Spooky and Swann stood, the Spook's arms folded and Swann's hands tense but not quite fists. Sometimes Simmons almost seemed to enjoy being watched while he worked the shake-and-bake.

"Easy there, Reaper." Zampana scratched under one of her thick braids, digging luxuriously with a crimson-lacquered fingernail. She'd taken to good cop, bad cop with a zest that surprised exactly no one except Minjae. "You don't want to hit his head; he'll get confused. Look, Walt—can I call you Walt?"

The subject, balding with a hard little hate-gut that certain types retain even when the rest of their frames are skin and bones, blubbered. His mouth was bloody from the first shot of the festivities, his nose drooling little bits of snot and crimson. A red firework, two days after the Fourth, which had been very quiet this year.

Nobody wanted any more artillery.

"I'm n-n-not W-W-Walt," the prisoner moaned. "I'm *Jim*. Jim Smith."

"Creative," Swann muttered, and glanced at Spooky again. Her expression didn't change. Dark hair thin and brittle at the ends because the malnutrition had grown out a bit, hazel-ish eyes thoughtful and fixed on the scene before her, she might as well have been a statue.

"Oh come on, now." The Reaper leaned forward a little. His high and tight, aggressively waxed, glowed under the fluorescents. "We'll ask the other guy, Pana. This asshole's small fry, he's useless to us."

There was a soft knock behind Swann, and the door opened by degrees. It was Lazy, his weak eye blinking rapidly. Swann glanced back, and the kid made the sign for *They're getting restless*—a roll of his good eye, left hand stroking an invisible cock. Swann just shook his head—nothing yet. Lazy looked like he wanted to come in and watch, but Swann resolutely turned his back. The kid didn't need to see more than he already had, for Chrissake.

"I-I have r-r-rights!" Potbelly stammered. "I'm an A-A-American!"

"Not until you're certified, Firster." Simmons grinned, full of obvious relish. Swann made a restless, uncomfortable movement, but Spooky just continued to watch, unblinking. In the dimness, she might have been staring at a movie screen, flickering lights telling a story. "Remember that? You assholes decided nobody had rights until you said so, and look where that got you."

"I'm certified!" the subject howled, his boiled-egg eyes, full of hot salt water, flickering side to side.

"Under a false name," Zampana pointed out, kindly. If you didn't know her usual tone, you'd almost think she was trying to be helpful. "Your real name is Walter James Eberhardt, and you worked at Re-Edukation Kamp Pilgrim. Personally responsible for eight summary executions we have witnesses for; that means you probably killed five for every one we—"

"He's useless." Simmons slapped the back of the man's head again, a jolly, nasty little swipe. "The other guy's singing like a boy band. Let's just go work with him." Another old trick—tell your subject one of his compatriots was already giving up the goods, adding a whole new layer of pressure.

"What other g-g-g-guy? Look, I d-d-don't *know* anything!" Walt's voice spiraled up into a begging whine, and Swann glanced at Spooky. She met his gaze, finally, and nodded.

He was going to break. Damn uncanny, how she could tell. Every damn time.

"Fine." Zampana pushed her chair back, its metal legs scraping harshly on concrete. "He's all yours, Reaper. I'm going to go watch the other guy's—"

Potbelly began to blubber. "Don't leave me in here with *him*! What do you *want*?"

Zampana appeared not to hear, standing and sweeping together the file folders spread on their half of the table. Most of them were stuffed with trash receipts or blank flimsy, but the subject didn't know that. Simmons leaned down and whispered in the subject's ear. He had a different set of phrases for each eventuality, and Swann wondered idly which one he was using now. Spooky's lips moved a little too, like she could hear, or was mouthing along. Or praying, though she wasn't a Christer.

"Oh, God," Walt moaned. "No, no, no. Look, I was following orders, that's all! I'll tell you—just don't leave me in here with *him*!" The stutter had vanished, and a ratlike gleam filled his rolling eyes.

Zampana paused. "I dunno, my friend. You've wasted a lot of my time already."

Simmons leered, whispered again.

"*Skelm!*" Walt almost yelled, and that was what Swann had been hoping for. "I can tell you where he went! He was in charge, not me!"

Peter Skelm. Not the most powerful man at Pilgrim Kamp, but one all the survivors whispered about, glancing around nervously, if they could be persuaded to talk. Skelm with his collection of ears, and the habit of locking himself in autopsy bays with bodies for a few hours at a time. Nobody knew what he'd done in there, and Swann didn't care.

He just wanted the bastard caught.

From there it was simple. Walt Eberhardt, one of the Three Butchers of Pilgrim, sang, in short, like a prewar boy band. Zampana took notes, and Simmons prodded whenever the flow of information seemed likely to choke itself. Lazy came back after about ten minutes, and Swann sighed, stepping out into a fluorescent-lit hall just like every other station they'd been in since the goddamn surrender was signed. He dug for a smoke before remembering you couldn't do that indoors anymore, and his face set itself sourly. There were still unpainted patches on the wall where pictures of McCoombs had lurked, grinning his self-satisfied, lacquer-haired, upside-down smirk at anyone who dared to come to the cops.

"What?" Swann said.

"Police dude getting nervous." Lazy's shoulders twitched, an approximation of a shrug. "Says he checked fucker's papers himself. Phone keeps ringing."

"Great." So Spooky was right, and the fat-ass motherfucker who passed for law in this slice of not-shot-up-enough suburbia was nervous because he'd been selling certifications. "Send a double to Poulson. Tell him we have a Section Nineteen and a Three-A." The former was your regular charge for selling certification, and not likely to get much of a response except for the beating they'd administer to the police chief for being a corrupt Firster-loving motherfucker. The latter, though, was a high-priority capture tag, and Poulson would know it was the Big Butcher of Pilgrim.

"Okay." Lazy's eyes—good and bad—widened, and he might have taken off at top speed if not for Swann's hand on his elbow.

"Don't just send the double—secure a call and verify." Swann waited until the kid soaked up the caution. "We're transporting this motherfucker."

"Aw, *shit*. Do we have to?" Lazy, like Simmons, was of the opinion that ferrying even a high-value target to a federal condo was a waste of time. Raiders weren't in the habit of taking prisoners, so the protocols for transport were…strict. They had to be, since most of the Blue Companies had feelings about acceptable wastage.

In every sense.

"Orders," Swann reminded him. "Pop Minjae, tell her to prep the nest for evac."

"Yessir." The kid bounced off, his shoes squeaking against old greenish linoleum. *Oughta be in school,* Swann had mumbled once, staring after him, and Zampana had elbowed him. *The war taught him everything he needs to know,* she'd replied, but he wasn't sure he agreed.

Swann rubbed his hand over his growing-in, steel-gray hair. No more head shaving. His hat was retired now, and sometimes he wished he could join it. This would make four they'd brought in, all relatively small and easy bags since plenty of Firsters were corralled at the filtration sites. Eberhardt was just a lucky find, and hopefully he'd lead them to Skelm, then to God knew who.

Maybe at a half dozen caught, Swann could tell Poulson he was getting tired, that it was time to…what?

The observation room's door made a small, forlorn noise as Spooky pushed it open. She peered out into the hall, blinking at the fluorescent glare, and maybe she'd once been pretty. The camp pallor was gone, but her cheekbones still stood out too starkly and her thin shoulders were perpetually hunched. Zampana bought girl stuff in the local black markets since rationing was still tight, but Spooky didn't seem to care that much.

Not that Swann blamed her, but it was a damn shame. Even the good-time fishgirls at the black markets, with their short skirts and eyelids smeared with grainy charcoal instead of anything so expensive as actual *makeup*, were getting rounder by the day. Zampana was solid, even when lean, Minjae was a round little bit of a thing too, but Spooky was a stick in a uniform. That was a fashionable look before the war, but nowadays even the nowcast starlets had some meat on them.

Spooky slid out and closed the door softly, like it was a hospital room or something. She never walked down the middle of a hall if she could help it, always sticking to one side or the other. Less chance of being noticed that way, maybe. A camp habit.

She stopped just out of arm's reach. "We dragging him?"

"Yeah." Swann rubbed at his face now. Christ, this made him tired. "We've got a nineteener."

Her bloodless lips curved a little. "Toldja." She straightened a little, waiting for orders. "He's repeating himself now. We have a direction but no contact name."

"Well, *shit*." That was half the reason to drag the asshole out of here, to pump him for more details about Big Butcher Skelm's destination, not just his travel direction. "You sure? No, you know, jogging his memory?"

She shook her head, a pained grimace pulling up one side of her mouth. "If he knew, or knew and didn't *know* he knew, maybe. But no. They're getting a little smarter."

"So are we." When you worked in cells, it was best if nobody knew any more than the general direction of their next contact. Old strategies were surprisingly durable when you were the insurgent instead of the empire.

She nodded. "Yeah." Her hair swung a little, and she stripped it back from her face with impatient fingers. It wasn't long enough for a ponytail yet, and Chuck had run out of red thread. "One at a time, that's how it's done." Quoting his own words back at him.

Swann sighed, restraining the urge to kick at the thick rubberized strip along the bottom of the wall. "Yeah, one at a fucking time." You couldn't drag the motherfuckers in wholesale. Or, you could, but not with refugees spilling out of the goddamn South, infrastructure shot to shit, electricity still intermittent, and the damage to the ports and all...not to mention New York. The financial nerve center of the whole goddamn world, even if it had slid under Firster mismanagement and the meteoric rise of the Chinese markets, now gone in a flash.

Spooky just stood there, patiently waiting. Finally, Swann sighed again, a deep one, coming all the way up from his heels. He ticked his head impatiently to the side, and she fell into step behind him.

It was glare-bright in the interrogation room. Walt Eberhardt jerked upright in his chair as the door banged open, and the whites of his eyes showed like a frightened horse's.

"Well?" Swann asked. The single word bounced off the walls, the false mirror watching with its silvery eye.

"He's being helpful." Zampana smiled, but it didn't reach her eyes. "Aren't you, Walt?"

"Please," Walt moaned. "Please, yes. I've told you all I know, everything."

Swann had heard that before, more times than he liked. Of course he had. Only nowadays he was hearing it in cop shops instead of forest hutches or RVs.

Any suspected raider, or person with "sympathies," or, God forgive, an immie brought here a few years ago wouldn't have been in one of these rooms. There was always a basement in buildings like this. Walt had it easy. Swann had seen the bodies; he knew what the cops—maybe the

very same fat fuck sweating on his phone in his office down the hall—
did before they handed you over to the Patriots for Reklamation or Re-
Edukation.

If you lived that long.

Simmons straightened. His face had gone blank, and the Reaper
lurked below the corn-fed aw-shucks regularity of a sweet Nebraska boy
descended from good-natured Scandinavians. His hand was on Walt's
shoulder, and his big blunt fingers dug in a bit.

"Minnesota," Walt repeated. "There's a man, I don't know his name, in
Minneapolis. In an old grocery store, but it's a house now. That's the only
safehouse I know!"

Zampana studied Swann's face. "We have the address."

"We don't need this asshole, then." Simmons's hand tightened again.

Walt whimpered.

"Simmons." Zampana, very softly.

Each time, it took a little longer for the Reaper to glance at Swann for
direction. The seconds ticked by. Finally, the Reaper's upper lip lifted, his
cheeks reddening. "Okay." When he did look up, it was at Spooky first.
She held his gaze, level and cool. "Well?"

Walt whined again. His face was puffing up, and his tongue probed for
what was probably a tooth loosened in the first go-round.

"Cuff him." Swann sounded tired, even to himself. "Zampana and
Spooky can prep him for hauling. I need you for something else."

"What?" Simmons didn't move.

Swann hooked his thumbs in his wide leather belt. He didn't reply, and
after a few more tense moments, Simmons turned Walt loose with a last
vicious squeeze.

The captain restrained himself from saying *Good boy*. There was a
word for a dog that didn't particularly care what it bit, and the word for
a raider gone into the red was the same. "We got a nineteener," he said
heavily, and Simmons's eyes lit up with that particular cold, sterile blue
glow. "I think we're gonna talk to him up close."

CHAPTER TWENTY-THREE

CURES GOD OF US

July 8, '98

"Reminds me of Texas," Zampana said, squinting at the road as the sun sank bloody orange. "Raiders there used RVs too. You could clear 'em out and haul an ultralight in one, or even a small prop plane. Miles of nothin', and we used the ham radio sometimes to bounce messages around before the Firsters got wise. Hit an installation with air cover, man, then vanish. They had the helicopters, but we could move the planes around...the only problem was getting gas—we didn't have any sleds or retrofits."

Spooky made a soft noise, just marking that she was listening. She liked it when Zampana talked like this, quiet and low, reminiscing. With the hum of the tires and a bottle of distilled water in reach, it was...nice.

Zampana sucked on her top teeth for a moment, then continued. "Nah, the retrofits only came after Second Cheyenne, when I hooked up with Swann. He'd been pushed all the way back there, one step ahead of the Reklamation Army. Those were dark fucking days, I tell you."

The first offensive, meant to take back the seceded Western States, had been breathtakingly successful until it ground to a halt near the Rockies. First Cheyenne had been called a Firster victory at the time, though the bloodbath had pretty much skimmed the cream of the RA. It took Second Cheyenne to do *that* army in completely. Of course Spooky had only heard about the latter piecemeal.

At Baylock, right before the bombing.

"Reklamation," Spooky agreed, a shudder shifting her hips in the seat. When the Fourteeners had gathered up all the "blood-pure" organizations, it was the Klan who gave the most lasting gift, putting *k*'s in everything and flipping words around. Patriot. Re-Edukation. Rendition. Blood. None of it meant what it used to in the dictionary, and all of it was horrifying. Out of all the words, though, *reklamation* was the worst.

If you weren't going to be a part of Greater America, well, everything on you and *in* you would be "reklaimed." The killing bottles and the bath bays were just a natural extension of that concept, that one little word.

Their RV slowed, Zampana sensing potholes ahead. It wasn't a difficult guess—refugees cluttered either side of the freeway, some moving in clumps, others collapsed atop whatever they'd managed to carry from their homes. Yellow dust rose in veils, bugs splattered the dry windshield, and the vehicle swayed a bit as Zampana slowed further. Some of the power poles around here had been splintered or lopped short by artillery, and great scars gouged the fields on either side, greening at their edges since the human beings had stopped blowing shit up everywhere.

There were still scattered pockets of Firster crap, sure. America was huge. Some of the Firsters down south had taken a few pages from the raiders' playbook, but with plenty of major cities shelled to bits and so many people deciding that leaving the smaller towns was preferable to starving to death, the assholes didn't have many to steal from, beg from, or kill except their own supporters.

"The RA wasn't at Memphis," Spooky finally added. They'd already been moving west by then. "But I heard, later. In the transit kamps."

The back of the RV was quiet. Simmons was sacked out on the couchlike bench along the strip of dining table, the only place big enough for him to rest. Sal was sleeping too, fussily buckled into a jumpseat and lolling with his mouth half open and a bubble of saliva collecting in the corner, his cheeks rough with stubble and his black curls tumbled. Minjae was in the overhead bed, curled around a couple pillows. Prink sat on the floor with his back to the door of the tiny bathroom, bent over a cheap paperback with a pink cover showing two women in a lustful and exceedingly gymnastic embrace. His carroty hair flopped as the RV's pads hummed over a series of frost hillocks in the pavement.

Swann, Chuck, and Lazy Eye had transit duty this time, and were on a sled with Walt Eberhardt trussed like a bird for roasting. The potbellied motherfucker was probably just glad Simmons wasn't along for the sled ride.

"Shitty." Zampana leaned forward, arching, stretching in the seat. Long trips were hell on the back no matter *what* you were driving.

"You could tell when the offensives happened." Spooky's eyes unfocused; the roadside masses blurred together. Skinny, wan women with sheared hair, some of them in long sleeves and skirts despite the heat, holding pleading signs a little higher as the RV passed, mostly variants of WILL WORK FOR FOOD. Plenty of the women had bruised faces, too—in some places, Firsters took a page out of the Christian Court playbook and branded "fraternizers." The women who had survived the Firsters' Scarlet Woman Initiative had longer hair, were not quite as thin, and were considerably less vacant-looking. The men, gaunt or stocky, were all hard-eyed and dirty, sitting in whatever shade they could find or trudging along with their thumbs out, shoulders hunched. "There would be a bunch coming in with flash burns or crushes. Lots of striping the day after."

"Jesus." Zampana crossed herself. In the camps, the lashes weren't counted like they were for Public Atonement. Instead, the flogging went until the flesh came off the bone, and kept going.

"Can I ask you something?" Spooky dug in a coat pocket, bringing out half a ration bar. She hunched, unwrapping it a little guiltily. None of the fugees outside could see her, but it still felt...wrong. She quashed the urge to look over her shoulder. There was no jar kaptain to grab the food, or singer to inform on her.

Habit was hard to break.

"Go ahead." It didn't look like Zampana minded. "Should get you some protein shakes, too. How's your stomach?"

"Fine." She flattened her free hand across her belly, dug her fingers in briefly, and really thought about it. "Yeah, fine. You a Christer? I mean, what kind? If you want to say."

"Catholic. Don't let it worry you, I'm not a thumper." Zampana grinned. Her hair, damp from a cold shower at the last stop, poured over her shoulders. In a little while someone else would drive, and she'd braid and pin the mop up. "You?"

A short, harsh caw of a laugh escaped Spooky's throat. "Kamps cured me of God, Pana."

"Yeah, but what cures God of us, *mi Abuelita* would say." Zampana slowed still further. "Look at this. They're all over the road."

They were indeed. A scuffle had broken out on the wide, dusty meridian, yellowing grass beaten down by foot traffic. Zampana whistled, a long low noise, the RV slowing to a nudging crawl as a tide of humanity blocked the freeway's ribbon. A sign to the right had a perfectly placed hole in the middle—looked like a mortar hole, but how did it hit perpendicular like that? God only knew. The shot had eradicated the lettering but left the fact of the sign itself, and someone had strung a tarp below to make a sort of tent.

"No," Spooky murmured. "Grenade launcher."

"What?" Zampana glanced over at the blasted sign. "That? Huh, yeah, looks like. What are they fighting over?"

"Can't see." Nibbling at the bar was soothing. When you were eating, there was nothing else in the world as wonderful or interesting. She leaned forward too, peering at the scrum. Looked like men involved, and a bright red flash of blood glowed fresh through the dust. They had one down and were stomp-kicking. "Maybe a Firster?"

"Not a lot of those advertising it anymore. Ration thief?" Zampana guessed. "Look at that, his head's...*ew*."

More blood spattered, and the growling crowd-noise took on a higher pitch. The disturbance spread, a clot of violence around a sodden crumpled mass that had once been a man fracturing into smaller pieces of shoving, yelling, a high short scream from a woman caught at the edge.

Swann might have made Zampana stop and tried to restore some order, but Spooky just watched as the RV drifted forward through the crowd. The sea noise of excited voices all babbling at once washed against the windows, and she bit off a good chunk of the bar, luxuriating in the tang of fresh cranberry. You could get new bars instead of old, crumbling ones now, and they were good. Some of them even had real chocolate shavings instead of carob stubs, but it was the vitamin C ones Lara liked best.

No. Not Lara. Anna, or Spooky.

Each time she caught herself, there was a slipping sideways motion. Inside, not outside, as if everything inside her had come loose for a split second and jolted to a stop on a protruding nail. Like the scar on their father's hand, a short sharp brutal pink hyphen.

"What's going on?" Prink, near the back, shaken free of his book by the change in speed.

"Crowd in the road." Zampana, losing a little patience, hit the horn once, twice. Light taps, but the blatting jolted Spooky. It sounded too much like roll call. "Looks like a fight. Or they caught someone stealing."

Prink made a low, chuffing, disgusted noise. "Prolly a nineteener." Certification was a slow process, and with records wormed or burned, you had to catch false certifications in interrogation or get witnesses. Funny, those who'd had Patriot pins and Party posts all seemed to have vanished, pictures of McCoombs were now torn down, and everyone was now someone who had resisted.

At least, that's what they wanted you to think.

"Who knows?" Zampana hit the horn again. "They should stay out of the road."

"Run a couple over." With that wisdom shared, Prink went back to his book, licking his dry lips and stretching out his legs.

"That'd make the cells sing." Zampana kept the RV nosing forward, counting on the whine and buffet of the pads to keep the crowd away. By the time Spooky grubbed the last crumb out of the wrapper, they'd broken free of the worst of it, and the refugees started to scatter for the sides of the road. Some tried to flag the RV down, but the festoons of barbed wire gleaming along the sides of the vehicle discouraged barnacles. At least this wallowing hulk didn't have tires that could be spiked by the desperate. The flat, reflective buffer pads along the bottom, full of glow from the kerro engines, were *way* better. Except when something fleshy got caught under them, and squealed.

"How many camps were you in?" Zampana's curiosity was thoughtful, not prying.

Spooky counted on her fingers. Baylock. A transit kamp, then another. Maybe another one before Gloria? "Four? They blur together. I got sick. Don't know why I wasn't selected into the bottle." *Sick* was one way of putting it.

"Dios." Zampana crossed herself, a quick reflexive movement. "Used up all your luck, *chica*."

"Maybe." Spooky folded the wrapper in half, folded it again. You could get them really small if you did it the right way. A pad of foil-ish wrapping was useful in several tiny ways, and it was habit not to throw away anything that could be repurposed.

They passed another road sign, this one shattered and hanging in curls of metal. A plank had been attached to one of the poles, proclaiming CAMP 2MI in sloppy white reflective paint, an arrow pointing drunken-crooked to the right toward a venomous glitter of bright blue water. Two sleds winked above the liquid gleam, circling slowly—maybe bringing in purification tabs; Christ alone knew what was in the groundwater around here. Or maybe they were just keeping an eye on a seething mass of humanity. At least the refugee collection sites weren't fenced.

Still, it was good Spooky wasn't in one of them. She didn't have to shuffle in line for rations or sit through certification questioning. Less mud, less crowding, less of the breathing crowd pressing in on her, shoving, forcing, screaming all at once. The only trouble was, before, she could pretend that the one voice she wanted to hear was in the middle of all the others, just drowned out by the cacophony.

Now the unsilence was deafening. How did people born in ones instead of twos *stand* it? All the…loneliness.

"But maybe not all," she added, as the RV accelerated past the exit, through the clogged artery of a smashed overpass. Gangs of refugees had been put to work clearing the roads, small human hands hauling chunks of unforgiving concrete. "Or maybe just the bad."

"That's a good way to look at it." Zampana rolled the window down a little, and fresh hot summer air roared past. "Light me a candy, Spooky."

"Thought you didn't smoke."

"They're not real cigarettes." Zampana shook her head, her drying hair raveling into curls. "Besides, after seeing that, I need *something*."

CHAPTER TWENTY-FOUR

TEN THREES

July 10, '98

He checked the map twice and decided yes, this was the place. The address numbers were taken off, and the streets were woozy staggers, some of them pocked with craters from drone attacks; their crumbling sidewalks, put down in the previous century, were too thin for the size-obsessed America that followed. Some of the trees had survived, and there were gangs of fugees sweeping the debris up into piles. Humans just like ants, scurrying back and forth to get things lifted, arranged, put away. Nobody took any notice of a skinny kid in a dusty tan sports jacket, loitering in the shade of a miraculously unhurt poplar, its leaves fluttering in a breeze redolent of dust, exhaust, and colorless kerrogel reek, plus the edge of rot from bodies trapped in ruins.

The only trouble was that it wasn't just Firsters dead under artillery but immie indentureds too, and the pets. Dogs were the worst, they wouldn't leave the dead assholes. Cats knew when to get out, but dogs were loyal, and that loyalty got them fuckered up but good.

Once, before Lazy'd joined up, he'd seen a dog sitting patiently by the hanging mess of stripe-flayed meat that had probably been its owner. Not licking at the steak or flanks, not sniffing the blood, just…sitting there, a brown dog with its head cocked, hoping its master would stop playing dead and stumble away so it could follow. He remembered every hair on the dog's head, its big liquid brown eyes, the paws surprisingly white and another pale patch on its chest like a target. Some of the Patriots on duty in the square had pointed their guns at it and laughed, making jokes, but the dog didn't care. It ignored them, and waited by the dead body of its master. The placard hung at the corpse's neck had read FAGGOT. Whether or not it was true, who knew? Homosexuality was fifty stripes for a male, and if you survived that they sent you to a Reklamation camp. Girls had it easier—you had to really *try* to get caught as a lesbo, and they sent you for Minor Re-Edukation for a couple months, figuring it was just a phase.

The worst thing about striping wasn't the whip cutting the skin. It wasn't the sound, or the pain during it, even though that was fucking bad enough. The worst was after, tied to the post and hearing flies buzz, whatever pants you had left soaked with urine—your own and God alone knew who else's, since some stripers pissed on their work—and the pain a gnawing until it turned numb, damage creeping through nerve and muscle down to bone. Striping didn't just fuck you up in the short term, oh no. It twisted your entire fucking body around and did funny neurological things. Like make half of your face dead and one of your eyes drop, twitch, or roll when you were least expecting it.

Or make everyone call you *kid*, even when you were halfway to your thirty dead Firster-fucks. One for every fucking stripe laid on a kid's back, sure, but even more, it was a mystical fucking number. Holy Trinity, dialed up to ten. Ten threes, right? Lucky three, like lucky seven. After he had his thirty, well, maybe he'd shoot for forty-nine. Seven sevens.

Lazy checked the hand-drawn map one more time, then tucked it inside his jacket. If he brought this motherfucker in, Swann might quit calling him *kid*, and might let him actually question the sumbitches like Simmons did. The Reaper was all-fucking-right, and didn't treat Lazy like a child. At least, not often.

He blew out between his teeth, running his fingertips over his face. Not a lot of twitching. He could see just fine, until things started jumping when the nerves on his bad side got confused. He was quick, and he was smart, and he did a lot more than Swann ever saw. Did the captain think it was easy, sweet-talking paperwork through one hoop after another?

Lazy ate last and got up first, dammit, not because he was young but because he was *committed*.

The kid stepped out of the shade of the poplar, aiming for the front door of the house. Its upper story had been hit and was probably closed off, but the cracked and frost-heaved path leading up a few tiny concrete steps was swept. Electricity out in the suburbs was generally good, but closer to the city centers it was kind of problematic, so he decided to knock the way the asshole they'd dragged in had specified—three short raps, a pause, then two.

He made it up to the door, the screens on the porch full of gaping holes. Overgrown bushes pressed against the side of the house, shielding the front from prying eyes.

Rap-rap-rap. Pause. *Thump-thump.*

Man, Swann was gonna be so fuckin' surprised when Lazy brought this fucker in. He even had his first line all prepped. *I'm here to see a man about a dog,* he'd say, just like in an old movie.

There on the overgrown porch, the kid smiled, hearing stealthy movement on the other side of the door and a grinding sound from down the street, where they were filling in a shell crater. Bringing this asshole in was gonna be the feather in his cap, all right. Even Zampana, with her pretty fingernails and long black hair, would have to admit he'd done something outstanding.

CHAPTER TWENTY-FIVE

GET OUT

Inside a ramshackle, vine-grown safehouse, painkillers thankfully blurring every edge, Gene Thomas blinked at the knocking. This room, its carpet stripped and a dentist's chair dragged into the middle of a flood of greenish light through the overgrown windows, was none too clean, but the doctor used an excess of antiseptic on his hands and surgical tools to make up for it.

Gene's leg ached, and so did his face. The shrapnel wound in his calf sometimes bothered him, but it was the head bandage that was the real irritant. Mild reconstructive surgery—probably the only benefit from his rank since Amerika had ended, but one he'd take—was unpleasant, but how else was he to achieve some kind of safety? He had new ID blanks with certification attached, yes, but now there were former partisans tracking down Patriots. All the traitors were looking to ingratiate themselves with the degenerates now, so better safe than sorry.

Not that there were many from Gloria who would recognize him. Except the jar kaptains, the midlevel guards, and whatever filth they hadn't cleaned up before the degenerates arrived. Had *she* survived? Probably not, and that was one more thing to hate.

There was no shortage.

The safehouse owner, a nervous big-eyed jackrabbit with a long flop of hair and a yellowing wifebeater wrapped around his skinny chest, cursed and flung open the door to a broom closet in the dusty, trash-stacked hall. His jeans sagged, clinging low on his hips, and he was barefoot.

"Get out," he snapped, and drew a long, familiar shape from the closet's depths. He racked, and the whine of a live plazma shotgun spiraling into forty-watt range buzzed softly under the words. "Out the back door, turn east on Polk, double back. Get to the next stop."

The doctor responsible for Gene's new looks—a lean hatchet-faced man in a plaid sports jacket despite the heat, who'd given his name as Johnson—shrugged on a backpack from the leaning metal desk under the small dusty window, his long-fingered hands quitting their nervous washing of each other. "What about—"

Their host, who'd been a low-level functionary in the state Party structure, headed for the front door. Barefoot, his stained tank top stretching across chicken-bone ribs, he didn't *look* like a warrior for truth, justice, and inviolate borders. "It's the wrong knock," he hissed over his shoulder. "Someone broke a node, but the asshole gave them the warning signal. Get *out*."

"Where's the next house?" Gene's jaw ached, the words slurring. He stumbled after the doctor, who glanced sourly at him, perhaps gauging how far his oath to a patient extended. Or judging how likely he was to see the results of his work if he ditched said patient now.

"North," was all Dr. Johnson would say, settling his backpack straps with quick, impatient jerks. "If it's any consolation, they're probably after me, Captain."

Gene didn't have the breath or the energy to point out that once they were caught, the question would be academic, since he was obviously getting his goddamn face altered. He followed the doctor's bobbing fedora-clad head, and they slipped out into an overgrown, humid backyard full of the whine of mosquitoes and the stench of rotting greenery, still water, and bodies trapped in shattered buildings.

There were no sleds circling, no rumble-whine of kerros lurking; the doctor headed across the yard for a small wooden door choked by raspberry vines. Inside, stairs went down into what had once been a dry cellar, but gave out onto a shell crater with a good foot of oil-shimmering water stagnant at its bottom. Dappled sunlight sent headache darts through Gene's head as he staggered in Johnson's wake.

A plazma blast tore the afternoon behind them, a boom that crackled at the end. Hard on its heels came a short, agonized cry, and the crisp clatter of pistol fire.

Gene put his head down, splashing through the shallow, noisome water, and kept going.

CHAPTER TWENTY-SIX

A RIGHT TO BE

A low, hard-floored box of a room, full of glaring fluorescent light, a bolted-down table, and three indifferent plastic chairs, was nowhere near big enough to contain this pile of trouble. "Two hours." The words forced themselves out through Swann's teeth, his jaw so tightly clenched a headache was no doubt brewing up his neck and behind his eyes. "You've been in town *two fucking hours*, Simmons."

The Reaper sprawled in a hard, uncomfortable chair, his face starred and speckled with drying blood. Handcuffed and sullen, his uniform shirt torn and bloodied as well, he lifted his lip and outright snarled. "She called him a nigger, Swann."

On the other side of the table, Chuck Dogg stared at the wall. He wasn't handcuffed. Of course, he hadn't tried to beat the shit out of the MPs hastily called to bring in a couple of un-uniformed men who, in a brawl, certainly *acted* like enlisteds. Chuck was spattered too, but only with beer and a few ounces of eye-wateringly strong clear liquor from the bottle he'd broken over some asshole's head as said asshole was attempting to blindside Simmons with a wobbling barstool.

The Dogg didn't look mildly inconvenienced, like he would have if that had been the whole story.

"Chuck?" Swann studied the man and decided that was definitely *not* the whole story.

Because Chuck Dogg looked downright *irritated.* "Bar ho. Told her I wasn't paying for no pussy. She up and called me nigger, like a goddamn Firster. Said I wouldn't get no white woman anyway."

Swann rubbed at the back of his neck. The MPs had run their ID chits and popped Swann a *Come get your asshole soldiers* flimsy, and he had no idea if the local commander was going to get sticky. Martial law was still the order of the day in previously Firster cities, and Minneapolis, white bread and Lutheran butter, had been prewar-tolerant only until the first round of McCoombs's registration legislation passed. Not like, say, Vermont, which had always been restless. More like Maine, where the nail that stuck out was to be hammered down, and sooner rather than later.

"I just tapped her," Simmons added, somewhat helpfully.

Swann reached for his hat, found out—again—that he wasn't wearing it, and took another whack at figuring this out. "And somehow that turned into a full-scale engagement? You carved one asshole's eye with the end of a bottle, Simmons. Might need an implant."

The Reaper shrugged. Swann glanced imploringly at Chuck, who spread his hands and shook his head. "They jumped us as soon as Simms slapped the bitch, Captain. Fucking bar full of nineteeners. We just wanted a drink."

"Uh-huh." The headache arrived, throbbing right between Swann's temples.

"I ent going in stockade." Simmons's entire face set, stubborn as frozen prairie sod. "She called him that, Swann. Shoulda cut her."

The woman he was referring to—a blowsy brunette, still loudly drunk and full of fuming imprecations—was being held in a cell, her cheek swelling up and turning purplish. She didn't seem to grasp how goddamn lucky she was. Unshaved, so she probably wasn't a campog or a scarlet. The Firsters had first publicly flogged, but later shorn and branded "scarlet women," like unwed mothers or the ones caught trying for a back-alley abortion. After liberation, it was the "collaborators" who got shaved, but Swann had an idea they were just the girls nobody liked, or who were unlucky when it came to choosing a protector.

Men didn't get shaved, and didn't have WHORE painted on their faces.

They were just striped if they were Party members, or shot if they were proven nineteeners. Or if they tried to jump a soldier. Or if ock troops—for *oc*cupation—didn't like the look of them. Just as in any war, the Federal front liners had been too busy—and too goddamn tired—for any bullshit, but second and third waves coming through conquered territory were just fresh enough to want a little of their own back.

Casualties hadn't stopped just because the surrender was signed and everyone was waiting to go home, either. Partly because of shit like this.

Swann gathered whatever patience he had left after a long day, and nodded thoughtfully. "So she called Chuck...what she called him, and you pimpslapped her?"

"Yeah." The Reaper set his jaw in the familiar mutinous line and let his bloodshot blue eyes bore into his captain.

"And then?" Swann glanced at Chuck.

"Then the whole damn bar went for us." *What you gonna do?* Chuck's dark eyes asked. *You gonna let this stand?*

It was the same question, just a different goddamn day. The war should have answered it once and for all, but there were *still* assholes who decided to test. "Well, six of 'em needed a medic, and the girl's locked up. Fine her for hate speech, prolly. Just...*two hours*, Sim." At least he'd finished the processing paperwork for Eberhardt yesterday. The rest of the Riders had RV'd into town just two hours ago; Sal was still asleep, Prink looking for funnybooks, Minjae getting supplies, Pana and Spooky looking for hot food, and who the fuck knew where Lazy had gotten himself to?

The Reaper couldn't have looked less repentant if he'd tried. "You sayin' I shouldn't've—"

"No. Not saying that at all. Just remarking on the timeframe." Swann reached for his hat, remembered—*again*—that he wasn't wearing it, and turned the movement into a spreading-his-hands gesture of resignation. "Okay. Sit tight, I'll get someone in here to take those off. Be nice, Simmons."

"Long as they don't call my man Chuck no names, I'll be a model fuckin' citizen." Simmons showed his teeth.

Chuck put his hands on the table between them, leaned forward to rest his head, too. He looked tired.

Well, he had a right to be, goddammit.

"Chuck? You all right?"

The Dogg didn't reply. It was stupid even to ask, Swann decided, and just as he turned to the door, there was a knock and it swept open to reveal a pale Zampana, her hair hastily braided and her uniform jacket thrown over a T-shirt and a pair of culottes that showed her strong, medium-brown calves. "Captain?" She barely glanced at Simmons, and Swann began to get a very bad feeling. "There's, uh, a problem."

CHAPTER TWENTY-SEVEN

WRONG KNOCK

"Look at this." Zampana peered into a stainless steel cabinet. "Sterigauze, opfoam…norpirene, opioids…"

Leaf-rippling greenish light filtered through boarded-over windows webbed with raspberries, ropy stems and thorns thick with summer. Spooky stared at the dentist's chair the fucker had obviously used as an operating table. "And we were making do with bandannas and whiskey."

"Waste of whiskey." Zampana's nose wrinkled. "How did he *get* all this stuff?"

"Firster." It was all that needed to be said. They got the best, inside their own borders. If you were white and your membership number was low enough, or if you were good at "organizing," you could be the first stop on the distribution pipeline. If you were a Firster, the Selekt Shops were chock-full of things to buy.

It was only the immies, the non–Party members, and the raiders behind the lines who had to make do with soylon instead of cotton, carob instead of chocolate, chicory instead of coffee, sand instead of blood. Spooky's fingers ached; she shook her hands out. The lamp over the dentist's chair was a high-intensity glare, and there was a tray of bloodied instruments on a trolley. Used gauze, surgical thread. Something had been interrupted. "Huh."

"What you think?" Zampana's eyebrows were up, and she pushed at her hair, settling the braids more securely. "Since you got the degree and all."

What would Lara say to that? Spooky didn't have to think very hard. "No residency, though."

"Unless you count stitching up raiders with pine needles and spit." Zampana's hip brushed the edge of a slumped-sideways, rusted metal desk as she looked out the dust-coated, vine-choked window. The entire house was covered in greenery, a cave full of liquid shadows and a chronic reek of disinfectant just barely big enough to stretch over the smell of blood and cheap canned food cooked over jellied gasoline. "What's this asshole doing?"

Well, it was obvious, really. "Plastic surgery." If your records were wormed, all they had was ident photos and biometrics to go off, or not even that. Eyewitness testimony was unreliable, and what better way to make it even *more* so than by changing your entire face? Even just a few millimeters could mean your certification was safe. "Motherfuckers."

"No shit?" Zampana studied the room, the green-lit window at her back shadowing her face. "Oh yeah, I see. Can't do real work on a chair like that."

Spooky pointed at the floor, where a congealed mass of something that looked like cat litter was soaking up blood and op disinfectant. No wonder the disinfectant didn't cover up the smell. How had the fucker gotten his hands on *litter*, for God's sake?

They hadn't used litter at Baylock. They hadn't had to—the surgical suites were fully equipped. Cracking open the thoracic cavity? Sure. Trepanning? You bet. Endoscopic neurosurgery? No problem. Administering syringe after syringe of gene-edit serum? Of course! Shock treatments after hair-fine intrusions through the dura, arachnoid, and pia mater? Child's play.

And afterward, the tests with patterned cards, dice, oscilloscopes. *Make the dial move.*

Oh, she had. The dial was spinning now, motherfuckers.

"Hey. You okay?" Zampana was suddenly *there*, right next to her, and Spooky flinched away, her knee barking on the chair with a heavy *thock*ing sound. "Oh, shit, sorry."

Nothing in here was trapped, but it was still good to be cautious. "It's all right." Spooky sounded very far away, even to herself. A familiar rushing filled her ears, but she forced herself to look at the headrest, wobbling because the clamps had been loosened. Looked like he'd added padding to keep the head still. "Just thinking about it."

Prink tapped twice on the doorframe, his carroty hair sticking up in clumps. "Everything okay?"

"Yeah." Spooky rubbed at her knee. There was gonna be a helluva bruise there tomorrow. "What else we got?"

"He didn't write anything down, if that's what you're asking." The redhead's hands washed each other, an unconscious motion, the stub of his missing finger twitching. "No notes, no nothin'. Swann called yet?"

Zampana shook her head. What Prink was *really* asking was completely different. "Motherfucker plazzed Lazy in the gut. I don't know, Prink. Nobody can tell with a wound like that."

And even gutshot, the kid had managed to shoot the skinny-ass Firster bastard with his sidearm, then ping for backup. It was a damn good thing he'd been carrying a comm cell. Minjae was at the hospital waiting for news while Swann argued Proustinek, the military governor this entire pisswah had landed on, into turning Simmons loose again. Proustinek was a one-eyed bastard—literally, he'd taken shrapnel to the face during the Topeka Offensive, and it had soured his disposition.

He was, alas, no Crunche. He wasn't even a Poulson.

"Well, the kid got him." Prink pushed on either side of the doorframe. "What was he doing here? You think he was, maybe, warning 'em?"

Spooky rubbed at her knee. It would be fine, but that gave her a reason to look down instead of at Zampana, whose silence turned as fierce as the sunlight assailing the outside of the tumbledown house. A few long, unhappy moments ticked by, all the fine hairs on Spooky's body rising, her shoulders drawing up almost to her ears. Her uniform trousers were breaking in really well, even if she had to cinch them double tight with a regulation-issue webbing belt.

It was funny, sometimes she wondered if she'd ever really worn a skirt, felt material sliding against shaved legs, bared her shoulders. She knew she *had*—she could remember dresses, and the pink soylon dress *he* had brought her. She could remember holding up one or two falls of shimmering material in the sorting shed...and the gentle swaying of a body in a blue-and-yellow floral summer frock.

"Yeah, you're right," Prink said quietly, as if Zampana had yelled at him. "Prolly came to get the fuckers himself. Him and his fuckin' thirty."

Spooky's head jerked up. What was that?

Thud-thud. A pause. *Thud-thud.*

"It was the wrong knock," she muttered. "Shit."

"What the fuck?" Prink turned on his heel, his hand dropping to his sidearm.

It was Zampana who caught on first, though. "Shh!" She waved a hand frantically. "It's a Firster, Prink. Maybe the fucker we're after. Go pretend you're one of them, get him inside." Her other hand dropped to her sidearm too, and her upper lip lifted, showing her strong, horsey white teeth. "Spooky, come on."

The tension snapped, a shower of cold relief inside Spooky's chest. A strange chill certainty settled behind it. She could tell herself she only suspected who was at the door. It would be a lie, because she didn't "suspect."

She *knew*.

CHAPTER TWENTY-EIGHT

TO MEAN SOMETHING

Peter Skelm's mouth felt like a wool coat, fuzzy-thick and at once too dry and uncomfortably sweaty. He shivered in the shade of the overgrown, cavernous porch. Standing in the sun was worse, his armpits and thighs greasing up under the heat. This place had better have some goddamn antibiotics, or his wanderings were going to come to an inglorious end. It wasn't right for a man who had served his country to die of tetanus, but the world was an unjust place at best, his grandfather always said, and this just proved it.

He coughed, twice, into his left hand. Have to wash up as soon as he got in. He stared at the green-painted door—chips and cracks, a few thin glass panes a little above eye level, the doorknob of blackened metal sitting indifferently cockeye. Why even bother knocking?

Oh, that was right. There was a code. Good way to get shot, knocking on doors these days. Salesmen were probably having a tough time of it.

His vision blurred, the fever slipping him through time and memory, and for a moment the door was another one—a trim white-painted slab of wood neatly set in its frame, with two black-clad guards on either side.

They always saluted him, even though he wasn't *precisely* a soldier, but McCoombs said any man who did the disagreeable work of keeping the peace was a soldier in *his* Amerika, and God if that wasn't good to hear. It was good to *mean* something. He'd read the history books, he'd signed on to all the Fourteen Words message boards when he was a kid, and for ten goddamn years, the Fourteen Words had been gloriously adhered to.

Now, of course, they were back to being a dirty little code. Seeing the way things shifted made a man think. Meaning was slippery; it changed from day to day. Not like a bullet, or the lock on the door of a killing bottle.

Maybe the fever was tetanus. He didn't know. All he knew was the shrapnel flickering through the air, like the end of a whip, cracking and then the pain in his thigh, and the *smell*. It was probably the cut on his foot, oozing a bright green-yellow pus, that was the bigger problem, because *that* was the injury sending red streaks up his ankle and his calf, branching veinlike fingers.

The green-painted safehouse door shuddered, bringing Skelm back into the present with a jolt. It opened a crack, and a hook-nosed red-headed idiot, his muddy eyes a little too close together and his hair too long for a real Patriot's, peered out at him.

Skelm's own hair was too long, and filthy besides. He tried to keep himself clean, but staggering through fugee camps full of degenerates and immies wasn't good for your health.

A short, barking laugh escaped his thin, pale lips. "Amerika first," he croaked.

He heard movement on the other side of the door. For a long, hideous moment he was afraid he'd somehow bungled the password, or hadn't found the right house. With everything shelled and fuckered-up, it was hard to navigate, and the fever…

"Amerika always," someone husked from the other side of the door, a low sweet voice. The redheaded idiot pulled it open and beckoned him inside with one limp hand. Christ, were they even using faggots on the underground railroad now? *Sensitive*, his mother called it, but Pete knew what that meant, yes indeed. It got your file marked and made the Army a no go, because don't ask, don't tell was one of the dark-age liberal victories.

Looked like the fuckers had won in the end, though. Won all the way to DC, and the big man probably spirited away, hiding in the mountains for a while. At least, that's what Skelm hoped. McCoombs was the only hope for this goddamn country. They'd regroup. Fight back. Somehow.

He tacked gratefully through the door. There was a doctor at this stop, they'd told him. That meant antibiotics, and stitching up his foot, and maybe even—

It wasn't until there was a slam behind him and he saw the two women, one a goddamn immie with a broad greasy taco-bender face and the other a pale stick in a brand-spanking-new Federal Army sweater despite the heat and an unholstered 9mm pointed right at him that Peter Skelm, the Big Butcher of Pilgrim, understood there was no safety here, and he'd been caught at last.

Funnily enough, he didn't mind so much, as long as they had some goddamn medicine. He smiled weakly, charmingly, and lifted his shaking hands. "I surrender. Don't shoot."

The stick-woman's hand tightened, her finger tensing on the trigger.

Skelm smiled drunkenly and collapsed against the wall.

CHAPTER TWENTY-NINE

PALLIATIVE

July 12, '98

The world swam back into focus, one piece at a time. The heavy, funny, floaty feeling was new, and so was the smell—clean, bleached cloth. Sheets. *Hospital* sheets.

"I ain't gonna babysit," a familiar voice said, hard on the consonants, clipped on the vowels. Simmons, with the buckle of the Bible Belt rubbing through every syllable. "Give me that."

"It's not *babysitting*," Chuck Dogg replied, a deep rumble. "And you've done enough drinkin', my friend."

"Fuck." Simmons was just visible, a large blond smear, his gray-green fatigues a blur underneath. "I think he's awake. Hey, kid."

Lazy's chin dipped slightly. He stared into the man's familiar face—stubbled now, the tip of each small aggressive hair flaxen pale. "Sim," he managed, through a throat dry as the back porch that summer he burned the pages from the Bible in the backyard and his little sister Connie's face, white and awestruck, lifted to his like a sunflower's. "Hey...man."

"Definitely awake." The Reaper made a quick motion with one hand, a sketch of a wave. Chuck Dogg's face swam into sight as well.

The Dogg's hair was damp, moisture caught in its woolen, red-knotted curls. Underneath the incipient 'fro, he looked grave and thoughtful. "Look at that. You a regular cowboy, Lazy."

"Amen to that." Simmons jostled Chuck, reaching into the other man's fatigue jacket pocket, digging. "Here it is."

Chuck's mouth turned down at the corners. "Man, you shouldn't drink no more, Sim."

"It's not for *me*." The Reaper uncapped a silvery hip flask. Nobody knew how Chuck kept it full; it was enough that he did, and there had been a few times, right around Second Cheyenne, that everyone had taken a shot because fuck it, they were probably gonna die anyway. "Jesus Christ, Dogg, you ain't my mother."

"Damn straight. You too fuckin' ugly."

A tired, slow laugh bubbled and burped up from Lazy's dry, dry throat. It sounded like he was playing monster again, a flashlight under his chin and Connie giggling, horrified. A good little sister, only moderately annoying.

If Connie hadn't told Dad about him burning the Bible, he might not have gotten striped. Did she think about it, did she even remember? Was she even alive anymore? How old would she be? Ten? Maybe?

Why was he thinking of Connie? It never ended well. That was, in Simmons's terms, a *fucking bad idea*.

Simmons held the flask to Lazy's mouth. The liquid burned going down, but that was better than nothing. When the coughing settled, Lazy's eyes watering, he heard the various sounds of medical machines. *Beep, boop blurt,* rinse and repeat. One was soughing across the room, sounded like his uncle's breathing when the cancer rolled through his lungs and they couldn't afford the hospital. Their dad's application for Party membership had been denied for the fourth time. No reason given, but right after that, Connie had blurted it out at dinner. *Bobby burnt a Bible,* she'd chirped, *and nuffin' happened.*

"Thought you were gonna get a Firster on your own, huh?" Chuck's teeth were very white, splitting the lowest third of his dark face. He generally looked fresh as a daisy, and Lazy couldn't figure out how the hell he did it. Even during the retreat, the Dogg's pants always had a good crease to them. A real raider. "Swann gonna give you what for."

"Shit," Lazy whispered. "Gotta get my thirty, man."

"Amen." Simmons lifted the flask again. "You want some more?"

Lazy shook his head. Even that small movement tired him out, and he drifted away again, into a cloud that reminded him of the backyard. Sometimes, the sheets had smelled kind of like this at home. He really missed the sun-dried ones, though. There was nothing like hanging your goddamn laundry out to dry; even though he'd bitched endlessly to himself about his mother making him bring it in, now that he thought about it he'd actually be happy to do it for her. It was really funny, if you stopped and considered. All sorts of shit he used to bitch to himself about, he'd be kind of happy to do now. Like wash the dishes. Even pick up the dog shit, if she told him to.

It would mean she was alive, and maybe still loved him.

"He wake up?" someone said, a soft, female voice. Zampana, he'd know her anywhere. Sometimes, way down deep at the bottom of his brain before he went to sleep, he thought about how nice it was when she stood close to him. Her body heat was different than the others'. Warmer, somehow. Or just more direct.

"A little bit." Chuck sounded grave. "What's the word?"

Lazy drifted away. Funny, nothing hurt except his throat. The clear, fiery liquor burned, a rasping irritant. There was a *poosh*ing sound, and a few moments later, a wonderful warmth slid up his arm to his shoulder, paused there, and spread through the rest of him.

He didn't hear Zampana's whispered words as she flipped through Lazy's chart, especially the ones that turned Simmons's mouth into a hard, pursed little line that meant trouble.

Morphine, Sim. Palliative.

CHAPTER THIRTY

VICTIM'S LUXURY

The IV pole rattled as Peter Skelm settled in the chair. A bare concrete cube, just like all the other interrogation rooms, with the same one-way mirror along one wall. There was no tripod for a vidcaster, though that didn't mean much—there could be a tiny lens up near the fluorescents, a little wireless dealie for flushing out degenerates and immies. Stick one of those with a rechargeable battery to a ceiling tile, sit back and watch them incriminate themselves.

If you had nothing to hide, you had nothing to worry about, the saying went.

How many raiders had been held in rooms like this? Only the ones they wanted something good out of. The others would be taken downstairs, to the windowless concrete rooms with stains worked into their walls and floors.

Spooky leaned back in her own uncomfortable seat. Stretched her legs out under the bolted-down table. *His* chair wouldn't move; it was bolted, too. Zampana checked the Big Butcher of Pilgrim's IV again, glancing at Spooky with reddened eyes. The older woman's gold hoops glittered fiercely as she moved, her braids pinned high and savagely tight.

Spooky cleared her throat. "Thanks." The single word fell, flat and uneasy, against the drain under the table. Right in the middle of the room.

You could hose this fucker down, no muss no fuss. Easy cleaning, the housewife's friend.

Skelm's fever was abating. You could see it in the way his eyes were brightening, the sickly flush retreating, antibiotics working overtime to clean his bloodstream. His left leg was bandaged almost all the way to the hip. He would probably lose it below the knee, but the doctors would do their best, even if he *was* a Firster.

Even if he was a complete waste of skin, muscle, and breath.

A faded, bleached hospital johnny and loose cotton pajama pants completed the picture of a patient. One slip-on shoe, the other foot closed in a sheath to keep the bandages full of antibiotic and steri-gel on the newly cleaned wounds. Norpirene was a goddamn wonder drug, cleaning out infection and burrowing in. You could pair it with antibiotics or add it to plasco—it didn't care, just went quietly about its work.

Just like a fellow raider, one whose presence you took for granted until he was on a hospital bed, drifting in a morphine haze.

The Big Butcher was a skinny man now. A smudged ident picture, rescued from a burning file cabinet, showed a much heftier frame. In the picture, Peter Skelm stood near the proud, high-arched gates of the new Re-Edukation Kamp Pilgrim, grinning, a whip tucked under his right arm. His high boots shone, his hair was cut in the universal Patriot fashion—shaved on the sides and back, loose and floppy up top if he was young, bristle-stubbed if older. There was still an echo of the erstwhile healthy, committed Amerika Firster in the collection of bony, grinning, twitching, eye-rolling male across from her.

Swann had asked her if she wanted the file. She'd just shaken her head. Now Spooky settled herself, and really *looked* at him.

The chairs were uncomfortable—hers by default, his by design. The clear liquid dripping into his veins from the IV bag would feed him, fight the dehydration, fill him with yet more antibiotic to kill the infection raging up his leg.

She didn't have to look through the testimony in the file to know none of his victims ever had that luxury. She also didn't need the scrawls in the medical section of the paperwork to know the grinning and twitching were probably not an act. Swann's team had brought him in, so they got first crack at questioning him; Zampana had suggested waiting until the fever was under control and he wasn't high off his ass with pain meds.

"Spooky just set her jaw and insisted.

Anyway, she settled her ass against the metal seat, hands dangling off the ends of the chair arms, the back of her head against the top of the chair. That meant she could stare at him from under her lashes. Spooky filled her lungs, let the breath out.

"Hello." The left side of Skelm's face twitched once, twice. "Which are you? Internist? Psychologist? Or are you entertainment?" The last word cracked halfway through. His grin was a death's-head grimace. "You're not an immie. A sympathizer, maybe. A blood traitor, I'll bet." He leered, almost drunkenly. "I already surrendered. You can't do anything."

Maybe that was so. Prink had been all for shooting him first and making the ID later. Pana had stopped him. *We gotta question him, we gotta get* something *out of this.*

The Butcher was a big fish, but there were others in the food chain—both vertically and laterally. No shortage, as Swann often muttered.

Spooky let her gaze unfocus. A flutter of something inside her skull, right in the center of the brain. *Corpus callosum,* Lara's knowledge whispered. The smell of burned bone from a saw as it carved through the skull, lightly, lightly, so curious students could peek below. The brain felt no pain; most headaches were from neck tension.

Swann was no doubt watching. All he would see was Spooky in her chair, staring at the Big Butcher of Pilgrim. Who stilled, staring right back at her. The little shudders and shakes of an overloaded nervous system cracking its whip at bone and muscle eased. Skelm's mouth dropped open, his stubbled cheeks relaxing, and his pupils dilated.

An analog clock hovered over the mirror, wired to the wall. Its ticktock filled the interrogation room, Spooky's breathing regular as the marching seconds; a dull brick-red flush worked up her scrawny neck to her thin cheeks. The fingers of her right hand spasmed open once, flicking invisible water away.

Peter Skelm, after five and a half minutes of Spooky's steady gaze, began to shiver. The shivers increased, his head bobbing back and forth, his hands batting ineffectually at empty air. After another ninety seconds, he began to scream, hoarsely, and claw at his own face. The rankers on guard outside the door rushed in, which was not usual—they heard all sorts of things during interrogations.

But Skelm's howls were pure animal, echoing down the hall. One guard grabbed him, trying to contain the Butcher's hysterical strength. The other yelled for an orderly before attempting to help. The IV ripped free of the Butcher's hand, blood droplets hung in the air before spattering down; they lifted him bodily from the chair, the bandages on his leg jarred loose by his writhing. He kept screaming, those awful, chilling, grating cries, even when vessels in his throat burst and blood sprayed from his mouth.

Spooky, still as a statue, watched the struggle. The orderlies arrived, and a military doctor with a syringe full of tranq. It didn't matter; when it wore off, the result would be the same. Heavy iron warmth filled her nose, but she sniffed twice, deeply, and the blood slid down the back of her throat instead. In any case, the nosebleed didn't last long.

They carried Peter Skelm away. The door banged shut. Behind the glass, Zampana's fingers dug into Swann's left biceps, hard enough to bruise, as she exhaled a long, uncharacteristically soft obscenity. Swann, rigid, simply stared, his mouth a little open like he'd just had a good idea and was testing it inside his skull before letting it out to play.

Spooky, still sprawled in the interrogator's chair, smiled—a soft, pretty curve of thin lips, the flush dying and a faint sheen of sweat glistening on her forehead. She now had everything, willing or not, he could give during interrogation.

It was getting easier.

CHAPTER THIRTY-ONE

BUSINESS FROM GLORIA

July 14, '98

"I need you," Spooky said.

Minneapolis Base, the complex of what had been the prewar Army and Air Force Reserve stations out on Federal Drive, had an actual enlisted bar set up, with cobbled-together pool tables and a flatscreen playing some wartime movie full of candy-colored girls dancing in a rosette. The Firsters had tried to make Florida into a new Hollywood, but the only movies McCoombs liked were Westerns. Hollywood, of course, kept right on keepin' on, and musicals had turned out to be their biggest money-maker. It was worth a stint in Re-Edukation to run pirated non-Firster DVDs in, or T-rent the movies over encryption.

That was, if you were *caught*. Now both Hollywood and Florida were already making quickie movies about the surrender.

For his money, though, Simmons preferred musicals. They were just easier to look at. You could let the colors and sounds wash over you, especially when you had a bellyful of bourbon burn.

"What?" The Reaper blinked, blearily. "I'm on post, big man said."

That wasn't all Swann had said, but Simmons had buttoned his mouth and taken it. If you were gonna follow a man into hell, the least you could do was sit still when he gave you a chewing out. Swann never went overboard with the toothing, which was partly why Sim had signed up with him. That, and the day at the ranch. The fire, and the screaming, and the choked sounds when their throats gave out or the smoke…

When the raiders had melted out of the undergrowth, too late to help, it was Swann who said, *We can make 'em hurt, big fella*.

But that was a fuck-all-no-thanks to think about, so it was bourbon for him, please and thank you. At least he didn't have to suck down back-woods moonshine or engine cleaner anymore. No, if he wanted to blind himself, there was actual, *real* bourbon.

The Army had benefits, now that the fucking surrender was done.

Spooky, dead pale, ignored the noise from the wheezebox and the glances from male soldiers bellied up to the rankers' bar. Some of the fe-males gave her a going-over too, but her disinterest was palpable. Instead, she leaned closer to Simmons. "I need you," she repeated.

He almost asked *For what*, and almost added *I don't fuck where I eat*, the first because it was the thing to say and the second because he had a hazy idea—more like a wish, really—that maybe she wanted to ride. Through the fumes of five doubles, their glasses lined up neatly in front of him because he snarled when the 'tender came to take them away, he rethought both things, and ended up just staring fishmouth at her, candysmoke haze riding knee-high in the bar. The new cigarettes wouldn't give you fucking cancer, but the vapor from them sank in-stead of rising.

Which was, Simmons thought, pretty much the story for the whole goddamn country over the last decade or so.

It was difficult to believe this was the same girl he'd found sitting on a camp brothel bed. Instead of that terrible blankness behind her hazel-to-dark eyes, someone was home, and that someone had a fierce, watchful, hungry stare. Almost one he recognized.

The only thing worse than seeing that thousand-yard look on another soldier was watching it in the mirror.

Simmons contemplated the next double, sitting squat and amber in its misshapen glass in front of him. Then he considered Spooky, who just stood there silently, waiting for him to make up his mind or already ex-pecting him to say *Fuck it* and go along for whatever she had planned.

"Where you goin'?" he asked finally.

Now it was her turn to make him wait, the brittle ends of her hair frizzing. Humidity was going up, the land of a thousand fucking lakes beginning to breed its thousand million mosquitoes, and summer thunderstorms were on their way, too. "Business," she said. "From Gloria."

Well, there was only one thing *that* could mean. Simmons lifted the glass, tossed the bourbon far back. It stopped working so well after you took down too much of it over too long. *Resistance,* the science-heads said. Even your own body could fight shit off. There wasn't ever any rest. It was one long battle until finally you took a plasma burst in the gut and ticky-tocks of morphine dripped into your veins.

The Firsters would've already pulled the plug on the kid. *No drag on the system,* they said. Then there was the old way of putting it: *useless eaters.* Oh, they'd dressed it up, and they called it different things, but those motherfuckers were just the same shit from different days.

It was no use. He wasn't getting drunk enough. And the goddamn new medic—easier to call her that, mostly, since Zampana was *the* medic—just *stood* there, her birdlike shoulders sharp-rubbing through her green-gray fatigue jacket, like she was cold even in July. She was thicker than she had been, but when you started so far down, it took a while to even get to the bottom of normal. They didn't have much in her size, so she made do with a tight belt and rolled-up sleeves.

For a couple seconds Simms tried to imagine being that small and having a hole instead of a dick.

It didn't work. He cracked the empty shot glass down on the bar and waved away the bartender's anxious look, digging in his pocket for writs. Spooky, however, already had a handful, counting them out with her thin spidery fingers, knuckles too big and her fingernails chewed back to raw pink crescents. She also gave the 'tender a tight, apologetic smile, ducking her head a little. It was more a grimace than anything cheerful, an approximation of politeness.

"Don't need no woman buying me drinks." Simmons considered sweeping the empty glasses off the top of the bar, but Spooky already had his elbow with those clever, capable little paws.

"I'm not," she said, coaxing him along, a bossy tug chivvying a much larger battleship into port. "You're getting the next round, after we come back."

That was good enough. Simmons concentrated on one foot in front of the other, and thought hazily that if Swann found out, they were both going to be bollocked. Maybe Spooky had a plan for that, maybe not.

Outside, a thick summer dusk, purple skied and wet, pressed against every inch of exposed skin and dragged down every wrinkle in his fatigue jacket. From above, if you could get up there, the lakes would be blue-jewel compound eyes. Out in the woods, the skeeters were hatching in every still puddle. They'd get big enough to kidnap a small child. "Better be good," he mumbled at Spooky. "Skeeters carry you off."

She didn't reply, just took them down the pavement, her bony fingers pressing into his upper arm. Not hard, she didn't have the strength for it, but he could still *feel* them. Did she think he was gonna try to escape, or was he weaving? Fuck no, he wasn't weaving. He was steady, right down the line, goddammit.

Even when he didn't *want* to be.

After two blocks, she pulled him to a stop next to a pea-vomit truck, the canvas on its back rent from shrapnel but its hood undamaged. The silver fangs of a kerro retrofit lurked on its grille, grinning their knowing little grin, and it had pads instead of wheels. "I've got a line on something." She indicated the truck with a jerk of her head. "I've also got this. Maybe nothing; maybe a fucker there needs erasing."

"Shit, girl. Why else would you want *me* along?" It was only July, and it smelled like summer's armpit. Fight and bleed halfway across the damn continent and end up in *Minnesota*. It was fucking insulting. The Great White Lutheran North, full of wax cheese binder and people who said *Dontcha know* and *Uff da* while they voted for McCoombs because he promised to keep the brown people in their place, cross his heart, hope they all die. The universities up here had died on the vine, too, after the student protests in '93. Except the Firster ones.

"Your charming personality?" A glimmer of her teeth.

A kerro rumbled by, its pads flickering with static and its headlight beams slicing across a freshly repaired shell hole. Filled in, there was only a dip to show where explosive had torn through pavement, dirt, and anything else in its way. Were there atomized bits of human meat mixed in?

Some of the mountain partisans had used horses. They could go places cars and kerros couldn't, but when the shelling hit, the animals' screams were enough to give a man nightmares.

"Fuck that," Simmons murmured. He checked his sidearm—of course, a raider didn't go in unarmed, and they'd stopped trying to make the Blue Companies turn in their weapons. The knife was in his boot, right where it was supposed to be. "Anything good in there?"

"Just us." Spooky's eyes narrowed as she peered up at him, maybe blinded by the splash of headlights, maybe not. "If you're coming."

He shook his head, though that made the entire world reel for a few minutes before the cursed, awful sobriety came back, sour sweat prickling in his armpits and a hideous mineral taste of blood touching the back of his mouth. "If there's killin', I'm in."

"There might be nobody there."

Christ, he hoped it wouldn't turn out that way. "Then you owe me another fucking drink."

CHAPTER THIRTY-TWO

GET YOUR HANDS DIRTY

With the preliminaries over and the "Sorry for your soldier" dispensed with too, Buckley got right down to business. He was higher on the ladder than Crunche or Proustinek and knew it, a bullet-headed quasi-martinet who wore his uniform loose and his watch a little too tight, the edges of its scaled metal band digging into his brawny, hairy wrist. "How many is this?"

For all that, Buckley was *almost* good folk. His office was spartan and rigidly organized, but he didn't give Crunche—or the raiders, by extension—a hard time. This gave Swann some comfort, even though he suspected he was going to get a bollocking for Simmons and his goddamn temper.

At the same time, there was nothing else the Reaper could have done and kept some self-respect. Refusing to stand by while Firsters and assorted other bigots shat on everyone around was how a raider got into this whole fuckhole in the first place. So Swann contented himself with a nod and a bare statement of fact. "Five, sir."

The shades and blinds were drawn tight against a heavy-breathing summer evening, the office door was half open, and another man sat in an armchair near an empty bookshelf—a youngish Italian-looking fellow with shoulders not as wide as Simmons's. His stripes said captain, and the way he wore his fatigues said he'd earned them. His face was mostly nose, with a couple of raw dark eyes, the kind always looking weepy and pink rimmed even if the owner was a tough fucker. His hands lay discarded on his knees, left one cupped over his folded hat, bent fingers the only part of him not completely military. A line of scarring ran across his left knuckles. Looked like a burn; he was lucky to still have the digits.

Swann had a couple ideas why this man was sitting there. Neither of them were exactly comforting.

"Good work." Buckley bobbed his bullet head, staring at the papers spread before him. Confirmed captures, four of them. The fifth, a confirmed kill.

Swann shook his head slightly. "Too slow." And how did Chuck feel? The man had slogged through hell fighting the Firsters, and he couldn't even drink in peace. *Too slow* was only the beginning; they'd signed the surrender too goddamn early. Should have burned every fucking Firster city off the map, dumped every surviving fuckhat into their own killing bottles and bath bays, and started fresh.

Except it was the kind of thinking, on the other side, that started this whole mess of shit and blood and mud and death.

"Your close rate's good. Pretty phenomenal." The West Point ring on Buckley's left hand—married only to the service, it looked like—gleamed dully. At least he didn't rap the fucker against the desktop. "About your team…"

Swann waited. Christ, he hated this petty back-and-forth. It didn't help that he was good at it, and as much of a free agent as could be expected in this shit-sucking world. Finally, though, he bit. "What about 'em?"

"Well, you know, a close rate like this…higher up is wondering about inside information." Buckley dipped his chin slightly, twice, still shuffling through the papers, not looking up.

Swann gazed at him for a few moments, mildly, deciding whether or not to consider that offensive. It was a close call. "We raiders got our methods, sir." What would this spit and polish say if he'd seen what Swann had—a skinny woman in a too-big uniform, just staring at the

Butcher of Pilgrim until the skeletal, twitching son of a bitch started to howl like a lunatic?

"Sure." Buckley nodded, spreading his hands as if to apologize. "But we'd like to embed a fellow with you to study your methods. Some of our other teams, they could use a little help."

"A watchdog." Swann had to work to say it flatly, calmly. Now he was glad he hadn't acted insulted before, because the time to do so was now.

"A liaison, Swann. Captain Hendrickson here is highly decorated." He indicated the young fellow in the armchair, who popped to his feet like he was on springs.

Swann barely glanced at him. "We don't take to outsiders." *Outsiders*, because he was too polite to say *spies*. Anyone who knew their ass from a hole in the ground should have grasped that right away. When you operated behind enemy lines, strangers were worse than a liability.

"Sir? If I may?" Hendrickson was a bright-eyed boy. Straight-backed, clean-shaven, and far too young for this kind of work. "Captain Swann, sir, I worked with raiders. Kellogg's group, in Missouri."

Oh, yeah, Swann knew about *her*. "Kicker Kellogg. You know she crucified Firsters? Right up on telephone poles."

"Yessir." Even though they were technically the same rank, Hendrickson had the sense to use his manners. The youth now held his folded hat at the regulation angle, in that scarred left hand. His Adam's apple bobbed. "I…I don't blame her."

Now *that* was interesting. "Why not?" Swann turned a little, planting his feet and regarding the young fellow closely for the first time. Someone coughed in the hallway outside—Zampana, from the way the sound caught in the middle; she hated giving her position away. It was probably hard for her to stand out there, wondering how Swann was doing in the lion's den. *Let me in there,* she'd said. *Can be the bad cop this time.*

But Swann was where the buck stopped, and if there was a shoutdown, he would be the one to take it.

Hendrickson met his gaze squarely. "I know what they did to her wife, sir."

Swann nodded thoughtfully. "Lotta rumors about that."

"Not rumor. I was there when she found her." Another convulsive movement in his throat. "There, ah, wasn't a lot left. We ID'd her from her dress. And her wedding ring."

That wasn't the whole story, not as far as Swann had heard, but it was close, and about all that could be said about that kind of business. "You ever get your hands dirty, son?"

"Dirty enough." The way his eyelids flickered and that left hand tensed, it might even be true.

Swann wished he had his own hat. Something to throttle would be mighty welcome. "You come in, you be lower than a private. Any of my crew tell you to jump you don't even ask how high, you just bust your ass doin' as high as you can. You all right with that?"

"Yessir." Hendrickson didn't glance at Buckley. That was interesting. Dollars to doughnuts the boy had been briefed beforehand. "I'm no watchdog, sir. Unless it's to watch how you do it so I can show some of our teams how to catch 'em quicker."

Our teams. It could have meant the Army's teams, leaving the raiders out. Or it could have been a sign that he lumped himself in with the raiders. Really fraternizing of him.

Swann's hands itched to close into fists. He didn't let them, just nodded and looked at Buckley. "Anything else, sir?" There was a way to make the honorific as dead and disrespectful as possible, and Swann came close. He didn't like this one goddamn bit.

"Just that you do good work, Captain Swann." Buckley's face lit for a moment, a flush creeping up his slablike cheeks. "Real, lifesaving work. I'm proud to know you."

Well, wasn't that sweet of him. "Thank you, sir." Swann didn't bother to salute, just stumped for the door, not bothering to glance at Hendrickson, either. He caught a flicker in his peripheral—the young man's hands stowing his hat, the scarring across his left fingers shiny in the golden incandescent lighting. It was past dusk, and Swann didn't feel any better about today than he had about the last week as a whole.

He had some thinking to do, and none of it was particularly pleasant. At least he got out of Buckley's room without Spooky being mentioned at all.

How long, Swann wondered, would *that* last?

Zampana, her boots shiny, her black braids in place, and her expression as sour as Swann felt, peeled herself away from the wall and fell into step beside him, lengthening her stride to keep up. She didn't ask who the tagalong was, and she didn't jump on him with any other bad news.

It was time, Swann decided, for a fucking drink. And to see if any more of his Riders had managed to get into trouble.

CHAPTER THIRTY-THREE

SAD LITTLE STIFF

It took Spooky a half hour to match the prewar map to the shell-pocked, ghostly terrain. It was easier than figuring out what the fuck in a forest, and the place was only five miles from the base's eastern border. Bumping along in the passenger seat, Simmons smoked, his eyes half lidded and the used-sugar reek of bourbon greasing his skin. He said nothing, even when a civilian jalopy, belching clouds of cheap petrol smoke, sped through a prewar stop sign and almost hit the truck sideways. Headlights glared, Spooky leaned on the horn, and the seatbelt cut cruelly across her hips. She blew out between her teeth, downshifted, and muttered a long, entirely new word that had *fuck* as every other syllable.

War damage fell away on either side, the road smoothed out, and they slid into the northeastern quadrant of suburbs, where the surrender of the city's Firster garrison had shielded structure and infrastructure alike. The streets were still narrow and cracked but much less bumpy. You could almost pretend it was a normal neighborhood, if you ignored the dead streetlights and the flickering bright points from only some windows. Candlelight, or another open flame, because this part of the grid wasn't turned on.

The victors needed what electricity there was, and didn't feel like sharing.

There were even uninjured street signs, standing tall and regular, glittering under headlight glow. Several of the houses and other buildings hurriedly blacked their windows, sensing nothing good in a vehicle out after curfew. Spooky began to count, and found the one she wanted. It was like groping around in a dark room, one where you knew *sort of* where the furniture was. Enough not to skin your shins, but not enough to avoid bumping into a lamp. She missed the place on the first pass, circled another block, and cut the lights.

Simmons crushed his candy out. He sat up, ran both hands back over his buzz cut, checked his sidearm. In the subtle glow from the dash, he looked peppier than a man who had taken down that much alcohol had any right to. "Blue house?" he said, and she nodded. Plenty of people had taken the numbers off their walls, but the mailboxes still stood sentinel over the ghosts of reflective paint lingering on high narrow curbs, most of the boxes holding tiny gold stickers pronouncing the numbered slice of real estate they belonged to.

The blue house, thin with a high-peaked roof, frowned neglected at the street. The yard was weed-choked, the slim driveway plunging to a garage set below. Probably a split-level, which meant a tactical nightmare. He studied it as they rolled to a stop, the kerro dying with a faint whine. Two of the bottom windows were boarded, but the plywood was worm-eaten and caked with dirt—which meant it had been lying on the damp, warm ground until recently. Simmons peered past her, and now that his eyes were dark-adapted, he could see it too.

"Girl, you are a ninth wonder." A short, bitter little laugh. "We gonna get shot at the front door, like Lazy?"

Spooky considered the house. Her hair, scraped and clipped back, the fried ends crinkling, was an inky cap in the dimness. "Not if we go in the back?" It could have been gallows humor, or it could have been an honest suggestion.

Simmons paused, one corner of his mouth twitching before he sobered, staring at the house. "You think he's gonna make it?"

"I don't know." And she didn't, because she didn't *want* to. Plazma to the gut, at close range? They'd be lucky to salvage some of his intestines.

The way plaz went for bone, he'd be lucky to be able to feel his legs ever again, much less use them.

"He better." Simmons reached for the door handle, easing it open and sliding free. The overhead light didn't turn on, and Spooky was just as quiet on the driver's side. The house on the left—a ramshackle brick number—exhaled a cold breath of neglect; the one on the right, like the small one across the street, flickered with candle- or lamplight. Either the residents hadn't noticed a kerro out after curfew, or they were just glad it hadn't stopped in front of them.

The walkway gritted underfoot—old concrete, full of pebbles, weeds forcing up through gaps, wooden spacers rotted and providing nutrition for creeping bits of trashlife. Not like the mud of the camps, sterile and baked dry in summer, deep and sucking when it wasn't steel-hard frozen in winter. Even dandelions and crabgrass refused to grow inside the electrified fences. The misery soaked into the ground and blighted everything.

Simmons had vanished into a damp-breathing postdusk, the sky turned indigo as a fresh bruise. A really deep one, with serrated crimson teeth at the edges. *Name that contusion,* Lara whispered inside Spooky's skull, but she ignored it. It was kind of uncanny how the big blond Reaper could simply disappear, even in gloaming when it was easy to blur.

The house drew nearer, reeling her in. The boards over the lower windows, clotted with drying dirt, were wart-scabbed eyelids. It dozed, unaware of the woman creeping to its door. A seashell held to her ear, the song of blood moving through veins, but she strained to hear the other, subtler sounds.

Heard nothing.

The front door was unlocked; she pushed it open by degrees. The smell—ripe, gassy, hot weather spurring decay in the house's hollows and crevices—boiled out. You couldn't shut your nose off; death crawled in and greased your sinuses, thick and slick and heavy. A slight creaking, the house settling as it cooled, and she heard, suddenly, cricket song rising and falling all through the neighborhood. Tiny insects rubbing their little legs together, screaming for mates.

It was a split-level. She waited until the *feeling* changed upstairs, like a storm front—Simmons was in. Stealth served raiders better than kicking down doors, especially when you knew there were only one or two hostiles. Any more, and the house would have *felt* different.

Besides, a raider worked with what she had, and what Spooky had was Simmons and her own creeping catlike sense of danger. That was all.

Simmons appeared, his face a ghostlike smear at the top of the stairs. Shook his head. He could smell it too, and pointed down. Spooky, flattened against the right-hand side away from the door hinges, slid down step by step, the reek growing thicker. The carpet was squishy—damp burrowed in, and a place without occupants started to fall apart quickly. So he'd come back, boarded up the windows, and…

They found him on the lower level, in what had once been a comfortable finished half-basement. "Well, shit," Simmons whispered behind her. "Someone beat us to it."

The corpse, bloat-squeezed into a Patriot uniform with polished buttons, sagged sideways in a straight-backed wooden chair. All around the edges of the basement ran shelving, dipping and rising crazily, swelling and shrinking, for a model railroad. It buckled and warped with the damp; the small trains and tiny painted trees and houses were discolored too.

Spooky's boots squelched afresh on the carpet, now alive with small moving things drawn to food. She peered at what remained of the puffy, blackened face under its slick of thinning reddish hair, strands sticking in the mess his head had become when the bullet tore through the back of his skull. "Bricks," she murmured. Sergeant Brixon.

He'd watched over what they called the quarry, digging for rocks to break in the swampy bottoms, and this guard's favorite game was to force jar kaptains and other high-ranking prisoners to pile the stones in the press—a board sandwich with human filling and a crate on top for the stones adding more and more weight to whatever luckless prisoner hadn't greeted Sergeant Bricks with alacrity, or who *had* greeted him when he didn't want it, or had smiled, or had *not* smiled, who had ignored him, or who simply caught his eye.

Sometimes they lasted a while in the press. Once or twice, even overnight.

"Huh?" Simmons leaned down, studied the way the left eyeball bulged free, already shrunken. The Brick's mouth was slack and teeming with foulness, and it was a wonder the uniform hadn't split. It was one of the old high-quality wool ones, far too small for the towering, furious, fat figure he'd been at Gloria. Cross-country travel might have melted a few pounds off, but the flora and fauna in his gut were doing their best to add inspiring girth to a sad little stiff. A piece of gore-spotted paper fluttered from his knee to the floor, and Spooky tweezed it up, delicately, between index finger and thumb.

"He was at Gloria." She straightened, a slow unfolding. "That kamp you found me at."

"There's an old woman upstairs." Simmons turned carefully and stepped across the squishy carpet with the caution of a raider. He examined the tracks running around the room, a circuit of tiny disciplined machinery. The wires were probably corroded. "Laid out on her bed, one in the back of the neck."

"Probably his mother." It seemed fantastic to credit that even the Brick had a parent. Someone had given birth to him, wiped his nose and ass, held his chubby little hands as he took his first steps. Maybe he'd even emailed or written to her from Gloria. *Hi Mom, I'm a murdering bastard.*

"Looked old enough. He even put flowers on her. Fake ones." Even a hushed tone was too loud for this hole. "How you know how to find him, huh?"

"Papers. From that paperhead asshole in Chicago." Plus a little help from Skelm's head, but she didn't need to say that. In any case, the Butcher had only heard a rumor of a man from Gloria using the pipeline. He hadn't given her anything *new*.

"Huh." Simms sucked on his front teeth for a moment. "This place likely to be trapped?"

"I don't think so." She lifted the soggy note. Her fingers ached with tension, but she had to hold gently or the paper would tear. "Why write a note if you don't want it found? We should look around."

"Okay." Simmons's hair glowed. He didn't sound too happy with the notion, but anything they got here would be a hedge against a Swann bollocking if the old man found out about him going off post.

"Then," Spooky said, "I'll buy you a drink."

CHAPTER THIRTY-FOUR

REAL FUCKING EGGS

July 15, '98

A migraine-pink dawn found Spooky in the rankers' bar, hunched over a plate of substandard huevos rancheros on a bed of toast and a large mug of coffee spiked with cheap whiskey. The huevos were at least fresh, none of the powdered bullshit that had been the bane of the early war infantry. The cook, McCorkle, one of his eyes swallowed up in plazma scar tissue, said that shit had been pure protein powder, meant for blocking up the intestines of anyone foolish enough to eat it in bulk. Which was pretty much what the early rankers had to do, since most of the MREs had been in depot when the West had declared McCoombs the "Caudillo of DC" during secession.

Spooky listened to McCorkle's spiel with half an ear, sliding her coffee mug toward the cook every once in a while for a refill. He waxed rhapsodic about finally having *real fucking eggs* again; the next step was cheese, but he'd organized some damn fine hot sauce and the whiskey was finally coming in real bottles instead of pots and pans dipped in whatever dirty bathtub the soldiers could find. Over the other end of the bar, a flatscreen was jury-rigged to the wall, its blue glow full of nowcast news, a blonde in a red jacket talking in front of a hastily covered Patriot seal that used to be standard on the cable talkies. The white sheet hanging over the seal was a ghost, and the lower curve of painted plastic poked out, as well as the penile stub of the musket the figure stamped in it held. The chyron underneath was full of names—politicians, mostly, from the reconstituting Senate. They were certification hearings going on, and new elections to organize.

When Zampana showed up, hitching one hip onto the barstool to Spooky's left and wriggling the rest of herself up with a sinuous motion, she sniffed at the plate of eggs and fixed the cook with a baleful glare. "You better have some fuckin' corn tortillas to give me with that, Cork."

"Where'm I gonna pull 'em out of, woman? My ass?" Cork's mouth twisted, his scar-socketed eye turning into an evil, leering wink. "*You* try gettin' masa up here in the Great Northeast. Ain't even got real lard in the depots, just that shitty guvmint cheese."

"Hunt down the long pigs and render 'em," Zampana muttered. "Plenty around. You have coffee, at least?"

"Yes ma'am." He poured her a tall one in a battered old Navy mug, added a healthy dollop of the aforesaid whiskey, and slopped it onto the bar. "I'll make you pancakes instead?"

"Nah, I'll have what she's having." Zampana curled her hands around the mug. Even on a scorching summer day, hot coffee was to be treasured. Especially if it was *actual* coffee, and not freeze-dried or chicory. "You got in late last night."

"Business." Spooky's arm twitched, wanting to slide around her plate. It took a conscious effort to sit up, to leave the food unprotected for even a moment.

"Yeah, well. Get what you went for?" The other medic stared into the dark liquid. Her sidearm sat easy on her hip, and gold glinted in her ears. Most of the martinets knew to leave the Blue Companies alone by now, but some of the enlisteds might have made a mistake or two. *Buddy up,* Swann was always saying. Not like before, when you could pass another raider on the street and never acknowledge, not even glance at them for fear of giving them away or breaking your own cover.

Spooky shrugged. Sitting at her elbow was a creased, battered file folder, heavy orange, filched in passing from a desk at HQ. Zampana didn't glance at it, but Spooky edged it toward her anyway. The gore-spattered, now crinkle-dry note she kept to herself.

Since everthing is lost I am resining in protest. She couldn't decide if it was funny or horrifying that a man who had murdered so many, playing God, didn't even know how to fucking spell.

"A productive night." The other medic made her peculiar sound of amusement, like a fox's dry gekkering. "Anything good?"

"Dunno. There's a jumper in there." A jumpdrive, one she'd turned over in her hands, thinking about it. "Could be nothing." It could even be loaded with worms, who knew?

"I'll take it to tech." Zampana glanced at the flatscreen before opening the folder to peer at its insides, and Cork, bringing her plate, possibly interpreted that as interest, or maybe was interested himself. In any case, he snatched a remote and turned the sound up.

"—Baylock," the blonde announcer said, and Spooky stiffened. "The complex, situated in West Virginia, is the center of allegations including human experimentation and gene editing in violation of the prewar Stark Act." Over the blonde's shoulder, an inset appeared, grainy footage of glass towers huddled together, their reflective faces glittering sharply under bright sunlight. "Authorities are—"

"Huevos rancheros, ma'am." Cork snagged the coffeepot too, and freshened Spooky's cup. "You want another jolt?"

Staring at the screen, Spooky didn't appear to hear. Zampana, paging through the papers, picked up the jumpdrive and considered it. Black, the length of her thumb, high capacity.

Cork, maybe used to soldiers ignoring him, just left it at coffee. He shuffled back for his makeshift grill and the eternal cleanup. There would be more to feed soon, and the day drinkers to think about. The announcer kept talking—she had been a minor celebrity during the war, with her smooth delivery of the news and her mane of golden hair. Now she was probably just glad to have a fucking job.

The inset footage had to be prewar. Spooky could never remember the sun coming out at Baylock, or any aircraft overhead until the drone bombing. Then again, would she have noticed either sunshine or sled? There was too much to occupy a kampog in sheer, stubborn survival.

"Hm." Zampana looked around for a fork, found one, and shut the folder decisively. "I think they're gonna be happy with this, Spook. You want to say where you got it?"

"No," Spooky heard herself say, her lips numb. The screen-image of Baylock vanished, and her stomach turned around inside her once, twice, a dog settling for the night. The blonde moved on to something about a USO concert given for the troops cordoning the New York zone, but Spooky kept looking at the flatscreen, glass towers vibrating in her mind's eye and the ozone-smelling white light of shock treatments blinding her in turn.

CHAPTER THIRTY-FIVE

OUR TIME NOW

The center of power in postsurrender America was a brick building that had escaped shelling, now wrapped protectively in a ring of sleds above and a block-wide cordon below, MPs and checkpoints grimacing at torn-up streets. The sign had been changed to say MCCOOMBS NAVAL BASE years ago, but drunken second- and third-wave soldiers had wrenched off bits of it or just plain shot the fucker to pieces. Now there was white paint on plywood, proclaiming ANACOSTIA-BOLLING again, thank the Lord and pass the ammunition.

It was good to be back, even if the Navy was a shadow of itself and the Air Force was howling about being reined in. Padgett was fulminating about bombing Texas to take it back, and continuing the burn in the South even though they'd done a thorough job of the latter to begin with. Some might even suspect Padgett of giving the order to burn the heartland of McCoombs-ism, but of that the head of the Federal Air Force was innocent.

Not that it mattered, now that the bodies were greasy ash and the skeletons heat-warped. *Innocent*, as always in wartime, was a relative term.

Inside, CentCom was a hive of offices, paper rustling, tablets blinking, secure lines buzzing, and all the necessary chaos of military bureaucracy. What remained of DC was under martial law, and the progressive layers of security got tighter and tighter until you reached the nerve center and this small windowless office that served as a retreat from its throbbing and stinging for the two highest generals in the land. Everyone else was catching some sleep or catching up on their drinking, savoring the luxury of being conquerors in their own homeland.

Rank, however, brought paperwork. And paperwork meant no fucking sleep for a long while.

"Where did this come from?" General Osborne wanted to know. Lean and lanky, with a full head of iron-colored hair he kept ruthlessly short, the architect of the victory—if you could call it that—at Second Cheyenne glanced at his tablet. The InfoSec boys were going floor by floor at Langley, with the help of a couple true blues plus a few turncoats anxious for certification and keeping their jobs. All that *can't operate on domestic soil* had gone out the window once McCoombs needed warm bodies to watch his serfs.

This particular bright-faced corporal wasn't one of *that* merry cleanup crew, however. He was an InfoSec boy in fatigues, rat-faced and poker-backed, clearing his throat. He had been signed in through all the layers of security, and was nervous for no good reason, but that was normal. His Adam's apple bobbed, as if it had to dredge up his surprisingly light tenor from a deep well. "Blue Company, sir."

"Which one?" General Leavy, the hazel-eyed darling of the moment, sat up straight and pain-faced in his chair, his crinkle of graying hair shaved close and his broad nose shining mellowly in the light from the incandescent lamp on his metal desk. The shrapnel in his back was only part of the reason for his sourness or his posture; the other part was sheer stiffneck distaste for the amount of killing he'd seen done, or ordered. Or so one or two of his underlings suspected.

It hadn't stopped Leavy from ordering, when he had to. Nothing did.

"Some outfit out of North Carolina. Or what used to be North Carolina." It was a smear pocked with burner-blasted holes now. The corporal consulted said paperwork, swallowing several times. He couldn't quite believe what he'd found. "Cohen, sir. Cohen's Fireballs."

"Fancy names." Osborne scrolled through a few more pages on the tablet, its blue glow lighting his mournful face from below. "Shit, he's still alive?"

"No, sir, Cohen died in the Uprising. But his band kept the name. They were involved in the—"

"Yes, I remember." North Carolina, what a shit show. Leavy blew out a long dissatisfied breath between thick, sculpted lips. "So, this all says Minnesota. Who's up thataway north? Of the Blue Companies?"

Osborne consulted a list. "Kellogg, Lancey, Swann—"

"Swann." Leavy nodded. "I know about him. Good fellow. Tough." He glanced at Osborne, who was apparently absorbed in the tablet. "Thank you, Corporal. Dismissed, and send in Haney, will you?" Haney was Leavy's adjutant, and the general had more than one task for the poor fellow now.

Relief turned the boy's ratty face into a child's disbelieving grin. "Yessir."

"Oh, and Corporal?" Leavy had to remind himself, every once in a while, that you had to grease the wheels to make 'em run smooth. "Good work."

The corporal visibly flushed. "Yes sir. Thank you, sir."

Osborne waited until the corporal had left. "What are you thinking, Pat?"

"I'm thinking we'd better jump quick, before the goddamn civilians get their mitts on any news of this fucker. It'll be hearings and votes and bullshit, and he'll get over the border. Or, God forbid, nabbed by the fucking Russians."

"They're opening diplomatic relations." Osborne managed not to sneer when he said it.

Leavy's expression turned even more sucked-a-lemon, if that were possible. The New Soviets' days of destabilizing America were done, but they didn't give up easy. What they'd succeeded with once, they'd try again. He stretched his booted, aching feet under the desk, thankful they were at least dry. "Of course they are. While loading as many Firster allies on the boats as they can. Entire city's like a kicked beehive."

"Be nice to get the Pentagon back." Osborne's laughter had a dry, unpleasant echo. "You think Kallbrunner's gonna end up President?"

"Probably." Leavy picked up his own tablet, hit the thumb lock, and stared at the most disconcerting document of all: an after-experiment report. There was a fifth of vodka back in his quarters, and maybe he could organize something decent to put it in if he ever got back there for more than a quick shower. "But what I know is, we've got to get on this *first*. And collect as many of these poor Baylock assholes we can."

"Gonna be tough. Fugees everywhere, certification going on, the Blue Companies tearing around hunting—"

"Which is why I want Swann. At least he'll keep his crew from killing this Doctor Johnson bastard." Leavy sighed, rubbing thoughtfully at the scar on his neck. "And martial law doesn't end until Congress says it does."

Osborne's teeth were strong and only mildly yellowed from bad coffee and old-school nicotine. "The Congress they'll have to elect in. Which will take for-fucking-ever."

"That's right." Leavy nodded. His broad, dark brown face was impassive, but a gleam of satisfaction could be guessed at deep in his gaze. "That's right, Joe. It's our time now."

CHAPTER THIRTY-SIX

A HISTORICAL DEFENSE

July 16, '98

In a ramshackle ranch-style house with a weedy front yard, the doctor, his gaze clear and steady, unwound the gauze around Gene's head. As always, he only looked happy when he was performing some medical function, or one that could be conceivably called medical if you didn't look too hard. "Where were you stationed?"

This safehouse, on the shattered rim of Duluth, held only food, water, and first aid. There was no "conductor" to help a Patriot or two along the way, but at least the place hadn't been looted, trapped, or broken.

Gene, perched on an ancient, wobbling metal stool, thought of shrugging and decided not to. The incisions were healing; his face felt less like a stiff blank mask and more like skin and muscle over aching bone. "Kamp administration. Missouri. You?"

The doctor's V-shaped smile under his narrow nose turned genuine for a few warm, satisfied moments. "Assistant Director of Research. West Virginia." He said it like Gene should be able to guess. His fedora, pushed back, revealed a slice of thinning fair hair. "You're lucky, I wouldn't have known what to do with you if I hadn't witnessed some of the experiments. Mostly, my work was in the lab."

It was small consolation that Gene had heard…rumors, about West Virginia. Certain undesirables matching certain criteria were sent there, though not from Gloria. The Western drone-bombing campaign had scored a few hits on the kamp system in that area too, though the official newscasts said the damage was negligible. "Everyone does their share," he muttered, trying to keep his cheeks still.

The doctor's mouth puckered, a bitter asshole transplanted onto a thin face. His sport jacket was far too heavy for the season, but he was probably glad of it at night. "Do you have a thought that's not a slogan?"

"Plenty." Gene weighed showing him. First would be standing up, and second would be kicking the older man's knee. It would give with a sound like dry wood, and while the snotty motherfucker sucked in a breath to scream Gene could grab the wobbling metal stool and bludgeon him. Done quickly and correctly, there would be little noise except the hollow sound the stool would make when it hit.

"Then try to express those." The doctor smiled a little, a thin curve of startlingly pink lips. "I didn't serve that grease-haired turd in the White House. I served *science*. Maybe you wouldn't understand."

"I never liked him either." Trying to talk while the other man peered and dabbed at the incisions with vile-smelling, stinging antiseptic was difficult. "It was just a job." A good one, even if he was stuck in the deep end of beyond. There had been space enough to organize a few comforts at Gloria, and the pink room, his own glowing little secret.

"Just following orders, were you?" A sardonic grin, the doctor taking back his superiority with visible relief. "A historical defense."

"So's yours."

"So you weren't educated in the usual manner, to know as much." He dabbed behind Gene's ear, and it stung afresh.

As if anyone with half a brain would have trouble figuring out how to get past the Big Firewall. The only thing stopping you was the danger, but if you were a Patriot officer with a good record and enough organizing skill to pay off a few superiors, you were all right. "Not stupid, Dr. Johnson. Just cautious."

"Would that more were so." A few more cold, repellant dabs at the incisions. "We'll let that breathe a bit. The norpirene is wonderful stuff. Does it hurt?"

It felt like being painted with fire ants. "Not much."

"Good, good." Johnson stepped back, examining Gene critically. "Well, Kaptain. I must confess, I wouldn't recognize you. There's a mirror in the bathroom, see what you think."

"Thanks." He eased off the stool, shuffling like an old man himself. Killing the supercilious fuck would be stupid; the doctor was the one who knew where the next stop was, and the secret signs. The existence of a network for after the surrender didn't surprise Gene much, really; the brass took care of their own. Nobody close to the top could have been astonished at the eventual outcome, not after the bloody draw that was Second Cheyenne, or after Mexico started grabbing whole chunks of Texas with help from the Federals.

The arrests had sped up then, and so had the work at Gloria. Fingers in the dam, like that story about the little Dutch girl on the cleanser canisters.

The bathroom was a dank little hole, but the last place had given them flashlights with good batteries. Gene switched his on, playing the beam over the mildewed ceiling, and glimpsed himself in the spiderweb-cracked glass.

There was some puffing and bruising around his eyes, and the scars along his jaw were livid instead of pale like they would be when healing was complete. Behind his ears the major incisions glared, his hair prickling from presurgical shaving.

Not bad. He'd barely recognize himself, either.

Would *she*? Christ. He should've gone back for her; nobody would suspect a couple. Or would they? At least he'd have her here, breathing and quiet, turning to him for protection. There would be a way to pass the time that wasn't listening to the goddamn doctor go on and on about how fucking smart he was.

"Well?" the old man called, waiting for his pride to be stroked.

"It's good work," Gene said, watching the stranger in the fractured glass his mouth. "You're a genius."

"I know, I know. Help me pack; it's a long way to the next station."

"Where's that?" Not that the old fuck would tell him more than absolutely necessary. Johnson was smart enough for *that*, even if he wasn't half the genius he thought he was.

"West." The doctor's sneering little laugh bounced off the floor, fell flat in the corners. "The last thing they'd expect. Right into the dragon's mouth."

CHAPTER THIRTY-SEVEN

MUCH THE SAME

July 17, '98

From above, a refugee camp is a city in miniature. Instead of skyscrapers, low medical and administrative buildings were the tallest structures. Packed-dirt avenues rayed into straggled ends; tents and ramshackle temporary huts hunched under a pall of yellow dust. Movement was swift and furtive, more a seething herd than a group of individuals. Spooky rested her forehead against the thick, gritted glass of the porthole, watching the camp fall away as the sled wheeled. The new guy—Hendrickson, thick dark hair and a vicious five-o'clock shadow—was at the controls, keeping up a soft running commentary as Minjae, copiloting and with her eye on the main seat, asked questions. It would be good to know how to drive one of these, Spooky decided, but she didn't want to learn from *him*.

It wasn't just that he was new, and Army, and therefore a question mark at best. It was more that he was tall and uniformed and unknown; glimpsing him in her peripheral was enough to make her heart drop into her guts with a splash and the bitter metal of adrenaline fill her mouth. Simmons, for some reason, was not nearly as dangerous.

Swann, his legs splayed into the aisle and his face slack, had fallen asleep as soon as the sled began to whine. Prink was in the jumpseat behind Minjae, his ears all but lengthening as he listened. Simmons and Sal were dozing too, Simmons with a still-sealed bottle of bourbon tucked in his lap, his hands wrapped around the neck. His right hand was bruised and puffy, and when he moved, his hangover sent out a pulse of sick-sweet post-alcohol fume. Sal had his fingers laced over his belly, his legs drawn up, and his eyes gleamed a little under mostly lowered lids. His hair was a tangle of darkness, lovingly combed whenever he had a spare moment. Soap just stripped the natural oils, he said. He'd offered to trim her hair.

Look at this, he said, pointing at her head. *It could be pretty. A little curl, and va-voom!*

Zampana's hands were palm to palm, her eyes closed, and her lips moved soundlessly. Her earrings gleamed, and whenever the sled jolted, her fingers pressed together a little tighter. She was the only one who *didn't* want a window seat, so Chuck Dogg sat to her left, looking out thoughtfully, his profile an Egyptian prince's, unblurred by time or desert sand.

It was hard to say which Spooky preferred, Chuck's blessed quiet or Zampana's well-disguised, bitter determination. Both of them were accustomed to thinking, and didn't shy away from it with distraction. Not like Simmons, who actively loathed the sensation of his own brain working, and Prink, who was not dim—quite the opposite—but was used to simply coasting along.

There was a hole in the tight, cohesive unit. It was the size of a lanky young man with a twitching face and paddlefish hands. He should have been sitting there, nervous with excitement and pestering Simmons, or bouncing slightly in his seat and bursting with barely concealed satisfaction at another sled ride.

Or maybe he would be in one of his rare quiet moods, sitting and blankly staring, his skull full of an expectant hum. It was every teenager's trick, still available to a kid of twenty-one or twenty-two, letting the mental engines idle while a healthy young body trembled with trammeled energy.

All wasted now. Spent. Slipped away quietly in a hospital bed, morphine trickling in until the flood gently, sweetly eased him into the beyond. Nothing to be done when three-quarters of your guts and a chunk of your lumbar spine were gone. It was a miracle the shock hadn't killed him, but the kid was tough.

Had been tough. Lasted four days. At least the end had been painless.

Spooky drifted, just like the sled. High up, the buffeting of the underside cells passing over rough air smoothed out. A six-and-a-half-hour glide, enough time to catch up on last night's sleep. Still, she didn't relax all the way. How could she, when underneath the sled's cells, the ground was maybe slices she'd traveled once, the *thock-thock* of the wheels on the rails jolting her bones, the inside of the cattle car packed so tight nobody could sit or lie down? Crammed in with the mass of humanity, her skull aching, the surf roar of hungerthirst misery wringing her out and making her just a rag of skin and bone with no thought other than survival. Yelling was no use—everyone else was asphyxiated or screaming as well—and reaching the transit kamp had almost been a relief.

A shit-smeared, staggering-from-weakness, just-as-cacophonous relief. Which meant no relief at all; just trading one sort of hell for another.

Her eyelids fluttered, pupils shrinking.

It was ice she saw, gigantic shards and splinters falling from the sky, piercing a metal skull frozen into a winter wasteland. The skull leered upward, its shattered cervical spine pointing north, and in the distance its ribs rose full of flapping, rotting meat. Her nose twitched slightly, and the smell was the kamps again.

No, not any kamp. It was Gloria, the deep silty mud and a fug of wet cotton dungarees decaying on scrawny flesh-rag bodies, the thin "soup" with its scraps of vegetable protein at the bottom, the salt-sickly fumes from the bottles and bays vented through tarnished portholes in the sides of the squat buildings. The faded, dusty warmth of the sorting sheds, where clothing was searched and baled; the alcoholic smear of the joyhouse with the whirlybird jukebox. The faded fustiness of the pink room, and the sourness of a man's hot breath against shrinking skin drawn tight over her own bones.

When the sled jolted and began sliding downward, she thought she was still dreaming. Everything underneath glittered, and her bladder was suddenly two sizes too small. There it was.

It had shattered, the big glass building looming over the rest of Baylock's marching barracks. Unlike later camps, every prisoner at the Big B had a cot instead of a bunk, and the work, while brutal, was clearly meant to keep the place running. There was always the chance of light duty in the hospital, too. Rumor was the upper floors were soft living and blood tests before you were released with a Retraining instead of Re-Edukation stamp on your ident, which meant a bad job at the low end, but you wouldn't starve.

Who spread those stories? Were the jar kaptains told that, so it would filter out through the laundry, the generators, the road-repair details, the long wide fields of tobacco and sweet potatoes? No need for machines when there were prisoners to tend fields by hand, and no need to drag prisoners into the hospital when they showed up on their own.

It was on the upper floors of the great glass beast that the horrors began.

No, it wasn't that the Baylock Kamp and Medical Center had been bombed. The problem was, of course, that it looked pretty much the same even after the explosions had ripped through: a wasteland of glass and suffering. Tender green crept through the fields on every side, getting ready the swampy back half of summer to settle down over furrowed earth. From up here she could see the hop-skip marks of the bomb payloads as they'd come down. Most had been harmless, unless you counted whoever was in the goddamn fields at the time.

It was almost a relief to see the bomb marks. But then, she'd never seen Baylock from the air before this, so how was she to know they hadn't been there all along, waiting to be uncovered?

She had only fuzzy, confused memories of that day. Staggering out into the hall, ripping the needle from her arm and the bandaging from her shaved head, the floor shifting and tilting, nurses and doctors peppered or ventilated with broken glass. Blood, screaming, and the fire...wait, was there fire? She remembered smoke, and the sick-sweet smell of burning flesh.

At first she'd thought the shock treatments had started again, only instead of the white light filling her skull they had wired up the whole world and given it a jolt. It took a while afterward for everything outside her own skin to acquire any coherence.

Landing. Whine of cells powering down. Her bladder hurt, a short sharp spike of pain. Hard to tell if it was hers or not. Hard to pull every scattered bit of herself back together, not even sure whose body she inhabited.

"Open the door," Simmons said, already unbuckled and uncurling. The rest of them began to move too, Zampana crossing herself and touching her lips. "I gotta piss."

CHAPTER THIRTY-EIGHT

NOT A KAMPOG

The "conference room" was simply one of the insulated barracks, its doors closed despite the stifling lack of windows. Nevertheless, there was air-conditioning, a gigantic luxury. A broad-chested InfoSec colonel, his uniform full of knife-sharp creases in all the regulation places, didn't turn up his nose at Swann's crew, but he didn't speak directly to them either, addressing Hendrickson's similarly well-creased uniform and regulation salute instead. "We know they had a plan for after the surrender."

"After we beat their asses," Simmons muttered, leaning back in his chair, and Zampana elbowed him.

The colonel didn't crack a smile *or* wrinkle his nose. "They had safe-houses and routes for the higher-ups. We've cracked most of them, enough to predict some of the others with worm algorithms. And of course, the Blue Companies are boots on the ground—your lot has the best record for closures. That's why you've been brought in. What I'm about to tell you is top-level classified—"

"Have anything to do with the mutants?" Prink drawled, cutting across the pontificating. "Like on the news? This is where they made 'em, right?"

"Genetic experimentation was practiced here, yes." The colonel blinked several times. "The administrative head of that experimentation division shot himself right before surrender, when a group of raiders happened by but didn't have enough support to do much. We managed to get partial records, but the problem is—"

"Someone who didn't shoot himself," Minjae supplied. "We get it, speed up."

The colonel—his name tag said FRYE—did not unbend enough to roll his eyes, nor did he bark at them. "One of his scientist assistants is in the pipeline, carrying a full copy of the data. All of it—prisoners, experiments, protocols, effects. I don't have to tell you what that information is worth, or what will happen if the New Soviets get hold of it."

"Again with the goddamn Russians." It was Sal's turn to mutter.

The colonel *again* didn't roll his eyes, but it was close. "They were the ones who handed that fucker the presidency, soldier."

Spooky sat in a hard wooden chair, her hands down and clasping each side of the seat. Punishment for being caught in the guards' barracks without authorization? Ten stripes. More if you were suspected of theft. It didn't have to be proven, because why else would a kampog be in a guard barracks? The guards weren't supposed to have pogs run errands or shine shoes, but they all did. Other things, as well. If you were lucky, there was food to be had when they finished with you.

"Let the man talk," Swann said, and the raiders subsided. Simmons uncapped the bourbon bottle and lifted it to his lips, glancing at Spooky. After a healthy draft, his throat bobbing, he peeled it away from his lips, leaned over, and offered it to her.

She had to work to unclench her fingers from the chair seat. *Not a kampog,* she kept reminding herself. She wasn't a prisoner anymore. She was a raider, she was one of Swann's crew, and the war was over.

It just didn't feel like it. The burn of liquor in her nose as she sniffed the bottle helped, but only a little.

"Thank you." Colonel Frye managed to avoid a supercilious snort. He still addressed Hendrickson, who sat straight in his own chair, knees together and uniform cap resting on one, looking mildly interested and freshly shaven all at once. "About all we know is that the assistant's heading west."

"Sir? How do we know that?" Hendrickson's left hand twitched, like he'd just restrained himself from raising it. "Or should I not ask?"

"We have…well, some of the experimental subjects were kept here. The drones only got the top of the glass block; they moved the subjects down into the basements once they cleaned up a bit. The 101st got here a week after the surrender, and what prisoners survived Sam Johnson— that's our target—were glad to talk. One of the subjects let us know where he's going and what he's carrying."

Hendrickson glanced at Swann, whose eyebrows had shot up. Swann waited, though, and finally Hendrickson asked the question. "Uh, you questioned a prisoner, and…?"

"The intel is solid." Colonel Frye's expression bore more than a passing resemblance to a brick wall. "We need this fellow and what he's carrying. It is absolutely vital that we catch him. We need him brought back intact for questioning, which is why your group was chosen." His chin pointed in Swann's direction, magnanimously taking notice of the man who might have been, to him, just another civilian contractor.

"What a compliment." Minjae didn't bother to say it quietly.

Bourbon stung Spooky's throat, made her eyes water. She handed the bottle back, nailed firmly in her own body again. Her shoulders relaxed a little, and she studied Frye critically, her heart hammering thinly in wrists, ankles, throat. An acrid whiff of her own sweat reached her, and that jolted her just as the booze did.

It had been a while since she'd had the extra energy to sweat simply from fear. She couldn't decide if that was comforting or not.

"West." Swann reached up as if to touch his retired hat, let his hand drop. "All right. Last known location and everything you know about the feller, any personal items he left behind, give us that sled we rode in on and clearance to get us through any hassles, and get out of the way."

Now Frye almost goggled, his mouth dropping open a little. Minjae grinned, and Prink popped a stick of black-market peppermint gum in his own mouth.

Captain Hendrickson stood, settling his uniform cap firmly on his head. "Do you need a flimsy of our authorization, sir?"

"No, that won't be necessary." Frye cleared his throat, glanced over the papers scattered across the raw-lumber table. He'd expected to go over them with the raiders—not for the irregulars, in their shabby clothes, to requisition every-damn-thing and show him the door.

Swann's expression was best described as bland, but his left cheek twitched once, almost dimpling with amusement, and Zampana softly let out a pent breath.

Spooky leapt to her feet, headed for the door. The walls were shifting, pushing in on her, and the release of Swann's tension freed her arms and legs. She hit the door at almost a run and staggered out into a bright, hot July afternoon full of a soft wind coming over turned earth and ruffled, emerald plants.

Only the fact that liquor was precious calories kept her from retching it back up onto the familiar packed gravel of Baylock's pathways, fraying at the edges because there were no pogs to rake it back.

CHAPTER THIRTY-NINE

GOOD MORALE

This room had once been the kamp administrator's office, and there was a spot of unfaded paint on the wall where the obligatory picture of Mc-Coombs had glowered. It smelled like it had been closed up for months, which might have been the case, since it was in pristine order except for the safe crouching in one corner, its door neatly cored by a plazma cutter. The darkness inside was a watchful pupil.

The office's window was inadequate. It was stifling in here, because the AC was only on in a few of the cushier barracks.

"Well?" Frye lit a candy, his fingers none too steady. His hair was a limp animal, plastering the top of his skull. Damp patches bloomed under his armpits. He was really just a glorified doorman, meant to keep order and make sure the site wasn't looted to the bones.

"Not much, sir." Hendrickson stood at ease. His left knuckles ached a little, the old burn remembering what this smell—floor wax, despair, pain, regimented cruelty—meant. They trained you for escape and evasion, but they couldn't make you forget. "They're a tight group. Good morale."

"What about the—the girl?" Frye's forehead glistened with sweat. It could have been the simmering outside, but it was more likely a result of the classified footage.

Hendrickson almost pitied the poor bastard. Getting suddenly saddled with something this hush-hush was bound to be bad luck, one way or another. "Hard to say. Haven't seen any signs. They call her Spooky."

"Spooky?" For some reason, the colonel found it funny. At least, he laughed, a short, hideously high-pitched giggle, and took another long sucking drag on his candy.

Hendrickson's hands itched, the old familiar feeling. It wasn't this asshole's fault, he told himself. He didn't know. "Well, she's strange. You could say the same about any kampog, though, and it's clear she was in at least one kamp no matter what her paperwork says."

"Is that what they call themselves?" Frye's nerves were *not* steady, no sir, not at all. He was a timeclock puncher, and this was not in his rules-and-regulations book.

"The kamps had their own language, sir. It'd be a miracle if survivors—or just plain raiders—didn't display some trauma." *And I should know.* The thick, pink scar tissue on his fingers twitched. Or maybe it didn't—maybe he just felt it again, the red-hot crackle, smelling his own flesh charring before the red haze descended and he came back to himself covered in blood and brain; hearing a knock at the door, and the sure knowledge that he'd be executed filling him with the raw unsteady faux-courage of desperation.

It wasn't bravery if you were just doing what you had to. And it was only luck when the guards were drunk and there was a hole in the electrified fence.

Frye swabbed at his shiny forehead again. "Well, you keep an eye on her. If she really is X-Ray, the higher-ups want her nice and whole. Not even a scratch, you hear?"

How long would *that* last, Hendrickson wondered? "That was made clear to me, sir. Yes." For all they knew, Spooky could have been in another kamp, then broken out with the raiders before Wyoming or even earlier, even though Crunche hadn't seen her. Things got...fluid, out in combat.

"I'd've cashiered the lot of them," the colonel said, inhaling a deep draft of candy smoke. "No discipline."

Funny, since Swann's crew had been called in because they were regarded as the most likely to bring their quarry in alive. "Raiders, sir." Hendrickson concentrated on relaxing his fingers. If she *was* X-Ray, or even just one of the Baylock escapees, God alone knew what she'd do if she somehow guessed his primary mission. Even a fellow kampog was a threat. Hunger and brutalization made everyone a question mark at best. "Should I take this and the authorization to them?"

"Go ahead. Good work, Captain."

"Sir? One question." Not that he suspected the man knew, but he might as well ask.

"Go ahead."

"What exactly is X-Ray? Do we know?"

"Oh, *they* might, upstream. All I know is what I saw when we pulled the lid off this shithole." Frye shook his head, a galvanic, tossing movement. "Christ. They did things, Captain. The goddamn fucks did things you wouldn't believe." He inhaled again. The candy smoke didn't seem to be doing much to calm him down, despite the fact that the docs swore it was a mild sedative. "You'd better get on back to them. Take whatever you want. Good luck."

"Yes, sir." That answered that, then. The man hadn't just seen the footage. He'd seen the actual subjects, the ones lucky enough to survive to the end.

Hendrickson paused outside in the hall to settle his cap. If the girl was X-Ray, and he pulled this off, his career was probably made. Either that or they'd put him in a hole, depending. How she'd gotten involved with the raiders was probably a long story, and one he'd have to piece together just as if he'd wriggled out through the fence again and found himself in the middle of nowhere, the kamp behind him, his hand a bloody, roasted mess, and his entire hide prickling like a hunted animal's. Ears open, face blank, letting the world think he was stupid while the meat inside his head went into overdrive.

He made sure the papers were neatly stacked, set his shoulders, and headed back for the sled.

CHAPTER FORTY

LIVE AND LEARN

"I don't like it." Zampana crossed her arms over her ample bosom. Her fine, poreless cheeks tightened as her mouth pursed. "Smells setup-y."

"These are Federals, not Firsters." Minjae tapped up a candy, considered it, shoved it back down in the crumpled pack. Her ink-black hair gleamed, standing up in a short ruff since she'd stopped shaving, and her round face was set, thoughtful, and distant.

Chuck Dogg held his hand out. His fingertips, pinkish and callused, curved upward a little. "Yeah, well, rank is rank. Remember that bastard before Leavy?"

"Oh, how could anyone forget." The casualties had been almost as bad as Second Cheyenne. Minjae handed Dogg a candy and dug for her lighter. "Looks like Sal has a new customer."

Sal had Spooky settled on a knocked-over kerro drum, and the scissors flashed as he combed and snipped. "Can't take it anymore," he repeated, every once in a while tossing his own shining black curls. "Been bothering the fuck out of me." The frayed ends of her hair drifted on the breeze, and every so often he touched her shoulder or adjusted her head with gentle fingers.

Spooky, her eyes glazed and her mouth slightly open, submitted patiently. Simmons crouched in front of her, watching her face. He rocked back and forth a little every so often, occasionally taking a jolt from the bottle and offering it politely.

She didn't move. Barely even blinked. Only her hands twitched every once in a while, an arrested shiver.

Minjae considered this tableau, scuffing her left foot back and forth meditatively. "You think she was here?"

Her hip bumped Chuck's gently, and his eyelids slid down to half-mast while he took a drag. "Huh?"

"The Spook." Minjae didn't sound impatient, like she would with anyone other than Pana or Dogg not following her leaps. Too much mental horsepower made her uncharitable with lesser mortals sometimes. "You think she was here?"

Zampana, her arms still crossed, had a line between her crow-feather eyebrows. "Looks pretty goddamn likely." The gleam of a gold chain at her neck was new, but nobody remarked on it. "On the other hand, all the fuckin' camps look the same, right? Could just be that."

"This one don't look the same." Chuck tipped his head lazily at the giant, shattered glass glitter. "Musta made a helluva noise. What you think they did in there?"

"Christ only knows." Minjae shuddered, though the day bordered on hot when the breeze fell off. "Experiments, right? Mutants. That's what the news said."

"Genetics," Zampana murmured, but softly. Then, louder, "Who cares *what*? Firsters. Bound to be bad."

"Better question." Prink slunk around the front of the sled, his hair a slicked-down copper flame. He scrubbed his hands together, the sharp sudden smell of rubbing alcohol stinging the breeze. "How many Spookies out there?"

Minjae looked to Zampana, who drew back into the shade a little. Chuck did too, his free arm snaking down and around Min's shoulders. She didn't shake him off, and Prink's expression turned sour before he swung back toward the sled's nose, exhaling hard. He kept rubbing, as if his finger stump pained him. It probably did, phantom limbs being what they were.

Pana finally finished whatever long train of thought had boarded at her station. "Pretty sure we got the only one." She cleared her throat, working up a good wad, and spat. The gobbet glittered in midair, splashing onto weedy gravel. "Why else they ask for *us*? And give us that Johnny Quickstep."

A chorus of scoffing noises rose at the mention of Hendrickson. He wasn't an active irritant, true, but he wasn't a *raider*. When the Federals slipped one of their own in, the best you could hope for was that they didn't think they were gonna take over and do something stupid, like provoke the fucking Firsters when there was no call. Command and control, they called it, but the raiders knew what it was: bullshit plain and simple. More precisely, bullshit that could get an entire raider band wiped out in a heartbeat.

"Maybe we just got the only *sane* spookbunny." Chuck took another drag. His 'fro, its top arc hanging out in sunshine, was a halo cut in half.

Prink tapped on the sled's side, testing the metal. "Sane?"

"Well, I mean, compared to Simms." Dogg took another very long drag, pulling the smoke all the way down. It wasn't nicotine, but it would do.

"You got a point." Zampana laughed, a sharp bark of wry almost-amusement. It cut the odd silence drifting over the bones of Baylock, and brought Spooky's chin up.

"Pfft, pay no attention," Sal said, lightly tapping the back of her head. "Just a few minutes and we'll be done. Another trim or two and you'll be a model."

"Skinny enough." Simms rocked back on his heels. "Gnat bites and no hips. Got to eat more, woman."

Spooky didn't reply. But some sense came back into her wide dark eyes, and she stared fixedly at Simmons, who took another hit off the bourbon and grinned, his cheeks flushing high and hot with alcohol burn.

"Yes, yes," Sal said, snipping and stepping back critically to evaluate his work. "Soon your hair will be like Pana's. Warrior braids."

"Gonna take a while, Sal." Simmons kept rocking. His eyes were bloodshot.

Spooky focused past him, at the tall, spike-crowned glitter of broken glass and twisted metal. The damage was old; dandelions and vines forced their way between fallen girders and chunks of debris too big for even a full work gang to shift. To her right, an uninjured chunk of the building had been reroofed and a double door had been added. The glimpse she'd managed to get through it showed a guard hutch and a bank of elevator doors, also newly added. They gleamed mellow in the cool dark, but the strip lights overhead weren't dead, just dialed down.

Instead of rebuilding, they'd burrowed, while she was shuttled from one transit kamp to another, becoming not even a name or a number, just a blank space inside shivering skin. They hadn't even magtatted her in the transits, just used indelible ink on her arm when they loaded the cattle cars. Then there was Gloria.

"Through the cracks," she murmured, her lips barely moving. Slipped through, vanished, a rabbit chewing its way out of the hat and searching for a dark, quiet corner to hyperventilate in.

Simmons either didn't hear or chose not to respond.

"And voilà," Sal said, ruffling her hair, vastly pleased with himself. "It will grow in with the layers, they will give it life. I was a hairdresser before the war, you know."

At least he wasn't using one of the burring, buzzing razors; you had to plug those in. If she ever heard that nasty grinding sound again, she'd vomit.

"Shit, Sal, you already said that. Like, twice." Simmons unfolded, rising and rising. His shadow fell over her, and she sat very still as Sal brushed her shoulders, her nape, dusting away stray hairs. "And you, woman, are gonna itch all day. Don't ever let him cut your hair in the field." He offered his large, callused bear paw, and she took it. There didn't seem to be any reason not to, and he pulled her to her feet. "Live and learn, Spookster. Live and learn."

CHAPTER FORTY-ONE

SNAIL SAFE

"Whaddawe got?" Minjae stretched her fingers wide, balancing a slim Dell deck on her lap as Swann handed her a stack of file folders. The other box sat, taped and silent, prissily holding its secrets. With the seats up, the interior of the sled was roomy enough for all of them, and it was as good a base as any with the hatch closed and the kerro core humming to fuel some AC. Better than many, many spaces they'd worked in. "Ooh, look at this. Personal correspondence, how I love the personal correspondence. And thumbdrives too! It's like Christmas."

"Feliz Navidad." Zampana hefted the other box. She gave Swann a significant look, her eyebrows rising. "Scan 'em first."

"Teach your mama to make kimchi." Minjae was at her happiest with intel to work. She flipped through a few more pages. "God damn, tell Lazy to…"

A stung, sharp silence fell inside the sled. Min's hand flew to her mouth, and Simmons's shoulders jerked as if he'd just been gut-punched. Spooky, eyeing the second box from the very back corner of the sled, drew her knees up and hugged them.

Sal cleared his throat, awkwardly. Swann opened his mouth, but Simmons beat him to it.

"I keep looking around for him, too," the Reaper said quietly. He hunched near the sled hatch, absurdly broad shoulders straining at his uniform T-shirt. He hadn't given up on his high-and-tight, and his scalp was pink with sunburn through the blond scruff. "Fuckin' kid. Why'd he have to do that?"

"Wanted to make us proud." Prink blew out a long, unhappy sigh. "Fuck, man, hand me that bourbon."

"We ain't holding a wake for him tonight." Swann picked up the second cardboard box. "Make a hole."

The box thumped down in front of Spooky. Hendrickson, up in the pilot seat, wisely said nothing, but he had half turned, his knees uncomfortably bumping the center console. Zampana—short enough she could walk fully upright inside the cramped confines—stood with a brief, huffing sigh and leaned on the bulkhead, blocking his view.

"When are we holding it, then?" Pana examined her nails. The cheap polish—bright but so terribly fragile—on her left middle finger was chipped. "Because we need to organize more than Simms's daily stash of firewater to do it up right. I feel the need to get blinded."

Swann crouched, put both his hands on the sealed box, and looked at Spooky. She nodded slightly. He straightened, almost clocking himself a good one on a weapons rack. "God *damn* it. Well, I believe as soon as we catch this motherfucker, we'll hold the wake proper." He paused. "A *raider* wake."

"Too many of those." Prink dug in the box ahead of Minjae. "I'll get his deck out. You got his password?"

"No," Simmons piped up. "I got it. *Pastorburg.* With an *o* and a *u*."

"*Pastorburg?* No numbers, no symbols? Jeez." Minjae's cheeks had blotched with red, and her eyes were suspiciously bright.

"That's the name of the shithole he was born in." Simmons hit the hatch release, and was gone into the late-afternoon glare outside. The hatch closed behind him, sealing itself with an uncomfortable hiss, and Prink swore, a low, vicious obscenity that had nothing to do with the zipper on his deck bag, already looking worn despite the fact that he'd picked it up near Jackson when supply restrictions started to ease. Minjae's was already dotted with Zampana's nail varnish, a sloppy red heart on the flap and some salvaged tinfoil turned into glitter beads tied to the straps and buckle.

"A raider wake," Swann repeated as he finished unfolding and half turned, looking for a seat.

Spooky hugged her knees harder. The box crouched in front of her, patient and mute, its top trisected with regular Army sealtape. The bar code stamped onto a bed of waterproof was attached to an inventory number, and that number would call up a list of items in the box. This article was so long, that article weighed so much—dimensions neatly measured and described, and no doubt anyone with enough clearance could peek at the list and fool himself into thinking he knew something.

There was more talk, but it fell away into a low humming inside her skull. Spooky watched the box. If she loosened her arms, her hands would be free. She'd have to dig out the pocketknife in her medic satchel and slit the tape. Then she would have to reach in, and see if weighing everything by fingertip and palm would give them something.

She rested her chin on her knees. Curled up like this, she was a snail safe in its bony home. You could step on it, sure, but if the shell shattered it could throw shrapnel.

Could she? Finding a way to test that hypothesis was a dilly, as Lara would say. Her sister out in the woods, carrying filched medical supplies and food to lean, fire-eyed raiders. Everyone in town called them *traitors*.

To her, they were patients.

Hannah. Lara. She exhaled softly, tensed every muscle. Even *Anna* was too close. *No. Spooky.*

The creaking of a rope, a blue-and-yellow skirt rustling. A face no longer like her own, but purpled and swollen, the neck at a grotesque angle.

Spooky closed her eyes.

Pretend to be me.
  But why?
  Because they might know.
  Know what?
  What I've been doing. Out in the woods.

You shouldn't. It's dangerous.
I know.

The inside of the sled was dark and quiet, and somehow, while Spooky was lost in the past, they had lifted off. Minjae, buckled into a seat now, had her deck balanced across her knees again, and was chewing at a fingernail as its screen bathed her with blue light. Cables snaked across the floor, the sled batteries charging electronics as well as fueling internal processes.

Simmons slumped in the jumpseat closest to Spooky, dozing. On his other side, Swann, buckled in tightly, stretched out his legs, his hair showing little streaks of gray. Hendrickson was at the sled controls again, this time taking Prink through procedures; Zampana sat cross-legged on the uncomfortable metal floor, humming a little and biting her lower lip as she poked at a torn pair of uniform pants with a curved flesh-stitching needle. Seen from this angle, in the low light, Pana's profile was serene and stern, a goddess concentrating on a mortal task for no other reason than the pleasure of seeing how her worshippers lived.

Sal, stretched sideways across two of the seats, snored lightly. Spooky's back itched, and her legs were numb. Her fatigue knees held a damp spot, either drool or condensation. Had she slept or just checked out, become what the kampogs called a blanker? You saw them, walking around with their jaws slack and their eyes useless and dull, withdrawn into their own little worlds.

They didn't long. Once they completed that inward revolution, they stopped even trying to keep clean or eat, and if they didn't die of starvation they were swept into the killing bottles during the next roll call.

It felt different in here, she decided. Less like there was a Lazy-size gap, and more like the shaky, sickened half hour in whatever aid station a medic could organize after the casualties stopped coming in and the triage was done. Sooner or later the flood of wounded ceased, and there was a moment where the internal balance shifted. You couldn't stop, but you could take a deep breath in the middle of a task, and some hair-fine inner thread would relax just a little.

Spooky uncurled just a little, too. The box was still there, but someone had cut it open. Probably Simmons. Whoever it was hadn't raised the lid at all; the top with its bar code and the slashed tape was a sly cartoon smile.

Her hands shook a little. She poked at the flap, glanced at the front. Hendrickson's attention was all out the front bubble, attending to the business of flying. The radio crackled, and Prink gave the call sign and heading in a bored monotone.

Spooky wormed her aching, almost-numb fingers into the dark interior, and set to work.

CHAPTER FORTY-TWO

MIRACLE

July 18, '98

They landed near what used to be the Kansas border, settling on a pad in the middle of a bivouac base, and as the sled powered down Minjae was still tapping at her deck. "Big old goddamn heap of nothin'," she told Swann. "Lemme alone for a bit."

"I'll stay," Zampana offered. Prink was already shoving his way through the hatch, desperate to get out and find a patch to piss on.

Hendrickson eased himself out of the pilot's seat. He was looking a little worse for wear, his black hair slicked down and his eyes bloodshot. He tried to stretch, almost braining himself on a bulkhead, and let out a jolted curse that brought Spooky's head up, her eyes glittering feverishly under half-lowered lids. A smear-trickle of darkness on her upper lip gleamed wetly. Both her hands were in the box of personal effects, and her expression, half hidden, was somewhere between a dreaming woman's and the uncomprehending stare of a tired animal.

"Hey." Captain Hendrickson pushed forward, despite Zampana's broad hip suddenly in his way. "Shit, she's bleeding!"

"Nosebleed," Swann said. "Happens. Probably the cabin pressure."

"But—" The captain swung forward, around Zampana, who slid a foot back but not in time to trip him. It was Simmons, stretching his legs out, who fixed him with a baleful look, bringing him to a halt right in the middle of the sled. Sal snorted, surfacing from his doze, probably sensing a feral current sliding through the cramped space.

"Oh hey." Minjae glanced up. "You. Dogboy. Bring me some coffee. And a bacon sandwich."

Hendrickson chose to ignore her, and pointed at Spooky. "There's a med station here. Should get that looked at."

"She's *fine*." Zampana sniffed. "Side effect of temporary malnutrition. Gets a little self-conscious when people point and stare, though."

"Yeah," Prink piped up. "Don't be rude, asshole."

The glimmers of Spooky's eyes faded as she blinked, reappeared. Her mouth, slack and slightly open, was a dark downward curve, full underlip trembling a little.

"Fine." Hendrickson pushed past Simmons's legs, heading for the hatch. A damp, burning breath of warm summer night flooded in, and he filled the doorway for a moment before hopping outside, his boots heavy on the stair grating.

"This ain't gonna end well," Swann said softly, in the charged silence that followed.

Spooky's pale tongue flicked out, licked at the smear on her upper lip. She blinked again, slowly, her hands moving inside the box with little rustles.

"Lots of accidents can happen, hunting Firsters." Simmons leaned his head back against the sled wall. It could have been a joke, except for the flat shine on his blue bloodshot eyes.

"That's your answer to everything." Zampana rolled her shoulders back, holding up the T-shirt she'd just finished repairing. She could probably draw a new one—the Federals had no supply shortage—but working behind the lines meant you learned to fix everything you possibly could. "Why don't *you* go get us some coffee, and something to chew on? I'm hungry."

A soft, hissing exhalation was Spooky, as she drew her hands out of the box, clutching a knotted length of material. It was a uniform tie, black polyester with the red embroidered eagle of Firster service peeking out from the tangle. "This is his," she murmured. "Look for Project Carpet." She shook her head, banging it against the sled wall behind her, a solid, painful sound. "No. *Flying* Carpet. Look for that." Another hiss, a labored breath, sweat pasting strands of dark hair to her forehead. Her shadowed face contorted.

"Oh." Minjae nodded, staring at her screen. "Yeah. Okay."

"Fuck," Prink breathed. "Man, oh man."

"Remember Franco?" Swann kneed Simmons's legs, and the Reaper pulled them up again. "And that redheaded Firster bastard?"

Apparently Sal was now awake, because he pushed himself upright, stretching luxuriously. "The one with the glasses?" He rubbed at his oily hair, tumbling it just so. "Yeah. Scary fucker, cracked Cowboy Bill, and leapfrogged his whole band. And Franco, with his sniffing out patrols. Swear he *could* smell 'em, just like he said."

"Weird shit in the world." Swann headed for the hatch. "We've all seen it."

"I'm a problem," Spooky said suddenly, her chin jerking up and her tone shifting from dreamy to flat and uninterested. She rubbed the back of her head against the wall, her hair sliding against slick metal. "Right?"

"You're a raider." Three little words, loaded with significance, as Swann's gaze rested on her. "One of our crew."

"Well, technically speaking, you're both." Minjae stretched her arms. Little crunching noises echoed as she stretched her neck too, popping it and sighing. "But to be fair, most of us are. Right, Simms?"

"Fuck your mother," was the Reaper's equable reply.

"See?" Minjae's short, bitter laugh was echoed by Zampana's fox snort and Sal's rich, fruity chuckle. "Don't worry about Johnny Fed, Spook."

Swann continued out the hatch, into darkness full of damp heat and cricket singing. Spooky's face tipped back down, but it was impossible to tell if she was comforted or simply exhausted. "Flying Carpet," she mumbled again. "Look for that."

"Thanks." Min bent back over the keyboard. "Simms, you gonna get me some coffee?"

"Yes ma'am." He unfolded, and on his way out he paused for just a second in front of Spooky.

She didn't look up, and he didn't say anything. Still, the humming tension hunching her shoulders and keeping her knees rigid relaxed a little, then a little more.

"And bingo," Minjae whispered. "Oh, Spooky, you are a miracle. Any ideas on the decrypt key?"

Spooky wound the tie around her right fist, licking again at the blood on her upper lip. "Not yet," she said softly. "But soon, I will."

CHAPTER FORTY-THREE

CHEMICAL LIE

Swann held his peace until they were past the sentry at the edge of the concrete pad, ident shown and directions to the depot listened to. He further held it until they were inside the depot foyer, poking the sleepy, lanky, cornrowed first sergeant on evening watch behind the desk into yawning action. While the console booted up, though, he had to say *something*, and he settled for the obvious. "You're not makin' any friends."

"Never been one of my strengths." Hendrickson passed his chipped wrist over the reader and was rewarded with a green light, a soft modulated tone, and the touch screen on its pedestal filling with a dizzying menu of options. "Coffee, right? Be nice to have it in the sled. What other supplies do you need?"

"Firsters almost burned Spooky at the stake. We're kind of protective." The first half was sort of a lie, unless one counted camp internment as immolation. Which wasn't far off.

Hendrickson's chin dipped a little. That was all. "So the nosebleeds are normal?"

"Not so much anymore."

Hendrickson nodded as if he'd expected the answer. "MREs? Protein packs? Ammo?"

"For Chrissake." Swann leaned in, began scanning and tapping. "Gonna need another sled to carry all this."

"Well, at least I'm useful." Hendrickson's teeth showed, a semicircle rictus. "Want to know how I got this?" He lifted his left hand a little, displaying the scars. "My unit got taken by the Reklamation fucks in north Colorado, during their first big push. Sent us to Pilgrim. I wasn't shoved right into the bottles there, for some reason."

That made Swann pause, turning his head to regard the other man steadily.

"They were big on branding there." Hendrickson's tone had turned thoughtful, distant, just the same as Spooky's when she mentioned something about fucking Gloria. He looked at the burn scar, fingers closing slowly, opening again. "One of the Butcher's boys did it. Made a mistake, though. Didn't tie me down enough."

Swann looked down, tapped at the touch screen. No reason to pass up a resupply chance, and people had an easier time talking when you weren't staring at them. "That so?" He was getting really good at not looking at soldiers while they told him horrible shit.

Of all the skills wartime had given him, it was one he liked least.

"Yeah. I hooked up with Kellogg's crew after I went through the wire. Saved me from a patrol sent to drag me back to Pilgrim." A faint hitching sound, clearing his dry throat. A thin sheen of sweat on his forehead could have been the heat outside, or something else. "What I'm trying to say is, I'm not the enemy, okay?"

Never said you were was on the tip of Swann's tongue, but he decided that was probably not what Minjae, or even Prink, would call tactful. Besides, it was a damn lie, and while this fellow might be a watchdog, he wasn't a Firster. "Okay." There. That was a reasonable response, he decided. He caught himself reaching for his hat again, and finding nothing but skin and his own hair.

Fuck it. When he got back to the sled he'd root through his luggage and find the damn thing. If he wasn't allowed some goddamn retirement, neither should a piece of soggy-ass, leathery felt be.

Maybe it satisfied the Army man, maybe not. In any case, Hendrickson pointed at the screen with a thick, callused finger. "You done?"

"Think that'll do 'er." Swann nodded at the depot sergeant, whose eyes glittered a little, like Chuck's.

"Hell of a Christmas list." The sergeant stretched, a long lithe movement, and scratched at the side of his neck. "Take me a little bit."

"No hurry." There wasn't, until they had a good direction. Which Spooky and Minjae would give them. Sometimes all you *could* do was wait. That was 95 percent of the goddamn war, waiting around. The other 5 percent was sheer terror, and all of it was sickening.

Hendrickson made a short sound that could have been a laugh, or his own impatience, as the console powered down and a flimsy printer whirred into life, producing a paper list with checkboxes. "Don't tell him that, we'll be here all night. Let me through, Sergeant, I'll help."

"Sir?" The sergeant stiffened. "Are you sure, sir?"

Swann thought it pretty likely the fellow didn't want Hendrickson seeing any bare spots on the shelves. Selling from the depot on the sly was a good way to make a few writs or a lot of friends, but if an officer came by, you were looking at some uncomfortable times indeed.

"Very sure," Hendrickson replied, and his faint steely smile, sly as a Sicilian farmer's, made it obvious he was thinking along the same lines.

Swann left them to it, heading back out into the damp, breathing night. He took a few steps sideways from the door and lit a candy. It was time for some thinking, and he didn't like the way said thinking was already tending.

The world was full of problems. There was Simmons sliding further and further into twitchy violence, Prink and his shaky hands, Sal and his unspoken but sensed desire to quit this goddamn shit work and go *home*. At least Sal had a home to go back to, but he was a calming influence, and Swann hated to lose anyone.

Which brought him to Lazy. The fucking kid, going off and getting himself gutshot. The surrender was supposed to put an end to that bullshit. The crew needed a wake, but were they going to have to drink everyone else they'd lost into the ground, too? How many times until it took?

There probably wasn't enough rotgut in the world to keep all the dead quiet.

Lazy. The stupid kid. The stupid, lovable, goofy-ass kid.

Last of all, the two big problems, which were really one: Spooky. The Federals certainly suspected she'd been at Baylock, so they'd sent in this nice little captain with raider credentials to gather what intel he could? It was just sneaky enough to be possible.

Candy smoke wasn't as harsh as tobacco. It was no Camel, that was for damn sure. He listened while he inhaled, drawing it down deep in the lungs. It just gave you something to do with your idle hands, really. Sedative his *ass*.

Night insects singing, crickets and what-have-you. Whine of kerro engines to the east, swords of white light jutting down from the slow-moving drift of sleds. Keeping an eye on things; there was probably a refugee site over there, to judge by the smoke. Other kerro whines and the deep grumble of a gleeson slightly to the south, more bright lights and the sounds of construction. Either they were digging this temporary base in deeper or they were hauling away leftover crap from a battle. Twisted metal, burned-up junk, shell casings—a rich magnetic harvest. At least the Firsters hadn't used much in the way of mines.

Mines and IEDs were a raider trick. You used everything you had to even out the playing field, behind the lines and running hard.

Swann stood, and smoked, and thought about all of it. After a few minutes he stiffened, the candy's glowing-red cherry tip jerking.

If the Federals didn't already know Spooky had been at Baylock, they suspected strongly enough to keep an eye on her. And there was no goddamn way they would give raiders, even ones who had signed up and did good work, this kind of carte blanche unless someone else was after this Dr. Johnson, too.

And let's just say, Swann thought, for the hell of it let's just say his raiders caught this bastard. The Federals probably wouldn't hang him. Someone who could make Spookies? They'd scoop him up and set him to it. Imagine that, a bunch of soldiers who could do…what she did.

It was enough to give you nightmares.

There was no way around it, Swann decided, tossing the candy away as if it were foul. They tasted sugary, true, but that was some kind of chemical lie. Probably give you a new kind of cancer.

He was gonna have to have to think about how to make Lara, now Anna, their Spooky, disappear from Federal sight.

Just in case.

PART THREE

GLORIA MUNDI

CHAPTER FORTY-FOUR

A FINE SUBJECT

July 20, '98

Another day, another shitty little hole in the ground in some godforsaken flat stretch of the Dakotas. A clapboard house set far away from anything resembling a town or civilization, but only two miles from the charred remains of what had been a frontier kamp. Not a Reklamation site, but a short-term, dig-up-the-sod piece of prairie—Retraining, for those who had the proper racial heritage but, for one reason or another, needed a little convincing about contributing to the Greatest Society. The last safe spot had given them a rusting old petrol-burning piece-of-shit truck, and while it was a relief not to be staggering along behind the hatchet-faced son of a bitch, the cloud of stink made Gene long for at least a hybrid.

It was all academic, because something wasn't right. Gene's legs wouldn't quite obey him, and the high whining in his ears made sleep or coherent thought almost impossible. The doctor gave him some capsules, and he washed them down with mineral-tasting ditchwater without thinking.

This place had a bedroom full of liquid prairie light, its only furniture an ancient iron-framed bedstead the doctor pushed hard against the wall before setting to work. The world went away for an indeterminate time, becoming a droning buzz and smears of weird color. As soon as Gene opened his eyes, he knew he had a fever, and the hard pinch on the inside of his left arm was a needle pushed into a vein. A sharpish, sour smell of rotting potatoes warred with a vomitous stink, and he tried to roll onto his side.

"Now, now," a familiar, leathery little voice said. It was the doctor, his face swimming into view. "It will pass; it's a common reaction."

Christ. What had the bastard *done* to him? *Antibiotics,* he'd said. *I don't like the way that looks.*

It wasn't Gene's face; it wasn't the wound in his calf either. It was the small rusty-knife incision just above his left wrist, swelling hard and black now under a thin pane of stretched, pink, shiny skin. A dirty wound. Splashing through mud and oily, infested water hadn't done him any favors. Red streaks crawled up his arm, he sweated when he wasn't shivering, and he'd passed out in the truck. Amerika had died, now *he* was dying, Eugene Thomas understood as much.

"Oh, don't be so dramatic." Something cold probed at his wrist. "We just have to drain this." Poking, prodding. The stink grew worse. "You really should have said something before now. Not so long ago, you'd probably lose the arm."

"Gee," Gene heard a drunk man with his own voice slur. "Thanks, Doc."

"He thanks me." Amused, the doctor pulled the needle out. "No, don't thank me, young Patriot. As it is, you might just lose the hand."

Gene starfished, arms and legs thrown out, but he was feeble and feverish. Besides, the doctor had strapped him to the bed's convenient, heavy frame.

"*Stop* that." Sharply now, and the doctor's face changed, stretching like a reflection in a funhouse mirror. "Or I'll leave you tied here to rot."

Gene quieted. He suspected, even in his state, that the Baylock man would do it. Christ, if he could just get on his feet…

Johnson turned away, rummaging in something set on a plain stripped-pine nightstand pulled close to the bed. "Much better," he mumbled. "You know, I've always wanted to…never got the chance in med school. Sequencing and editing are all very well, but sometimes you want to get your hands dirty. Right?"

The crazy fucker. Gene tried to *think*. All he could summon, though, was a croaking groan as something warm spread up his arm. He saw *her* again, those hazel-dark eyes and her dark hair, the full underlip. Standing up in the quarry, straight and graceful, those eyes catching his, that gaze burrowing into him … *"—naaaaah,"* he moaned, the last half of her name. She never seemed to listen when he called her by it, responding to direct commands only but also submitting to whatever he wanted.

Anything at all.

"A little cocktail of my own devising. Is it pleasant?" The doctor leer-grinned, thin mouth stretching, and the world distorted sideways. A cold probing at Gene's left wrist, a sharp spike of pain breaking the warmth for an excruciating second, a jet of foulness. "It isn't for me. Christ, this stinks."

Gene shut his eyes. Whatever the doctor had loaded him on *was* pleasant. The world went away for a while, except a faint, persistent tugging on his arm and a nose-scouring wave of disinfectant.

With the young man finally resting comfortably, the doctor could stand in the front room of the old farmhouse, looking at his grandfather's sagging armchair. The red corduroy upholstery held both damp stains and the round, mean little eyes of cigarette burns, and if Sam Johnson concentrated he could see the old man himself lounging there in one of his yellowed wifebeaters and overalls, legs stretched out and a mug of exquisitely hard homemade cider to hand. He could even almost see little Sam, rolling one of his beloved Hot Wheels along the worn carpet and listening to the television bark out the staccato rhythms of old war movies, his grandfather every once in a while laughing or saying, *That's right, git 'em!*

It was a risk coming here. Perhaps the incident in Minnesota had been a coincidence, perhaps not. Science demanded methodical thinking and precision, and caution was handmaiden to both. If it meant he obsessively checked the lump in his traveler's money belt, strapped securely under whatever approximation of clean clothing he could find in his bag on any given day, well, a little obsession showed a certain strength of character. Discipline, a commitment to ideals. All things his grandfather might have approved of.

Approval might be too strong a word, though. Certainly the old man had hated little Sam's father.

The chair was moldering, and the entire house had been shut up for too long, but it was better than the bedroom reeking of foul-smelling pus squeezed from a wound. Who would have thought the young blond man could have so much infection in him and still manage to remain upright? At first Captain Thomas had been protective camouflage, but now Johnson was thinking he could be useful in other ways. The early Patriot recruitment drives had high standards of both genetic and ideological fitness, and while Johnson sniffed at the latter, the former was nearly ideal for research purposes.

Assuming, of course, the young captain survived, and further assuming they both reached a place of safety.

Sam Johnson turned sharply and headed for the kitchen. There were still dishes in the cupboard, dusty now but perfectly serviceable. What he was aiming for, however, was the mudroom, with its connecting door to the long, low garage holding the old tractor and the ancient Chevy, acquired near Duluth, that had belched and farted them the entire way here.

And the workbench.

Johnson wrinkled his nose at the smell—somehow, old garages always smelled like chicken straw and dry-rotted vegetables. There was an old CB radio on the workbench, shrouded in canvas. With a few minor adjustments, it could be made serviceable and wired in to the old antenna going up the side of the house. The pulse would communicate that he was alive to certain…interested parties. He'd rendered quite a few services; now was the time to call in a favor or two. At least those interested parties would provide him the means to continue the experiments. Hell, they'd even pay him handsomely to do so.

Johnson twitched the canvas aside, sneezing at the dust. Data flashed through his head, patterns cropping up just like on a monitor. They'd been so *close*. So few successes, the most intriguing one lost in the drone bombing. But they'd carried on, burrowing under the shattered glass bones of Baylock's hospital building and scouring the entire shrinking country for subjects and supplies.

Only around 20 percent of the subjects survived, and of *those*, only 40 percent showed any promise at all. Those were bad odds if you wanted a whole corps of Enhanced, but considering that each one was worth a good ten *ordinary* soldiers if researchers could just standardize the application…

Well, the solution was there. All he needed was enough time with the data, and enough supplies to continue. If his former friends didn't see fit to rescue him, he could at least carry on his work in some forgotten corner until he had something definite and inarguable to show. You worked with what you had, especially when the stupid called your work *illegal* or *unethical*. Silly words, both of them.

The young Patriot, once his infection was cleared, would make a fine subject. And the good doctor thought the fentanyl he'd just injected would no doubt help keep the fellow manageable.

Johnson smiled and took a look at the radio. The first step would be scavenging enough power to turn it on.

Fortunately, the truck engine had a battery.

CHAPTER FORTY-FIVE

NONE OF US RIGHT

July 21, '98

"Just what are you fucking saying?" Minjae whispered, a fierce hiss usually reserved for someone interrupting her work.

Prink glanced over his shoulder, hunching defensively. "I'm just sayin' we should think about things. That this isn't right."

"Isn't right? What's so right about what you're—"

"We don't *know* she was a raider." There. He'd said it. He was dead pale, and his coppery hair was slicked down with damp from the showers. Finding Min in the hallway, wrapped in a towel and dangling a pair of pink rubber flip-flops from one plump hand, had been a stroke of luck. She had her boots on, tied loosely, and she was probably looking forward to hot water. But dammit, he'd been chewing on this for a while, and besides, with the way she looked at Spooky, maybe she was thinking the same thing?

Minjae's chin went up. She regarded him for ten long, ticking seconds. "Oh. I think I get it now." Nodding, her black hair standing up in an aggressive ruff. It only made her prettier, not that she needed any help. "You think Firsters put a spy in a kamp whorehouse and raped the shit out of her just so she could be picked up by us before the surrender, on half-wormed data. Gee, Prink. That's amazing. I don't know why anyone didn't figure that out before."

The sarcasm was painful, but Prink persisted. "Think about what she can do. Who's to say she wasn't—"

"Prink." Minjae glared at him, still dead level. "You want to stop. Right there."

"I'm just sayin'—"

"Remember her hauling you out of that fucking house at the burning camp? You *do* still remember that, right? She ain't no fucking Firster, and you want to check yourself, man." Minjae pitched forward, on her booted toes. You could go around in just a towel, sure, but a raider knew to take care of her feet. "You're going all Reklamation, and it ain't attractive."

"I don't think she's a Firster." Now he was regretting he'd ever opened his stupid mouth. "I just, I dunno, Min. She ain't *right*."

"Yeah, well, Zampana's a Christer, Simms is a psychopath, Swann don't like sleepin' if he don't have a hat, and you and me, we twitch all the fucking time. What the fuck you think about that? Huh?" Minjae's round cheeks flushed and her dark eyes flashed. "We ain't none of us *right*, Prinky. Cut it the fuck out."

He stepped back, raising his hands in surrender. "Fine. But if shit goes down, Imma say *I told you so*."

She rolled her eyes. "You do that. *I'm* gonna go take a shower and forget we ever had this conversation." She pushed past him, and he could smell the healthy, oily shine to her hair as well as the simmering of an angry woman. Halfway to the door of the girls' locker room, though, she stopped. "Prink?"

"Yeah?"

"I like your suspicious little brain, you know? It got us out of some trouble in the woods." Teeth flashing, that slow sleepy smile that turned him inside out. "Just keep it on a leash, okay?"

"Okay." Now he felt like a dipshit. She was right, of course. Minjae was pretty much *always* right. He watched her hips move under the towel, and couldn't help but think of nights when she'd slept between him and Chuck, huddled for warmth, and he'd been able to pretend…well, it didn't matter.

Not much mattered anymore, now that the war was over. *Go home,* all the Federal regulars were saying. As if *home* wasn't bombed, burned, leveled, scraped flat and pissed on by black-clad Patriots and the fucking Firsters. Nothing left but this shitty work sifting through the cesspool for the biggest turds, eating leaves and drinking to blackout when he could. The war took all the good ones, and left the dregs, like Simmons, and the fucking uncanny, like the Spook.

He *also* couldn't help thinking Spook wasn't what she was supposed to be. Something was wrong as fuck—Zampana had said as much. Had Spooky done her thing to both Pana and Swann? They didn't seem any different, except Swann and his hat, and he could have just gotten tired of wearing the fucking thing.

Prink found he was rubbing his hands together, over and over, dry-scrubbing. Again. Each time, it felt like his fucking finger was there, and the germs were crawling over his skin.

Yeah, Min was right. He was jumping at shadows. Suspecting everything and everyone kept you alive behind the lines, but it also fucked you up royal.

Prink shook his head and dug for a candy. Smoking inside was technically against regulation, but he was a raider, for fucksake. And if he waited long enough, Min might come out, and he could walk her back to the sled.

With that prospect in mind, he almost cheered up. Still, it nagged at him.

Everything did.

CHAPTER FORTY-SIX

RIOT

July 22, '98

Nobody was in any kind of a good mood when dawn came up and they drifted over a fugee site turned into a cauldron of smoke, screams, and flapping canvas. Spooky huddled in a seat, her hands clapped over her ears, even though the sled was high enough that the noise was only a faint scratching murmur through the radio. "—in progress." The air controller's voice crackled over the comm. "Do not, I repeat, do *not* land on the east side!"

"Get us over the base," Swann said. His hat was back—clamped on his head like an old friend—but featherless. "God *damn* it. What the fuck they fighting over down there?"

"Want me to ask?" Hendrickson steadied the controls. "We need a recharge."

"What's the holdup?" Zampana called from the back of the sled. Even *she* was getting twitchy.

"Riot, looks like," Swann said over his shoulder. "The base is only a half-klick from the fugee site; fugees are at the fuckin' gates. We'll be down soon."

A general chorus of groans rose, with Simmons's taking on words. "Then what are we doing hanging over the goddamn—"

"Simms." Swann pinched the bridge of his nose. "Not helping."

Hendrickson was close to losing his temper, finally. "It's the only approach that wasn't jammed." A popping, whining *zing*, and the sled lurched. "Son of a *fuck*!" Hendrickson yelled. Red lights bloomed across the console, and Swann, tossed sideways, began cussing too.

The sled spun, something crunched, and Minjae, still buckled in, let out a yelp of furious irritation. "Lost a panel!" Hendrickson yelled, a mad edge of glee to the words. "Hold the fuck on!" Swann was tossed again, but he managed to fall sideways into the copilot hole and clutch at the sides for dear life. Gyros whined, something else cracked, and the Federal laughed, the high, insane sound of a man facing something he'd trained for but never realized he'd have to actually *do*. World turning over, Zampana's cry transforming into a prayer at the end, Sal yowling as the seat harness pinched his balls unmercifully, Simmons and Spooky deadly quiet, Prink jolted awake from the floor and breathless-cursing.

Somehow Hendrickson got the sled level, but by then it had plunged dangerously close to the burning fugee temporaries. The sled spun on a vertical axis, canvas ripping outside the sled as it tore through the tops of large tents, guy wires snapping with musical *twang*s and smoke belching in through the vents, the whickering chaos filled with steam and thicker vapors.

Spooky shut her eyes, going limp. The straps were too big, so she jolted inside the chair's indifferently padded cradle, bumped and bounced. Round and round, spinning, trapped, anything not tied down turned into a missile, safety glass breaking, more snapping impacts as Hendrickson fought the whirling. A kaleidoscope, and softer bumps were human bodies as the sled cut through the heart of the riot, scattering fear-maddened human beasts in every direction. Screams bubbled and boiled, oddly faint outside the sled's hard carapace. More flame belched, the cells on the sled bottom whining. The unbroken ones, sparking and overstrained, failed; the instant they did, their whine cutting off sharp and clean, the sled stopped spinning and simply dropped.

Crunch.

It wasn't the initial crash that did the damage, though. It was the flip afterward, the edge of the sled digging in and the rest attempting to continue on its trajectory. Up and down changed places, dancing like water flicked across a hot pan, a sudden hot stink, and right before everything went black, Spooky thought, *Oh, Lara, I'm on my way.*

"Easy. Easy there." A familiar voice. Zampana's bloody face swam into view, her hand cupped under Spooky's head. "Attagirl. Look at me. Look." Checking the pupils. Hot slick nastiness coated Spooky's face. She coughed, feebly trying to bat away Zampana's hands as the older woman clicked a small flashlight. "Okay. Easy, Spooks, it's Pana. It's *me*."

Spooky subsided. Burning. Smoke in the air. Was it the drone bombing again? No glass breaking, but the screams and the groans, and the smell of blood and bowel and...

Everything faded away, came back again as she was lifted like a child. Where was her sister? If it was bedtime...

"All right," someone said. "Over here, over here. There's another one."

"Shit. What happened?"

"Firster in the bread line, they're saying. Shoved an immie, and the whole thing just—"

"Over here! Still breathing!"

They picked through the wreckage, human ants swarming at a fiery hill. Screams of pain, softening as medics, camp staff, and soldiers pressed into cleanup duty kept working. Zampana, shaking off a male medic trying to get a look at the blood on her face, waved Simmons to the tent set aside for them. Spooky, cradled against his chest, was heavier than she looked. Anyone was when they were deadweight, not even conscious enough to help. He swung from side to side, staggering, but got her in through the flap.

"Set her down there." Hendrickson, his arm in a sling and his uniform torn into jagged strips, pointed at an empty cot. "Gently, goddammit!"

"Shut the fuck up," Simmons snarled in return.

"They find Swann?" Chuck, ghost-chalky under his melanin, clutched at his shoulder and hobbled closer, a crutch socketed into his armpit. He'd lost some blood, and his uniform trousers were missing their right leg. At least, missing most of the material, cut away so medics could get at crushed muscle with norpirene and foam. Thankfully, the bone was still intact.

"Not yet." Simmons, bloodshot eyes blazing and dust in his short-spike hair, glanced sideways. Minjae, crumpled on a cot and clustered by two field medics and a surgeon, coughed weakly. "No Prinky either."

"*Shit.*" At least the Dogg's boots were in good shape, and they hadn't cut the right one off, just yanked it free because it had been unlaced while he slept. Small miracles, the only kind that ever happened.

Sometimes, even a small one was enough.

Hendrickson hovered over Spooky's cot, collaring a passing surgeon with his good hand and barking something. Nobody was sure whether they should treat him like a hero for bringing the sled down with everyone inside it in human-size chunks instead of bite-size, or clap him in irons for going down in the middle of a full-fledged riot and spreading fugees around like paste. The brass inside the base was, at this very moment, hearing about how someone had fired a rifle at a military flier.

A trigger-happy soldier or a refugee who had a piece—who knew? The wreckage was still burning, along with half the fugee site.

Spooky surfaced hazily a little after that. Hendrickson loomed over her head, his black hair wildly disarranged, glowering at a skinny, horse-faced male nurse taking her blood pressure.

"Don't care *who* you have to save, Sergeant," he told the man, low and fierce. "This one gets priority care, and that is an *order*."

Spooky had enough time to look at the underside of his chin, blisters marching along a deep burn, before someone outside screamed, a high, agonized cry that halted all activity for a moment. It trailed off, raggedly, and Spooky pushed the nurse's hands away, fish-flopping to get out of the blood pressure cuff.

She knew that voice. It was Zampana's.

CHAPTER FORTY-SEVEN

INESCAPABLE WEIGHT

It wasn't Swann, though Pana'd seen the hat and let loose that gawdawful cry. No, it was Prink, smeared into a paste because he hadn't been buckled down. Swann's lunge into the copilot's seat had saved him, but his hat had been knocked free, fluttered around, and ended up over Prink's face and the charred remains of his coppery hair.

Minjae, burned over most of her body and both her plump pretty legs broken, was finally airlifted into the base, where there was a hospital in a Quonset. She held on for sixteen hours. Zampana passed out at her bedside from shock and blood loss, but it was Chuck who took it hardest, turning his face away from any visitors and going mute. Swann, almost miraculously untouched, was with Min until the end, between her bed and Chuck's; Zampana's bed, with her black, black hair swallowing the crisp white pillows, was on the far side of Min's.

Min—and Prink—had come through the war, only to end up biting it in the middle of a shitty fugee riot.

Simmons, one eardrum ruptured and packed with norpirene and sterigel, his face set and white when it wasn't madly twitching on the left side, had to be physically restrained. He swore he was going down into the camp to find whoever had fired on them, and nobody who heard him say it thought he'd be particularly choosy about the evidence used to convict.

But it was Sal, seemingly unharmed except for a black eye and his merci-lessly squeezed nuts, who went down into the camp and began shooting every adult male he saw.

At least he left the women alone, Swann said dully, staring down at Min-jae's torture-breathing form. Pana was sedated, but Chuck turned away, pulling his own pillow over his head.

Swann lit a candy and stood there, smoking. Every time someone came to tell him it wasn't allowed, they got the fierce, dull glare of a man who has had *enough*, and decided to go enforce the rules elsewhere. When they came to take Min's body, he let them, but he didn't move away. Just smoked, staring at the empty bed, his face stippled with blood and bruised up the right half. His lean nose had been broken and set; he sometimes touched the throbbing bridge gingerly, as his eyes puffed and he peered through the slits.

It was Hendrickson who talked Sal down and got the base brass to turn him loose, and Hendrickson who got Spooky and Simmons moved into the Quonset hospital next to Chuck and Zampana. He even dragged the Reaper to a chair and set him to keeping watch on Spooky, though it wasn't anything the big blond bastard had to be pushed too hard for.

Through it all Swann stood, staring down at Minjae's empty bed.

"Sir?" Hendrickson, red-eyed, stopped at the foot, his full, chiseled mouth pulled tight and bitter. "Captain Swann, sir?" As if Swann out-ranked him.

Swann swayed. His rawhide-tough shoulders drooped alarmingly. He'd worked his way through two packs of candies and just...*stood* there, staring.

"Sir, they're all settled." The Federal eased another step closer, around the corner of the bed. His sling was a white ghost, floating. Simmons sat at Spooky's bedside, his head in his hands, possibly asleep. Zampana, still sedated, tossed and muttered. The darkness, lit only by night-lights and the bright bulbs at the nurse's station, was full of the rustling of wounded soldiers at 0400, just past the long, breathless lagoon of time the old and the gravely ill succumb during. Soon there would be reveille, and the able-bodied would sort out more of the mess in the fugee site. "You should eat something. Or maybe some coffee?"

Swann made no reply. He just stopped moving. In the dimness, only the glitter of his eyes, almost swollen closed, showed he was conscious and not just asleep on his feet like a horse.

"Sir." Hendrickson tried for Zampana's firm-but-immovable tone. "You've got to eat something."

A faint whistling inhale, and Swann spoke softly, reflectively. "Dead men don't get hungry, kid."

Hendrickson's arm ached, but it was only physical. If he could just get Swann down, both of them could rest. "You're not dead yet."

"Oh yeah? How can you tell?"

"Because I'm alive, and you're—"

"Oh, kid." Wearily. "You are, too. You just don't know it." He patted dreamily at his top right pocket where his smokes should be. Not finding them, he reached for his absent hat, ran his palm over his gray-bristling scalp. "This war, man. This fucking war."

"Come on, sir." Hendrickson took another step closer. "A little coffee, and then you should get some shut-eye."

"Can't fuckin' sleep after coffee; you know that." Swann shrank again inside his clothes. Funny how that could happen, a man turning inward all at once, cloth that fit him before suddenly deflated. "Go to bed, Lazy. I'm fine."

Hendrickson opened his mouth, maybe to say *I'm not Lazy*, but stopped. It reminded him of Kellogg, standing in the ashes of what had been a pretty farmhouse amid rippling waves of blasted, dead corn, looking up at the hanging rag that had been her wife, remnants of long blonde hair moving in a blood-drenched clump as the dusty wind came up. The same movement—a human being crushed under an inescapable weight.

Instead, Matt Hendrickson approached Swann sidelong, the same way he'd seen Kellogg's lieutenant—quiet, feral, ebon-skinned Popper Grainger—step close to *his* commander. Matt put his arm around the taller man's shoulders, and was momentarily surprised by Swann's solidity. Packed with lean muscle, the older man smelled like candy smoke, blood, pain, and a thin thread of old-fashioned aftershave. Smelled like English Leather—all the men wore it or nothing at all.

Christ. How you could remember old advertising jingles and forget your own mother's voice, remember things you'd rather cut out of your own brain and forget…well, all you really forgot was how to be a goddamn human being. It got burned out of you, somewhere between your first tangle with a Firster patrol and the sick knowledge that if you'd just changed course a couple degrees, someone might still be alive.

Swann leaned into him, and Matt guided him away from the empty bed, its thin blue-striped mattress naked and glowing faintly. There was another empty mattress on Spooky's other side, and he eased Swann down. The man tensed when Matt began loosening his bootlaces, picking with his good hand.

"Don't worry, ain't gonna take 'em off, sir." Nice and quiet, that was the way to do it. "Just easy 'em up. Watches are on and the pickets are full."

"Good kid," Swann mumbled. "Fucking war. Good kid."

Matt understood. "Fucking war," he murmured back. He wanted to add something else—like *Easy, old man*, or even an absurdity, *I've got this*. But instead, he just drew a light, scratchy regular-issue blanket up over the raider captain, booted feet and all. Swann was going to feel this in the morning.

They pretty much all would, Hendrickson thought, as he cast around for somewhere to lay his own goddamn weariness down. He ended up on the floor next to Swann's bed, his head on his good arm and his entire body twitching, still believing it was in the sled's thumping, bucking, spinning hell.

CHAPTER FORTY-EIGHT

THE GOOD AND THE INNOCENT

July 23, '98

"Well, speaking frankly, sir, you're the only choice." General Joseph Osborne sat at the plastic-covered dinette table in a scrubbed-clean bachelor's kitchen, his back straight and his old dress uniform starched to within an inch of its life.

"No." Kallbrunner's clothes weren't starched. Nor were they the set of shabby dress blues he'd worn all through McCoombs's tenure. Instead, the Hero of Arlington wore a faded flannel button-down over a thermal undershirt and a pair of gray wool trousers, ironed but so old they were butter-soft. "I have no desire to be a military dictator."

"The true test of that statement would be whether or not you handed power over after the elections." You had to give Osborne credit for trying, at least.

Kallbrunner's dark eyes were faded, but still sharp. "Which aren't scheduled yet."

"Have to get international observers." Osborne tented his fingers. "Everything aboveboard. Congress has to be cleaned out, too. Legal challenges about certification and voting rights." Joe sighed. "I don't blame you for not wanting to. You're just the only person everyone will follow."

"Right off a cliff," Kallbrunner said heavily. "Like my Parris Island boys."

"Sir…" There was nothing to say, so General Leavy, sitting gingerly in a rickety tube-metal chair, shut up after the single word. The Marines, cadets and teachers alike, who hadn't died defending the installation had been hanged, unless they were ringleaders and went in front of a firing squad. The ones who hadn't been shot weren't dropped cleanly, either— the gantry had been lifted to strangle them instead of giving a good swift neckbreak.

Osborne tried again, his gin-blossomed cheeks pale except for the broken blood vessels. "America needs you."

"America *elected* that piece of shit." Kallbrunner was not having it, but at least he was looking at them now, not off into the distance with the set, constipated expression of *I'll hear you out, but don't expect anything*.

That got Osborne's hackles up. "Not by popular vote. And then the New Soviet hackers—"

"New Soviets? Is that what they're calling themselves now? Ask them for another hand puppet." It would have been difficult for the old man to sound more pissy-bitter.

Patrick Leavy didn't blame him one goddamn bit. The New Soviets were indeed in town, wining and dining and using chaos plus diplomatic immunity to the hilt. It was all the British could do to keep the ruins of their Continental Union together now that Russia had swallowed Ukraine and half of Poland again, Germany and France rearming as fast as they could, and the smaller players nervous as cats in heat. China, as usual, was waiting to see who would come out on top, while selling to both sides and making diplomatic protests about New Soviet "border incursions." Japan was not seeing the benefit of pacifism anymore, and North Korea...well, without America minding the store, Leavy thought, the entire thing was going to hell. Independence here, commie bootlickers there, Hawaii seceding even from the West Coast bloc, the Middle East in flames because petroleum wasn't what it used to be...

Yes, the New Soviets would probably love to finance another Mc-Coombs. If they couldn't find one willing to take the job, they'd make him out of spare parts. "I'm sure they'd supply one." Leavy couldn't quite match Kallbrunner's bitterness, but he could try. "Christ knows they'd love to take Alaska too, if they think we're not looking."

"One problem at a time," Osborne said grimly. He'd suggested rounding up the goddamn Russkies and interning them before shooting the whole bunch, but that was just blowhard anger talking. He quit when Leavy made the point about that being a classic McCoombs strategy, though not gracefully.

Working this closely with a man rarely turned out *graceful*. Unfortunately, he and Osborne were where the goddamn writs were stopping nowadays. Leavy had no idea there would come a time when he would *want* politicians dealing with this crap just so he could get some sleep. The South Americans were all relatively helpful, though, except for Venezuela, and God alone knew what was happening in Cuba anymore.

Their host pushed away from the tiny table and shook his head, still thinking about the goddamn second-to-Last Election. "We should have been smarter. I was there, young man. I saw it go down."

"So did I." Leavy leaned forward. The chairs were cheap metal and flowered vinyl, and he had the unsettling thought that the Marine had deliberately kept two of the more unsteady ones for guests. Or *made* them unsteady. "You did the impossible, standing up to him. And surviving."

"You call it surviving? The fucker kept me around like a lapdog." Kallbrunner rose, with an old man's finicky care to each part of the gesture—straightening the knees, easing the hips, pushing the shoulders back. "Let me ask you this, son. You ever regret enlisting?"

The correct answer was, of course, *No sir, I love the Army, sir*. Anything else was unpatriotic…and yet, wasn't that how they'd gotten in this whole mess in the first place? The desire to love your country turned into a car salesman's cheap shill and ended up a goddamn black hole.

His neck hurt. The shrapnel in his knee, from the Topeka debacle and the retreat after, throbbed. The scar on his neck made it hard to look over his fucking shoulder too, so Leavy decided to tell the goddamn truth. "Several times. It's not every goddamn day, but it's close."

"Second Cheyenne," Joe Osborne said, in the heavy silence that followed. He was staring at the flowered plastic tacked over the tabletop, but he still felt Leavy's glance. "What? I know what they say about it. Have to be fucking deaf not to hear. It bought us the time we needed, but I stay up at night and think about them." A heavy pause. "All of them. My boys and girls, dying to buy us minutes. Hours."

Kallbrunner paced across the kitchen, stared out the window into the ruthlessly cropped weeds of the backyard. His thin shoulders had dropped, and his spotted hands rested on the lip of the enameled double sinks. Tendons stood out on the backs, his fingers spidery but the tips blunt and spatulate. "I wonder." After a long pause, his head drooped a little. "I wonder what my daughter would say."

Amy Kallbrunner. Human rights lawyer, part of the First Wave of opposition protest. Vanished into the first Reklamation Kamp—Marikopa, plunked down in Texas wasteland and run by that bastard who used to lock immies up in tin boxes during Arizona summers. The Firsters had razed it once the tide turned, before the Mexicans got close enough to liberate, and the data was so wormed...well, maybe the old man hoped.

That was another thing. Mexico had taken all they were going to, and getting Texas back from them would be a headache. Assuming America even *wanted* a rump of it back. Miles of fucking nothing, and where it wasn't the Mexicans themselves, it was inbred Firster don't-tread-on-me fucks the Mexicans were welcome to deal with in their own way.

Hard.

Osborne, for once, didn't venture an opinion. Leavy looked down at the table with its faded yellow flowers, their green stems puke colored now. What was it like, he wondered, living in this shitty shotgun shack, brought out for rallies where you were spat at and held up as a disgrace, wondering when the black SUVs were going to come and take you away, probably to the same death-hole they'd put your child in? And that was another thing—being helpless to protect your buddies, your troops, your own goddamn kid?

A man's nightmare. Even worse for an officer. That is, if you were any good as an officer. The stripes meant service, not royalty.

The old Marine shook his head. His shoulders came back up, a straight bar of duty and pain settling right where the neck began. Once you carried that load, it sank in. You couldn't wash it out or wriggle away. "I know what she'd say," he continued meditatively. "'Get back in the fight,

Dad. It matters.'" It was a good imitation, even if it was rasped out through a throat more used to barking commands at swabbies.

Apple didn't fall far from the tree. Amy Kallbrunner had been all over the internet, that viral video where she blasted McCoombs. Clicks didn't give you immunity. Not when the Firsters had both houses and the entire swollen Homeland Security department, the CIA, FBI, NSA, TSA, all the alphabet soup too craven to stop the slide into bloodshed.

"You're a good man." For once, it didn't sound like Osborne believed himself a better one.

It was fucking uncharitable to think of your fellow soldier that way, but when you worked this close to someone, you saw the cracks. They saw yours too, but at least Osborne had the decency not to point Leavy's out to him. The least Pat Leavy could do was return the favor.

"No." Kallbrunner did an about-face, and Leavy wasn't surprised to see the old man's faded eyes were wet. "The good and the innocent are dead. McCoombs saw to that. We're what's left, gentleman, and I suspect this is just the first in a long series of unpleasant things you have lined up for me."

If he'd still been able to flinch, Leavy might have done so. Eventually, they were going to have to talk about Baylock, the missing Dr. Johnson, and X-Ray, as well as the fact that the New Soviets, god damn their pseudocommunist asses, and anyone else who had heard a whisper of what the Firsters were doing in North Carolina, were in the race to scoop up Johnson and his data, too.

And the worst part? Due to a fucking two-bit refugee riot in the Dakotas taking down Swann's team, it looked like someone else might manage to pick the prize up first.

CHAPTER FORTY-NINE

THOUGHT IT WAS PERSONAL

July 26, '98

"I dunno." Sal kept arms folded high over his beefy chest. His hair hung, lank and oily, over his bruised face; his right eye was puffed shut. His legs were a-spraddle, probably to let his junk breathe after the beating it'd suffered, and his boots were double tied, raider fashion. "Maybe. Eventually."

"Yeah." Swann kept his thumbs hooked in his belt loops. Every part of him hurt, and if he focused on that, he wouldn't have to think about Minjae's tortured breathing winding down, inch by inch. "Me too."

"It's not that I don't want to keep up." Sal tested one of his legs, then the other. Built low and wide, he had an advantage in brawling, and could wire a charge in seconds flat. There was that one time in the Rockies, hitting a Firster pharmacy, and the front window lighting up with the red-and-blues that meant police. *Leave? Not yet, I came to blow this fucker up,* Sal had said, and did just that. A timed charge, calculated on the fly to let them get out the door and the Firsters in before the fireworks started. "It's that…"

"It's that you don't want to," Swann supplied. "Yeah."

A bright, beautiful summer morning folding over the temporary base and the fugee site still reeked of smoke. "It was supposed to be over." Sal stared at the haze on the northern horizon, glimpsed between rows of Quonsets. "The whole shitfucking thing was supposed to be *over*."

"Yeah, well." Swann leaned back against the front of the hospital building. The candy smokers' corner here was deserted, for once. The sun felt good, sinking into hematomas and pulled muscles, skin stretched taut over tired meat. Up in the mountains, the breeze would be full of pine instead of burning.

That is, if the fucking Firsters hadn't torched a house, or held one of their bonfires to get rid of seditious literature. The pines would still be fragrant even if there were a hanging, like the one that started Swann on this whole fucking merry-go-round. Little bodies, swinging back and forth. What was the name of that old song, sung in a raspy, throaty ache of a woman's voice? Something-something fruit, hanging in the trees.

"Why ain't it over, Phil?" Sal's fingers sank into his meaty biceps on either side. Holding on to whatever pieces hadn't already been jolted free. "They signed the fuckin' papers, why ain't it *over*?"

"I don't know." Papers never meant much, except to a Firster. The right ones could get a raider through a checkpoint, though. Could stave off suspicion, could get you extra rations. But you always had to worry and wonder about the times when some asshole wouldn't abide by the stamp or the order because he had a gun, and gun meant God. "I wish I could tell you, Nicos. Hell, I wish *I* knew."

Nicos Salvatore's shoulder touched just above Swann's elbow. How many times had they stood like this, looking at terrain or turning over alternatives? Too many to fucking count, and there was one thing Swann had never asked. Maybe he should have. "Nic?"

"Huh?"

"I never asked, but—"

"I never asked you either." Quick, a slamming door.

"Okay." Let it be, then. Let the man have his own reasons.

But then, as he usually ended up doing, Sal surprised him. "You'll think I'm an idiot. But there's no reason. Not a goddamn one."

Swann freed his thumbs. Dug for a candy. Again surprising him, Sal let go of his arms and made a *gimme* motion, so Swann gave him the first lit one, lit another. He said nothing.

"Not a single thing," Sal continued finally. "Packed up and left my shop in San Fran to sign up with the first raider crew I could find, because it was right. I thought it was, anyway. You remember that? Knowing what the right fucking thing to do was?"

"Sometimes." Swann closed his eyes. Took another drag. How could the sun still feel good, after all the blood and pain and artillery?

"My grandma. She used to watch this old show, space cowboys. There was a priest on it, and he died, but when he did, he said something. *You can't do anything smart, so do something right.* She always used to say that."

"Wise fucking woman." Swann felt the story rising in his throat, swallowed hard. "You know what, Nic?"

"What?" Sal didn't look at him, and Swann knew, miserably, that he was going to confess.

"I did the same fuckin' thing. No family, nothing. Lived by myself and was damn happy with it." A sigh caught him by surprise, fetching up from the bottom of his aching ribs. "One day the Firsters hung some kids. Bullshit stuff—fucking twelve-year-olds, playing at raiders. Hacked the school district's network, wormed it to show a donkey's ass on Mc-Coombs's face during morning announcements." He shook his head. "Hung 'em. For Chrissake." But only because they were brown; white kids would have gotten off with a warning.

Everyone knew, nobody said it. Standing under a flood of sharp thin autumn sunshine, all Swann saw when he looked at the gallows were...kids. They were hooded, of course, but the bruising down skinny, scrawny kid necks glared at him. A man couldn't look away from something like that.

Plenty had, though. Swann had told himself for a long time that it didn't matter. He didn't vote, he kept to himself, and as long as he did, there was no reason for him to get involved. So he'd stood in the crowd, staring, and it happened all at once, like someone flushing when you were in the shower. A cold bath of hating himself for not bringing a gun. Hating himself for gawking, hating himself for doing goddamn *nothing* while the pronouncement was read and the lever pulled.

Nothing made a man as furious as his own fucking cowardice. Everything after was atonement, really.

"Damn." Sal coughed a little. He was used to tobacco, not candies. "Thought it was personal."

"Ended up that way." Swann sighed. He couldn't even remember the kids' names, and it bothered him. "I'll get the paperwork for your pension. If the asshole here won't sign off, I'll get Spooky on him."

"Shit, bringin' out the big guns for little ol' me?" Sal leaned in a little, bumping Swann's arm. But gently. Almost kindly.

Sal had been with him since the beginning.

Swann's throat hurt for a few moments. He pretended to take another drag from the candy. "Don't think it means I like you, motherfucker."

Sal's laugh, startled at first, turned into a genuine chuckle halfway through. "Feeling's mutual, but don't bother."

"Huh?" The feeling of missing something was uncomfortable.

"I mean, don't bother signing me out. Come this far, might as well stay in." Sal took another drag off the candy. "I gotta think this is worth something. Even Min. And Prink."

"Franco." Shot, then gangrene.

Sal's eyes were half lidded. "Popper John." Cyanide tab in a holding cell, died without giving up his fellow raiders.

"Wills." Choking on his own blood after Second Cheyenne.

"Mary." Town contact, taken in a sweep, vanished without a trace.

"Hogan." Running fresh vegetables to the raiders, caught by a patrol, again vanished.

Sal probably couldn't take it any more, so he skipped to the end of the roll call. "Lazy. The goddamn kid." They could have gone on, really. The raider dead were numerous. If it went to fucking civilians, they'd be here all week reciting them. *Kaddish*, Hogan would have called it.

"Yeah." Something inside Swann's chest eased. Just a fraction. A fraying rope, slackened right before it broke completely. The release was almost as painful as the strain.

But not quite.

Sal turned, almost limping. "Come on. I need my shears."

"Fine where I am, thank you." Swann planted his feet to prove it.

"No. You are *not*. Look at the scraggles." The Greek drew himself up to his full height and glared at Swann with his one good eye, waving a blunt-fingered hand at his captain's head. "Zampana needs a trim, and so do you."

"Fuck," Swann groaned. But not very loudly.

CHAPTER FIFTY

SEEIN' THE SNAKES

Inside another hastily dropped Quonset, in a large, bare commandeered room smelling of sawdust and plastic just brought out of a warehouse, it was stuffy but not overly hot. Spooky hunched in a heavy regulation-issue office chair, cupping her elbows in her palms. It was nice to feel her own arms pressing against her chest, to squeeze a little tissue over her bones. Gaining weight was hard, but she was managing. Her ribs were beginning to recede.

Finally she spoke. "Maybe." She eyed Minjae's laptop, sitting closed and prim on the table. It looked secretive, and maybe she *could* put her hands on the keys and tell what Min had been able to dig up. "You should wait for the others."

"Don't know if we can." Hendrickson slumped in the other chair, babying his left arm. It had bashed pretty good against the sled wall as he fought the spin. His hair wasn't quite as combed as usual, and his fatigues were wrinkled.

Through the grainy, temporary plastic of Quonset windows came just enough sun to tell her it was a beautiful afternoon. It would be nice to go stand outside, if she could find somewhere away from people. Nice to feel the sun and the wind and listen to something other than a confusing mishmash of terror and screaming and…

He was sitting that way, she realized, to make himself smaller. Less threatening. He wanted her to dive into Minjae's deck and give him something.

Spooky fidgeted once, twice, settling herself inside her skin. Examined him, from his floppy-topped short-on-the-sides black hair to his boots—not shiny anymore, full of dust. He'd been out to the wreckage of the sled. A faint odor of burning clung to his uniform. His dark eyes were bloodshot, but unlike Simmons, he didn't reek of unstable alcohol and colorless agony.

Still, Spooky decided, she preferred the Reaper.

Hendrickson waited, his broad coppery face set. So did she. If she was silent long enough, he'd start. Most people didn't know what to do with quiet; they had to break it. Like fresh-fallen snow, someone had to trudge across it just because it was there.

She concentrated on her breath. If she did that, sank into her body, it muted the chaos outside. Focusing on one sensation made the others fall back. Lara would have been fascinated, full of ideas to test and verify.

I'm Lara.

She hunched even further. No. *No.* She was *Spooky*.

It was getting easier to remember.

When Hendrickson did finally speak, it wasn't what she'd expected. "I'm not here to hurt you, Spooky. Or is it Anna? Which do you prefer?"

She shrugged. It didn't matter; both names were merely slips of ident paper attached to a ghost. Her arms tightened.

"I'm here to help." He leaned forward, elbows braced on knees, shoulders rounded even further. If it was uncomfortable, he didn't show it. "Okay? I want to help you."

He was a Federal, which made it just one step above what usually happened when a Firster offered to "help." Like a big-shouldered blond man staring at her in the quarry, and a small hateful tickle in her head.

"You want X-Ray." Whatever that was. It was always so confusing and piecemeal, the flashes, even when they were hypercolor saturated and sharp-edged. Pouring yourself into someone else's skin took time. Distinguishing what was useful or true from what was self-image or just assumption took energy she didn't have right now.

He didn't move. "Orders aren't what a soldier wants, Spooky. You know that."

Maybe he was right. Orders were just what they followed, whether they thought it was a good idea or not. That was fine for the black-beetle Patriots, the Firsters, and even the Federals. Raiders, though...they were different.

Weren't they?

It smelled of dust and sun-warmed plastic in here, with a faint edge of moss baking to death. They'd dragged this hut from somewhere rainy, and it remembered. Spooky pushed herself upright, her arms still wrapped tightly, digging her fingers in. "X-Ray's your orders, then." Her head began to ache, right in the middle of her brain. No nerve supply there, so was it psychosomatic? It wasn't the only thing that hurt. Shoulders and knees, her neck—all from the sled's whirling.

He finally straightened, the *I won't hurt you* posture sliding away. "Huh. Fine." The chair scraped as he turned it, and he opened Minjae's laptop carefully. "You gonna give me anything to go on in here, or—"

Voices echoed outside, in the long hall running down the center of the Quonset. "...shady motherfucker," Simmons finished, twisting the doorknob viciously and sweeping it open. "Shouldn't leave him alone with— Hey, Spooky." He limped through the door, his outline fuzzing with that same sullen, cold almost-hatred.

Her relief might have shown if Baylock, then Gloria, hadn't taught her to keep her expression neutral. Her face was a mask, and the watchful animal behind it curled up a little tighter.

Zampana, working a hefty black bobby pin free to resettle one of her braids, bumped into Simmons to get him to speed up. "Spook, I need an extra finger or two. Move your ass, Reaper."

"Oh, the jokes just write themselves." Chuck Dogg piled behind her, but his wan smile dropped completely away when he saw the table, the laptop—and Hendrickson. "What the *fuck* you doin', man?"

"Looking for—" Hendrickson started, but Chuck had already shoved Pana aside and was bearing down on him, the crutch jabbing the floor between long strides. He'd be all right—the norpirene would see to that— but still, he shouldn't be up and moving.

"Don't fucking touch her stuff," Chuck growled. He'd found red thread and attended to his afro, this time tying off a few hanks over his left temple. "You hear me, boy? You don't *fucking* touch Min's stuff!"

Swann, his eyes swollen and his nose a mess, trailed through the door. Even Sal was walking funny. A collection of bruises, pulled muscles, bodies crying out for rest and good food and maybe even some sleep unbroken by aches. The tighter the group got, the more Spooky could tell who hurt where.

"Aw, shit," Simmons began. "Chuck, man—"

Hendrickson's chair legs scraped the cheap vinyl flooring again, hard. He backed away from the table, and it might have gotten ugly if not for Chuck's crutch slowing him down.

Spooky took two steps. Her head only came up to Chuck's chest, but he stopped on a dime, almost overbalancing.

"You're gonna have to work her deck, then," she said quietly. "If we're gonna get him. The scientist." The *doctor*.

"Shitfire." Zampana's lip lifted, her hands still working at her freshly trimmed and rebraided hair. "That your vote, Spookster? We keep running this fucker down?"

Like there was a choice? Spooky didn't reply, staring up into Chuck's face. Traces of bruising lingered on his cheeks, and his stubble was as fierce as Swann's bristling scalp. She didn't push, or spill out of her skin and into his. She just *watched* him. When his mouth crumpled, hers did too, and slowly, Chuck leaned forward. Spooky held his gaze, and she stood very still as his forehead touched hers. Gently, so gently.

Swann arrived softly at Chuck's shoulder. "We ain't got to decide anything just yet."

"Oh, *I* decided." Chuck's pupils had turned hot, blurry because he was so close. "Motherfucker flew us right over the riot—"

"There wasn't any other way to go." Swann's weight shifted. "They *put* him on that approach. Right, Sal?"

"Heard it myself," the Greek confirmed.

"You seein' the snakes, my friend," Swann continued. "Okay? Settle down."

Chuck leaned on the crutch. "It ain't right," he said mutinously. "It *ain't right.*"

"No, it ain't," Simmons said, just like he had during Second Cheyenne. "It ain't, and ain't ever gonna be."

It was Zampana who moved close and put her arms around Chuck, then Spooky. Gingerly, Swann hugged the three of them as far as he could reach, and Simmons—sour-sweet alcohol fumes sliding off his skin—did too. Sal was last, resting his face against Swann's biceps, his knee behind Zampana's. Hendrickson, closed outside the breathing circle of body odor and pain, said nothing. He looked away, at the half-open Quonset door and the simmering sunlight outside.

Ninety seconds of dead silence, then Chuck moved, and they became individual raindrops again, clear and tight inside their watery surface tension. Spooky was pale, and her throat worked. She edged for the door, Zampana heel-and-toeing after her, one of the older woman's braids coming loose.

"Come on, man." Simmons beckoned Hendrickson. "Come on."

They left Chuck with Minjae's deck. Swann was the last, and before he shut the door he glanced back.

Chuck, his head in his hands, sat in Hendrickson's chair, the laptop open and its blank, innocent screen bathing him in blue light that fought with the fall of sunshine. It made ticking sounds as it booted up.

Swann closed the door gently, and settled down to wait.

CHAPTER FIFTY-ONE

LISTEN TO REASON

It was warm, and full of the scent of a dark-haired woman. Right at the nape, where you could brush the hair aside and move your lips gently over shivering, creamy skin. Even though she was skinny, once you pushed aside the harsh orange of the camp uniforms she looked…soft. Like you could dip your finger into the curve of her hip and come away with something delicious—a serving of whipped cream. Soft except for the chapping on her hands from the quarry work. He'd brought her rationed, expensive coconut oil to smooth, working it between her fingers, pretending she actively liked the touch instead of suffering it, her chin turned away except for when he gave the command.

Look at me. Smile.

And she would. Each time, without exception.

The warmth drained away, though. With it went the memory, and a fuzzy thought rose. Why, out of all the women he had access to, had he chosen a kampog? A scrap of dark, frizzing hair and hazel eyes, who barely spoke except for when he demanded it? Who never once put her hands around his neck unless he told her to?

In the quarry. That afternoon. Why, in God's name, had he even bothered, instead of shooting her? Or letting her bolt for Suicide Alley and the electrified fence? There was a reward and furlough for catching a kampog attempting "escape." It was even a game, to throw one of their headrags or a crust of dense WonderAmerika soybread and watch them try to resist obedience or hunger. Or both. *Go get it, pog!*

Gene moved restlessly. A clanking noise, and his left arm was arrested halfway through the motion. So was his right. Light danced and dilated, and the heavy, strange feeling that something was not quite right poured through him and away. He vaguely remembered an iron bedstead, unfamiliar but necessary because…

Fever. He'd had a fever, right?

A shadow drifted over him, prairie light blocked. It wasn't a cloud; it was a man.

The doctor, with his long nose and funhouse smile, teeth and eyes both gleaming.

"Oh, hello," the doctor said. The words stretched out, long and deep, time and sound not behaving the way they should. "Don't worry, my friend. You're doing very well, all things considered. Very well indeed."

There was a tapping. That weird clanging noise didn't stop when Gene tried to move. His arms kept getting jerked short of what he wanted. There was a sharp stink of urine, and the sensation that something was not *very well*, that it had gone pretty fucking bad, and he was too goddamn drugged to realize it.

"Shhh, now." The doctor leaned over him, another funhouse distortion turning him into an insect in a plaid sports jacket, claws clacking and compound eyes refracting. The gleam in his hairy black bug-hands was a syringe. "A little more rest will do you good."

Gene struggled, but it was no use. A sharp pinch, another wave of that clinging, cloying warmth, and the doctor turned into *her*, leaning over him in a soylon slip and smiling just a little.

Don't worry, she said, her full underlip moving with the words. Her mouth, it was so pretty. *Everything's going to be fine, Gene.*

Which she had never called him. Just *sir*. Because she was a kampog. Sometimes, though, he'd fantasized…

Let me help you, Gene. Let me take the pain away.

It wasn't until he woke up six hours later that he realized why his left arm felt so funny.

It was shorter. Just a little bit.

Just a handspan.

"You *son of a bitch*!" The subject raved, and tossed, but Johnson had him well strapped down, right arm at the wrist, left arm at the elbow. The bedstead rocked a little, but it was quality construction; they didn't make beds like they used to. "What did you do to me? *What did you do?*"

"Saved your life." Johnson's nose wrinkled. "The wound was already septic. Everything below it had to go." Really, the idiot should have known better than to question a *doctor*, but he didn't seem too overblessed in the decorum department. It was fascinating, even if depressing. Once they became subjects, they tended to lose all sense of decency. Johnson sometimes wondered at it, and concluded that Science, being a harsh mistress, liked to test her apostles. To retain one's faith in the midst of spitting, cursing foulness took a certain intestinal fortitude. "You should be thanking me."

"My hand," the young Patriot whimpered, his blue eyes like poached eggs rolling, rolling. *"My fucking hand!"*

"You still have the right. Your dominant." Johnson shook his head. The iron bedstead rattled again, but there was little chance of the subject getting loose. "Your dominant, and I should think, your masturbatory. There's no reason to complain." He should have kept the subject catheterized; the loss of bladder control was faintly disgusting.

Fieldwork was always a little messy, though.

Great drops of clear sweat plastered corn-gold hair to the soldier's forehead, and his eyes were wide and bloodshot. Even a few days of bed rest had melted muscle from his frame. He thrashed again, and Johnson clicked his tongue. "You'll only tire yourself out. We have a long way to go."

"You *fucker*!" was the only reply. Johnson sighed, eyed the restraints once more, and plodded away to check on the truck. Once he put the battery back in and let it run for a little bit, they should be in shape for the next leg of the journey.

It was a long way to Boise. That was as close as his contacts could get, the situation being what it was. The situation wasn't ideal, but he could test a fraction of the precious XR editing serum he had left on the subject. He hadn't decided yet. There wasn't enough for a full treatment, not if he wanted to retain some of it for insurance, and he had no access to anything but jury-rigged electroshock to start the gene cascades.

Eggs in one basket was a shitty way to run anything, but *especially* an experiment.

With the battery safely seated and the truck belching and burping to charge it, he went into the kitchen and looked through the rations they had left. You could drive to Boise in a day before the war, but now things were likely to be a bit more difficult. The Rockies were in the way, as well as the Stokes Border. Just because the Federals had won didn't mean they would dismantle the checkpoints or the Demilitarized Zone. There was a safe route through Bozeman, but it was up to him to get there.

Upstairs, the soldier yelled and thrashed. He'd tire out soon enough and begin to feel a few pangs. Johnson had plenty of opioids, knowing they would be worth a lot in trade. It had become habit to squirrel such things away for a rainy day, even in the first weeks of the war when he was just finishing his work for BernaDyne Pharma. And hadn't *that* been exciting indeed.

The drugs would also keep the soldier's appetite down. He'd have to watch carefully for more signs of infection, but norpirene was indeed wonderful stuff. Out of the woods, the stump would heal well, and if the subject knew what was good for him, he would listen to reason.

If he didn't, Johnson thought, slowly unwrapping a raspberry protein bar as he gazed out the window over acres of prairie sod, pressure on the recent surgical site could be utilized to enforce compliance.

So could withdrawal.

CHAPTER FIFTY-TWO

WHAT WE WERE FIGHTING

July 28, '98

They propped the doors open to bring a warm breeze inside the hospital Quonset. A chorus of shuffling and low conversation filled it to the roof, but as 1700 approached, a couple of orderlies wheeled out a cart with a flatscreen lashed precariously to its thin metal top. Trailing power cords, it dragged and squeaked to a mostly central position; plugging it in produced a low hum *and* a prickle of expectation.

When Long Joanna's mournful face came on, her brunette bob shimmering under studio lights, a weak cheer rippled through the room. The face of the Federal Forces News was a little older now, a little more worn, and never possessed the high gloss of Firster talking heads on the propaganda whirl of ROXNEWS. Blonde, skinny, and big-eyed, the ROX girls had sagged visibly all through the war, as if the crap they spewed distorted them from the inside. They were replaced, one after another, and rumor had it McCoombs kept a harem of the leftovers just a few doors down Pennsylvania Avenue for days when the strain of governing grew too heavy.

But good old Long Joanna was still going, and she gave them the same tired, louche-mouth smile. "Good evening, everyone. Welcome to the FFN's *Dinner Hour*."

They'd tried to replace her once or twice, but each time a howl of protest had gone up from the troops and they had to put her back on the air. Even the faint Los Angeles flavor to her speech was much admired. *Now that's a real fine forty-eight,* they told each other, for the section in the codes that gave a soldier furlough to get married. *She wouldn't go behind a man's back.* No Dear John letters from Long Joanna, no sir.

As usual, she got right to it. There was an epidemic of whooping cough and diphtheria sweeping the South. Since the Firsters had been anti-vaccination, that was hardly a surprise. The northern borders of Tennessee and North Carolina were being held in force, and patrols along the Mississippi were shooting rafts full of fleeing people unless they were immie-colored. New Orleans, miraculously left unburned, was jammed full of former plantation workers who had first priority to be brought out by the truck- and gleeson-load. If you didn't have a shade of black or brown, a star-shaped scar, or a plantation tag, you were out of luck. There were even some coastal refugees on makeshift boats trying to make it through the Cuba Embargo.

Which showed history had a sense of humor, maybe. A bleak, black sense.

"Leave the fuckin' South rot for a few years," one pale, walleyed soldier, his leg in a cast all the way to his hip and half his blond head shaved, muttered. "Let all the cracker Firsters die off."

A general murmur of assent went up, only slightly less audible from those viewers who had people over the border. Chuck Dogg, reclined with his own leg held up on a gantry-like thing so the norpirene wouldn't smear off his calf, lit a candy. Minjae's deck, balanced on the mini-table over his bed, was open, and he barely glanced at the news. Zampana, checking Hendrickson's arm, peered over her shoulder. Spooky, cross-legged on Sal's bed, watched as the Greek cleaned and sharpened his hairstyling shears, going over them and other tools with finicky precision. The repetitive movements were soothing, and so was his soft running commentary, but that petered out as the newscast got under way.

Long Joanna continued about a small food riot in Arkansas, another larger one in Nebraska. Crews working overtime to get the rail and road systems repaired so goods could begin to flow again. A Firster patrol, taking a page out of the raider book, had been caught near Saint Paul. All six of its members were to be tried by a military court.

That was when the first real, grainy footage of New York began coming out.

The skyline was still there, but the bridges were wrecked. The fires were still going, roaming and ravening unchecked. Drones sent in to look for survivors found only…strange things, misshapen hulks of tissue that struck out blindly as they slouch-slumped through the smoke-choked streets. There were other glimpses—a man running, on fire but curiously unburned, screaming and whipping gobbets of orange flame off his wildly gesturing hands. Another one, ripping at his shirt while bony spikes tore outward through his back and legs. There was no audio, but you could almost *hear* the cries. A woman stood atop a burning building, her arms spread, and leaped, appendages on her back working furiously but not hard enough to keep her from meeting the pavement twelve stories below—and, amazingly, she staggered upright afterward, tacking off drunkenly down a garbage-choked Brooklyn avenue.

"These images are not doctored," Long Joanna said, heavily. "The last act of the Firster government was to release some type of biological weapon on New York, and these are the results. The mutations are quick, and those not immediately fatal are, from what we can see, excruciatingly painful. New York is gone, my friends." Her bloodshot eyes narrowed, and her mouth firmed. "The entire metro area is being contained, and the victims inside quarantined until the nature and type of the biohazard can be determined. A joint Federal and Canadian task force has upstate New York under control at the present time."

"Wow," someone breathed. "Look at that shit."

"I heard about this," said someone else. "Mutants. They were making 'em. Farting around with genes."

"The weapon used in New York was, we are told, the result of human experimentation in the Reklamation and ReEdukation camps." Long Joanna paused. When she continued, her husky, pleasant voice had lowered slightly, and she had to force the words out. "The footage we're about to show is extremely disturbing, but Federal Forces News believes you should know just what we were fighting. I can only say, if you are a sensitive viewer, you might want to look away."

The Quonset hospital went still. Blue light from the flatscreen bathed nearby faces. Sheets and blankets shifted. One of the orderlies, a wide-shouldered kid with a scarred cheek, stood scratching at his left forearm, staring at the moving, flickering images. "Oh God," he whispered. He had a snubbed nose and freckles, and for a few moments he looked very much like Lazy Eye.

Only Zampana noticed that particular resemblance, her hands on either side of Hendrickson's left elbow as she craned to see the flatscreen. The images were pitiless, filming adding depth and texture. Hendrickson pitched forward a little to see past her, and what he glimpsed made his gorge rise.

Spooky, her pupils dilating, slithered off Sal's bed with dream slowness and rose, staring at the flatscreen as well. It blocked the view of the bandaged soldier on the bed behind them, and he let out a sobbing, unconscious sound of relief. Her eyes round and her head cocked, she dropped a roll of ACE bandage she'd been winding. It hit the ground with a flutter.

Shaky but crystal clear, the camera focused down a long hall, hospital beds on either side bearing shrouded, misshapen bodies. "—Camp Baylock," Long Joanna said. "This footage was smuggled out in the last days of the war, and acquired at great personal danger by FFN reporters—"

The camera shuddered, the screen went black. When it came back, the footage focused on a child. A girl of about eleven, with a solemn monkeyface bespeaking malnutrition, held her hands up. Rudimentary sixth fingers wiggled on both, and as the girl spread them, her starveling face contorted. The camera panned away, showing the object of her scrutiny—a glass beaker on a small, flimsy table. The girl's profile twisted afresh, and a thin bead of blood—black because the screen's color mix was off—slid from one nostril.

The beaker shattered, and the girl's mouth dropped wide in a soundless scream. A white-jacketed orderly with Patriot pips on his sleeve rushed in and was thrown back, an invisible fist socking him squarely in the gut. The camera spun away, showing a whole ward of emaciated children, watching apathetically. Most had bandaged heads, sterigauze glaring white.

"I must warn sensitive viewers again," Long Joanna said.

The White Room. Spooky's lips shaped the words, but nobody was looking. Instead, spellbound, they stared at the flatscreen, even Chuck pulled out of his concentration.

It was replayed over and over again in the weeks afterward, the FFN chyron reading ORIGINAL IMAGES—NOT ALTERED scrolling across the bottom. Everywhere it was shown to civilians no few people vomited, and at least one passed out. Plenty of the soldiers turned green, and the young floppy-haired orderly ran for the door, almost not making it before he blew chunks.

Growths all over helpless, naked, skeletal bodies. Eyes bulging and bleeding, scalpels wielded. Seizures coursing through a woman's body as she was held down and a syringe was plunged into either arm, a thick liquid forced into her veins. Blood, bile, a pile of still-twitching corpses, one or two in scraps of papery hospital johnnies, all of them disfigured and deformed. A grafting surgery, masked doctors sewing a blackened hand onto the stump of a man's arm while his eyes rolled and he screamed, obviously not anesthetized.

"Turn it off," someone said, thickly. "For God's sake, turn it off."

Nobody moved. Long Joanna's face came back. "I regret to say there is even more disturbing footage from the Baylock camp. Captured along with it were several drives of badly wormed data, which are now publicly available on the FFN website and mirrored on the DOR network so the world can see the crimes committed by former dictator McCoombs and his so-called Patriots." Her gaze swung away from the camera, and scuffling sounds came from offscreen, as well as voices. "We were asked not to air this, but after so many years of bearing your public trust, I felt we could not remain silent. Thank you, ladies and gentlemen. We're being forced off the air now. Thank you, goodni—"

The 'cast cut off, the screen went dark. Outside, the orderly could be heard retching.

"Holy shit." A sergeant with thick, sturdy plaster on her arm and dreads just beginning to come in since they had relaxed the buzz restrictions shook her head. "Holy fucking *shit*."

Spooky was already heading for the door. Her shadow in the sunshine wavered, and she pushed past the vomiting orderly into thick sunshine. Her own retches echoed, but she didn't slow down.

CHAPTER FIFTY-THREE

AN UPGRADE

July 29, '98

Swann, a dark crumpled shape in his left hand, palmed the hospital Quonset door open, lengthening his stride. "Riders!" he bellowed, and no few of the soldiers in the hospital jerked out of a doze or outright sleep, reaching for a missing weapon. "Saddle up!"

Zampana, stretched out flat on her back, slammed into wakefulness, the jolt wringing a groan out of her. She'd stiffened up. Chuck Dogg thrashed, the gantry thing holding his leg wobbling, before Sal, who had been sitting reading a funnybook, got him free and found his crutch. Simmons was already out of bed, tightening and tying his loose-laced boots with quick jerks. "Where's the Spook?" the Reaper barked.

"Johnny Fed's got her," Swann replied. "We're leaving in five. Get everything you need."

"What is it?" Zampana, wrapping her braids around her head, dug in a pocket for the long black bobby pins that had seen her through the war. "Swann?"

"Got a flimsy—they've pinged that motherfucker. Get scrambled, we're due at the landing pad."

"Oh Christ," Chuck moaned. "Not another sled." He hopped to the end of his bed, scooping up Minjae's deck case; Sal grabbed Chuck's duffel and his own.

One of the orderlies, a rangy blonde sergeant, bustled up. "People are trying to *sleep*!" she hissed.

"Sorry." Swann sounded not very sorry at all. "We've got a Firster motherfucker to catch."

"Yeah, we'll be out of your hair in a hot minute, *chica*." Zampana grabbed her bags—duffel in one hand, medic's hip sling in the other. "Sim! Help Chuck."

"I got his bag." Sal all but hopped from foot to foot. "Flimsy? The doctor?"

"Not here, asshole." Swann, his scalp glowing through his gray buzz cut, squinted at the door. "Get moving, let's go."

A warm, breathing just-past-midnight enfolded them, Simmons all but carrying Chuck *and* his crutch. Sal swore as he moved, a familiar song from other hurried exits, patrols breathing on their necks, someone's nerves twitching, uneasy.

Swann shook out what he was carrying. "He's in the Dakotas. Got some sort of ping. We ain't the only ones after him."

"Duh." Zampana, breathless, ducked through her medic-bag strap. "Other raiders?"

"Nope. The fucking Russians. And God knows who else." Swann stuck a candy in his mouth, chomping the filter viciously.

"What?" Both Simms and Chuck said it, a harmony that would have been funny in another situation.

"Fucking New Soviet fucks." Swann chewed on the candy filter. "It was all over the flimsy. Johnson's been selling to them for years, I guess. He's supposed to strike west. We're gonna pick up the trail and slide one step ahead."

"West? Why…Oh." Zampana exhaled sharply, her boots crunching gravel. "Seattle?"

"Maybe. Got to get through the DMZ first."

Simmons hauled Chuck along with a grunt. "Why not north? Canada, Alaska."

"Might be able to get into Canada, but good luck shoving into Alaska." Swann would've sounded outright happy to have a direction to run if his entire body wasn't aching so badly. "Border there's locked up tighter than a whore's cashbox."

"Russians." Sal almost spat, visibly thought better of it. "Ain't they done enough?"

Zampana's dry fox-laugh echoed through the wet darkness. "Well, you know, it could be worse. Could be the Chinese."

"They're fighting the Russians, though." Chuck sucked in a breath as his leg was jostled. "Ain't they?"

Swann's boots ground into gravel. The candy was a shredded mass against his teeth; he spat it and grabbed another, remembering to light this one. "Not our problem, and doesn't mean they don't want to fuck with *us* for extra credit. Anyway, that's what's up."

"Christ. Can I at least pee before we go?" Zampana didn't think much of this.

Swann jammed the dark blot in his hand onto his head. It was a new hat, a felted slouch number. No feather. It was, no use denying it, kind of a relief to them all to see his head covered. The adrenaline and high singing awareness of danger, time to move, take only weapons and what you can carry, zing-popped through each raider.

"You can pee aboard, Pana." Now, and for the first time in a long while, Swann sounded grimly amused. "Johnny Fed got us an upgrade."

Long and sleek, with raked-back lines and active cells glowing along its underside, the new sled was much bigger—and much quieter—than anything they'd seen before. "What the fuck?" Sim pulled up short, which meant Chuck had to as well.

A skinny Federal pilot in a mottled greenish flight suit poked her sleek black head out the side hatch, over a set of folding iron stairs that looked too delicate for real use. "That you, Captain, sir?" A high, sweet, very young voice, piercing the evening. The whites of her eyes were startling, and so were her small perfect teeth, except the missing canine.

Pana halted, too. "No. No *thank* you." She shook her head. "Who the fuck is that?"

"Driver." Swann didn't bark at them to hurry. "Came with the package."

"Don't even look old enough to jill off," Chuck weighed in, the red-tied hanks at his temple bouncing as he shook his head. "She gonna drive us over a goddamn riot, too?"

Swann didn't bother repeating that had been a *mistake, so stop fucking mentioning it.* "Advanced prototype. Feds been workin' on this down in New Mexico for the entire war. Hendrickson pulled a few strings; some-one's ass is gonna get busted for giving us an old sled when this was available. It was supposed to meet us two bases ago."

"And it has a shitter aboard?" The way Sal said it, that was the over-riding consideration. Maybe it was.

Swann headed for the hatch, his boots crunching on gravel before he hopped onto the concrete landing pad. "It's us, Ngombe. Hendrickson in there with you?"

"Yessir, and the medic, sir. She's, uh, sir, she's throwing up, sir."

"Spooky?" Zampana shoved past Swann. "Shit. Still?"

"Sir?" Ngombe, now visible in the backwash glow of the cells, had a small, squished-in face on a head too large for it. Her dark woolly buzz cut, plastered down with heavy sheencream, only added to the smushed factor. Her smile was electric, and her eyes danced. "Is that everyone, sir?"

"Jesus Christ." Simms glanced at Chuck. Sweat stood out on his pale forehead, and his blue eyes were bloodshot. "They just get this kid out of basic?"

"Not our problem," Swann reminded them, not bothering to explain. "You comin'?"

"Long as she don't smash us," Chuck said. He was sweating too, but whether it was from effort or the idea of getting back on a piece of flying iron was debatable. "Simms?"

"Fine." The Reaper hauled him forward. "You crash us, you little fuck, and Imma cut you' arms off."

"Sir?" the driver squeaked, and Sal's thin laugh was lost in the quiet, powerful humming of the Z-Stat 32 prototype.

CHAPTER FIFTY-FOUR

HUMAN ROCKETS

Spooky heaved again into the galvanized bucket Hendrickson held. She was producing nothing but bile, and her stomach wouldn't quit trying to turn her inside out. She barely knew she was on another sled, weightlessness as it rose setting off another round of retching.

Then Zampana was next to her, the older woman's hand on her back, and the heaving stopped all at once. "Easy, *chica*." Pana peeled up the closest of Spooky's eyelids, then used her thumb to scrape back sweat-slick hair.

"Found her halfway to the fugee camp," Hendrickson said. "Almost had to tackle her. Got her cleaned up, but she can't stop yarking."

"Electrolytes." Pana dug in her bag. The gold crucifix at her neck glittered, not tucked below her shirt. "Shit. I need—"

"There's pouches in the med cabinet. I'm on it." The dark-haired Fed rose in one swift smooth motion, and Pana's sudden, ruthlessly quelled realization that they were in a sled again, and furthermore unbuckled, spilled through Spooky's aching, wide-open skull, threatening to bring up another round of retching.

She had to keep her *self* inside herself, but it was hard. So hard, and she was tired. Finally, Spooky sagged in the jumpseat, head hanging, shivering like a tired horse. Her clothes were damp—she hadn't even used a towel after the shower Hendrickson dumped her into. "S-s-s-sorry…" she began.

"Shhhhh," Zampana soothed. Stray strands of black hair floated around her face, worked free of her hasty braids. "It was the newscast, wasn't it."

"Baylock," Spooky moaned. *"Baaaaaaaaylock."*

Hendrickson's boots clanged. His hair was wet too; he'd held her under the shower like she was a kid who hated bathing, rinsing away vomit splatters. Now he had a whole armful of electrolyte pouches, their foil shining in the pitiless glare from gleeson-fed overhead lights. "What flavor? Cherry, grape—"

"Unflavored." Pana snatched one from the selection, popped its bubble, and thumbed the straw out, all with one dexterous brown hand. The sled leveled, Swann talking to the young pilot in a monotone—bearing, speed, altitude double-checked. "Here, Spook. Just a sip, no more."

"Baylock," she moaned again. "The kids. White room. Little kids." Experimental Ward D was right next to the White Room, and the screams came through the wall each afternoon when testing time rolled around. Strapped to a gurney and rolled past the room toward the electroshock bays, you could hear some of the kids sobbing, or—even worse—the deathly silence when the doctors, marked by their pristine white lab coats and their ubiquitous cotton breathing masks, came through.

Spooky could *smell* it again. Disinfectant, shit, pain, and the sick-sweet exhalation of the killing bottles. Which was where you were bound after they finished experimenting on you, and the fumes soaked into every part of the camp except the fields of growing tobacco or sweet potato. Maybe she was strapped down, and this was a hallucination after the electroshock.

Don't worry. Lara's face over hers. *I'll take the pain.*

Sal groaned, too. "Shit," he whispered, uneasy with the clutch of gravity and the sled's slipping upward.

"It's okay. You're here, Spook. You're here." Pana offered the straw. "A little sip, okay? We got to get you back on track."

Finally it quieted down, and Spooky sagged in the jumpseat, sucking at the pouch of electrolyte, her eyes still showing their whites like a troubled horse's. Pana pushed herself upright and made it across the sled to Chuck, who was harnessed unhappily in, his bum leg stretched out as far as it could reach. "Should've stayed in bed," she grumbled at him.

A tight laugh, Chuck smoothing his slick forehead. His hair, dreaded up nicely, bounced a little as the sled jolted. "Not gonna stay with a buncha Feds when you running around havin' fun." Minjae's deck bag, clutched to his chest, sparkled a little.

Pana swallowed, hard. "Simms? You buckled up?"

The Reaper snorted. "Gonna ruin my threads. Yeah, Pana, I'm buckled. You sit your sweet Mexi-ass down, aight?"

"Gonna." First, though, she made it to the med cabinet, got it squared, and checked the head. Yes, there was a commode in there, thank God. A tiny in-flight one, with blue chemicals instead of water, but *that* was a secondary consideration. *"Gracias, Dios mío."*

"It's all right," Hendrickson repeated. He made a short movement, like he wanted to smooth Spooky's shoulder, and she flinched. "Whoa, okay. It's all right, Spooky. You're safe."

A jagged little giggle boiled out of her acid-burned throat. "We're in the sky," she husked. "How is that *safe?*"

"Amen." Sal flipped open his interrupted funnybook, sweat glistening along his forehead under his flattened curls.

Hendrickson didn't give up easy. "Well, this is a new kind of sled. Super stabilized. Even if someone takes out the cells, we'll glide." He dropped his hand back into his lap. "It's got fire protection. Baffles. The whole nine."

"Little late," Simmons muttered. Just loud enough.

"Yeah." Hendrickson chose to answer him, lifting his chin and staring at the Reaper dead-on. "I know."

Spooky took another mouthful of the electrolyte. It tasted awful, but it got the nastiness of bile and vomit out of her mouth. Her entire midsection was tender. "The White Room. At Baylock." A shudder worked through her. "That was where they had the kids."

"Spooky—" Simmons shifted restlessly.

"He's not gonna turn me in." She cut her eyes at Hendrickson. "Are you?"

The Federal shook his head. "I'm not here to turn anyone in, goddammit." The sled rattled a little, bouncing through turbulence, and every one of them tensed.

"Dios mío," Zampana yelled, behind the thin hatch to the head. *"Cut it out!"*

Chuck, still clutching Minjae's bag to his chest, narrowed his dark eyes. "What's this turn-in bullshit, huh?"

"Mutants," Spooky said. "Right? Firsters, Feds, they both see the same thing." Were they all fucking stupid, not to see it? "Weapons. Feds just want Dr. Death to work for *them* instead, making more Spookies."

Simms opened his mouth, maybe to say that wasn't true. He shut it again, as Spooky sucked on the electrolyte pouch. Hendrickson had turned pale, but maybe that was the sled rattle.

"Better us than the Russians, right?" Chuck shook his head, winced as his leg twinged. "Motherfuckers never learn."

"They did that after the big war." Simmons cracked his knuckles. "Read about it. Bunch of Nazi motherfuckers building rockets."

"Building human rockets now." Spooky rocked back and forth in the jumpseat. Her stomach turned over again and her cheeks puffed out, but this time nothing came up.

Thank God.

CHAPTER FIFTY-FIVE

BOSS

July 29, '98

The ancient blue rust-spotted truck jolted and rattled. Gene stared out the half-open window, a burning-redolent afternoon breeze brushing his sweat-stiff hair and stubbled chin. It was like an ancient 'cast, a road trip movie. A crazy doctor and his loyal sidekick, across fields of waving grain.

Except it wasn't grain—it was smoking grassland, summer fires hitting their stride amid war drought and lightning strikes. Plenty of Wyoming was aflame, and Montana's big sky was full of burning. Refugees clotted the road around any town large enough to have more than one stoplight, kerchiefs knotted around their faces, jalopies piled high with mattresses and home goods, all flowing west. Soon they would splash against the DMZ, collecting into scabs of desperation, heading for the golden land of the coast. PC, they called it, Practically Canada. A fabled land full of tolerance, milk, and honey. All those things the immies and degenerates used to seduce Amerikans and turn them into traitors.

Gene had to admit, though, the sky *was* big around here. It went on forever, the truck inchworming on a ribbon road, a beetle crawling on the back of a beast too big for reckoning.

It was probably just the drugs talking. The good Dr. Johnson, his hatchet face a grinning mask, seemed to have an endless supply. Warm and forgiving, chemical fire crawling through his veins, it was almost enough to make Gene forgive the man.

Almost.

Then he'd look at his left hand. Or, more precisely, where his left hand *should* have been. The stump, wrapped in sticky norpirene-smeared gauze and a blue senso-wrapper, ached and tingled. The doctor checked it at every stop, and sometimes pressed on the end with a gloved finger, enjoying Gene's grunts when agonizing bolts of lightning jolted up to his shoulder, detonating in his head. Each time, he tried not to react, and each time, the sound pulled itself out of him almost by accident.

The dashboard was blue too, molded plastic, clunky and antique. Every once in a while the doctor would consult a similarly antique yellowed atlas and pull off the highway, sometimes even bumping through clusters of refugees who scraped along the side of the truck, their eyes squinting above knotted, soot-stained kerchiefs or filthy surgical masks. When the crowds thickened, you could tell there was a checkpoint ahead, and the doctor would sigh, turning stained pages and bumping over a network of old-fashioned roads, from blacktop to macadam, sometimes off both and onto gravel.

"Help me with this, will you?" The doctor leered through Gene's window, sweat gleaming on his long nose.

Creaking in every joint, the once-Kaptain Thomas climbed out of the truck into slumberous golden sunlight, all the more vivid because of the looming black clouds. You could see the weather coming a long way out, here. "What?" His tongue didn't quite want to fit behind his teeth *or* work properly. Cottonmouth, a dry rasping going down his throat too.

The filling station was boarded up, its plate glass windows filthy with dust and flyspecks. A soaped drawing on the front was full of pumpkins, snowflakes, a scarecrow, and the invitation to COME ON IN! In the western distance, the bruise-dark clouds thickened, diamond flashes stitching their undersides. Gene stared for a long moment before he realized the doctor had seized his right hand and put it on the old-fashioned nozzle, pumping petrol into the truck's sloshing tank.

"Hold this." Johnson made a spitting sound, arranging Thom's right-hand fingers to suit him. "Good. Don't splash it. I'll check your dressing when I get back." With that, he strode away, hurrying for the side of the building, his fedora bobbing. He was prissy about pissing, the good Dr. Johnson from Kamp Baylock.

Gene blinked several times, trying to *think*. The pinching on the inside of his elbows, where the needles went in. When the narcotics wore off, he could *feel* his missing left hand, fingers spread and painfully cramped. Sometimes he thought it was a mistake, that Johnson had just tricked him into believing his hand was gone, showed him the jar with the floating flesh-spider in it, thumb curled like a monkey's, ring finger abnormally short because the tendons—

Splish. Petrol fumes simmered up, crawling into his nose. Hard to think with the buzzing in his head. *I saved your life,* the doctor said.

Was it true? His arm had been infected, but…

Of course he's lying, someone whispered, her breath brushing his ear. *He just wants a body to experiment on. Any body will do.*

Gene jerked the nozzle out of the side of the truck, splattering colorless petrol in a wide arc. How was this pump still working?

Gravity, silly. A low, caramel laugh. *Her* laugh, but he'd never heard it. She'd barely said ten words to him. Why was he hearing her now? Hallucinations. The drugs.

Dr. Johnson had drugged the fuck out of him. Gene shuddered. His feet were wet, and when he looked down he found out why.

He was in his sock feet, standing outside a shitty little boarded-up fleabite in Montana, splashing gas on his toes while he pushed the stump of his left arm into his chest. Amputation was a guaranteed out, the Patriots wanting only the whole and the healthy. Even if your genes were right, a missing limb was a no-no.

It took him two tries to figure out how to shut the pump off. His head was full of hot fudge, hard to stir, thoughts sticking to the sides of his braincase. There was the truck. If he put the nozzle in the window…how would he light it? He didn't smoke. Was it worth the risk of catching on fire himself? Maybe he could douse the doctor, and—

No, she whispered in his ear. *He's meeting someone. He has something they want; he's probably carrying it.*

So, no fire on the doctor. Not yet. There were other ways to skin a cat, like his mother might have said. A shudder raced through him. He hadn't thought of the old bitch in years. Skinny and dishwater-blonde, her raddled breasts hanging as she looked at herself in the mirror, she'd caught him in the hall that day and whaled the fuck out of him. Just for accidentally seeing her body eaten up with the cancer. No insurance, not for hardscrabble coal country. The Patriots and their Guaranteed Citizen Care had come along too late for old Ma Thomas.

Gene shut his eyes, breathing deep. The smoke smell intensified, a burning wind. Had he already lit the damn thing on fire? When he looked back up, the inkstain to the west had drawn closer, or maybe his gaze was just focusing properly now. The stabs from the pendulous cloudbelly were brighter, too. Lightning. Too far away to hear the thunder, a storm on the other side of nothing. The wind sharpened, freshened, brushing aside smoke for a moment. Light-headed, he jammed the nozzle back in its holder and tried to think, again.

When he lay down at night, the doctor didn't take his trousers off, or his undershirt. Wrapped around Johnson's thickening, stiffening waist was a black smear—a travel belt. He never took the damn thing off. If he was carrying something good, that was where it would be.

The only thing Gene had to worry about, he thought, leaning against the ancient gas pump with its bubble top and faded, chipped red paint, was figuring out who to sell it to. And, of course, making sure he searched Johnson's corpse thoroughly for every drop of drugs the man was carrying.

Then, Eugene Thomas told himself, *then* they'd see who was boss.

CHAPTER FIFTY-SIX

NGOMBE'S HANDS

"Practically drives itself, sir." Ngombe's slim thumbs caressed the yoke. "Never thought they'd let someone like me take this baby up. Isn't she a beauty?"

"Real cute." Swann rubbed at his grainy eyes. His stomach wasn't too happy at the feeling of being aloft again, even though the ride was surprisingly smooth. "What you mean, someone like you?"

"Well, you know." She flipped a couple toggles until the lights dancing across the displays suited her. "They don't like raiders taking shit out of the hangars, sir."

"You a raider?" He took another look at the girl's profile. "With who?"

"Nana Bona." A cheerful wink, and she rubbed the back of her close-cropped head against the pilot cradle. "Hung around in Texas, grabbing shit, running intel. Got sent to Mississippi twice, got loose and went back each time. Rattled around in RVs with ultralights chunked up in the back, scout an airfield, load 'em up, drop shit on 'em. Drones, sir. I can build you a drone. It flies, I like it."

"Huh." He'd assumed she was Army. This was a welcome surprise. "Pana? This lady says she was with Nana in Texas."

"No shit." Zampana, free of the head, edged her way cautiously up the middle of the sled. "Which band you with, then?"

"Desert Rats," Ngombe said, turning her chin slightly. From that angle, with the instrument glow playing over her features, she looked childish instead of squished. "Scrounged everything, sir-ma'am. Hit the depot in Amarillo last year."

Pana's grin, startling and good-natured, widened. She scratched under her braids, peered out through the sled's front bubble at a vicious red sunset sky. "How the fuck you end up flying this?"

"Big man come down, said any raider sign up gets rank. I said, get me in that air force, let me fly some beauties!" Her teeth peeped out, strong and white except for her upper left canine, knocked out. "They didn't want to, but Nana hollered at someone until they got me in an old junker of a sled and I turned that thing upside-*down*, let me tell you. Then they couldn't get my sweet ass in somethin' good fast enough."

"I can believe it." Pana leaned against the bulkhead behind the girl's seat. "I'm Zampana. Pleased to meetcha."

Her head bobbed, the salute of a soldier with something in her hands. "Likewise, ma'am. It true what they say?"

"Depends on what they're saying." Swann tried to relax. "Can the *sir*, we're all raiders here. Pana, buckle yourself *in*."

"Yeah, yeah." She dropped into the jumpseat on Spooky's other side; the Spook kept sucking at the electrolyte pack. "Now that I'm a few ounces lighter, I'd be glad to."

"Thanks for sharing," Simmons weighed in.

Ngombe's laugh was caramel, a deep rich chuckle. The sled evened out. "No shit, though, is it true? Y'all hunting those motherfuckers?"

"Yeah." Swann rubbed at his eyes again. Why the fuck had he taken the copilot chair? The controls were like a regular sled's, but not *enough* like, and he wanted to catch some shut-eye. All the same, he didn't want Hendrickson up here. Let the asshole sit next to Spook and think about things, dammit. "Got some notched up already."

"Sir, and they *pay* you for it?" She let go of the yoke to wave her right hand. "It's like fuckin' Christmas!"

There was no way Swann was ever going to get as excited about *any-thing* as this girl seemed to be. "Keep it steady, all right?"

Her grin didn't alter in the least. "Hey, you don't need to worry, sir. You couldn't crash this baby if you tried. Raider's honor."

"Fucking shit." Simms settled himself more firmly in his own seat. "Does she ever shut up?"

"Be cool, man." Chuck checked the catch on his own belt again. There was a doodad that folded out a flat surface from the sled wall, and Min-jae's laptop fit right in a shallow well, plugging in just like it was designed to. "Look at this. High-class. Min would *love* this shit."

Uncomfortable, humming silence descended on the sled interior. Simmons shut his eyes, stretched his long legs out. Spooky cautiously leaned aside, away from Hendrickson. Jumpseats didn't have armrests, so she could put her shoulder against Pana's, sinking down, alert for any sign the older woman minded.

There was none. Solid and soft at the same time, Pana just settled her weight to accommodate. A few tendrils of freshly trimmed hair fell into Spooky's eyes, but she didn't move.

Ngombe sobered. "My name's Kelly, y'all," she said finally. "Kelly Ngombe."

"Pleased to meetcha," Zampana repeated. "You know Swann. This bitch with the big eyes is Spooky, and that Johnny Fed, well, he answers to *Hey, you*. The big reader there is Sal. Big blond bastard is Simmons, and that's Chuck Dogg." It was a painfully short roll call.

"Hendrickson," Johnny Fed said, but not very loudly. In any case, presumably, she already knew.

"So, I got the coords," Ngombe nodded, sucked in her cheeks, popped her lips. "I ain't gonna ask about anything else, aight, sir? You tell me when I need to know."

"Ain't that a goddamn relief," Simms said. "Johnny Fed there like stickin' his nose in."

"They can't help it. Way they're built, sir." But Ngombe glanced back, as if troubled. "That heavin' one, she gonna be okay?"

"Just fine," Pana said. "Nervous stomach."

"Man, I can't imagine gettin' airsick. But don't you worry, sir-ma'am-y'all. Gonna get you there nice and smooth. No weather all the way there, so get some rest. You in Ngombe's hands now, mothas."

"Stick to *mothas*," Swann said. "Instead of *sir*, all right?"

"Yessir." And Kelly Ngombe laughed again.

CHAPTER FIFTY-SEVEN

NO CHANCES

July 30, '98

Dawn rose over farmland gone fallow. A smudge on the eastern horizon flushed bloody, reflecting a sullen haze. The newscasts, starting at the top of every hour, were full of burning on the plains, wildfires out of control and the DMZ swamped with refugees—and others—splashing against the Rockies. In between, music crackled softly over one frequency, air traffic headings read monotonously over the other. The pilot hummed along with all the songs—old favorites like *"Cubano Sol"* and Bi's "Dear Momma Don't Cry," famous as the most-requested tune during all of the Second Western Offensive; newer ones like Tribe Banyo's "Federal Stomp" and Cucaracha's *"Bailando Segundo,"* with its call-and-response about the hated *Migra Negra*, the Patriot "border patrol." *Go back where you came from,* Adamo Lisandro wailed over the mariachi strum, *you fucking conquistadors.*

Swann dozed in the jumpseat next to Spooky now; Zampana, fully rested, was in the copilot seat, reading off verified instrumentals when Ngombe asked for them and sometimes humming along herself. There was an all-corrido channel the pilot favored, and they alternated every half hour between that and AF-KROC for the 'casts along with Top Forty and oldies. Once or twice, the signal fuzzed, the last time with a Christer frothing about Revelations and the fall of America. "Could get that fucker quick," Ngombe muttered, her face distorting for a moment. "Lock onto his 'cast and run it down. Give him nine grams."

"If he's still there when we come back," Pana murmured in reply. She didn't add *and if he's not using a relay*. The old days of bouncing 'casts all over to hide from the All-Amerika FCC were full of bad memories.

They banked over a small, deserted South Dakota town, a blip on the landscape—shell-burned church, broken glass glitter-winking at mid-morning from the ruins of feedstore and gas station windows, gutted homes. Raiders or regulars, who could tell? For someone to fight over this shithole must have meant something was worth it, one way or another.

Or maybe someone hated the local Party members, or they burned the downtown because it was a raider hole. Whoever could tell them any different was probably in the DMZ with other concerns right now.

"Coming up on coordinates. We going hot?"

Pana glanced back. Better safe than sorry. "Captain?"

Swann jolted out of dead sleep, twitching as if he wanted to leap up-right, stopped by the restraint harness. "Fuck!"

That brought everyone else up, even Hendrickson, whose knee bumped Spooky's, hard. Chuck, his head tipped back, surfaced midsnore. Simmons, reaching for his knife, swore like Swann, but more creatively, ending with a term of surpassing anatomical impossibility.

Spooky opened her eyes but didn't twitch. Only a thin crescent glitter showed beneath her eyelids, and that was the mark of a kamp survivor. You learned not to betray anything, even balanced on the gray edge be-tween sleep and waking.

"Get your hat on, Captain." Zampana tried not to sound amused and failed miserably. "We're almost there."

"We got fifty cal and a couple missiles," Ngombe said cheerfully. "You want them loaded up?"

"Christ, no." Swann rubbed at his face. "Set us down about a mile out. Quiet like."

"Aw, shit." The pilot's grin didn't change, wide and fetching. "I was hopin'."

Swann hit the release catches on his harness and stretched, rubbing at his head with one hand. "Head up and fuel up, monkeys. We got a run."

"Aye, Captain." Simms rubbed at his face, clearing away sleep. "This thing got a coffee machine?"

"Look next to the med cabinet." Ngombe whistled out between her teeth. "Which angle you want on it, sir?"

"Got any eyes?"

"Maybe. Techie? Dial in, we gotcha full stats." A full sensor array, infrared to UV, cams, bouncers—well, maybe they'd just stuffed everything on the prototype it could hold.

"Fuck me," Chuck groaned, opening Minjae's deck. "I'm no good at this shit."

Nobody asked him why the fuck he wouldn't let anyone else's hands on Minjae's deck. It had a certain fittingness—she wouldn't want her gear in a nonraider's paws, and Chuck was about the only person, other than Pana, who didn't irritate her.

Hadn't irritated her. Poor Prink could never figure out if he was coming or going with Min, and Pana sometimes thought Min liked it that way. In any case, they didn't need much in the way of intel crunching now that they had a direction. When it came time to let go, maybe Chuck would.

"I could try." Hendrickson unbuckled. "Or I'll just bring you coffee," he continued, pretty much sure of rejection.

"Let him look." Swann stretched, joints creaking. "Motherfucker, this is uncomfortable."

"I miss the goddamn RV." Simms banged back for the restroom. "Could piss off the side of that."

"What, you want a fugee hanging on your pecker?" Chuck snorted. "All right, Johnny Fed. Help me out of this shitty-ass chair and point me at the coffee maker, and Reaper, if yo' ass spends more than five minutes in the head, Imma comin' in to help you shake off."

"Never knew you cared," Simms cracked back, and vanished behind the flimsy partition.

A few minutes later, Spooky edged for the bathroom, and the boiled reek of instant coffee filled the sled. Hendrickson, his hair stiffened from a few days without soap and crinkle-dried from the shower he'd dumped Spooky in, hunched his broad shoulders and tapped at Minjae's laptop.

"Farmhouse," he said. "Two stories, probably a cellar too. Garage. No heat signatures outside. Fuzzy, probably has asbestos in the walls." He tapped a few more times. "Nothing moving except wildlife, Captain."

"Why not just blow the fucker up and look for bones?" Simmons slurped at too-hot boiled instant and spluttered a little.

Zampana stretched, doing her best to touch the sled ceiling and not even close. "Sure. Melt whatever he's got the data on, too."

Simmons rolled his eyes. "Might be best."

"He's not there. The ping's almost a week old; motherfucker's moved unless he's stupid." Swann accepted his own tin cup of instant. "Christ, this smells like balls, Chuck."

"You'd know." Chuck tapped on the bathroom partition. "Spook? You want coffee?"

She reappeared and accepted a cup, wrapping her fingers around its warmth. Chuck clapped her shoulder, too. But gently, so she didn't spill. All of them moving and breathing dialed the temperature up, and humidity, too. Ngombe pointed at the dash, and Swann found the temp controls. Cool, dry air soughed in, an unexpected relief.

"Even has AC," Simms crowed. "We come up in the world."

"Not very far." Pana stretched again, joints cracking, her face contorting as bruises and muscles protested.

"A shitter right there, coffee, and air-conditioning." Sal cackled, straightening his legs in defiance of all manners or good sense. "I'll take it."

"Set us down a mile out," Swann repeated. "No chances. Sal, you got the demo clips?" Best to treat the entire structure like it was trapped.

"Sure thing."

"Brush 'em up." Swann touched the buckle on his harness, and decided he could wait to piss until they were safely on the ground.

Just in case.

CHAPTER FIFTY-EIGHT

CHECK THE WELL

Nothing was trapped. The place was full of mouse shit and dust, skeletal antique furniture standing lonely guard in otherwise empty rooms. Front door, untrapped. Back door, unlocked. Living room, dining room, bedrooms upstairs and the one bathroom downstairs, clear.

The kitchen, full of midmorning light, was bare and clean as if a farmwife had just stepped into the hall. A chipped enamel double sink seemed luxuriously out of place; the oven, sturdy and avocado-colored, was a useless cave. The floor had been swept but not mopped, though the water was obviously on. Probably a well—Swann glanced through the window and yep, there was a ramshackle well shed. Two mismatched water glasses, upended in an ancient dish drainer of plastic-covered wire, sat mute and unobjectionable. A long-dead houseplant, its leaves gone to powder, perched in a little yellow pot on the windowsill.

The puzzle deepened with the second bedroom upstairs, with a narrow iron bed pushed against the wall and a large, still-damp stain on the wooden floor, scattered with a double handful of clay kitty litter. A thin, ancient mattress had been hauled out back and left in the sun, flies crusting large soaked-through stains. Urine, it looked like, and shit as well.

The garage, just as ruthlessly bare, held a fresh slick of dripped oil from a petrol-burner. Simmons studied the disarranged gravel outside the big garage door. "Truck," he said, finally. "Bald fucking tires, too."

Zampana, balanced on an old, handmade wooden step, peered into the mudroom. "Huh."

"What we got?" Swann, inside, examined the narrow room, floored in peeling yellow linoleum. Wooden racks for scraping your boots clean pressed down the lino's loose edges, and the big utility sink still held a trace of moisture near the drain.

"Simms says a truck. Looks like a gas-burner. What you make of this?" Pana indicated the dish rack on an anemic slice of jury-rigged counter next to the sink, cluttered with bone-dry metal and glass. Wicked edges gleamed.

"Surgical tools." Swann's face set as he holstered his piece. "Sweep that fuckin' garage twice, Pana."

She swallowed a sharp reply, contenting herself with a simple "Wait until you see this." She crossed herself again too, for good measure.

Near the ancient, dust-sheathed window, a worktable lay shrouded in canvas. Twitched carefully back, the cover revealed an old radio, its buttons and dials clean of dust, and a stack of paper with spidery handwriting in blue pen. Other tools were arranged neatly, some hanging on pegboard to the left and right of the window, but the thing the raiders gathered to stare at was a tightly capped specimen jar full of clear liquid.

Inside, a hand floated, the ring finger grossly shortened. Neatly shorn at the wrist, a meaty seaweed, its palm cupped and its nails blunt but clean, it pointed toward the lid. The specimen jar glittered once the canvas was pulled away, sunshine showing finger ridges and whorls, the lines on the palm, a fading ring-indent on the distorted third finger, the cicatrix of a burst blister on the pad under the squat, broad thumb. Sparse hair on the back and knuckles stayed frozen, no ripples in the fluid as they stood and stared at it.

"Jesus fucking Christ," Sal finally said. "Wait until Chuck sees *this*." The Dogg was probably almost beside himself at having to stay with the sled and pilot.

"It's fresh," Hendrickson said. "Look at the tied-off veins, right there. Jesus."

"He did it upstairs in the bedroom." Spooky, in a monotone. She pointed

at a wooden box, knocked free of dust and set carefully below the workbench. A thin line of staining at its bottom edges was blood, the spatter and
drips starting at a sharp angle. "Had something over that to catch the blood."

"So he holes up here, cuts off his hand…"

"Someone else's hand." Zampana shook her head, a restive movement,
trying to fit this into the catalog of Firster horrors and finding a place
without too much difficulty.

"Someone else's," Spooky agreed. She swayed forward, but subsided
when Swann flashed her a warning glance.

"Do we look for a body? Maybe in the well?" Sal squatted, examining
the lower shelves of the workbench. "This ain't trapped. Maybe he didn't
have time."

"But he had time to take someone's arm off?" Simmons peered at it
more closely. "Priorities, man."

"There's something about the angle." Hendrickson folded his arms,
sucking in his cheeks. His five-o'clock shadow was coming in early,
matched only by Simmons's. "Why do it that way? Huh."

"Magchip," Spooky whispered. "It's a left hand." A hectic flush spread
up her thin throat, staining both cheeks.

The Fed nodded. "Makes sense. Except why take the whole hand off?"

"I still say we should look for a body," Sal grumbled. "Check that damn
well."

"Papers." Zampana pointed at the pad next the radio, with its blue-pen
hieroglyphs. "Looks like code. What you want to bet he hooked up that
old-timey box there, and that's where they got the ping from?"

"Lo-fi Firsters. Now we seen everything." The Reaper's laugh bounced
against the garage walls. "Well, if he's haulin' around in a gas-burner, we
got a chance."

"Wish Lazy was here." Sal rocked a bit, easing the strain on his
haunches. "He'd probably get that thing hooked up and working, tell us
something."

Spooky stepped forward, her knee touching his back. She leaned, and
her small, quick, capable fingers closed around the specimen jar.

"Jesus *fuck* be careful!" Swann yelled, but she already had the heavy silica-infused plastic, lifting it free. The hand bobbed gently; the lid had a pressure lock she was careful not to touch.

It was exactly the type of jar they had shelves of at Baylock. The ward they'd stuck her in after the electroshock had a bank of them, human brains floating in the same colorless solution—some in cross section, some whole, each neatly labeled. When the bomb hit, they'd gone up in volatile flames. Even the toughest jar would crack under that kind of concussion.

"I *told* you it's not trapped." Sal hunched his shoulders. "Christ, Spook, *warn* a man next time."

"Sorry." She held the unopened jar at arm's length, like a kid with a frog to carry home and scare a sibling with.

Simms took his hand away from his sidearm, with a visible effort. "Whatchu thinking, Spooky?"

"Fingerprints." She stepped back gingerly. "Right?"

"Well, goddamn," Hendrickson said in the thunderstruck silence. "That's a good idea. Let's go."

Sal hauled himself up with a grunt. "Imma check the well."

PART FOUR

MISERICORDIA

CHAPTER FIFTY-NINE

BLOOD SOONER

August 1, '98

The 'cast went live on a bright, beautiful summer afternoon. Drones whirred over the Supreme Court building, dipping and rising to pan over the crowd spilling down the steps and into the street. Stone-faced MPs kept most of the crowd back, and the drones served a secondary purpose, scanning for weapon thermasigs. Whether they suspected Firsters attempting a rescue or any other group looking to assassinate was an open question.

Some people carried signs, mostly with requests to let the traitors swing. "Crimes against humanity" was a popular phrase. Immies clustered, safety in numbers, a holdover from the sweeps during McCoombs's first few years, when the only hope of breaking free of Patriot cordons was to rush their batons and riot gear. Waves of chants went through the restive crowd, and if there were any leftover Firsters, they chanted along with the rest.

To do otherwise might have been fatal.

As it was, scuffles broke out around suspected Firster or Patriot sympathizers, the crowd's mood turning on the thin edge between relief and the desire to bite the kicking boot of the last decade.

Inside, the cameras watched as the prisoner was settled in an uncomfortable, straight-backed chair. His sober-suited lawyers, their faces set with the disagreeable duty of defense, conferred quietly, shuffling papers from leather folios. The right side of the prisoner's face was a mass of packed bandaging, snow-white and taped down; the eye on that side was a deflated, rolling grape. Half his jaw was gone, and rumor was he had to be fed protein shake through a straw, barely able to swallow past the esophageal damage. It was probably true, because his suit, as ill-fitting as usual, hung on a slimmer frame than his former jovial bloat. What could be seen of the prisoner's face had paled, the false tan leaching away to jaundice. An IV pole stood behind him, a bag of tinted liquid swaying gently whenever he shifted.

A gavel struck. It was the Old Court, elderly men and women squeezed out by Firster appointees under the Emergency Acts. The New Court were in their respective cells at Annapolis, awaiting their turns. The youngest of the Old Court was Kavannen, and she was seventy; nevertheless, her dark eyes behind thick glasses were bright and sharp. The judges' faces were set too, but a gleam could be discerned here and there—a hand tightening, a lip threatening to curl.

A complicated dance of legal rhetoric ensued. Precedent was quoted, prosecution arguments listened to, defense counterarguments heard. Another flurry of paperwork and procedural wrangling. Finally, the Chief Justice—ravaged by untreated throat cancer, her eyes swimming behind steel-rimmed spectacles, her proud nose pointed straight ahead—allowed a further argument, on the proper trying of high treason and crimes against humanity. An international court was considered.

Outside, the crowd waited. Organizations that hadn't been legal for years—NAACP, ACLU, SPLC, all sorts of acronyms—announced their renewal on makeshift stages buttressed on the steps, and called for the prisoner to face international trial *and* a public trial before the people of the United States, sea to shining sea despite the rumbles of the West Coast "join Canada" plebiscite. Breathless rumors raced through the mass of people, growing by the hour. Lunchtime became late afternoon and edged into a soft slumberous evening, a cool breeze whistling riverward. A candlelight vigil massed at the Lincoln Memorial, the statue unhooded and cleaned, Firster graffiti even now being scrubbed from marble and the building's facing. Old polymer matting had been dragged out to cover the grass on the Mall; rationed water had been drained from the pool, and glimmers of handheld candles showed from the bottom.

Who among them had been at the rally where McCoombs declared total war and bathed in the hysterical screams of his worshippers?

Some went home; new people arrived. The crowd lived, breathed, moved.

Finally, a rustling roar went up. Anyone with a handheld popper or a cell dialed into the 'cast turned to their neighbors excitedly. A decision had been reached.

The rustle became a grumble. At the Lincoln Memorial there was singing—old protest songs, war ballads, and finally, as the moon rose, someone blew into a harmonica. The first few bars of "America the Beautiful" breathed melancholy, and it was taken up from the back of the crowd, sweeping for the front.

It was at that moment those on the steps of the Court learned that Mc-Coombs would indeed stand trial in international court for genocide and war crimes.

After he faced a Federal military trial for treason.

The protests against giving the bastard his day in court started immediately. General Leavy didn't exactly *blame* them—of course civilians would want blood sooner rather than later. He'd just been afraid the geezers in black robes would decide to ship McCoombs off to some candy-ass European court that would give him life in prison or some shit. Nobody was going to be happy with anything for a while.

That, Leavy had decided, was *democracy*.

He walked heavy-footed down the hall, salutes snapping from every side. He had to go slowly—Kallbrunner's stride was firm but unhurried. A new set of old-style dress blues had appeared, and fit the acting President as if tailored. Maybe they had been; this was DC and there was an army of unemployed ready to provide any-damn-thing. The higher-class call girls—and boys—were probably bathing in Federal dollars and writs. Patriot money had collapsed, the breadlines were getting longer, and earlier that evening some Firster bastard who had slipped through the nets had fired at a shed holding three immie refugees. MPs hadn't been able to keep him out of the hands of an angry crowd, and the Firster asshole hadn't made it any better by screaming slogans straight from McCoombs's last rally.

The report was on Leavy's desk, along with other bad news. A whole avalanche of it. He almost preferred the fucking war to this.

Not really.

Dr. Hovins, his round reddened face shining faintly under the fluorescents, stood just outside a half-ajar door. This wing of the hospital was under the tightest security possible, patrolled every quarter hour, everyone checked and double-checked at every hallway.

It was just like McCoombs to fucker up his own goddamn suicide and cause problems for everyone, Leavy thought sourly, and plastered what he hoped was an interested expression on his face. "Evening, Doctor."

"Good evening, good evening!" The doctor bobbed up and down a little at Kallbrunner. "What an honor, Mr. President."

He probably said the same thing when he checked McCoombs's colostomy bag. Leavy quelled a grimace.

"I hear you're doing good work," Kallbrunner said urbanely. "Do you know what was in the capsule yet?"

"Well, we're not quite sure. The burns are somewhere between acid and caustic—it's hard to discern. He won't say, of course. There's a great deal of compromising of the facial structures—"

"Thank you, Doctor." Leavy cut across the nattering, motioning Kallbrunner along. If you got this asshole going, he'd be telling you the composition and color of his patient's stool before you knew it. "Mr. President, this way."

The room was dim except for the counter along its left side, where the sink glowed metallic and the cabinets were full of medical supplies tucked quietly away. The whole place reeked of disinfectant and yellow-brown pain collecting in pus-pockets. The bed, its upper half tilted so McCoombs didn't drown in his own saliva, stood in the very middle, the windows covered with bombproof netting instead of curtains. With all the ordnance lying around, someone could send a rocket-propelled grenade through the glass, if they had a mind to.

Leavy almost wished them luck.

Kallbrunner stopped at the foot of the bed. A monitor showed a pulse; the sheets were crisp and clean. It was a far cry from the field hospitals during Second Cheyenne, or the chaos of the immie clinics in Arizona or New Mexico.

A gleam showed under a pouchy, bruised-looking eyelid. The bastard was probably awake, doped up on pain meds.

"Well." Leavy swept the door closed, right in the face of the two guards supposed to follow Kallbrunner at all times and take a bullet for him if necessary. "Here we are."

"The best of care." Kallbrunner approached the bed, still ponderously slow. "Hello, Doug."

Leavy folded his arms, his back against the door.

Douglas McCoombs gave no indication of hearing, but the pulse on the green-hued monitor picked up a little.

"Heard you were in court today." Kallbrunner stepped along the side of the bed. Stopped, examining the slack, half-bandaged face. "Must be nice to get a trial, instead of being dragged out of your house and shot in the street. Or hung." He paused. "Or starved to death in a shitty little camp."

Leavy's fingers dug into his arms. The old man didn't sound angry. Instead, he sounded a little...wistful. Envious, maybe? Or just tired.

The body on the bed raised its eyelids. Bleary, bloodshot, one half clouded as if by cataract, the gaze of the man who had once made the entire world afraid of nuclear winter stared at Kallbrunner. The cheek bandage twitched.

Kallbrunner stood for a few more moments, then turned sharply, almost clicking his heels on a face-left. He took three steps and opened a cabinet door, then another. He found what he was looking for, and when he turned around, his spidery, veined hands held a thin hospital pillow. "General Leavy?"

"Yessir?"

"You might want to wait outside."

"Is that an order, sir?"

"No." Kallbrunner approached the bed again. McCoombs exhaled, a soft gurgling sound. What was it like, to have your voice gone after you'd spent years bludgeoning everyone around you with it? Leavy could remember the breathless magazine articles, the screaming at the election rallies, the sick thumping realization that his country had gone to war against itself. Every single night afterward, wherever Pat Leavy happened to be, hoping he could sleep despite the crushing, feverish worry, the nausea returned. "Not in the least."

Leavy set his jaw. The man had a right, he supposed.

McCoombs's eyes flickered. He looked from Leavy to Kallbrunner, and the pulse monitor spiked. Even in the dimness, beads of sweat turned visible on his high-domed, yellowing forehead. Christ, he looked small lying there. Not like the huge posters of him in any Amerika First rekreation kourt, or the flickering images on Patriot newscasts, shot from slightly below to make him appear taller.

This was just a rancid old wreck in a hospital bed. And yes, he had shat himself. The sudden stink was almost monstrous. It was a wonder anything in his bowels had made it past the stoma.

"Let me ask you." Kallbrunner leaned over McCoombs. "How do you like this, Dougie? *How do you fucking like it?*"

Goosebumps raced up Leavy's back. His underarms, for the first time in a long while, were damp, even though it was a steady sixty-eight degrees in here. His throat was dry, but he forced himself to watch.

McCoombs gurgled.

CHAPTER SIXTY

AMONG FRIENDS AGAIN

August 2, '98

The truck rattled along, rolling at a good clip over macadam and under a bloodred, smoky sunset. Moving by day was a risk, now that the fringes of the DMZ grasped and waved along freeways and larger roads. Working south was a risk, and so was too far north. Another risk was moving at night—headlights shouted your location, especially to overflight patrols. Which thickened the closer you drew to the invisible line the Federals had drawn as soon as McCoombs signed the Good Neighbors Immigration Act barring all "undocumenteds" and "undesirables." Right after that was the executive order criminalizing protests, and the West Coast had gone berserk. *Not Our President* was their response, a bumper-sticker side order of secession drenched in hippie sweat.

Johnson sometimes snorted quietly, thinking about it. McCoombs could have gotten much more cooperation by using the old, familiar terms. Nobody *really* wanted a tide of immies and degenerates swamping America, but the bumbling, misguided Man of the People had been too impatient.

So Johnson and his subject rattled and rolled toward the Continental Divide, listening to the patchwork of coded talk and silence you could find on AM radio, if you knew where to halt the dial and how to winnow the lip service. Before McCoombs, they'd called it old-people analog.

Evangelists, sports, and right-wingers, the lonely voices crying out about the slow strangling of a shining city on a hill. Sometimes you were even mocked for listening to it, like Johnson's grandfather. The goddamn Federal liberals made fun of honest working people all the time.

The good doctor had gone to college, but he knew what was what, as his grandfather might have said.

There was an orange stain on the horizon—Rosebud, if he was reading the maps right. Maybe he should risk going farther north? Occasionally he regretted the necessity of medicating his companion; it would have been nice to have the soldier read the map and verify one or two small things. Christ, all Johnson wanted was to get to Boise. He hadn't had a hot meal since Duluth.

To make it worse, the subject splashed gasoline each time he refueled the truck, and the smell was making Johnson light-headed, even with the windows down. The smoke riding the wind scratched at his eyes and throat; even the subject had developed a hacking cough.

Maybe that was why Johnson didn't spot the checkpoint until they were almost on it.

It was a shoddy little affair, but then, you didn't have to do much to choke off a lonely two-and-a-half-lane Montana road. Just plonk down a couple of scavenged, rusted carcasses that had once been trucks like the one Johnson drove, add a rough crossbar of splintered, weathered fence posts lashed together with barbed wire, more reels and rolls of the wire tangling off to either side. The road funneled inexorably toward it, old-style guardrails on either side, and Johnson hit the brakes a little too hard. The subject, held back by a mere lapbelt, folded in half, and woke from his daze with a strangled sound. His hair flopped, dark with oil and grime—really, you'd think a Patriot would be more fastidious.

Everything still might have been all right, if not for the pothole. The front left tire dropped in with a sickening *crack*, and the pop of the threadbare tire blowing was just the thing to set off itchy trigger fingers. The truck, which until then had performed with many groans but unflinching readiness, jolted; the doctor, confused, jammed his foot all the way down, stiffening and pressing back into the bench seat. His hands jerked, a completely instinctive action, and the moment of weightlessness as the back end lifted gracefully was strangely gentle.

It was the habit of not wearing a seatbelt, married to the wrenching of the wheel, that crumpled Dr. Johnson and flung him halfway through the musically shattered windshield. His companion felt the forward jerk, then gravity and sky changed places. Crunching, more rattling, a great painless blow in the middle of Johnson's belly, and when the men at the checkpoint approached with guns drawn, they found a one-handed blond man with a cut on his forehead grinning and tugging at the mangled lower half of the driver's corpse, freeing a travel belt that held no greenbacks or Federal writs. It was a pity; they could have used them.

The small black jumpdrive was already stashed in Eugene Thomas's fatigue pocket, and he let the men pull him from the wrecked, hot remains of the truck, gasoline pouring from its ruptured tank. They even thought he was brave, because once he shook the dizziness out of his head, he kept running back to the wreck despite the risk of fire. They thought he was heroically trying to rescue a comrade. It took at least a half hour for Gene to realize they weren't Federals or reservists manning a DMZ checkpoint, but Patriots intent on fleecing fleeing refugees for every spare valuable they could, and when he did, his grin widened to nothing short of maniacal.

Johnson, almost severed at the waist, had bled out in seconds, but Gene had found where the man stashed the narcotics.

And he was, after all the struggling, among friends again.

CHAPTER SIXTY-ONE

INSIDE THE RIDE

August 1, '98

Swann gave the okay for Ngombe to bring the sled to the grassy, neglected swath of what had been the farmhouse's front yard. It took the rest of the day and half the night to shake the place fully, going over each inch. Finally, Swann decided they weren't going to get any more blood from the turnip, and they gathered inside the sled's air-conditioning.

"I ain't opening that shit." Chuck set his jaw, rubbing at his injured leg. "Nuh-uh."

"I don't think we have to." Zampana tapped the lid just to see him flinch. "A 3-D'll do 'er."

"Casper's closest," Hendrickson told Swann. "They have the resources."

Spooky chewed on her right index finger, working at a nail that, despite all her efforts, still showed a sliver of white. Her canine, with the funny groove near the tip just like her sister's, was the perfect tooth to shave with, and she kept at it, staring at the spiderlike piece of meat and bone floating in the jar's cold chemical embrace. Scanning it with a 3-D would indeed work; the only problem was, there wasn't one aboard the prototype. It had *everything* else, and that was, she mused, just the way things went. If you needed a knife, all you'd find were sporks.

Sal was only mildly upset that they hadn't found a body. "All this fucker's family were dead before the war. And he's going *west*, for fucksake."

"The DMZ's sewn up tight. He's got to have a contact." Simmons, buckled in though they were still on the ground, stared at the hand like he'd seen it twitch.

"Sure, we can get to Casper." Ngombe nodded, thoughtful and solemn for once. "It's right at the edge, though. We'll need a charge there."

"Get on the bouncer and tell them to expect us." Swann pointed at Hendrickson. "Get us in the air and headed there, Ngombe. Sal, Pana, get everything buckled down. Chuck?"

"Yessir?"

"Get on Minjae's deck, paw around, see what you can find on that paper the asshole left. If you ain't got nothin' in an hour, I want Johnny Fed to try. Spook, move over next to him, work your fuckin' magic. Talk to the goddamn hand if you gotta. Simmons!"

"I'm right here; y'all don't have to shout."

"Yeah, just want to make sure the wax ain't filled your ears. Weapons check, my nose is twitchin'. List everything we got."

"And my swinging cod?" The Reaper hit the release on his harness, with only a token hesitation.

Swann snorted. "If you gotta," he repeated.

The sled rattled as Ngombe began the prelift sequence, the hatch closing with its eerie slow hiss. "You expecting trouble, Captain?" Bright and chirpy, like she was asking if there was a good restaurant in town.

"Pays to be prepared." He mashed the new hat more firmly on his stubbled head. "If'n *I* were the Russians, I wouldn't sit and wait for Dr. Zed to come to me. I'd send someone to *fetch* him, and if that someone's heading for the ping same as we are, well."

"Think he'll ping again?"

Spooky stood, dreamily, slow. She scooped up the jar and headed for the seat next to Chuck's; he shook his head, dreads bouncing. "Don't let that motherfucker touch me, woman."

Her grin, pale and tense, was surprisingly mischievous instead of pained. "Not even the jar?"

"That's the other thing," Swann said grimly, still mashing at his hat. "If *I* was him, I'd move and ping, then double back. We may be chasing this fucker all over the continent. Or a ghost trigger, like we used to do."

"Playing tag with the Firsters." Zampana pushed Spooky's shoulders. "Sit down and buckle in, *chica*. Chuck, how that doin'?" A short jab at his leg.

The Dogg smacked at his thigh, a light glancing blow. "Itches like a motherfuck."

"Soon's we're up and level I'll take a look at it." Pana headed for the med cabinet, and Spooky buckled herself in, the jar clasped firmly between her knees.

"Great." Chuck dropped the sheaf of papers in Spooky's lap; she darted him a venomous glance, struggling to get them all together. "Just hide that shit, okay? I don't like it."

For once, she had an easy response. "I'll put it in your sleeping bag."

Pana's laugh, a bright little cackle, bounced off the sled's interior. Even Simms smiled.

"Bitch, *please*." Chuck shook his head, nascent dreadlocks bouncing. "You don't want to know what I'll put in yours. Do your thing. What those numbers for?"

Spooky bent her head over the papers full of their quarry's blue-ink scrawls.

The prototype hummed, rattled a little, and began to lift. "Keep yo' hands and feet inside the ride, chillun," Ngombe crowed, and Swann groped into a jumpseat, his forehead damp. Sal, already buckled in tight, opened his mouth to say something—and closed it, his gaze catching on the captain's hat.

Swann, God knows where, had found a feather.

It was black.

CHAPTER SIXTY-TWO

THANK YOU AND A CITATION

August 2, '98

Sunrise was a raw red blister behind the mountains, and even inside the sled's filtered atmo there was a tang of smoke. Sleds were slower than helicopters, slower even than prop planes or drones. Short bursts of speed were all right, but fast flying ate up the charge like a mofo. They made up for it with robustness, and fuel costs were minimal, but the flight time was a shitpile of passenger boredom.

Out of habit, Kelly Ngombe flicked the specters. You didn't really need 'em over an ass-empty slice of Montana, but they were fun to play with, and like Nana Bona always said, squinting into the sagebrush distance, every once in a while you had to shake things to see what would fall out.

In the copilot seat, the Johnny Fed with his greasy black hairdo glanced at the stat screen. "Neat, isn't it. Never thought I'd see one of these in the air."

"They was workin' on it the whole war, they said." She frowned at the round spec screen. It wasn't lighting up like it should. Her right-side ribs hurt a little, old injuries acting up. "Still got kinks to work out."

"Doesn't everything?" He had an easy smile, that white boy, and didn't seem to mind the way the raiders treated him—like he was a booger, or a splinter under a nail. Which could mean he was an asshole just waiting to show it, or that he was eyes and ears for someone they didn't give much of a shit for.

Ngombe still hadn't made up her mind which it was, but it didn't matter. She was right where she wanted to be. Flying. Except the damn specters were making her uneasy. "Yo. Dial up your specter, willya?"

"Yes ma'am." They'd been up awhile, and the Chuck guy was still staring at the laptop, determined not to let the Fed have a crack at it. So far, Swann hadn't said anything, but sure as shit he'd noticed, Kelly thought.

He didn't seem the type to miss much. He and Bona both had the same expression: sour and watchful, smarter than the average bear but unwilling to let it show. Quiet and steady was what you looked for in a raider leader.

Oh, some would follow a flamboyant motherfucker, like McCall and his Harpies, or that creepy-ass Madam Gulpa in Florida with her voodoo and her habit of sending water moccasins in boxes to the local Firsters. That sort of shit was funny as fuck, but it also got you sloppy, and sloppy got you killed.

"Shit." The Fed tapped at his round specter screen with one blunt, dirty fingertip. "That's..." Back in the sled's quiet cavern, Spooky flinched, her dark eyes flying wide open and her legs stiffening like she wanted to push herself back through the seat *and* the wall as well.

Ngombe needed only Hendrickson's first syllable to confirm what she was seeing. *"Incoming!"* she yelled, and everyone who wasn't mainlining adrenaline yet got there in a hot half-second. She had no time to wonder if they heard her or were strapped down, because tracers stitched in an arc ahead of her and she had to pull up, sharply, the prototype whirring and rattling as it took vertical strain. The cells whined in their sockets; Kelly tasted iron and salt and the brass-licking chill of *Hooo boy we might gonna die tonight,* sunset flashing across glass coated with UV and break-resistant tapfilm. This was when you found out if the tube of steel and plastic and thrust and lift you were in really liked you, or if she'd just been playing along.

The prototype hummed under Kelly's hands, tracers splashing too wide, gyro control and cloaking systems coming online like they were designed to. Easy-peasy, if the bastard in the seat to her right had any sense. "What we got, what we got?" What a time to find out if your copilot had his head screwed on straight. Lord.

"Fuckit, propseekers!" Johnny Fed barked, and he already had the popfusers online. "Prepping, prepping, ready!"

"Engage." The world shrank to a single point—left hand on the yoke, fingers tight but not *too* tight, right hand snapping sideways to punch subsidiary control over to the Fed, since maybe he could handle it—and paradoxically expanded, horizon and ceiling distant smears, *down* becoming any way her feet were pointing. "Hot loaded, put it in the bucket, amen!"

"Amen," he echoed, and there was a yell from the back as the sled jerked aside, Kelly sensing more than seeing the pop-flare of a heat-seeking missile. Old ordnance, and not a problem for *this* baby, oh no, but there were newer ones locking onto the sled's propulsion stream. Johnny Fed already had the countermeasures live, readouts flashing as one cell dropped to 30 percent capacity. *Shit.* Blown fuse? Cracked casing?

Who the fuck cared, when they was still shootin' at you? Jacking emergency power, the buffering under the cells taking a beating as propseekers detonated a critical distance too short, caught in an electromagnetic net. The specter showed a blurred profile, zipping little bumblebees jolting up and down underneath the prototype. She veered again, to the left this time, and they fell away in the backwash.

The stupid motherfuckers were on the *ground*, shooting at her. "Oh hell no." She bit down, her tongue poking where her missing canine should be. On the *ground*.

Comms were lit up like a Christmas tree. She had to jag the sled aside again, *hard*, avoiding another streak of tracers coming from the wrong direction. "What the *fuck*?" she screamed.

"—Cobra One," Johnny Fed repeated into his headset. "This is *Cobra One* out of Grafton, Federal Armed Forces, we are friendly, repeat, we are friendly!"

"Not to us you ain't!" Crackle-squealing, the funny blur-static that meant jammers. "Got us a chickenshoot, motherfuckers!"

The Fed popped over one channel, to the backup bounce instead of radio. "This is Cobra One out of Grafton, FAS. They're jamming other channels. We are friendly, repeat, we are friendly."

"Well thank fucking God," came the answer, crystal clear. The other sled, not quite as rakish as the prototype and bristling with armament, dropped down to parallel them, its underside glow a furious pink instead of blue. "This is Juliet Niner out of Malmstrom, what the *fuck* are you doing?"

"Heading to Casper, getting shot at."

"You loaded?" The shadow of the other sled pilot behind tapfilmed glass moved.

Johnny Fed didn't wait for Kelly's nod. "Yessir, we are."

"Good. Come about with me, bearing—" A long string of numbers. "We gonna drop down and erase those Firster motherfuckers. Been chasing them for two days now."

Kelly added the coordinates to the bucket in her head, but she didn't change course.

Not yet.

"Firsters?" The Fed sounded baffled, but only a little.

"Yeah, comin' south, for fucksake. You comin'?"

"Hold on that." Johnny Fed glanced at Kelly, who shrugged.

Nothing else coming up on the specter, so they could peel off and head to Casper instead. "Captain?" she called over her shoulder. "We got time to kill a few fuckers?"

"Man, I like this girl." Simmons pried one of his big hands loose of his armrests to wipe at his forehead. Chuck, his leg still stretched out, was sweating too; between them, Spooky was a tiny big-eyed bookmark.

Swann, tangled in a seat harness and jolted rudely out of the first good sleep he'd had in days—mostly courtesy of exhaustion—swore viciously. "What the fuck?"

"Feds. Waitin' on a reply, Cap." The Fed's fingers were already dancing, prepping and loading in case Swann said yes.

"We got enough charge?" Swann wanted to know.

"Yeah." It would be close, really, but Kelly wanted to see what this baby could do. "Pop back, blow the shit out of 'em, get a thank-you and a citation."

"All right." Swann coughed, rackingly. "What you need us to do?"

"Not a goddamn thing 'cept sit tight." Kelly toggled her own mic. "Juliet Niner, this is Cobra One. We hear you. Coming about; let's light it up."

Spooky, clutching at the jar, pushed her shoulder as hard into Chuck's as she could, and squeezed her eyes closed.

CHAPTER SIXTY-THREE

SOMEONE ELSE'S BAD LUCK

They did have to glide the last half hour into Casper, but the Malmstrom boys had called ahead, so they were cleared for immediate come-down-and-shut-down. Hendrickson sagged and rubbed at his face once the charging cables were attached and Ngombe stretched, unbuckling. His eyes were grainy-hot. It was a different thing, to pop midgrade cannos from a sled and feel the explosions juddering below. The other pilot told him the motherfuckers had come over from northern Idaho. Now that the war was done, it was the Firsters who were the raiders, and the Federals bombing the shit out of small bands possessing insufficient support, ammo, and weapons.

Shoe on the other foot, and all that. If he wasn't so goddamn tired, Matt Hendrickson'd be savagely triumphant. How did the motherfuckers like it now?

"I ain't gettin' back on this fuckin' thing until I get some real sleep," Simmons announced. "And Chuck ain't either."

"Yeah, well, it'll take a while to charge this motherfucker." Swann stood at the hatch, gesturing them out. Heavy, silky, soaked evening air pushed into the sled. "Don't get into any fucking trouble, all right? Be back at 0600."

"Yassir."

Next off was Sal. "I'll keep an eye on them," the Greek said, yawning. "Be nice to sleep on something horizontal."

"Grab some food that ain't paste," Swann told him. "I'm gettin' tired of ration bars."

"Aye aye." The black-haired man made it heavily down the surprisingly strong iron steps and caught up easily with the other two, Chuck's crutch beating an exhausted tattoo on tarmac.

Zampana laid the back of her hand against Spooky's forehead, wrinkling her nose at the jar and its pale, distorted occupant. "You gonna sleep with that thing, Spook?"

"No." Spooky's skinny throat worked once or twice. "Gonna go with *him* to the 3-D." Her chin jerked in Hendrickson's direction.

"You not a bad copilot, man." Ngombe clapped him on the shoulder, a good-natured, bruising punch, as she slid out of the cockpit. "Don't have to tell you what to do."

"No ma'am," Hendrickson mumbled. All he wanted was sleep, on a bed that wasn't moving. And yes, something to eat that wasn't a ration bar. The only thing stopping him from sleeping in this goddamn seat were those dual prospects, and the fact that he had to piss like a racehorse.

"Good work." Swann, warm and approving, shook her slim dark hand. "*Good* fucking work, raider. Be back at 0600."

"Yassir." A gap-toothed smile, a bounce up on her toes, and she rocketed out of the hatch, already whistling.

"Good God," Spooky said softly. "She's intense."

It was so unlike her a laugh came out sideways, taking Hendrickson by surprise. He hauled himself upright, almost clocking his aching head on an overhanging shelf of equipment, and eased, one joint at a time, out of the cockpit. Maybe they had hot water here. A bath would be nice. When was the last time he'd done anything other than grab an insufficient, tepid shower?

Career prospects or not, he hated this fucking job.

But Swann stood right in the middle of the sled, blocking his path. "You did a helluva job there, Matt. It's Matthew, ain't it?"

"Yessir." And Simmons, that asshole, would probably find a way to mock it. *Johnny Fed* was just fine, for fucksake.

"Matthew," Spooky said dreamily, stretching one arm, then the other. "He's tired."

"We all are. You got another hour left in you, son? Spook here wants her goddamn pet 3-D'd, and you're the one with the paperwork."

Spooky pushed herself up. She didn't look ready to start yarking again, which was good. Hendrickson was getting around to thinking she didn't need any looking after, X-Ray or not. "I want to know," she said, and peered up into his face. "Please?"

Shit. What could he say to that? Orders were orders. "Sure." Why the fuck not? He was only ready to fall over from exhaustion, he'd only just almost gotten shot out of the sky again, he was only the odd man out in their tight little group. All Ngombe had to say was *I was a raider*, and they fell all over themselves making her feel right-at-fucking-home.

But not him. Even Kellogg's Kickers hadn't been this insular. Spooky didn't move, looking up at him like he hadn't already agreed.

"I gotta go brief on those fucking Firsters." Swann patted Hendrickson's shoulder, much more gently than was his wont. "Just get the damn thing dropped off and catch some rest. I want you two back here at 0630, all right? Take the extra half hour and get some hot chow, a good shower, and whatever else you need."

All Matt needed was sleep. He nodded, rubbed at his eyes again, and wished he could step sideways to get away from Spooky. She cradled that goddamn jar like a baby. "It's all right," she said. "You made it."

Whatever the fuck that meant. He decided asking would be stupid. "Let's go find the 3-D so I can get some sleep."

Evening had given way to a cool, hay- and smoke-scented night. Most of Casper proper was dark, holding only flickers of campfires and jury-rigged lanterns. The slices glimmering with electricity were given over to the military; the MPs at the edge of the airfield called for a jeep and tried not to stare at Spooky and her cargo. Having to stand in the heat and bullshit with obviously uncomfortable soldiers was almost a relief, especially since they didn't treat him like an encumbrance or a possible spy.

The ride to Intel was bumpy and swerving, the jeepster driving with a candy hanging half out of his mouth and keeping up a steady string of obscenities laced with *Pardon me, sir*s. After the sled ride, though, it was pretty tame, and they were pulling up to a repurposed brownstone almost before Hendrickson had a chance to get nauseated.

Inside, it was warm and bright and full of sleepy murmuring even at this hour. Chatter to be coded, decoded, and filed, flimsies arriving and hot-printed, coordination with civilian authorities to fine-tune, and as soon as Hendrickson's clearance was discovered he and Spooky were whisked to a long cluttered room stacked with equipment, including a clunky old 3-D scanner that took up an entire four-foot counter. The nervous tech private responsible for it, rousted out of bed and brought on the double, eyed Spooky's jar with some trepidation, but snapped a smart salute at Hendrickson and got to work.

"You can go," she told Matt, gazing at his cheek instead of into his eyes. "You're tired."

"I'm also curious," he half-lied, and immediately regretted it. She could probably fucking tell.

"I've got a bad feeling." She kept staring as the tech calibrated the 3-D, its humming electric noise just high enough to raise all the fine hairs on a man's arms.

"Great." He watched the narrow-shouldered, tousle-haired tech visibly try to decide whether or not to open the jar and take the thing out to scan it, or try to aim the scanner past the glass. "Don't open that, we don't know what it's floating in."

"I wasn't *gonna*," the private returned, his mouth set in a tight line of distaste. Despite that, he knew his stuff. "It'll take about an hour if you want a fine enough scan to get fingerprints."

"We'll come back." Hendrickson glanced down at Spooky, who hadn't moved, still looking at his cheek. "You should get some sleep."

"So should you." She shook her head. "Go ahead. I'll wait."

"Fine." But he hesitated. "What kind of bad feeling, Spook?"

"Personal." She tried a smile, a thin, pale expression. "Don't worry. I can generally tell when it's someone else's bad luck."

He should have asked more. Any information X-Ray gave about the effects was to be passed along to higher-ups. At the same time…what had she said? *He's not gonna turn me in.*

Fuck it. His right eyelid had begun to twitch. "Fine. Don't get into any trouble, okay?"

She nodded assent, and it wasn't until he was outside that he realized he'd unconsciously imitated Swann.

CHAPTER SIXTY-FOUR

NO SPOOK FACTOR NEEDED

It took forty-five minutes to get the prints. Spooky propped herself in a corner and slid down to sit, her legs straight out and her head tilted comfortably. She watched her boot toes, scuffed leather broken in and dark with grease, dirt, oil. Filthy with gravel along the bottoms, too. They were still too big for her, but a double pair of thick socks, plus hard use, helped. Her eyelids dropped halfway; she watched the tech's legs move under the counter. He walked back and forth, his own kickers spit-shiny and a stain along one edge of his uniform trou cuff. Looked like mud. He'd probably get a Swann-size yelling from a CO during inspection.

Peacetime was a bitch.

She should have been able to nap. Raider sleep, soldier sleep, snatched wherever you found it. Her stomach still ached, her head full of an uncomfortable prickling. It wasn't the same feeling that drove her into the house at the burning camp to drag Prink out.

Poor Prink. Poor Minjae. Poor everyone.

No, this was different. This was the sludgy, dozing roll of train wheels inside her skull, thockety-rockety, the big drafty metal box used for hauling stock or merchandise stuffed to the brim with human cargo. The fraying pavement roads couldn't hold the kind of traffic rails could. Funny how transportation hadn't changed since they laid the iron down coast-to-coast. When you wanted to move a lot, it was the railroad.

Along with the rumble-rocking, the discomfort. A blowtorch in the stomach, thirst a red raging at the back of the throat, flesh and minds pressing through tissue-thin personal boundaries, the smell, dear God, the *smell*. On some of the early trains there were kids crying, until they figured out it did no good.

Later transports had no shortstacks. The young, the old, the weak, they went to the bottles and baths first.

Her burning, grainy eyes wouldn't close. She watched the tech's legs. Back and forth, checking the armatures and poking at the keyboard, watching the greenish, flickering screen and fine-tuning parameters. If she concentrated, she could *hear* what he was doing, what made the machine work, all his knowledge hers for the ride-along.

If it weren't for the nausea and the inside of her skull burning from being poured into someone else's head, it might even have been useful.

Why was she thinking about Gloria? She could still *see* it, whenever she blinked. Maybe she was still there, and everything else was a hallucination. Maybe she was still at Baylock, hallucinating after the fever, white-coated doctors and bustling well-fed staff moving among the bandaged scarecrows, hovering over her bed. The tests—*What card is this? What card is this?*

Stupid-simple, all you had to do was use their eyes to look at whatever painted plastic they were holding—and ignore how the distortion of looking through an alien mind turned your stomach inside out. It got easier the more you did it.

It was no use. Gloria returned, memory python-wrapping her. The roll-call yard, the stage built of raw lumber. No scaffold, like there at Baylock or the other camps—troublemakers went right into the killing bottles, thank you, goodnight. Jar kaptains leering, the struggle for a few extra calories turning them into monsters; regular kampogs looking down on the politicals; the man shot right next to her in the quarry whose brains splattered all over her shoulder and face and...

Survived. Made it out. Didn't matter. It was that day in the quarry, folding over her again and again, impossible to escape.

Straightening, her back a bar of pain from the lifting and hauling. The quarry was just a jumble of boulders and slightly smaller rocks, a pile at each end of a gluey sea of frozen mud. They were supposed to be paving it, but the overseers couldn't decide which end they wanted all the rocks piled at first. On some days it was the north end, others it was the south, and the only constant was that you had to haul at top speed. She'd worked her way to the edge, the battered red wheelbarrow with its half-flat tire zigging and zagging drunkenly. As soon as she arrived on the far end, she realized why she'd fixated on this one particular rock.

Suicide Alley was right there, the strip alongside the electrified fence. She could bolt, and if they didn't shoot her before she reached the beaten-flat dust, she could throw herself on the wire. A little zap, a little muscle firing, a lot of burn, and she could be done. Electrocution wasn't gentle, but at least the fence was quick. If she gripped it right, the muscle contractions would keep her there for long enough to overload her heart. Oh, they'd shoot her too, and the smell of roasting flesh would puff out in steam-smoke coils. Just two days ago—or was it three, time moved so strangely she couldn't decide—another kampog had taken that way out, gone almost as soon as he touched the wires. A collection of bones, jitter-dancing on the current.

The most sickening thing was that it smelled like any other meat. Pork roast, to be precise, and the mouth would begin to water before disgust crashed through every nerve.

Disgust couldn't stand up to the hunger. Some of the prisoners had rosy cheeks and imperceptibly shaking hands, pariahs who didn't mind the loneliness as long as they could get their teeth into flesh.

Any flesh at all.

Fear, rising from a slow simmer to a roiling boil. Stupid, coppery fear, adrenaline flooding her thin tired body again. All she had to do was take the first step. Then she'd be committed, and if they shot her, fine. It would hurt, but everything did. She could put up with it, as long as she knew it was going to end. Maybe, before the curtain fell, she'd feel the tickle and dreamy slowness of Lara's thoughts through her own head, hear their secret language given breath again, feel her sister's fingers in her hair. Gentle braiding, her own hands moving slightly as if she felt the strands.

Just one step. Move. Do it now.

Why didn't she? Why did she just stand there, straight and trembling? Why?

Her legs refused to work. Her idiot body simply refused. There was no reason to keep going, Lara was gone, her sister was dead and swinging from the walnut tree and there were no take-backs, no do-overs. She was utterly alone, even with the blaring sirens of other people's shouting brains splashing against her, a starfish's leg torn away from the body. Salt stinging along the wound, idiot cells growing and dividing, bodily processes going on with dumb plodding stubbornness.

No. Get moving.

Her legs wouldn't move. The longer she stood here, the more chance one of the jar kaptains would notice and stroll over with a sickstick to hurry her up, and there went her plans of a . . .

. . . dignified?

No. A relatively painless exit. It was too much, all of this was too much, she was stupid and weak. She was a coward. Had always been.

Even a coward could loathe herself enough to finally do something about it.

The wind picked up, cold and raw despite the thin sunshine, the frayed edges of the rag around her stubble-bristled head brushing her nape and forehead with tiny sweat-stiffened fingers. A black uniform oozed across her peripheral vision, and her right foot twitched.

Something inside her skull twitched, too.

The guard—tall, blond, pale blue eyes, a recruitment poster in impeccable black wool—turned his head. Stared at her. The twitching inside her brain intensified. Shoot me. Come on, shoot me.

He examined her, his right hand low at his hip where the pistol lurked. Habit hunched her over again, her rock-sore fingers curling around a chunk of stone. She lifted it, without a grunt—wasted energy, and she couldn't afford any of that.

Not if she was such a fucking coward she had to go on breathing. The chance was lost now. Frittered away, gone.

Spooky jerked into wakefulness, her right hand digging for her sidearm. The private wisely froze behind the counter. "It's ready," he repeated. "Easy there, ma'am. Easy."

She licked cracked lips, shook out her hands. Her ass was numb, and her legs would hurt once she hauled herself up. "Okay." A dead husk of a word. Her mouth tasted like Gloria mud.

"You were dreaming." He had both hands up, palms out. "Okay?"

"Yeah." She very carefully took her hand away from the gun. "Sorry." She began working her way up to standing, wincing as her legs reminded her nerve compression was *not* happy, and they could just as easily refuse to carry her, thank you very much.

His shrug said *Don't worry about it*, but the faint gleam of sweat on his forehead said *Shit, that was close, trigger-happy raiders, goddammit*.

"I got the prints isolated and packeted to CentInt." Sheepishly, he lowered his hands. He'd taken his jacket off, and his undershirt was wilting fast. "They told me it'd take a little while to run, even with Priority One."

"Okay."

"You should maybe get some sleep?" Tentative. *So you don't shoot someone,* his expression shouted. No spook factor needed to decode *that*.

"Yeah."

"Want me to call someone?" A simple, decent human kindness. Out here, they could afford it.

After Gloria, could she? "No."

In the end, she went back to the landing pad and thumbed the lock for the prototype's hatch. Climbing inside, she stretched out on the metal grating floor, her head pillowed on Minjae's empty laptop case, and fell, finally, into mercifully dream-free blackness.

CHAPTER SIXTY-FIVE

GOOD NEWS, BAD NEWS

August 3, '98

"We have winners!" Hendrickson, flimsy sheets flopping in his hands, thumped down on the cafeteria bench next to Swann, who blinked over the rim of a zinc coffee mug and tried not to choke.

Simmons, across the table, bent over a mound of eggs and bacon. Real eggs, real bacon, and he was consuming a small mountain of each, his clean damp hair slicked down. Sal had a stack of pancakes roughly the size of manhole covers, his unoiled curls flopping as they dried, and Zampana had contented herself with scrambled eggs and a stack of the same gigantic flapjacks, drenched in syrup for her sweet tooth. Ngombe, shoveling down buttered oatmeal in a truly prodigious quantity, reached for a saltshaker with the quick, darting speed of a ferret. Between her and Zampana, Spooky picked at a smaller bowl of oatmeal, hunching a little guiltily and spooning up more whenever Pana glanced at or elbowed her.

Swann swallowed half-aspirated coffee, cleared his throat, and wished his nose wasn't stinging so badly. "You get some chow?"

"Gonna. Got possibles on the prints from some half-wormed kamp system shit. Also got some good news." Hendrickson, showered and shaved, looked altogether too energetic for the amount of rest he'd probably had.

"Eat first." Swann made a grab for the flimsies.

Hendrickson surrendered them willingly. "I *will*, in a second. The hand's got a couple pings from the kamp system—they finally have most of it batched up. But the really good news is those numbers."

"Numbers."

"The pad near the radio? I looked at them for a little while, went to sleep, and when I woke up they made sense." Hendrickson outright *beamed*. "They're coordinates and place-names, along with code words, a whole fucking dictionary. I req'd another laptop and did some crunching. The safehouses—they're mapped out. And that's not even the *best* news."

"Jesus." Simmons paused just long enough to pour something from his flask into his own coffee mug. "You're a wonder boy, you know that?"

"Damn *straight*." Nothing could bring the Fed down this morning. "Swann, sir, I know where the motherfucker's going. CentCom's gonna be *so fucking pleased* with you."

Swann's graying eyebrows rose. "With me?"

"Yeah, well, you can break it to them. I didn't want to ping without getting your thumb on it." Hendrickson bounced upright, knocking his knee against the table. "Ouch. Anyway, I've got the safehouse locales mapped, and the laptop's working on timetables if he's in a gas-burner. I'll tell you the bad news when I get back."

"Great." Swann forked up more eggs. He would've preferred the bad news *first*, but the Fed was excited. Hendrickson swung away, heading for the steadily growing chow line, and the set of his shoulders shouted satisfaction.

"Huh." Simmons glanced at Pana. "That Henny, he's all right."

"Looks that way." Zampana's tone clearly said she was still undecided but willing to be convinced.

"I don't like him," Chuck muttered.

"You don't like anyone." Sal reached for the tin syrup jar.

"Come on, *chica*. You need the fiber." Zampana elbowed Spooky again. Of course the most dangerous time was right after you got out of camp; you could rupture your stomach, eat yourself to death. The second most dangerous was when the trauma started catching up.

Food wasn't always food. It could be comfort, safety, control; it was never just plain, simple nourishment.

When Hendrickson returned, the spot next to Swann was still open, and he was greeted by Simmons's crooked morning grin. The Reaper set his flask carefully on the table halfway between them, next to the white plastic saltshaker. "Want a little pick-me-up?"

"Don't mind if I do." The Fed sniffed the top before he poured a splash into his coffee mug, though, and returned the flask with a nod. "Okay, so the bad news is, remember those Firsters?"

Swann shoveled in a mouthful of real bacon, salt-crispy and loaded with fat. Jesus, it had been a long fucking time since he'd had something this good. "Which ones?"

"The most recent set. They caught a few of them jackrabbiting after we plowed their bikes under. Holding them at Malmstrom. They've been doing rolling roadblocks, you know, fleecing fugees. Possible they may have seen our good doctor or know more about the goddamn network moving him around. I told 'em to keep the mofos able to talk for us, if you want."

"That's bad news?"

"Well, it's all the way up at Malmstrom, and they may be a dead end. You never know."

"Huh." Swann thought this over.

Zampana elbowed Spooky again. "You need some bacon, too. Get some fat back on."

"Get some *mamacita* hips, eh?" Simmons stuffed a gigantic clump of egg into his mouth and grinned, jaws working furiously.

"Shut up, Reaper." Pana rolled her eyes. "Come on, Spook. Good stuff."

"I know," Spooky mumbled, staring into her bowl like it held a universal secret or something. "I know."

"What are the chances they saw our fellow?" Swann filled his mouth with too-strong boiled coffee. It was heavenly. He began to shuffle through the flimsies, scanning each and deciding which ones he should spend a little more time on.

"Fifty-fifty." Hendrickson began to apply himself to his plate, barely pausing to chew. "The route matches up."

"And where's he headed?"

"Boise."

"Boise." Past the DMZ. "Now that's…"

"Whole lotta shit in Idaho before the war," Sal said suddenly. "North in the panhandle. Fucking Nazis and Minutemen. Practically screamed to join the Firsters, the whole shitty lot of them."

Swann sucked in his cheeks. Took another deep draft of coffee. "So we got us a bunch of Firsters deciding to head to Seattle or some shit?"

"Alaska." Hendrickson started shoveling chow. "And we all know who's there."

"The fucking New Soviets kayaking across the strait. Why didn't this bastard go east?"

The Fed shook his head, washing down a barely chewed mouthful and grimacing slightly at the engine cleaner in his coffee. "What, right where all the Feds are checking everyone? It's kind of smart, actually. Head back to the DMZ, figure out a way across now that it's peacetime, and hop up to Alaska. Then the Russkies'll pay for what he's got."

"Pay him nine grams right in the back of the neck."

"Not necessarily. They'll need him to help sort and apply the data. He's got more in his head, probably. They'd want someone who worked on it to help them. And if it looks like the Russians'll get nasty, there's always the Chinese to sell to. Fuck, even Japan would take this, and offer some kind of immunity." Hendrickson sobered. "I send this in, CentComm'll want to do a gigantic fuckery-up all over the DMZ, and that'll muddy the waters. Part of why I held off."

"The Russians gonna get themselves some Spookies, huh?" Simmons made a face into his demolished pile of henfruit and pig. "Fuckers."

"Simmons, shut your fucking mouth." Swann didn't quite bang his fist on the table, but it was close.

Spooky's spoon settled in her bowl. She sat, staring at the oatmeal's lumpy gray. A thick pat of butter—*real* butter, not margarine, since the front lines had moved on and second echelon had plenty of time to get things rolling again here—had turned into an oily golden blob. A spot of sunshine on a lunar hellscape. There was dust on the moon, wasn't there? Thick and powdery, with no wind to stir it.

"Could you be any more of an asshole this morning?" Zampana's arm settled over Spooky's shoulders. "Come on, Spook. That's barely a quarter."

"I could." Simmons sucked in his cheeks again. "Sorry, Spooks. I don't mean it."

"I know," she replied numbly.

"Huh." Swann shuffled the flimsies again. "Not a lot of safehouses in the DMZ. Except that Helena one, right there, Christ, right near the base. And then fucking Idaho."

"Yeah. You wanna question the motherfuckers in Malmstrom? Two male, one female."

"It's right there, close." Swann thought about it. When he straightened slightly, it was only to reach for the saltshaker. "I think we can squeeze it in."

Spooky picked up her spoon again. Ngombe, on her other side, was barely restrained motion, moving to a beat inside her head, jittering like she'd overdosed on coffee already. She didn't care where they were going, as long as she was flying.

Steadily, Spooky dipped the anonymous stamped stainless steel spoon, lifted it to her mouth. The bad-luck feeling was still there, and the longer it went on, the more she wished she'd taken that step in the quarry. Just the first step.

Everything, *everything* would have been easier.

CHAPTER SIXTY-SIX

ALMOST SURE

The sled leveled off and Simmons quit white-knuckling his armrests; Spooky unbuckled and pulled her legs up on her seat. Hendrickson was now ensconced in the chair with the laptop station; he bit at his upper lip every once in a while, then his lower one, as he concentrated. Chuck, with Minjae's deck safe inside its glittered-up case and held on his lap, glowered in the Fed's general direction, but without the edge he might have had yesterday. His leg was better, though he still kept it stretched out and often scratched at his thigh, not daring to get at the bandage on his calf and risk Pana's ire. He even unbent enough to call the man Henny, and the Fed was wise enough not to object to the nickname.

Spooky peered over Hendrickson's shoulder, watching while he collated data and checked subprograms. Nobody quite *said* things would have gone easier if Chuck had given up the deckwork to the Fed, but then again, nobody needed to because it was *thought* loud enough to make for a low-level tension, a knot in a string of yarn that only the right angle of careful pressure would loosen.

Sal took the copilot seat because Zampana and Swann had their heads together, low mutters rising and falling as the sheaf of flimsies passed back and forth. Zampana didn't like the idea of splitting up, but then again, she *never* liked that idea. *I worry too fucking much about what stupid shit you'll do without me around,* she told him more than once.

But Swann was Swann, and he carried his point. Pana shrugged and spread her hands. Then they settled down to examining each sheet of flimsy, turning it around and upside down. Occasionally they called a question over to Henny, who blinked owlishly each time he was jolted out of digital space.

Spooky, her seat shifted forty-five degrees and locked, watched the screen blur and change over the blond soldier's shoulder. Her stomach was stretched full, warm, and she was sleepy now that the sled was moving. Her chin rested on her arm, her elbow against Hendrickson's nape, but he didn't complain. It was enough that they weren't calling him Johnny Fed anymore, maybe.

"What's that do?" she asked.

His answer was a bare mutter, all his attention elsewhere. "Got a batch of partials from CentInt. Running through them one by one, in case Malm has our targets waiting for us."

Spooky froze. She stared at the laptop screen. Her breath touched Hendrickson's hair. "Stop," she whispered.

"Yeah, those aren't our guy; they're tagged for—"

"Go back," she said. "Go *back*."

He did. She shook her head violently, almost hitting the back of his. "One more."

The picture was wormed, blank pixels irretrievably gone, just a fuzzy arc that might have been a cheekbone and the ghost of a flag in the upper left corner, a drape of fabric. Several fields were blanked, the data wormed right out. The name had remained, though, a few of the vitals, and in the right middle third of the screen, there it was.

K GLORIA REK/NRET.

"Spook?" Simmons, across the sled's central well, his blue eyes hooded and his fingers paling again on the armrests as he bore down. "What you got?"

"Nothing." Her tongue had turned to quarry dust, her throat furred with its dry grit. "Kamp fucker."

"Someone you know?" Chuck hugged Minjae's bag.

How could she answer that? You couldn't really know anyone, even if you could peer inside their skulls and finger the matrix of memory and weird symbols, shifting through assumptions by instinct. "Maybe."

"Well, that's our missing-a-hand bastard." Hendrickson maxed the window, studying what was left of a personnel record after worms had been at it. "E. Thomas. Hardcore Patriot, he's an R3. File's flagged, so there's more somewhere in the system. I can run down everything on him if you want, Spook. Don't know if he's one of the assholes held at Malm yet."

Her ears were full of rushing. Was this the bad luck? A shudder worked down her back, and the oatmeal threatened to crawl up from its warm, dark home and lunge for escape.

I love you...Wait for me. "Is he certified?"

"I was gonna check."

"Okay."

"What are the chances of him being our dude?" Simmons wanted to know.

"Pretty definite; we've got an eighty percent match on his digits. The only uncertainty is we're working off half-wormed shit here, but I can—"

"Track it down," Swann said over his shoulder. "If Spooky pinged it, run that motherfucker down."

"Amen to that," Zampana added. "So that's our hand boy?"

"Looks like it." Hendrickson began to tap the keyboard in earnest, halting every so often to work the touch-responsive screen. He very generously didn't point out that he'd found the fucker first. "Man, wouldn't that be something if he was waiting at Malm for us?"

Spooky couldn't move. She was close enough to smell the soap from Henny's morning shower, close enough to catch a faint breath of the booze in his coffee metabolizing out through pores. Close enough that the edge of his body heat touched hers. Her arms trembled, her legs seizing up.

It would be something. The shivers finally receded enough to let her drop a hand to her sidearm, the same one Zampana had organized before they left Gloria.

It wasn't him. It *couldn't* be him.

But if it was…well, Spooky decided, she was ready, and this time she could take that first step.

Her entire hand itched. Her fingertips caressed cool metal. She didn't have the strength for the full list. Not now, and maybe not ever. But she had enough in her guts to carry her through *this*.

The first act would be cleaning *him* up. The second would be cleaning herself.

CHAPTER SIXTY-SEVEN

WE FOUND OUT

Swann stood on the metal sled floor, though he'd prefer to be buckled. Better yet would be squatting, his group in a loose ring and a stick in his hand, jabbing at the dirt while he mapped out the run. "Pana. You take Spook and Sal, look around here, get the lay of the land." He squinted, one hand clutching overhead cargo netting and the other at his side, full of his new hat. "Chuck, you run the home office for them. Henny and Reaper come with me—we're gonna go up to Malm and take a look at those Firsters that fired on us t'other night. See what they can tell us."

"You ain't takin' Spook?" Chuck's hair was dreading up nicely, and his eyebrows almost vanished into the soft blur above his forehead.

Spooky, hunched behind Pana, didn't protest *or* look up. Instead, she stared at Henny's laptop screen, a random series of green loops running as the screensaver thought its electric thoughts.

Swann shook his head, mashing his hat down with a quick, impatient motion. "Nope. Malm's not that far away. Might take more than overnight, though, if the assholes are cagey."

The Reaper moved a little in his chair, a gentle swaying. "Won't be cagey for long," he muttered. Swann pretended not to hear.

"Strap in," Ngombe sang from the front. "We're coming up on Helena, chilluns. Sit down so I can land, willya?"

Everyone hopped to obey, with maybe a little more alacrity than was *strictly* necessary. Spooky didn't buckle in, despite Zampana's prodding; she just sat down and bent forward, her head on her knees like she was going to start heaving again. Hendrickson began shutting down the laptop, and the heavy tension in him had receded quite a bit. Sal, in the copilot's chair, closed his eyes, his Adam's apple jumping as the prototype bounced a bit.

It took an hour on the ground before Henny could get all the paperwork in place, and another two and a half before the prototype was at full charge again. Which left Zampana, Sal, Chuck, and Spooky on the landing pad late on a bright, warm afternoon, watching the sleek black sled rise gracefully and loop around the pad once before climbing arrow-swift, pointed north.

Zampana, her arm over Spook's shoulders, sighed heavily. "Ain't gonna end well."

Sal hitched Minjae's bag up higher on his shoulder, glancing up at Chuck. "Reaper's gotta let off some steam."

"Prolly gonna do it on the Fed." Chuck's frown wasn't quite as deep as usual, though.

"Nah, Henny's okay." Sal patted at his freshly oiled hair, making sure every strand was in place. "Tight up, though. Maybe gonna end up a Reaper Junior."

For some reason, Spooky found that funny. At least, she laughed, a thin, pale sound lost in the rattle-whine of another sled cycling up, the next slot over. Pana hugged her a little tighter, only letting go when Chuck started moving along the safe line, his crutch *thock*ing steady time.

Spooky sobered, but only partly. Nobody asked what she found so fucking amusing.

A tiny cube of a room, its walls thick with successive layers of industrial beige paint, the bed pushed against the wall and a soft lump in its depths under a scratchy Army-issue blanket.

"Pana?"

A slight stirring. Fingers curling around a hilt, the animal consciousness of another creature's breathing.

"Pana?"

For a moment between sleep and waking, she was a child again, at her grandmother's bedside in the middle of the night. Abuela, abuela, *Pana-pana*... Only now Zampana *was* her grandmother, because someone else was saying that name, a tiny little-girl whisper.

Pana-pana, wake up.

Zampana lunged into full consciousness, the knife jerked from underneath her pillow and her head full of the past.

It was Spooky, her shoulders and throat ghost-white, her undershirt straps dingy and loose. She hovered out of knife range, her eyes huge in the dimness, her hair a mop. "Pana," she whispered again. "Can I sleep here?"

"Dios mío." Zampana's throat had shrunk to a pinhole. She coughed and nodded, loosening enough to lie back down on the bed. It smelled like damp disuse in here, but at least they were billeted in base housing instead of a barracks. "Sure, *chica*. No—" She put out her free hand when Spooky squatted, obviously intending to stretch out on the floor. "Come on up. Plenty of room."

Spooky was taller than Minjae, and her hips were not nearly as round. It took a little rearranging before both of them—still with their boots on, with the unspoken accord of women who often have to sleep near groups of men—were snuggled up, Pana's head on Spooky's bony shoulder, the fine thin shivers going through Spooky easing when Pana settled the blanket with finicky care. The radiator bolted under the window groaned a little. Old-fashioned still worked, especially out here in Big Sky Country.

When Zampana had everything settled to her liking, and her hair padded enough of Spook's shoulder, she settled and took a deep breath. "Bad dreams?"

"Yeah." Spooky shivered again. Her thin arms hugged with surprising strength. "Sorry."

"Nah, we all got them." Pana sighed. "Lucky we're not outside; I might've shot you."

Spooky nodded. Her cheeks were wet. Pana's arm, stuck uncomfortably between them, warmed quickly. The older woman's breathing deepened. There was no use in asking. You learned not to, learned just to wait.

Whatever was going to crawl out of the cave of another person in the middle of the night took its own time.

"I had a sister," Spooky whispered.

"*Sí.*" Pana's eyes were closed, her lashes sooty arcs against her high cheekbones. Her throat moved again.

"She was the brave one, helping raiders in the woods." Spooky paused, forged ahead. "They caught her."

Pana nodded slightly, her hair rubbing Spooky's shoulder. She knew this song. "My *abuelita*. She was a labor organizer."

"I keep seeing her," Spooky whispered. "Hanging."

"*Sí.*" Zampana settled her hip a little more firmly. The mattress was thin, the springs were worn, but it was far better than the ground. "They shot her. Hung her body on a fence." Each word slow, precise. "She would say, '*I am old, what can they do to me?*'"

"She said she'd meet me," Spooky whispered. "That we would go together."

"'What can they do to me?'" Pana repeated. Parallel tracks, moving into the night, both of them carrying cargo on rickety wheels. "Well. We found out."

"I hate them. I want to kill them. All of them."

"Oh, *sí.*" Pana sagged wearily into the bed's embrace. "And when they all gone, what you gonna do?"

Spooky didn't reply. She didn't need to. The answer hung over them, an invisible weight. Finally, after a long while, Pana turned over and dropped off, the knife back under her pillow. The younger woman, settling on her right side, her arm folded under her head and her back cuddled against Pana's warmth, stared across the dim room at the cafeteria chair she'd wedged under the doorknob until her eyelids grew too heavy.

For the rest of that night, neither of them dreamed. Or if they did, they did not remember.

CHAPTER SIXTY-EIGHT

DEGENERATES

August 5, '98

Rattling down the other side of the Bitterroots in a whine-celled gleeson hybrid bus, Gene rested his aching forehead against the slick, gritty glass of a window painted black on the outside—a precaution against nighttime strafing, the color peeling and chipping now that the surrender was signed. The umbrous atmosphere, full of the swampy breathing and heaving of other passengers, settled in his throat and coated his skin with grease. Immies, traitorous Federal soldiers in their slouchy uniforms, women with crying, probably illegitimate children—it was a tube full of degenerates, and he was a lone particle trapped three-quarters of the way back. An anonymous, foreign object.

Getting through the DMZ checkpoints was easier than he'd dared to hope. The ID blanks Johnson had carried were high quality; the only problem was getting the proper-sized photograph. Fortunately, the Patriots who'd buried the doctor sent Gene along with the appropriate signs to the next stop on the pipeline, a shitty little shack on the outskirts of Ralston, a mere fifty klicks from Helena. Waiting for bus service was the worst, between his stock of vials diminishing and the lack of a door to close and lock when he shot another jolt of sweet oblivion into his veins. When he got to Helena, he thought he'd start cutting back, but the sudden press of so many people after so long on the road made his nerves ragged. So he made himself another bargain: he'd cut back when he got through the DMZ.

Here he was, and Gene was thinking he wasn't going to make it to Boise. The bus rattled and scraped along on indifferently dipped gleeson cells that needed tuning, gliding over potholes but jolting every time the driver pulled back on the throttle to cut speed going downhill. Back and forth on curves designed to turn your stomach inside out, the heavyset immie woman next to him stinking of eggs and grease and cumin-seed sweat, the noise jabbing through Gene's head, and his arms itching, itching, itching.

His seatmate snored unconcernedly. Her flat brown nose shone; her cheeks were thick and pockmarked. Gene closed his eyes, leaning as far away as he could from the immie's fat arm relaxed along the ancient shared armrest. Summoned up a picture of the girl in the pink room— thin, those big hazel eyes, her dark hair growing out, a little smile he'd never seen her wear but could imagine. Standing straight up in the quarry, chin raised, her gaze an electric jolt all the way down his spine and into his balls. The electricity pulling, nagging, demanding, pressing buttons he hadn't even known existed inside his own skull.

Was she still alive?

Even when he could stick the needle in, what came in the middle of the blissful smeared haze was the scent of her nape, under her damp hair. So many little presents brought to her—extra food, the pink soylon dress, arranging for the room so he didn't have to share. She wouldn't recognize him now, with his new face. His right hand, slack against his thigh, turned into a fist.

His vanished left hand ached, too. The pain was a constant.

He'd washed the doctor's travel belt, and it was secure around his own thinning waist. Nothing in it but scrounged Federal cash, vials of precious unconsciousness, and a thumbdrive. It probably wasn't worth plugging the latter into a machine, even if Gene had access to one. Whatever was on it could stay there; he'd get to Boise and vanish. Whoever the doctor was carrying it for was going to be disappointed; the motherfucker hadn't written down the final destination.

Probably wise of him. If Gene had found out, he would've killed the fucker himself and shown up to collect whatever payday was offered. If it was a good one, it could've bought more vials, or something similar.

One of the babies on board began to wail, a desultory, hungry sound. Gene's ears popped, air pressure thickening as they descended.

Four and a half more hours to Boise, not counting whatever stops on terrible mountain roads the silver bullet of a bus found it necessary to make.

Gene wasn't quite sure he'd last that long.

The bus station was a roar of hustle and bustle, announcements blatting; domestic air travel was still curtailed so land transport was doing booming business. Gene sat on a hard wooden bench, his skin twitching all over, and tried to concentrate. Late-afternoon sunshine pierced high windows, bars of throbbing gold gilding the ticket windows and worn linoleum scuffed by thousands of trudging feet. Every time he made up his mind to get up and head for the closest restroom, someone else would go in, or a cop in a tan uniform would stroll by, eyes roving. Or a Federal would go past, in camo green or taupe. Even women wore the uniform, ugly when you were used to decently dressed females. Some of the younger immies waiting for a bus wore short skirts in bright bird-colors, probably to air their worn-out coozes. It was a cesspit, and he itched, itched, itched.

Every time he closed his eyes, the insect feet ran all over him, and they were sharp. When the gold bars falling through the windows turned buttery and rose above the ticket windows, filling the old-fashioned arrivals-and-departures board with glare, he decided it wasn't going to get any less crowded and managed to get to his feet, staggering on pins-and-needles legs into the bathroom. It had a handicapped stall—how long had it been since he'd seen one of *those*? In the real Amerika, the cripples went into the baths instead of eating good food and wasting space the healthy could use.

It wasn't the same, he thought, bracing the vial between his legs, tilting it to get the sweet nectar inside near the syringe tip. Missing a hand was a combat wound, right? It wasn't like he'd been born lacking. He'd done his duty, served his country…

Getting the air tapped out was tricky, and each time he wondered if it was worth just letting whatever bubble there was slide through his system. A tiny little particle, just like him, ready to clot somewhere and blow out an important vessel. An embolism for the fucking degenerates.

Sitting on the paper-clogged toilet—they had real paper here, no shortages on this side of the Rockies—and finding a vein, he pressed the plunger down and realized, a little too late, that he'd drawn it from the uncut vial instead of—

Soft blackness. He collapsed sideways, and it was a half hour before anyone found him propped against the stall wall, uniform pants around his ankles and the needle still stuck in his bared arm, a crust of foam drying around his slack mouth.

CHAPTER SIXTY-NINE

SUSPICIOUSLY LIKE HOME

August 4, '98

Neither of the male Firsters was missing a hand. They'd been softened up a bit by the soldiers on duty, but sometimes it took a raider to get the full chowder-to-cashews.

The skinny rotten-toothed one swallowed his own severed fingertip, the other was a gibbering, pulped-down mess by the time Simmons was finished, and Henny was looking a little green. Still, the Fed played good cop tolerably well, and when Henny said *That's enough*, Simmons didn't protest at all. He just smiled, a rather slow, sleepy expression, and leaned in close to the second Firster, a grizzled heavyset man with swastikas tattooed on both biceps. "Better hope you made my old man happy," the Reaper crooned. "'Cause if you didn't, it ain't gonna be a finger *you* lose."

"Come on, now." Henny made a show of pulling Simmons away. "Let's get some coffee, give the gentlemen a rest."

"Oh yeah. Nine grams of rest." Simmons showed his teeth, and the door to the interrogation room shut behind them with a bang, leaving Fat Swastika shuddering and sweating, sagging against handcuffs in a chair bolted to concrete.

Swann was in the fluorescent-lit, pea-green hall, his hat jammed firmly on his head and its feather a little more bedraggled than it had been. "Tell me you got something good."

"What?" Simmons stretched, sweat showing in half-moons under his long golden-haired arms. Muscle flickered; he had stripped down to his yellowed undershirt. "We got what we got."

"Let *me* guess." Henny, just as warm but considerably more dressed, scratched at his cheek with blunt fingertips. "That rear-echelon bastard who tried to keep us out is making noises."

"Careful, you're sounding like a raider." Simmons elbowed him, but not nearly as hard as he could have.

"Well, don't you get a prize." Swann's mouth turned down. "I think the finger sent him over the edge."

"I'll take care of it." Henny sighed. "No good news, I'm afraid. You want to tell him?"

"Nah, you go ahead. I want some water." Simmons set off for the end of the hall. There was a pisser on the other side of the bars and the bored sentry on duty. Simmons rarely missed a chance to wash up.

"The woman knows more than she's telling." Henny folded his arms, his mouth turned tight and unhappy. "Pretty sure it's nothing we need, though."

"Let *me* guess. Simms was a gentleman."

Henny made a wry little motion. "Yeah, well, he said you bitched at him last time he hit a girl. Okay, so they were running roadblocks to fleece the fugees, right? None of their group was missing a hand, but get this. Few days ago, a truck—a real old bastard of a gas-burner—almost ran down the roadblock. Swerved like a motherfuck and dropped into a pot-hole, and the driver took a header through the windshield. Splattered up *real* good. The passenger was a guy with—you ready for this? One hand."

"Shit," Swann breathed.

"Yeah. Gets better. One-Hand kept going back to the truck to get stuff. They thought he was loopy, trying to drag a komrade out. He vanished after a night in their shithole base a few klicks up the road; both of these fucks assume he was sent on down the pipeline because he was real Pa-triot material. They buried the driver, neither of them can remember just what mile marker."

"Shit." Swann closed his eyes for a moment. "Mother*fuck*."

"Amen." Henny rubbed at his face, scrubbing with salt-slick palms.

"You want to take one of them with us? I'd bring the skinny one; Fatso there is a much tougher nut to crack."

"And yet it's the skinny asshole who had to lose a fucking finger."

"Well, Simmons didn't have his *big* knife, he said. I'll go to this local general—what's his name?"

"Bretagne." And a stick-up-the-ass little French martinet that asshole must have been in another life, Swann thought grimly. His back hurt, and the hall smelled like burned baked beans and the sour sweat of men in pain.

"General Bretagne." Hendrickson nodded, rubbing at the back of his neck. "Wave the authorization in front of him. Smooth the ruffled feathers."

That was good news. "Worth your weight, Henny."

"I fucking well hope so." The Fed scratched at the side of his neck with blunt fingertips. "So, do you want to bring one of them?"

If Spooky were along, she'd have the location of the grave too, no need to drag extra weight along. How soon he'd gotten used to that sort of thing.

There was a lesson in that, Swann thought. You could get used to pretty much anything in wartime. Maybe peace wasn't any fucking different. There was just Before, civilian shit dogging you, and During. *After* was a lie. "Do we have to?"

"Prototype probably got a couple scans we can run to find disturbed dirt and something rotting. We know the general area, and they buried him next to the road. Gave him a cross and everything."

"What are the odds One-Hand's got the data?"

"Pretty damn good, if he knew what the doctor was carrying."

"Shiiiiiiiiit." Swann dragged the single syllable out, giving himself time to consider the situation. "Suppose we go scavenging at the shithole they were using for a base."

"Our boys burned it. Clean sweep."

"*Fuck.*" This was getting to be a real headache.

Henny looked like he had one, too. "I can go back and press the girl if you want."

"Nah. Just get Bretagne off his fucking fainting couch." Swann touched his hat brim, and from down the hall, he heard Simmons curse good-naturedly at the guard, who replied in kind. A barracks song, and one Swann could have sung with his eyes shut.

It was getting to where it felt suspiciously like home.

CHAPTER SEVENTY

IT'S PROTECTION

August 6, '98

The cameras didn't whir anymore, being digital, but enough of them massed in one place caused an electric susurration, almost audible. Leavy, standing at ease, stared across the crowd of journalists, waiting. Questions yelled in every accent, mostly from pirate outlets wearing badges, but a few resurrected big boys—CNN, KNAR, PBC—with ancient equipment jostling for a place. The good spots were taken by the proudly refractory—*Ma Jones*, the *National*, and that thorn in the Patriots' sides, *TeeVog*. It was strange to see them in the front of the crowd instead of in the shame-pen off to the side, spat on and screamed at by good Patriots whipped into a McCoombs-rally frenzy.

What's your reaction to the verdict?

Pride, the interim President said, unblinking. The military court had done a difficult job, and done it well.

No drones in here, not even the minis that would capture shots from near the ceiling. Some of the smaller networkers had headcams, live-feeding out in real time. It was going to be a golden age for access, the new administration bending over backward to prove it was different, better, a return to the good old days of media freedom and scrutiny.

What about the other trials?

Well, they would have to wait their turn.

Leavy was fucking glad he wasn't under the glare of flashes popping and round black camera eyes drinking you in. His foot itched, but he didn't move. Stone-faced, he stared at the back of Kallbrunner's head. Thinning gray hair over an eggshell-fragile dome, the old man's ears looking as cauliflowered as an old boxer's.

What is *the medical condition of the accused?*

He was getting the best of health care. The President didn't add that it was more than his victims had ever received.

It was Bauer from *Ma Jones* who asked what everyone was thinking. "Sir, there are several charges in international court. Will McCoombs be extradited?"

Kallbrunner, straight and natty in a dark wool suit, his tie good old Marine blue and his face filled out a little since rationing was being eased, looked as if he'd expected the question. "Well, son—Bauer, is it? Well, Bauer, I have to tell you, America is part of the international community, and has responsibilities. Mr. McCoombs has to pay for what he's done."

Leavy's back prickled with gooseflesh. He'd been goddamn certain Kallbrunner intended to put the pillow over that motherfucker's face and press down. So had McCoombs, for that matter, and the sheer abject terror had distorted the asshole's already messed-up face.

It was one thing to kill a man in combat. It was another to murder him in his bed.

Strangely enough, the thing Patrick Leavy had thought of that evening was his mother, standing in a clean yellow kitchen, her house shoes whisking over daily-scrubbed, worn linoleum and her mouth set in that particular way that meant she'd measured someone and found them wanting. *Patrick, I'm gonna tell you,* she'd said one day. *Some people just need killin'.*

When Kallbrunner let the pillow drop, dangling pendulous from one liver-spotted hand, McCoombs gurgled frantically, the faint steel-clad smile touching Kallbrunner's face enough to make a man's eggs crawl up into his body for safekeeping. *That's what I thought,* Kallbrunner had said. *You're yella, and you always have been, you son of a bitch.*

Leavy couldn't make up his mind whether he was relieved or faintly disappointed the old man hadn't solved the problem right then and there. He stood, stolid, under the flashing lights and other shouted questions: yes, the elections would proceed as scheduled; no, the uncertified would *not* be able to vote in them; yes, certification was proceeding; no, there was no truth to the rumors that Firsters were being hunted by extrajudicial teams.

The last was from the rail-thin, chain-smoking bitch from the *National*, the one with dyed-black scraped-back hair who had been in a camp or two, each time barely escaping after severe diplomatic pressure was applied. Canada, in particular, loved that particular loudmouth. Kallbrunner called on her, probably, to show he wasn't fucking afraid of the press any more than he had been of McCoombs.

"Sir." Her nasal voice carried without even trying, piercing the shuffle. "What about the victims of genetic experimentation being quarantined?"

Kallbrunner didn't even blink. "They're being given the best of health care, too. It's not a quarantine—it's *protection*. For victims of the Mc-Coombs regime."

Leavy swallowed a heavy, bitter taste. Kallbrunner thanked the press kindly for their time, and when he left the podium Leavy followed, trying to ignore the popping flashes and the shouting, heaving scrum.

CHAPTER SEVENTY-ONE

NADA, NADA

Breakfast time in the Helena base caf was full of shouts, horseplay, and the flat-edged reek of boiled-tar coffee. All normal, all usual, but Zampana was still uneasy. She kept touching the small lump right over her breastbone, her grandmother's crucifix tucked under her shirt and kept safe. The pancakes were just as good as in Casper, but there was a shortage of bacon. Good-natured grumbling at the lack went around each table like clockwork, as if there hadn't been rationing just a few short months before.

Sal was dumping syrup into his oatmeal, alternating bites of sweetened goop with buttered pancakes. Why the fool didn't put the syrup on the flapjacks like God intended was beyond her.

Spooky had vanished into the showers, since they were likely to be empty while everyone was eating. After seeing the killing bottles, Pana didn't blame her, but she also suspected the girl was avoiding food, and that was a troubling sign.

The raiders chose, by unspoken accord, one of the few tables with chairs instead of benches. Pana could see one entrance, and the boys the other. Just as usual, again.

On the other side of the table, Chuck Dogg tensed, and so did Sal. Zampana had to wait for the half-glassed door to their backs to swing closed before she could catch the reflection of two straight-edge Feds, one dark and one fair, both with the same haircut. The female was tall and willowy, her face set in the disgust of an attractive woman used to assholes seeing only her looks; the male, blond and squat, just needed a cigar chomped in his teeth to be a cliché. Both had starched creases in their trousers, and their uniforms shouted INTEL. A pair of pseudo-spooks.

Pana quashed the urge to hunch over her bowl. "Pair of Feds," she muttered. "Could be anything."

"Except they're heading this way." Sal's mouth barely moved. "Dummy up."

"Not a stretch," Chuck Dogg replied, and Pana snorted half a laugh into her coffee mug. This base had heavy industrial ceramic ware, a far cry from zinc or catch-as-catch-can.

She sensed them behind her before the woman spoke—a soft, deceptively quiet alto. "Swann's Riders? Blue Company, detached with a Captain Hendrickson?"

Sal blinked slowly up at her, playing the dumb-brown-immie card. Chuck's toe bumped Pana's boot under the table, twice. So that was how they were gonna work it.

Pana didn't mind, but *Dios*, it got tiring.

"Shyooooot," Chuck drawled, an outrageous thickening of an accent not his own. "Whatchu talkin' 'bout?"

"Copley, CentInt, SEC Three," the squat blond man said, right behind Pana. Almost breathing on her braids, and she contemplated scooching her chair back *hard*. "We're looking for one of your group. Anna Gray. Ring any bells?"

The Dogg let the question sit for a while, chewing slowly, letting his mouth open a little with each steady rumination. Finally, he took a long gulp of coffee, and smacked his lips. "Don't know no Annie. What 'bout y'all?"

Sal shook his head. "Noooooope."

The woman moved to Sal's right, examining the table. She peered at Zampana, probably counting on her partner right behind the seated raider to add pressure. Pana arranged her own face into a sulled-up mask, saved from outright hostility only by its watchful false stupidity, but not by much. She shook her head, slowly, her jaw working as she sloshed the overcooked coffee around. *"Nada, nada."*

"Come on." The woman tried a smile. "We know she was in the camps. This is just routine."

Pana's gaze met Sal's, but it was Chuck who jerked his head up, scraping his chair back with a squeal of legs on worn-smooth concrete. "You wanna know about the camps?" He leaned forward a little, as if he were about to leap out of the wooden chair. "I can tell ya. I was there, man. I saw 'em."

Zampana pushed her own chair back, slow but inexorable, almost running over the male's feet. He hopped back just in time, but she kept going until she had plenty of space, clipping the toe of a shiny wingtip at the very end of the motion. Chuck made a clicking sound with his tongue.

"Yeah, we was liberatin' the camps." Chuck wiped at his mouth with the back of one hand, tossed his fork to clatter on his plate. He fixed the asshole behind Pana with a steady glare, and a stillness spread through the caf as enlisteds noticed the tension. "Whatchu wanna know?"

"Easy there," the woman said. "We just want to talk to Specialist Gray, all right? We're in the east wing of the big brick building on Delta Drive. Just let her know, okay?"

Something told Pana this girl didn't play good cop all that often, but she was making an effort. So Pana just grunted and shook her head again. *"Nada, nada."*

"We come 'cross any Annie, we letchoo know." Chuck pointed at the male behind Pana. "Yo, mothafucka, she don' like crowdin', back yo' ass up."

"Come on, Copley." The blonde tried a smile. "Let's let these soldiers think about it, all right?"

Copley—it *had* to be a nickname—grunted. Pana rose slowly, just in case anyone decided going crazy was the way to head off these mofos. She turned, gave the man a once-over. He had the grace to look ashamed, and prickle-drops of sweat showed up on his forehead. *"Nada,"* she said again, and jabbed her fingers at him, like her grandmother warding off *el mal de ojo. "Malo suerte, cabrón."*

The gringo motherfucker grinned uneasily at her, showing a front tooth too white and shiny to be anything but an implant. Rear-echelon motherfuckers with time to get their teeth seen to, shit.

"Yassuh, we let you know," Dogg continued placidly, but he didn't scoot any closer to the table *or* relax.

It wasn't like dummying up for Firsters, but it was kind of funny. The Feds hurried out, pursued by the watchful examination of enlisteds and a few officers slumming a lunch for whatever reason. Pana settled back down, and Sal muttered a string of hideously obscene terms into his pancakes. "Shit," he said finally, reaching for the syrup again. "What they want with Spooky?"

"Nothing good." Pana grabbed a white plastic shaker. The coffee was only going to be palatable if she put a little salt in. "They're gonna watch us now."

"Oh, yeah. If they ain't been already." Chuck shook his head, his dreads moving softly. "Christ, Swann better come back soon."

"Hope Spooky stays hid, too," Sal added sagaciously.

"That girl?" Pana snorted. "Probably why she ain't here. Don't you worry about *her*."

It was good advice, really. But Zampana found herself unable to follow it, and from the look on his face, so did Chuck.

CHAPTER SEVENTY-TWO

SOME MAD GENIE

August 6, '98

"Fuck, man," Simmons groaned as soon as they cleared the stockade, stretching his legs to make his stride long and loose. "We got to get on that thing again?"

"What, you don' like my drivin', sir?" Ngombe grinned, hopping over gravel like she couldn't wait to take off again. "Gonna slide right through thunderstorms just for you. Boom boom."

"Fuck that shit."

Swann's neck ached. He was not in a mood to listen to complaints. "Oh for God's sake, Simms, just belt some booze and sleep on the way there."

Hendrickson shifted a new laptop bag from one shoulder to the other. Sleep had disturbed the circles under his eyes and given him a bit more bounce to his step. "So I gave him the clearance papers and he looked like he'd fucking swallowed a grenade. Sat back like he was afraid it was gonna go off."

Swann grunted. At least Bretagne had backed the fuck off and quit barking at him. If the jackass thought a missing fingertip on a Firster was unacceptable, it was pretty clear he'd never taken troops into combat. Fucking rear admirals.

Part of Swann's sour mood was the sunshine; another part was the uncomfortable sense of the situation reaching a boiling point. You didn't last long behind the lines if you couldn't sense when a particular set of circumstances was heating up, and this one had gotten there toot-sweet, as his daddy would say.

He hadn't thought of his father in years and wanted to keep it that way, so Swann quickened his pace. Ngombe was already ahead of them, moving along at a bouncing clip. Henny fell back with Simmons, the two of them bickering good-naturedly about what, exactly, General Bretagne resembled. Simmons said the man looked like Peter Lorre's ugly cousin; Henny disagreed, saying he looked more like a frog version of John Wayne. The two had apparently seen every ancient black-and-white movie ever, and a few that were in color, too.

It would, Swann thought, be fucking fantastic if they could find this one-armed fucker and finish this particular hunt. Why had he taken enlistment after the goddamn surrender in the first place? To keep them all together?

One fucking sled crash later he had 40 percent casualties. Some mad genie had escaped his bottle, and the dying wouldn't stop until he was crammed back in.

Swann's nape prickled, and he was in a crouch before he realized it, slapping his sidearm out of the holster and drawing a bead. Simmons, catching the movement, hit the gravel, and Henny did too. Ngombe, hearing the scuffling of three male animals disturbing small rocks, whirled and crouched at the same time, almost landing on her ass, her eyes wide and white-ringed. Simmons let out a short bark, probably digging for his own iron, and Swann realized the running footsteps were friendly.

The Federal private, out of breath and just barely out of school by the look of her, skidded to a stop a respectable distance away. Her boots were spit-shine, her dark hair regulation cut, her cheeks fresh and dewy, and her own sidearm was in a stiff new holster, obviously never used. She grasped a wad of flimsy and a small thumbprint catcher, and stared at them on the ground like she didn't quite believe what she was seeing. "PFC Malbrook, looking for Captain Swann, sir!"

"Fuck *me*," Simmons groaned. "Friendly. Friendly, everyone! Friendly!"

"Jesus Christ," Henny weighed in, breathlessly. "Jesus *fucking* Christ."

Ngombe, grinning, was the first to bounce back up. "Man, I thought we was gonna hafta shoot someone. You all right, Captain sir?"

"Captain Swann, sir?" The Federal private waved the flimsies. "Sorry, sir, looking for Captain Swann, sir!"

"Yeah, you said that." Swann's knees ached; Henny gave him a hand up. "I'm right here. Mulder, is it?"

"Malbrook, sir. Flimsy from CentCom, sir! High priority. Need a thumb."

Shit. It was probably more bad news. Swann took the flimsy, glanced at it, and the bottom dropped out of his stomach. He read it again, handed it to Simmons, and thumbed the small box with its heatfilm divot, acknowledging receipt. "Thank you, Malbrook. Good job."

"Yessir, thank you sir. Any reply?"

"Not a hand-carried one." Swann tried not to sound ungrateful. It looked like this soldier was upset about missing the war and applying herself wholesale to any job that got in her way. Christ, had any of his crew ever been that young? Had *he?*

No, just Lazy, and the kid had survived Second Cheyenne and running behind the lines only to get a bellyful of plazma from a goddamn hare-lipped Firster.

"Okay, sir, going back, sir!"

"Thanks, soldier." Swann accepted the salute, and the girl hurried away at a dead run again.

"Good Lord," Henny said. "I'll bet she enjoyed basic, too."

"Bite yo' tongue." Ngombe brushed dirt off her coverall knees. "What we got, huh?"

"Shitfire and save matches," Simmons breathed. "They pinged our one-handed friend. Somehow got himself certified under a fresh name. He was in a jail in Boise late as last night."

"Ngombe." Swann crushed his hat more firmly on his head. His knees throbbed. He was getting too old for this shit. "How fast can you get us there?"

"Had to fix the cracked cell, should be dry and socketed by now. Gotta do preflights and charging. Four, five hours? Maybe less." Ngombe thought it over. "We can stop in Helena to get t'others, sir, it'll take longer."

"Henny, get to the sled and bounce Pana, tell her and the rest to meet us on the strip down there. Ngombe, start the flight checks. Simms?"

"Yessir?" Simmons handed the flimsy to Henny.

"Get some booze, and get it on the fucking sled." Swann patted at his pockets, hoping to come up with a pack of candies. "We're probably gonna need it."

PART FIVE

SALVUS

CHAPTER SEVENTY-THREE

THE GREENBELT

August 6, '98

Gene squinted against harsh early-afternoon light, scratching at his left forearm. The itching would only get worse. His shirt was clean, though—they'd washed all his clothes before turning him loose. It wasn't a crime to overdose, but they'd taken all the vials. Assuming he was a freshly certified veteran hooked on painkillers, the hard-faced processing officer had given him a stern look and told him to check in for treatment. Even given him a slip for a methadone clinic.

In the real Amerika, he probably would have been sent to ReEdukation. Here, though, the holding cells were stuffed to the gills with fugees, petty ration thieves, drunken soldiers, and other flotsam. It was enough to make a man's skin *and* his guts crawl.

He scratched, and scratched, and walked. Downtown Boise throbbed with life. Pierced-face kids lounging on corners, boutiques full of unrationed goods, fat hippies scuttling around, Federals on leave swelling the stores, shiny-faced businessmen moving their soft womanly hips and asses. If there were any real, true patriots, they were well hidden, probably in the rural areas. Northern Idaho had *almost* stayed faithful, and if the goddamn cities hadn't been full of degenerates outvoting the real people, they might have had a chance.

They even called the heroes up here "terrorists." There were meme-posters lampooning McCoombs too, showing him in pearls and drag-queen makeup. Someone had hung an effigy of the real, true Amerikan President from a lamppost, and every time Gene passed it on that long syrupy afternoon, the rage rose.

Pollen floated on the breeze. Summer was in full luxuriant riot, the lindens were in bloom, green covered every bush. Despite that, the temperature dropped sharply as the sun did, and when dusk came, shivers added themselves to the itching. The streets he had been wandering drained, lamps buzzing into life.

The electrical grid hadn't been bombed to shit here.

Campfires began to glitter in the Boise Greenbelt. He worked his way downhill toward them, moth drawn to the flames, and discovered he should have been *there* all day. The refugees had moved in, close enough to strain the social services but far enough for the criminals to find soft shady spots.

Little tar-black ant feet stabbed and prickled all over him. His spine ached, his head throbbed, his pants sagged because they'd taken his fuck-ing belt at the jail. But not the travel belt. That had been returned to him, along with its slim cargo of cash—and the thumbdrive, still tucked in its secret little pocket. A useless bit of black plastic now, especially since he didn't have the vials.

Slipping and stumbling down a hill, he plunged into the Greenbelt and circled a few fires, looking for one with an empty space. It took a while, but eventually he ended up beside an elderly man stumbling back from a pissbreak. Gene caught at a sharp elbow with his good hand, righting the fellow reflexively. A heavy wash of body odor, sugary cheap alcohol, and indifferent asswiping wrapped around Gene, and he didn't push the man into a ditch because the geezer peered up into his dusk-masked face and said, "Sonny, thanks. Y'all can come to the fire."

"Come on over." The old man scooted sideways, a crab-like lurch, and made space on the rotting log. The campfire crackled, and the worn faces around its orange-and-yellow flicker barely glanced at Gene. It wasn't un-til he'd settled himself that he realized why the man had invited him.

All male. Two missing a leg below the knee; one with an eye patch and the last three fingers of his right hand gone; another slumped around a cave-in on the left side of his torso; one shaking, eyelids flickering every once in a while, a shaved patch on the side of his head growing back hair of a different shade.

"Cripples gotta stick together." The elderly man snort-laughed. He didn't look visibly deformed, but he certainly stank. "What's your name, son?"

"Johnson," Gene mumbled. It was good enough. He wanted to explain he wasn't a cripple, that this had been *done* to him, that he was really an able worker. All the excuses he'd heard before the kampogs went into the bottles and the baths.

A ripple of laughter went around the fire, quiet and comfortable.

Why bother? It was useless. He cradled the stump of his left wrist, squeezing it slightly every now and again. When he squeezed, the pain in his invisible hand retreated a little.

"Hurts, does it?" One of the legless assholes smirked. "Phantom pain, they told me. It's a bitch."

They didn't ask what battle he'd been injured in. Gene realized they were all soldiers, and to them, it didn't matter where he'd gotten his fucking hand chopped off.

The war was over.

Smoke rose lazily. The wood snapped and crackled. The authorities were even handing out firewood every evening instead of letting those who couldn't shift for themselves freeze. Typical, Gene thought. Make them weak and dependent. Well, he'd take the warmth.

The geezer's name was Fred, and he passed around a jug of cheap wine. It didn't stop the itching, but after a few hits Gene began to feel much warmer, and a little more hopeful.

Tomorrow he could start asking around. There was bound to be a way to get what he needed.

CHAPTER SEVENTY-FOUR

WE ALL STILL THERE

"Holy shit." Zampana squinted at the printout. She'd just found Spooky hanging around the back door to the kitchen, basking in thick golden sunshine and wolfing a plate of overcooked, rubbery mac and cheese someone had been talked into providing her. Smart move on the Spook's part, and Pana had been cautiously hopeful even when Chuck showed up with a sheaf of papers and a sour face. "When did this come in?"

"Couple hours ago." Chuck's hands worked, opening and closing. He was all right to hobble without his crutch now, as long as there was no emergency. "Bastards didn't come find us, for fucksake."

"Too busy looking for Spooky, maybe." Pana thought it over. At least they'd had a chance to wash their clothes. Her bloomers hadn't felt this fresh since before Missouri. "Captain gonna land here and load us come evening."

"Shiiiit." Chuck, spruced up and with fresh norpirene on his calf, was looking bright and perky, too. "Not another sled ride."

Pana heartily concurred. "Unless there's a Boise-bound transport. There might be."

"What chances those IntSec motherfuckers'll be watching it? *And* the airfield?"

Spooky's chin jerked up. She finished chewing, took a hasty gulp from a big ceramic coffee mug balanced precariously on the side of the Dumpster, and coughed a little. "I can get on without them seeing me." She blinked sleepily. Her clothes were still too big, but her cheeks had filled out. Now it was only the hunched, felon-shovel way she ate that would give her away.

"We can't keep 'em off you forever." Chuck sighed. "But we'll damn well try—don't worry," he added hastily, scratching uncomfortably at the back of his neck. "What you think they want?"

"X-Ray," she said, and took another giant mouthful. It had been a while since Pana saw her eat with such relish.

"Not even gonna ask," Pana muttered. "One problem at a time."

Chuck, taking the hint, moved on to the next one. "I set Sal to rustling up supplies, quicker the better. 'F I know the Captain, they're already halfway here."

"Okay." Pana sucked her cheeks in, thinking.

"It's fine," Spooky said suddenly, her spoon paused in midair. "I'll talk to them after Boise. It won't matter then."

"Talk to IntSec, or...?" Chuck's eyebrows arched. His dreads bobbed gently.

She shrugged and bent back down to her plate, balanced on one capable, deft paw while she shoveled with the other.

Chuck eyed her afresh. "Shit, girl, you tellin' me you know what's gonna happen?"

A slight, vicious shake of her head. "Not any more than you do."

"Knew enough to get Prink out of that house." A shiver ran through Chuck despite the baking heat bouncing off the side of the kitchen wall. "But not enough to keep Lazy from getting his ass shot up."

Spooky dropped her plate, and the spoon. Violently yellow elbow macaroni gooshed out onto baking dirt, splattering a few drought-corkscrewed dandelions. "Wish I had." She hopped over the mess and took off, not quite running but hurrying, her head down and shoulders turtled up.

"Good one, Chuck." Zampana rolled the printouts into a tight cylinder. "Just when she was eating."

The Dogg folded himself down, sore leg and all, and began to scrape up dirt, overcooked pasta, and waxy yellow glorp. Government cheese, familiar from before the war. He was sweating by the time he was done, wincing every time his weight shifted, but Pana didn't help. Instead, she dumped the coffee mug's contents into the Dumpster and stood, staring across a patch of Montana grass, mountains looming in the near distance, the sky overhead a thick bright canopy pressing every breath until it was too goddamn hard to fight and you broke down.

Just like everything else. Big Sky Country, they called it. A whole bunch of gringos and weeds was all she could see, with bonus shitty-ass Federals crawling over everything and complicating what could be simple. "Chuck?" It slipped out, surprising her.

"Huh?" He settled his leg with a heavy sigh.

She might as well ask. "You ever wanna go home?"

"What the fuck kind of question is that?" He craned to look up at her, his dreads moving a little as his head shifted.

"I mean, you ever wish the war hadn't happened? You ever wish that?"

"Don't waste time on that. You go crazy as the Reaper, or shit, crazy as the Spook, you start thinking like that." He took his time, scraping until every last bit of yellow goo was spooned onto the heavy white plate. "There ain't nothing to go back to. Ever. Sooner you get over that, the easier it gets."

"But when you started out—"

"That was then." Chuck began the slow painful process of levering himself back up. Pana, deciding she'd made her displeasure clear enough, gave him a hand, then bent to collect the loaded plate.

And this is now. She didn't say it. "You know what? I bet Spooky would eat it if it was like this."

"You think she got a taste for dirt?"

"No." Pana searched for words to explain. "We got her out of Gloria, right? But in her *head*, you know. She's still there."

He considered this, one hand spread against the Dumpster's blue-painted metal. Some joker had spray-painted a yellow happy face onto the fucker, with the eyes big *X*s, a dribble of rust from one corner of the smiling mouth turning the expression into a leer. "Or that other one she was at."

"Baylock." The name sent a shiver through them both. The newscast pictures were bad enough. Seeing it in real life, up close...*Dios.*

"Yeah." Chuck turned his head, a beaky profile as he stared at the mountains. Did the sky seem heavy to him, too? "We all still there, Pana."

"At a camp?" She scraped the mess into the Dumpster. Flies were already at work. Maybe Spooky had been sure nobody would bother her, eating here.

Or maybe, like a dog beaten too many times to ever trust a kind word, she'd thought to go through the Dumpster herself.

"No." Chuck shook his head, sadly. "The goddamn war, Pana. We ain't ever gettin' out."

"We will. Someday." She tried to sound certain. If Chuck got into a philosophical mood, Simmons wasn't around to jar him out of it.

"You think so?" Half a question, half sarcastic disbelief, even he probably couldn't figure out which one was going to win.

All of a sudden, Pana was tired of lying. Or of not knowing if she *was* lying because a medic had to stay steady. You started showing any cracks, and your patients would scent the fear. "I don't know." She tapped the plate gently against metal. The spoon scratched like fingernails on a chalkboard. "But I gotta think as much, at least some of the time. Otherwise, what's the point?"

"Yeah." Chuck wiped at his forehead with the back of one hand. A long pause, Zampana standing with the plate dangling from one hand and the spoon tucked into the coffee mug in the other, Chuck gazing into the distance like he was going to find an answer he liked better there. "Yeah," he repeated. "I ain't sure there is one, Pana. I ain't sure at all."

She didn't have an answer for that, even a lying one. So she stacked the plate, spoon, and mug on the shaky wooden step in front of the propped-open door. The kitchen boiled with the sound of KP duty—scrubbing, clinking, swearing both good-natured and not. She half turned and slid her arm around Chuck's narrow waist, resting her braided head against his stringy, scrawny, very strong biceps. They stood there in the sun for a few minutes, breathing in the reek of cooking and garbage on a hot day, hearing the distant rumble of afternoon thunder.

CHAPTER SEVENTY-FIVE

FUNHOUSE MIRROR

Ngombe feathered the prototype down, warm quarter-size raindrops smacking the canopy over and over. Lightning flashed, and the entire sled rattled. Simmons mumbled a curse, holding onto his chair arms with desperate strength, white knuckles, and sweating fingertips.

"Christ, relax," Henny kept telling him, and each time, Simmons came up with a new, breathtakingly obscene anatomical term in response. Sooner or later they'd get tired of the game.

"They're on Pad Four," Swann repeated, even though Ngombe had it and was clearly heading the right way. She verified, banked slightly, and fifteen minutes later had the sled touching ground as softly as a kitten landing in a basket of yarn. The hatch dilated, steps unfolding, and first aboard was Sal, spitting and sneezing, wet clear through and loaded down with supplies that should have gone into the cargo bay if they hadn't been in such a gawdawful hurry. Next came Chuck, all but hefted through the door with Pana putting her shoulder in his ass, and Pana herself, her braids soaked and rivulets running down her face. Last was Spooky, shivering and snuffling, hitting the hatch-close button and giving the all-clear. Spook helped Pana get Chuck settled, almost getting whapped in the face with his crutch, and dropped into the chair behind Henny's laptop station again like she'd never been away.

"Buncha drowned rats in here!" Simmons crowed. "Chuck, my *man*, you lost out on some interrogation action. Henny there had to play good cop."

"How'd he do?" Chuck mopped at his hair with both hands, ineffectually.

Simmons seesawed his hand, *So-so.* "You shoulda seen him when I cut that skinny fuck's finger off."

"We were gonna do some grave robbing too, but decided it could wait." Henny's dark eyes danced. "How the hell are you, Spook?"

"Cold." She snuffled up a wad of snot, her face contorting. "Wet."

"Grave robbing?" Pana crossed herself. "Where we goin'? Still Boise?"

"Yeah, Boise," Swann tossed over his shoulder. "Henny, dial 'em in."

"We got a ping." The Fed jostled his laptop, rubbing his hands together as Ngombe pulled up, the prototype humming happily and the heaters beginning to tick into steam-cabin territory. The dehumidifier was going to be working overtime if it wasn't already. "Our one-handed guy showed up in Boise in the bus station crapper, OD'd on highgrade he probably got from the dear dead doctor. They detoxed him and kept him in holding, let him go because they're full to the gills with fugees and displaced. CentCom's got their panties in several twists. Boise just put out an APB on him, we've got facials and everything else. No half-wormed shit, now we're cooking with napalm."

Sal wanted to get it completely clear. "So now we're looking for a one-armed man in Idaho?"

"One-*handed*," Simmons corrected prissily, and it was a dead-on imitation of Henny.

"Man, you can't make this shit up." Sal began to laugh, and after a thunderstruck moment—literally, a flash of lightning painted the front bubble and Ngombe squinted, her touch on the sled controls sure and soft as she rode the turbulence—the entire prototype was awash with chuckles.

Even Swann grinned, but that was of short duration, because Pana, in blithe disregard of procedure, leaned into the cockpit, her mouth near his ear, and began uploading at high speed in a fierce whisper.

Henny wiped away tears; Simmons all but howled, clutching at his belly; Sal shook his head, doglike, and spattered rain and hair oil everywhere. Spooky's mouth twitched, until she peered past Henny's chair and saw his laptop screen.

She bent forward and rested her forehead on her knees as if nauseous again.

The picture on Henny's screen was of a blondish, blue-eyed scarecrow with a prominent Adam's apple, his shrunken shoulders crossed by yellowing undershirt straps. Glaze-eyed, his hair a scrub-brush mess, bruises up one cheek, he stared. The profile shot showed his neck almost too thin to hold his head up; the full-front's eyes followed you at any angle like the best photographer's trick. Below, the name glowed.

EUGENE THOMAS ROBERTSON. Smart, to switch just a little bit of his name. But looking at the face gave her a funny floating feeling.

It was *different*. Had her memory failed her? Was she beginning to slip and blur like one of the given-ups, the blankers, the walking dead who wandered the kamps slowly, turned so far inward they couldn't find any way out?

How sane was she? How sane was anyone, after all this?

"Spook? You okay?"

She cringed away from Henny's hand, sensing more than seeing it. "Fine," she choked. "Tired."

"Shit." Chuck leaned way forward, peering around the console. "Pana? Spook's looking pretty raw."

Don't worry, her dead sister whispered inside her head. *Around his ears, those little white lines? Plastic surgery. He doesn't look the same, but it's him.*

"Spooky?" Zampana, softly. A familiar pressure against her damp forehead—the older woman's hand. "Your stomach bad?"

The sled rattled and bumped as it rose. "Pana!" Swann barked. "Buckle your ass in!"

"I'm fine," Spooky whispered. Cleared her throat, said it louder. "Fine. It was just a second. I'm okay." She even tried a smile, recoiling inwardly when she realized it wasn't *her* expression; it was Lara's. Or was it Hannah's?

She couldn't tell. Whichever one she was, she was wearing the other's face. For a few nasty, rattling, bumping, thunder-rumbling moments, the entire world stretched and smeared, Swann's Riders friction-rubbed into alien caricatures, the sled's interior full of sharp edges and blinking harsh lights, the storm outside a growling digestive tract swallowing a long sleek iron pill whole, not caring that inside the capsule were little fleshly blobs.

"We're medicine." For the world, or the storm? She couldn't decide. Her lips were numb. "Fine. I'm fine. Sit down."

Thankfully, Zampana took her hand away, and her worry no longer smudged and rubbed around inside Spooky's tired, shivering skull. Pana hurried away to her jumpseat—it was funny how everyone went back to the same place, though they didn't really have to. Slotted themselves into holders and returned to them, like birds seeking the comfort of their cages when freedom got too scary.

Spooky put her dripping head back down, because even with Henny in his seat the picture on his screen was glaring at her. Ngombe read off headings and protocols softly, Swann replied, and the sled pierced the storm, sliding through curtains of rain and rattles of thunder like a razor through bunched silk.

CHAPTER SEVENTY-SIX

AIN'T SLEEPIN' AGAIN

August 8, '98

"If they had proof, they'd show up with MPs." Past midnight, Swann rolled his head back, easing his aching neck. Below them, the forest tossed and wavered under the edge of the storm, but the sled was moving faster than the bad weather. The thunder's feet got tangled in the mountains, and the sled had stopped vibrating on flirting, unsteady air.

"Or Henny would get a nice little directive." Zampana, leaning against the bulkhead behind the copilot's chair, glanced back at the sled's interior. The Fed was asleep, tilted sideways in his chair, a screensaver bathing his face with weird bluish light. Simmons was snoring gustily, his chin on his broad chest; Sal nodded, drowsing fitfully.

Swann sighed. "He's a good kid."

"Yeah, I know." Most of them started out that way; Christ knew even Simmons might have. "But what's he gonna do if they give him a cuff-and-stuff order, huh? Got himself to think about."

Swann glanced up at her. "What am I not getting here?"

"Was waiting in the enlisted club for y'all to get here, so Sal could drink up." Pana's generous mouth turned down, and there was an old wary gleam in her dark eyes, one he knew well. "There was a 'cast on the screen. They're picking up all the poor assholes the Firsters experimented on. Quarantine."

"Quarantine." Swann repeated, heavily.

Zampana's face was an icon, bathed in soft glow from the controls. "For their own protection, Kallbrunner said."

Gather them up. How many were Spookies? "Sounds awful familiar."

"Don't it just?" Zampana's scowl deepened. "Beginning to think signing up for this was a mistake, Cap'n."

"The whole thing, or just *this* part?"

Zampana shrugged. "I'm in it, no worries. But I gotta tell you, I got a bad feeling. Spook needs fucking therapy. Maybe we *should* let 'em take care of her."

"Stick her in another camp?"

"I'm a field medic, Phillip. Not a fuckin' therapist."

Ngombe, silent and watchful in the pilot's chair, corrected course a fraction. She ignored them so pointedly even her eyelids were at half-mast.

Swann was silent for a long moment, watching the instruments glow and oscillate. Everything just fine, just as it should be. When they landed, the real scramble would begin.

"I don't want to lose anyone else," he said finally, half to himself.

Pana thought it over, shifting to her left foot to take some of the pressure off her hip. This was worse than sleeping on the goddamn *ground*. Finally, after a long pause, she spoke again.

"Yeah."

And that was that, apparently, because she turned around and went back to her jumpseat to strap herself in. Swann stared at the night, spatters of rain touching the front window and streaking away. When he was a kid, he used to count raindrops on his bedroom window. Watch them streak and meld, wonder where all the water came from. It really wasn't all that different. Except nowadays he could think about acid rain, about crouching in the woods in a downpour, shivering and hunted, or slogging through the mud and hearing the screams of the wounded, the pop of cannos, the heavy booming of artillery.

Growing up fucking sucked.

Ngombe adjusted heading slightly, recited the change in a warm, soft half whisper. Swann rubbed at his tired, grainy eyes, and went back to thinking about who would do what when they got to Boise.

"Let me get this straight." Major Wrickstett, liaison with the Sawtooth South Federal Army Reserve, ran his hands back through short, wire-stiff reddish hair. His office in the VA admin building was crammed with paperwork, an ancient coffee machine cooking down its current cargo into glue, and a heavy scent of Old Spice. "All this authorization and override, and you're looking for a one-armed dope fiend?"

"One-*handed*," Sal corrected, which made Simmons snort. Swann glared at both of them, a sobering look from under his shelflike gray eyebrows.

"I know it's a shitter," Henny soothed. The man was a born bureaucrat charmer. "He was in detox and holding; then they cut him loose. Don't worry, we're not here to add to your headaches—"

"Well, *that's* good, because I have a fuckton of them, with all the goddamn fugees the DMZ's letting through."

Henny rolled right on past the roadbump. "—but we do need some information. And a free hand to go look for this bastard."

Simmons snorted again. Sal's mouth twitched.

A quick gleam of curiosity sparked from the redheaded major. "What'd he do?"

"He was a high mucky-muck in the kamp system." Henny had decided that would get Swann's crew all the cooperation they needed, and he wasn't wrong. "Did a lot of shit."

"Huh." Wrickstett flipped the file of paperwork closed. "I saw the footage. Fucking Firsters."

"Amen," Swann added quietly. "There's already an APB out on this guy with the civvie police. We just need to know where a one-handed dope fiend passing himself off as a Federal vet would likely wash up here. Or if he's trying to get out of town and head Alaska-way, how he'd likely do that."

Wrickstett sucked in his cheeks, thinking about it. "Well, getting out of town any way but east is gonna cost him a pretty penny. We've sealed every road west, north, south—even the shitty dirt ones—as tight as we can. No further travel west, that's the word, unless it's by military convoy. We had some sovereign-citizen jerkwads during the war trying to blow up the Anne Frank memorial and IED the roads, so we've got checkpoints every five minutes. There's coyotes, sure, but they charge an arm and a leg, and there's no guarantee you won't end up raped to death somewhere in the mountains or in bumfuck Malheur. So this guy, if he's got any money—"

"Not a lot," Henny supplied. "And the cops took his stash."

"Huh." Wrickstett nodded, scratching at his clean-shaven face as if he felt stubble. Even at this hour he looked sharp, his pants creased just right and his shirt pressed. "Okay, well, I'll show you where to look. Come on over." He dug in the papers snowdrifting his desk for a pen, and had to jam himself against a filing cabinet to point at the situation map on the only bare patch of wall. "There's Hulls Gulch, and the Hollows." He pointed to the north and northeast. "But those aren't the real problem— they're just overflow. The *real* problem is the Military Reserve here on the east side, stuffed full of certifieds or nineteeners and wounded fugees now that the VA hospital's turned into a crisis medical. They've got fires and tents and everything, a real shantytown; the conservationists are beside themselves. Then there's the Greenbelt and Julie's Park and Ann Morrison, here in the middle of the city. That's where a lot of the druggies tend to congregate. There's even reports of motherfuckers shooting up over here, over on Morris Hill. A fucking cemetery—I *ask* you, who does that?" He shook his head, obviously not expecting an answer. "Military Reserve's pretty safe, but if you go into *any* of these, go armed. I can get you on with regular patrols, if you want."

"Simmons, Sal...you take the Military Reserve. I'll take this chunk— the Greenbelt, yeah? I'll take that with Henny."

"Which leaves the graveyard for me and Spook." Pana snorted. Spooky was still on the sled, staying out of sight until they got the lay of the land. She didn't seem to mind. "Unless you want us to head for this gulch-and-hollows bullshit."

"Figured you two would work downtown and social services first. If this asshole lost his stash he's gonna be looking to buy, and downtown's the best place for that, unless I'm wrong?"

Wrickstett nodded, glad he didn't have to spell it out. "Not really wrong, Captain. Ann Morrison's a hotbed for that shit too, though." The pen jabbed at another green space, and the Major was looking more relieved by the minute. "Shit, I can send you out with patrols, and comm support—"

"Can you plug in our sled? Ngombe can keep it warmed up and Chuck can run comms for us from inside, as long as we can get some of those little bouncer-popper things."

"I can go one better. We've got actual cells and the network up and running inside the city limits. Preloaded, GPS, the works. They'll use our towers, and we can get your sled talking to the towers too if it has C-Comm?"

"Pretty sure it does, sir," Ngombe said. "Got everything else."

"All right." Swann smacked his hat into his free hand. "That's a plan, then."

Now that he'd decided to be helpful, Wrickstett was swinging for the bleachers. "You guys want some sleep? Some chow?"

"Chow would be good. And coffee."

"We been chasin' this fucker since Minneapolis." Simmons showed his teeth, and Swann knew he was thinking of Minjae and Prink. "I ain't sleepin' again until we have him tied down."

"I believe you," the good major said, and hurried away to make arrangements.

CHAPTER SEVENTY-SEVEN

MABEL MOUSE PATROL

The night was getting old, gray false dawn rising behind the low dark blur of mountains. Sal sneezed twice, lightly, into his elbow, and followed Simmons along a winding dirt path. The patrol were regular Federals, mostly rear-echelon fish ready for a chance to prove they *could* have won the war, if they'd had to. The presence of a pair of hard-bitten raiders added to their swagger, and the rearguard, a squat woman with pock-marked cheeks and a red bandanna around her forehead that had never seen the real grease of fearsweat, kept up a low running commentary.

Shacks cobbled out of scavenged plywood, heavy evergreen branches, sog-sagging cardboard still damp from spring runoff and summer thunder-storm arranged themselves in dots along approximations of lanes and roads. There was stirring even at this hour—thin, frizzle-haired women in faded odds and ends hunching protectively near the embers in front of whatever small patch of land they'd managed to claim. The few men stirring were either poking dispiritedly at cold fires or lolling drunkenly in a rude door-way, clutching at gnarled sticks. No weapons allowed in fugee hands, but they made do, and no few of the skinny men wore faded Federal caps and military-grade scowls. It was anyone's guess whether any of them were ac-tual veterans, but the authorities had erred on the side of mercy this once.

To hear the grunts on patrol tell it, though, they'd done so just to piss said grunts off and make their lives miserable.

"Fuckin' animals," the rear guard muttered. "Yesterday they had a baby born right in the middle of the street. Just squatted down and *squirt*, out it comes."

Sal refrained from pointing out that it was sort of like the runs—when you had to squeeze out a pup, it wasn't a call from Ma Nature you could put on hold, even for a few minutes. He did, however, look at Simmons, and understood from the Reaper's set, thin mouth and narrowed eyes that the other man agreed.

"What happened?" Simmons had his best aw-shucks corn-fed-stupid tone on.

"Whatcha mean?" The rear guard looked from one raider to the other, visibly perplexed.

"To the baby." The Reaper placed his big feet in their worn-down boots carefully, avoiding trash or any disturbed dirt, stepping where he'd seen another patroller set foot. Sal found out he was doing that too— habit from the woods. If it hadn't blown someone else up, chances are it wouldn't detonate underfoot. Though they'd started using time delays and counters on mines, too, near the end. He'd heard of raiders biting it that way—a few of Schornach's gang before Second Cheyenne, back in the dark days when the Firsters were winning.

Schorn was a cut-corners type anyway, no discipline. He hadn't lasted long.

"Oh, it was one of those muties. Born with flippers. Mama was a campog." The Fed grinned, strong teeth jutting out, her cheeks almost swallowing her eyes. She rolled around a wad of cherry-flavored chewing tobacco, tucked it into her other cheek. "Took it to the VA. Don't know what happened, but she's back at work."

"Work?" Sal had a sinking feeling he knew.

"Sure. She was one of those good-time fishgirls. Sells it for candies. I'm tellin' you, man. Animals." The Fed shook her head and freed one hand from her low-and-ready rifle, hurrying them along. "Keep up, fellas. Don't wanna lose you in here."

Simmons opened his mouth, but Sal elbowed him midstep. That was usually Chuck's job, or Pana's; Sal had the strange sliding feeling that soon it might become his, and he didn't like it. The Reaper was part of the team, he was trustworthy, but still.

Mist cotton-wreathed the treetops, mixing with smoke. A few lone songbirds began to practice for the dawn chorus. "Missed that sound," Sal found himself saying, in a low confidential tone.

"Yeah," Simmons agreed. "Reminds me of when I was a kid."

Sal had been thinking of the pine barrens right before they found the first Reklamation camp, before the big push to end the whole pile of shit, and all the bullshit since. "Barrens" was a misnomer, since it teemed with tangled, overgrown life. Since the humans didn't want that slice of ground, birds and other small critters moved in and set up house.

There hadn't been any time for nature walks, though. You didn't really have time to think, either, while they were shooting at you or while you were a hunted animal. Or while you were in a hostile town, passing messages, carrying forged ident, and staying one step ahead of the patrols.

Sitting in the sled, or stepping along the tail end of this Mabel Mouse patrol, gave you too *much* time to throw things around inside your skull and feel your toes turn into icicles. *I'm in,* he'd told Swann. *Nowhere left to go* was more like it. With a healthy helping of *Who am I when I'm not around these bastards who saved my life so many times?*

Maybe if Minjae and Prink hadn't eaten the big burrito…it would've been nice to open a bar back in San Fran, have Prink dream up crazy cocktails and Minjae do the books. Customers could come in, get their hair done, drink a little. Great tips from tipsy hipsters and sailors. Maybe find a nice husband and settle down. Cake and wine and someone just for him, waking up in the morning to the salt fog and that wonderful smell of a living, breathing city that hadn't been bombed to shit. Living without the looming threat of electroshock therapy to "cure" him if he got a boner for another man.

A rail-thin man with messy dark hair and his left leg gone below the knee leaned on a crutch, watching the soldiers pass by. The scruff of a fast-growing beard darkened his cheeks, and his sullen expression was familiar. Sal had seen it on hundreds of civilian faces when the Patriots did spot checks. Crowd everyone together, let them out one by one. Immies in one line, secondary citizens in another, Patriots waved through. Stare at their ident, shoot anyone who looked at you funny or whose ident card had a blur, or even anyone with a skin shade you didn't like.

It was a new thing, to have that fucking look directed at Sal himself.

"We'll end up at Shed Two for the morning food ration, you can question anyone you want there." The rear guard's rifle was oiled and clean, in apple-pie order. She probably liked it better than most humans.

"How many generally show up?"

"There's three sheds, and by the time morning crowd clears out, the evening one's starting. All the aid workers got the picture of your guy; if there's a one-armed fella they'll chute him aside for pat down."

"One-handed," Simmons mumbled, but not very loudly. It wasn't worth it.

The patrol came out on a square of cleared ground, beaten into dust by refugee feet. In the middle, a spigot thrust up, just ten degrees off perpendicular. Women were already congregating there, filling buckets and talking in low sweet voices. One or two of them wore Christer bonnets and long dresses, despite being on the other side of the DMZ. Sal's right hand tensed, but he shook it out. Freedom of religion, he reminded himself. That was real America, not the bullshit McCoombs and his crew had tried to force down everyone's throat.

But Jesus, did they have to give it to the fucking Firsters, too? Those motherfuckers had only one use for freedom: taking away everyone else's.

Sal froze. Simmons, next to him, did too, and followed his gaze.

A body hung from a convenient fir branch. White man, with a hard little potbelly that wasn't from the gut bacteria throwing a party after death. The face was plummy, and liquid shit crusted the back of the legs. Bare, horn-toed feet hung slack and lifeless, and around the neck was a sign made of scavenged cardboard, bearing a big, black, painted 19.

Looked like they'd strung up two others before him, waited for them to stop kicking, then cut the bodies down and kept going. This fellow might have even seen the other two go before him. Sal, cold all over, squinted at the signs propped on them, like advertisements for cordwood.

One read RAPIST. The other said JUNKIE.

"Look at that," the rear guard said. "Someone snuffed Billy."

The CO of the patrol glanced back. "Huh? Oh yeah. We'll tell 'em to come in and pick up another load when we get back to the house."

"Who's Billy?" Simmons wanted to know. He jostled Sal to get him moving again, halted. "Which one?"

The Fed spat, a long stream of brown bacca juice steaming in the early-morning chill. "Junkie, there. Funny, he never touched the shit, just ran dope into the camp and out to the city. Pot's still legal under martial law, but a lot of shit isn't until the civil authorities get their say-so back."

"Huh." Simmons stepped, cautious and tiptoe, over to the bodies. He bent slightly, peering at the ones on the ground.

Sal knew that sound. "Whatchu thinkin', Reaper?"

"Billy ain't got a rope burn. Looks like he was stabbed."

"Animals, man." The rear guard shook her head.

Sal realized something else. "Where are all the kids?" It was early for them to be up, but he didn't even hear a baby crying, and none of the women at the spigot filling their buckets held a small bundle.

"Twelve and unders are all at the hospital outbuildings. They get care, even if their parents are fucking nineteeners." Madam Rearguard didn't sound like she thought much of the notion. "Shoulda seen when we had to separate them all out, it was a fucking nightmare. Kids crying, mothers screaming, you'd think we were camping 'em instead of taking them for vaccinations and food. Stupid fucks."

Sal glanced at Simmons again. The big man straightened, cast another considering glance at the hanging corpse and his friends, then shook his blond head slightly. Either getting rid of an uncomfortable thought, or, worse, shrugging off a few more casualties.

What were three more bodies, after Second Cheyenne or Gloria?

The horrible thing was, Sal realized, that *he* was thinking the same thing himself. He put his head down and trooped on. Each time the rear guard spat, a spasm of something not raspy enough to be hate scraped down Sal's back. It was just plain irritation, and it wasn't a reason to turn around and empty his sidearm into the Fed's round, self-satisfied face.

But he thought about it.

He thought about it each goddamn time.

CHAPTER SEVENTY-EIGHT

NOT HIGH AT ALL

The sun crested the mountains, a furnace of gold, and the river glittered. The first fury of snowmelt was past, but the river still ran deep and cold, and the banks were mush in many places since the dog days hadn't begun. Julia Davis Park was barricaded, but a few scattered groups of fugees got in anyway, and while the patrols were moving them along Swann and Henny eyeballed the shuffling, crusty-eyed rivulet of humanity. A couple amputees showed up, but not the one they were looking for.

Ann Morrison Park, easier to get into despite being on the west side of the river, was a different story. The body count at 1000 hours was thirteen and rising, since someone at morning rations pushed someone else in line, accusations of cutting began, someone pulled a contraband shiv, and the riot started. It took tear gas, water cannons, crisscrossing sleds, and sicksticks to get it sorted out, which left Henny and Swann questioning the wounded and whatever refugee community leaders weren't dealing with the mess. Finally, Wrickstett reappeared, and hustled them into a portable full of paperwork, arthritic coffee machines, and overworked volunteers.

One of them, a lean rangy woman with deep-tanned skin cracking like old leather, eyed the mugshot they had and cocked her short-shaven head, shivering as she pulled a brown woolen shawl—hand knitted, from its uneven look—closer about her lean-muscled shoulders. "Huh."

"This is Eddie Brunner, Refugee Control Board," Major Wrickstett said helpfully. "She's a native, did some raiding in Montana."

"Not enough," Eddie said softly, pulling the shawl even tighter. "Give me a second to look at this, it's on the tip of my brain."

"I'll leave you in her capable hands." Wrickstett accepted their salutes and hurried away, probably relieved to be done with this unpleasantness. Swann suspected he had way more waiting for him back at the VA admin building.

"You say he's a needle-rider?" Brunner's head snapped aside as a knot of Federals went by the door of her office, a screaming refugee man with his hands cuffed behind him. The fugee's hair, a wild matted mess, bounced. "Shit. Hang on a second." She hurried away, as the man's cries increased in volume. "He's a schizophrenic! Put him on the med transport!"

"Jesus." Henny shook his head. This morning he looked more rumpled than anyone who had seen his former Federal incarnation might believe. "This may take a while."

"You think?" Swann folded his arms, settling one hip against a listing but still sturdy file cabinet. His hat tipped back, a pale line of forehead that didn't see much sun anymore glaring out from underneath. "You want some coffee?"

"If I have any more I'll take off like that goddamn sled." Henny looked for a place to sit, found none, decided not to lean against the rickety plywood-and-sheet-metal desk filling most of this tiny space. "You've got something on your mind. Spit it out."

Another hurrying scuffle filled the portable's minuscule hall. *"No,"* they heard Brunner yell sharply. "Take her to the med shed! She's pregnant!"

Swann rested one hand on his sidearm. It was a normal, habitual movement, but Henny tensed slightly.

Just a bit.

There was no way to get rid of that habit. Swann had it himself. "Been thinkin'."

"I'll bet."

"When we bag this fellow, that changes things."

Henny considered this, his dark eyes half lidding. "It could. If you let it."

"Spook's one of us."

The Fed turned slightly, glanced down at the desk. "And me?"

"That's what I been thinkin' about." Swann's mouth set against itself, a perhaps-bitter expression that would have brought Pana to stand just behind him, braced for action.

"Have you, now." Henny kept his own hands very carefully away from his own belt. "I'm all ears."

"Should be all mouth instead, Captain." Swann watched the other man's face. He figured that was enough to give Hendrickson the layout, so to speak. And he wouldn't need much. A very sharp needle, was Henny boy.

To his credit, Henny didn't hesitate for long. "My mission brief is to render whatever aid I can, Captain. The classified brief is to keep an eye on her and see if she's what they suspect."

Which was pretty much what Swann had figured out on his own. Still, Henny got points for clarification. "Which is?"

"You really want to know?"

"Maybe." Too late to change his mind, his tone plainly said.

"The Firsters did a bunch of shit at Baylock. Nothing panned out the way they hoped, but they had a lot of…well, they pushed a lot of boundaries. There was a shining star—female subject, blew past all the barriers. They called her X-Ray. We're talking some scary shit—electroshock, gene therapy, heavy-duty drugs, sensory deprivation. The basic idea was to make a serum, inject it, and stress the organism into developing certain…talents." Henny shrugged. "You could figure that much out for yourself."

"X-Ray. They work through the entire alphabet to get there?"

Henny's face wrinkled with disgust. "Damn near."

"And that's what Johnson was carrying."

"Data, and maybe the serum formulation. Even if it's just the data, it's too much." Henny had turned pale. "You know eggheads. Once they know something's *possible*, someone'll keep pushing until they replicate it."

Swann's stomach was a pile of acid. "Build a better soldier."

"Intelligence, actually. Can you imagine an IntSec company of Spookies?"

"And what they'd do to get one." Swann's hands and feet had turned cold. His palms greased themselves with heavy sweat.

"If they could verify X-Ray, they might be able to reverse-engineer it, too." Patches of crimson stood out stark on Henny's cheeks, under his stubble. He fuzzed up quick. "Get her in a research facility, piece things together."

"Jesus." Swann's throat was pinhole-size now. "Jesus *Christ*."

"Primary docs disappeared after the drone bombing at Baylock. Primary digitals are wormed; there were papers that seemed to point a way, but those vanished. Administrative fubars, the end of the war confusing everything. The Army doesn't *know*, Swann, and what are the fucking chances that a Baylock internee would survive transit *and* extermination kamps and hook up with raiders? Your close rate was so fucking good, they figured either Spooky was X-Ray or you'd bring back Johnson's serum particulars anyway. Either is fine by them."

"And if we don't? The doctor's spread all over a shitty Montana road, and this one-handed fuck, who knows?"

"Well. Someone might have to take a fall for that one." Henny sighed. "Unless I can pull something amazing out of my ass."

Nice of him to suggest it. "What are the chances of *that*?"

"Not high, Captain Swann. Not high at all."

"Sorry about that." Brunner reappeared in the door. Her shawl was askew and her cheeks flushed to match Henny's. "It's been a morning. Can you show me the mug shot again?"

Swann let Henny unfold the glossy, high-quality paper with their quarry's flat stare peering out at the world.

There was a remedy, sure. With the entire city on the edge from the refugees, it would be easy for an accident to happen. Hell, he could even drop a quiet word to the Reaper, and keep his own hands clean.

But that wasn't what a raider captain did, at least not in Swann's book. This was the kind of mess you cleaned up with your own hands, because one of your own was threatened.

Swann listened to Brunner talk through maybe-recognizing-but-not-really. The coordinator was one of those who had to say it out loud to think it through, and they worked best with a neutral expression and some nonverbal prompting.

Finally, though, she hit on it, and when her leathery face lit up, she turned from mournful into pretty. "Down by the river—I can show you on the aerials—there's a spot where the nodders like to go. One of my informants said there was a guy with one hand asking about getting some horse, willing to pay for it. I'll point out where the shooting gallery is, and if he's been there, they'll tell you." She sighed, rubbing at her temple with one capable hand. "You may have to be...persuasive."

"We'll do our best to be gentle," Henny soothed.

Brunner straightened, fixing him with a general's paralyzing stare. "Don't be. Each motherfucker who shoots up takes resources from the ones who can be helped."

That, Swann thought, was one way of looking at it. Hell, it was probably even the *right* way. But something about it stuck in his craw. "Heard and understood, ma'am. If you can give us directions, we'll be out of your way."

Henny's chin jerked up, and he regarded Swann for a bare moment before bending over the aerial maps and listening to Brunner's clear, hurried directions.

Down by the river, Swann told himself, would be a good place.

He was hoping Henny would take the decision out of his hands.

CHAPTER SEVENTY-NINE

SOME FINE-ASS MEALS

"It's like the war never happened." Zampana took a huge bite of footlong, onions, sauerkraut, and chili sauce. Her eyes closed halfway, a blissful moan catching in her throat, and her knees loosened a little. "Oh *maaaaaaan*."

Spooky hunched her shoulders. The hot dog cart, with its bright yellow-and-red umbrella, was staffed by a sleepy, round woman with an electric smile and warm hazel eyes, keeping to the shade while she dished up a seemingly never-ending supply of don't-ask-what's-in-it tubes and homemade sauerkraut in the shadow of the Cathedral of the Rockies, bombed once by a Firster drone that later plunged into the Boise River trailing a long plume of grayish steam. Pana and Spooky were supposed to check with the needle exchange run out of the church's basement, and they would.

In a minute or two.

"Is it good?" Spooky's head swiveled, checking the street, an oddly birdlike motion.

Pana swallowed a hastily chewed wad. "Sure you don't want some?"

"I'm all right." A ghost of a childish smile crossed Spooky's face, there and gone like a cloud wisp or a Patriot's goodwill. The cathedral was Methodist, but Pana had still crossed herself before setting foot on the steps. That was before she saw the hot dog stand and decided all other considerations were secondary. Spook held a yellow bag of potato chips, and after a few moments opened it with a practiced movement. She peered inside like she couldn't quite believe what it held. "My sister loved these."

"What did you like?" Pana sucked on the straw of her RC Cola, her dark eyes almost rolling back into her head. "Oh *man*, that's good."

"I liked them too." But Spooky's eyebrows drew together, and she shook the bag a little, the rustle of its cargo lost in the sound of a mid-morning crowd and the hurrying of civilian feet. A police gleeson went by, its cells whining, and Spooky ducked her head, a raider's reflex. Dead giveaway in this crowd of soft faces and shiny ration-cloth clothes, but the war was over so it didn't matter.

Pana nodded. "It's okay to change. You know? I loved okra when I was a kid. Couldn't get enough of it. Now I can't stand the shit."

"Okra." Spooky made a face, and Pana's laugh was a bright scarf in the midmorning sunshine. "Do you think anything ever really changes, Pana?"

The older woman considered this, her braids gleaming. It was a relief to see them freshly washed and securely pinned, and to see the face under them unmarked by blood, gunpowder, dirt, or the set look of a medic expecting the worst. "Some things. Maybe not enough, but some." She took another huge bite of footlong. "I could swear, *por ejemplo*, this tastes better than I remember. But the chili sucks ass."

"We're in Idaho. Not exactly the land of habanero."

"Amen. Potatoes and sovereigns." Pana's eyes hooded. *I won't pry,* her eyelids said. *But I'm curious,* her cheeks replied. She took another gigantic, starving bite, but chewed this one much more slowly. "What I wouldn't give for some *queso fresco*. Or some good sauce."

"All I want…" Spooky shook her head. She tweezed out a single golden potato chip, held it in the sunlight. Crunched it with relish, the sting of salt, the oil it was fried in. "Oh. *Oh.*"

"I know, right?" Pana smiled. "Just when I think nothin's left, there's something."

Spooky pulled another one out. She watched as the cathedral doors, atop their high steps, creaked open. A thin trickle flowed up the stairs, mostly older women. Around the side, though, a line of thin-shouldered figures skulked in the shadow of a laurel hedge. The crunch of fried-crisp starch mixed with the salt, and she caught herself making a slow, satisfied noise deep in her throat.

"You and me, *chica*," Pana said. "We gonna eat some fine-ass meals together. But I'm full now, you want some?"

"No thanks." Spooky kept crunching potato chips while Zampana ditched the rest of the footlong. It took everything Spooky had not to run to the overflowing cement-sided trash can. Imagine, throwing food *away*.

If there was a measure of "peacetime," maybe that was it. Plenty enough to waste, and none of the civilians walking past stopped to fish something good out of the bin. Candy husks and filters ringed the bin's round bottom, ground into the dirt, not harvested like tobacco butts would be in kamp.

Was that "peace"? Enough to throw things away when you were full?

Still, Spooky finished every single chip, tipped the leftover fragments carefully into her mouth, and even tore the package open to lick the salt free. Others could throw away good calories. She wouldn't.

But there, in the sunlight, she decided she wouldn't go digging in the garbage for them, either. Not while she didn't have to.

That was her own measure of peace.

"Huh." The skinny flannel-clad man behind the counter at the needle exchange pushed his heavy black-rimmed glasses up on his forehead. "One hand?"

"Left hand's missing," Pana supplied helpfully. "Amputated a little above the wrist."

"Just enough to get rid of a magchip, huh? No wonder he's riding the whitemare." He made a soft clucking noise, tongue-clicking like a grandmother. Behind Spooky and Pana, the line stirred restively. Only a few people waiting looked like fugees—you could tell from the cropped hair and the circles under their eyes, as well as the worn-down soles. Shoe rationing hadn't been necessary on this side of the Rockies. "You know…"

He looked up and past them, at the line. Visibly weighed telling them more. Pana waited, so Spooky did too. So much of life was just waiting.

The man—his name tag read DAVID—finally reached a decision. "I got to hand these out, okay? If you want to wait, I can look through paperwork."

Pana glanced at Spooky, who tipped her head back, staring at the ancient overhead fixture. No electricity rationing, either. It might as well be a different planet on this side of the mountains. When her eyes rolled over slightly, she saw Pana still studying her expression.

Looking for a sign.

So she brought her chin back down and nodded. This, she could work with.

"Can you ask them if they've seen this man?" Pana spread the mugshot out on the tacky plastic counter.

"Sure thing."

The two women sat on a hard wooden bench to one side, watching the line as it moved forward in fits and starts. Spooky's eyes closed most of the way, only a faint glitter under her lashes showing she was conscious. Zampana kept a lookout for amputees. You never could tell when the bastard you were looking for would waltz right into your scope. Chance helped those who helped themselves, and all that.

There were a surprising number of people in line, and some of them were rounder than she'd thought needle-riders would be. Some of them even looked like professional civilians—ties, heels, styled hair. Several brought their used needles in plastic baggies. One girl with wispy black hair had a small zippered pouch with appliquéd rhinestones that gave Pana a pinch under her breastbone, thinking of Minjae.

Min would've had a few more things to say about this fucking state of affairs. Prink probably would too, but he was a bellyacher, and had been from the start.

So many lost. If she started thinking about one, it led her to another, a long bloody chain. Plenty of them had died in her arms, or holding her hand.

That was what "medic" meant.

Spooky was so still Pana almost thought she was asleep. The line showed no signs of diminishing. Glasses behind the desk shot them one or two nervous glances, and Pana was considering whether his was just the usual apprehension of a former junkie or the tension of someone with something to hide when Spooky twitched, her elbow smacking Pana's hard enough to hurt and her head knocking against the wall behind the bench with a soft *thud*.

A thin thread of bright blood smeared across Spooky's upper lip, and her dark eyes were glare-wide.

"Shit, is she OD'ing?" The girl with the appliquéd bag sidled like a horse, and Glasses behind the counter swore.

"She has epilepsy," Pana said, a little louder than absolutely necessary.

"And she's a *soldier*?" This from a man in a gray worsted suit, his own plastic bag held almost hidden near his leg.

"Hey, man." A T-shirted boy with glaring, healing track marks up and down his arms shook his dreadlocked head. "Everyone did their part in the war, man."

"Yeah, like *you* fought," Glasses snorted. "If she's OD'ing, get her out of here."

Someone farther back in the line objected. "This a *church*, man!"

Spooky's eyes opened wide, her pupils dilated so far the irises were a thin ring. They shrank as Pana rose to peer into her face, ignoring the rising noise of commentary. Spooky shuddered, and consciousness returned to her slack expression. *"—hill,"* she mumbled. "On the green hill."

"Spook?" Pana held her shoulders. "You're with me, Spooky girl. It's all right."

"You sure it's epilepsy?"

"Petit mal," someone else said. "Looks like it."

"You a doctor?"

"Trained as a nurse, fuck you very much."

"Hey, no pushing!"

"Hand out the needles, man, I got places to be." A skinny black man pushed up to the counter, glancing at the taped-down mug shot. "You lookin' for him?"

It never rained but it poured, Pana thought sourly, and looked over her shoulder. "Yeah. That's what we're here for."

"Dude has one hand, right? Saw that cracker in the Greenbelt yesterday, askin' around for Billy Bughead."

"Were you looking for Billy too?" Glasses sighed. "Never mind. I don't want to know."

The black man, his corduroy sports jacket once tailored but now a little too big, rolled his eyes. "Man, just give me the needles."

Spooky pushed Pana's hands away, but gently. She rubbed at her upper lip, smearing the blood, and blinked. "He knows," she said. "Go on. He knows."

"Give him his needles." Pana let go of Spooky, turned on her heel. "*Ese*, maybe we should talk outside?"

"There a reward?" The black man swept his packet of steri-wrapped needles off the counter. Glasses looked sour.

"Maybe, if you make us happy." Pana gave Spooky a hand up and made sure she could stand. "Come on."

CHAPTER EIGHTY

DRAGONFLY, CONSCIENCE

Nature was never really quiet. A hush generally meant humans were sneaking around looking to cause some hurt. All that said, it was still kind of peaceful along the river, frogs singing and insects buzzing, birds swooping and the trees rustling while they drank.

Henny didn't make any fuss about taking point. His back, bisected diagonally by the strap of his laptop waterproofer, bobbed as he edged carefully around the worst of the mud, and if his skin crawled at the thought of Swann behind him, it didn't show.

This was a reasonably well-traveled path, full of windings to take advantage of rocks and fallen trunks. Henny even shortened his long strides and took two jumps instead of one, so Swann could fit his stumpier legs into the rhythm.

Nice of him.

They walked in silence for a long while, alert for disturbed undergrowth, footprints, the subconscious tickle of *There's a mine around* or the hair-raising sense that someone was drawing a bead on you through the bushes.

Finally, the trail turned uphill a bit, weaving its way between dense brakes. A dragonfly zipped across Swann's vision, an iridescent jeweled alien with buzzing double wings. Prink might have even known its scientific name. Lazy might have tried to get one to settle on his hand.

Swann's fingertips touched his sidearm.

Lazy. Prink. Minjae. All the ones dead before the surrender, too. Was he going to add one more?

Shit.

Henny reached a small widening in the trail. On the right side, the river had taken a bite from the bank and ran smooth and fast past a screen of wild, thorny canes crumbling into its embrace. A quick shove from the brink would send a body crashing through and into the water.

The Federal halted, edged for the bushes. He pitched forward a little, peering over the brambles like he saw something caught in their flow. He stayed there, and Swann's fingers curled around the butt.

"Go ahead," Henny said, without turning. His hair was no longer buzzed so tightly at the back or sides. In a little while he'd have a raider's fuck-the-regs mop. "If you gotta, Swann, go ahead."

It wasn't like Swann hadn't shot a man in the back before, God knew. Traitors or Firsters weren't worth giving a chance to bite back. "You think I should?" Tossing a body in here…it could be an accident, a refugee armed with something and Henny in the crossfire. Probably wouldn't even be an inquest. It would piss off Henny's masters back in DC, but they were bound to know the doctor was dead already. Maybe he hadn't been carrying any data, or maybe they would find the one-handed bastard and have to make a decision about a goose laying a poisonous golden egg.

"Captain's gotta protect his own." Henny nodded, his shoulders settling. "And this is a pretty place, you know."

It was. You could almost believe the war hadn't happened. Or that it was really over, instead of echoing inside every shattered body, every frayed nerve.

Swann's pocket buzzed. The sound almost lifted him out of his skin, and his bootheel ground down sharply in gravel-laced mud. It was the handheld cell, and if it was doing its dance, that meant someone had something. Or a gigantic problem had reared its ugly head, probably in the Reaper's general vicinity.

When does the killin' stop, he'd asked himself, more than once.

Maybe it was when a man had a chance *not* to, and decided to take it.

"Get away from the edge." Swann fished the buzzing brick out of his jacket pocket, thumbing the screen to pick up. "Could be undercut."

Henny turned, slowly, his hands out and easy. He studied Swann, his expression somewhere halfway between disbelief and thoughtfulness, his black hair messy since branches had combed it during passage.

Pana's voice crackled over the connection, blasting on speakerphone. "Captain? We have something."

"Give it to me."

"Got a fellow who saw One-Hand in the Greenbelt hanging around a junk dealer. Spooky had a sort of seizure, and she keeps wanting to run off southwest. She says there's a cemetery—"

Swann dredged the name out of short-term memory. "Morris Hill."

Pana did *not* sound relieved. "Gotta be, she keeps saying 'the green hill.'"

"Where are you?" Copper adrenaline filled Swann's mouth, his heart giving its usual precombat prepare-to-get-the-shit-shot-out-of-you thump. "Right now?"

"The second needle exchange on the list. Cathedral of the Rockies." Pana swore. "Dammit, Spooky, just *wait a second!* Captain's orders!"

Swann shut his eyes, calling up the terrain.

Henny saved him the trouble. "We're halfway between them and the cemetery."

Swann was suddenly, deeply glad he hadn't pulled his gun. It might make problems later, and the whole thing was a shitbag and a half, but he found, with a cold gush of relief-sweat all over his body, that his conscience was pretty goddamn clear, for once. "Henny, get Ngombe on your phone, have her pick us all up back at those fucking portables. Pana?"

"Yessir?"

"Grab a cab or whatever you can; get over the bridge to Ann Morrison Park. They'll be waiting for you at the gates, all right? Call if you hit any snags."

"Yessir." Pana's relief was palpable. "Okay, Spooky. We're goin' that direction, work your magic and find us a fuckin' cab." The connection cut, and Swann found himself looking at Henny, who stared at his own phone's face, frowning a little as he tapped with his index finger.

Yeah, Phil Swann decided, conscience was clear. If he had to do something about Henny later, he'd do it to his face.

And he'd give the other man plenty of warning.

Maybe that was the beginning of peacetime—the luxury of a conscience. The rest of it might come when they caught this one-handed bastard.

But Swann wasn't gonna hold his breath.

CHAPTER EIGHTY-ONE

FORGOTTEN CORNERS

It was restful, Gene Thomas decided, in its own way.

The southeast corner of Morris Hill was where the buildings clustered, and most of the morons who thought this was a good place to camp were caught around there and dragged back to the Greenbelt or to holding for a night. Some of them skulked around the synagogue—wasn't *that* a fucking irony—hoping for a handout or two, or to slide in during their refugee food hours. But if you were quick, and quiet, you could slip through a loose section of fencing and into the cemetery to the north. If you didn't waltz right down the paved paths like you owned the place, and didn't light a fire, you could find a space to tack up a little camouflage cloth to keep the dew off, especially in the marshy northeast corner. On the other side of the low concrete wall and high iron fence spikes to discourage climbers was a bus stop, and he'd heard the rumbles all night while he tossed and turned under the verminous blanket he'd taken from the degenerate drug dealer's personal stash.

He didn't want to do his first solo cook-and-shoot at night.

The doctor's vials with their high-quality fluid were gone. Billy hadn't had any of *that* shit, but he had a brick of some fairly good stuff. At least, Gene had figured out as much, watching the man conduct business in the Greenbelt. He'd also watched some of the others in the gallery down by the river too, until he was sure he could replicate the process. The itching had faded, but the pain wouldn't go away, and what was worse, he hadn't heard *her* since the bus station. Even if he concentrated, he couldn't quite remember her face. Just words, like *curly dark hair* or *big dark eyes* or *pretty hips*.

The buttons in his head were bleeding, and he needed it to stop.

Midmorning sun thinned out as clouds came boiling in. Looked like rain, but under his cloth he was reasonably dry. Gene hunched, cross-legged, and shaved a little bit off the brick of strange, almost waxy white stuff. A stolen cotton ball went into the bowl of the spoon, and it took three tries to light the cheap birthday candle since he couldn't cup his left hand to shield the flame. Forget matches, he'd had to swipe a candy lighter.

Bubbling down. He had to pull his left leg up and tuck the spoon handle between thigh, knee, and calf, hoping he wouldn't spill the shit. He'd take a hit, and with the craving retreated a bit he could go and sell some of the rest.

Business. Entrepreneurship. The Amerikan way. In the kamps they called it *organizing*, but Gene had never truly liked the word. It was too…prissy.

Working the needle with one hand, he managed to get a respectable few cc's of oblivion loaded up. The wind had risen, and his stomach growled a little. Lunchtime, but he didn't want *food*. A faint faraway noise could have been traffic, or threatening thunder.

Rattling branches. He glanced up, fairly confident his hiding place was secure. The bushes weren't trimmed back here. It was amazing how you could find forgotten corners anywhere. A lot could happen in those empty, ignored places. They had all—Fourteeners, sovereign citizens, Christian culture warriors—been in forgotten places, before McCoombs brought them into the light with a rush. You could be proud to be one of the masters of Amerika for a few years, and Amerika was the master of the world.

Right now, though, Gene was going to see her again. He got the syringe tapped as well as he could, and wrapped the brick back up. Wouldn't do for that to get wet. The birthday candle sent up a tiny thread of cheap wax smoke, black and pungent, whisked away by a breeze full of the green echo of approaching rain.

"Oh," he whispered, pumping his left arm to make the veins pop. "Oh, yeah."

Dark eyes. The curve of her lips. The smell of her nape. The moment in the quarry when she stood up and looked at him, and something blind in her tugged at a string deep in him.

Gene pushed the needle in. His thumb rested on the plunger. He quelled a shiver, anticipation running along his skin, the fine small muscles around body hairs tightening to raise them.

"Hannah," he breathed, and pushed the plunger halfway. Stiffened, his head jerking up.

Footsteps. Drawing closer.

CHAPTER EIGHTY-TWO

AMONG THE GRAVES

"Slow down." Zampana grabbed the back of Spooky's fatigue jacket. "Wait for the Captain, Spook."

Spooky didn't bother saying she didn't fucking *care*. Henny, arguing with the civilian cop at the eastern cemetery entrance among a milling cluster of refugees and other homeless, jabbed his index finger into his palm, emphasizing a point. Swann glowered, but he let the Federal do what he was along for.

It didn't matter. None of it did. Spooky wriggled, tough canvas popped a few stitches but didn't tear. "This way," she said, straining.

It happened quickly. The cop was shaking his head, Spooky's midriff pressed against a barricade bar, Pana attempting to get a better purchase on her coat, the sled's cells making a low throbbing sound as Ngombe lifted it from the middle of a civilian road, pleased she'd been able to land so neatly and doubly pleased she'd been able to scare the shit out of a few cops.

Chuck Dogg, watching the situation with his dreadlocked head cocked at what Simmons would have recognized as his *I don't believe this shit* angle, decided it was time to *do* something, and cleared leather. He pointed his sidearm skyward and squeezed off a shot.

Refugees scattered, pouring across the street that was well and truly blocked now. The civilian cop flinched, Swann almost hit the deck, and Henny flipped out his badge authorization and grabbed the cop by his shoulder.

And Spooky, taking advantage of Pana's dropping into a protective crouch, tore herself away, ducked under the barrier, and took off at a run.

Cursing, scrabbling, ripping a fingernail on the concrete as she pushed herself forward, Pana followed, crossing herself as she lengthened her stride and plunged among the graves. Spooky stagger-stumbled, boots slipping on slick grass because she avoided the paved pathways like an animal conscious of human traffic. Adrenaline gave her the speed her trembling, starvation-wasted and barely rebuilt muscles couldn't otherwise summon. Later, she couldn't really describe what had pulled her on. *It was like a hot wire,* she would say, staring at something in the distance, her pupils swelling a little. *Red-hot, pushed through me and knotted up at my back.*

Zampana would always shiver and cross herself, thinking of small spatters of rain hitting the ground, a fresh rank green scent as the earth welcomed water, a sky-grumble somewhere far away. And Spooky, just out of reach, blindly avoiding standing gravestones and other impediments, her hands stretched out and her face a blank mask of suffering.

Still, it didn't occur to Pana to let the younger woman go.

Not then.

CHAPTER EIGHTY-THREE

COLD KISSES

Bushes rattled. Gene slumped sideways, eyes glazing, heartbeat a slow thundering in his ears like artillery pounding the hills. Something splatted on his lap. A bright, spreading crimson drop on his filthy pants. Another droplet fell, and he watched it change shape in midair like a glob of wax in hot water. A long time ago, there had been lamps like that—he remembered his grandfather had one, and child-Gene had been fascinated until one night when he touched the top and burned his six-year-old fingers.

Learntcha a lesson, didya, Eugene?

The drumbeat in his ears was soft and heavy. His fingers fell away from the syringe, flexing, releasing. He stared, the world a warm hazy blanket.

Finally, after all the struggling and the insect feet and the filth, there she was.

She looked different now. Put on weight, her cheeks rounding, her neck no longer straw-thin. It only made her prettier, and the deep itching inside his head arched and stretched under the claw-scratch of seeing her. Her hair was still short, but it had been trimmed, and blown curls framed her face. Her mouth firmed, and Gene tried to smile.

Here. She was *here*. This hallucination was a good one. He could see the texture of her canvas coat, the tough webbing of her belt, the Federal pistol hanging at her side. He'd wondered what she looked like as a raider, paging through her file when he organized sending her to the sorting shed first, then the brothel after he got one of those rooms cleared of its former inhabitant. He'd had to slip a fifth of good imported vodka to the clerk doing the selektion roster, but the killing bottles could always take one more.

She probably had no idea what he'd done for her since that day in the quarry, when she stood straight and proud as a queen gazing at a struggling worm.

More movement. The camouflage cloth he'd arranged so carefully trembled, collapsed. There was a wide-hipped immie behind her with a dark, round, stupid face, thick ropes of black hair crisscrossing her head. The immie said something he couldn't hear through the thud-thump brushing his ears, and the thought that this was no hallucination struggled through the warm blanket.

His mouth moved, slurring something. The immie bitch looked at him, squatting easily just out of reach. One of her brown hands darted out, snagged the travel belt—when had he taken it off? It didn't matter.

What mattered was that she was here, somehow, and he had a chance to say it again.

I love you. He tried to force the words out. *I came back for you.*

Surprisingly, when Hannah spoke, her voice didn't fade into the thumping. It bypassed his ears, arrowing directly into the center of his head. Crawling in on little insect feet, pushing those buttons again.

"You hurt my sister," she said, her lips shaping the sounds so beautifully. "You *hurt* her."

Sister? What the fuck? Maybe his bafflement showed, because she leaned forward, and she was *touching* him now, her fingers above the stump of his left wrist, bracing him. Her other hand straightened the needle; it pinched through the warm blanket, and Gene realized something was very wrong.

Her eyes had widened, they shimmered. Fat drops slid down her cheeks. Cold kisses touched his fevered forehead, hissed among the leaves. Rain? Or was she crying?

A single, convulsive moment.

Hannah pushed the needle's plunger down the rest of the way, sending the remaining three-fourths of the full syringe directly in.

CHAPTER EIGHTY-FOUR

FOLLOW SUIT

"Luffffoooooo," the one-handed man moaned. *"Lufffffffffooooo."*

Spooky let go of the needle. It stuck up, quivering as the one-handed man jerked, foam working up at the corners of his mouth, his eyes bugging out, his mouth open.

Pana's quick fingers turned the travel belt inside out with little help from her brain; it was reflex to strip a corpse quickly out in the woods. She palmed a small black stick—a jumpdrive, a heavy-duty one. There was cash in there as well, but Pana zipped it back up and tossed it onto the odiferous blanket next to the overdosing man. She crouched, her heart pounding, trying to get enough breath into her heaving lungs.

Spooky crouched too, still clasping the man's stump of a wrist. *You hurt my sister.*

What the fuck did *that* mean? Pana didn't know if she cared just yet. What she did know was that Chuck Dogg was going to be in a heap of trouble for firing on a city street, Swann was going to be pissy, and Henny was a question mark at best when he got wind of this jumpdrive.

Was whatever it held worth all this bullshit? Lazy? Minjae? Prink? Any of the others? Dead raiders, dead patients, bodies giving up in the middle of artillery barrages, soldiers screaming for their mothers—oh, male or female, proud or meek, bullshitter or shat upon, they all said the same thing when *Santa Muerte* came knocking.

Mama! Mother! Mommy!

Movement behind her. Pana watched Spooky as the one-handed man shuddered and choked his last. His eyes rolled up in his head and he fell over sideways, tearing his mutilated wrist from her grasp. A sudden sharp stink of loosened bowels shouted *Someone's dead here*, and his breathing hitched and shuddered to a stop.

Spooky tipped her head back. Her right hand dropped, working at the catch on her hip holster. She got her sidearm free, and Pana thought for a second she was going to put a clip in the bastard from Gloria just to make sure. Which would have been fine.

Instead, the pistol Zampana had scrounged for her on the outskirts of Kamp Gloria rose at the end of a skinny, bent arm, and it became obvious what Spooky was going to do.

She'd found this one-handed asshole, and killed him, and Spooky looked like she'd decided to follow suit.

Another gunshot, its sharp crack end lost under another rolling drive of thunder sweeping down on the city, filled the northeast corner of the cemetery.

CHAPTER EIGHTY-FIVE

SOMEDAY, SOMEHOW

Henny tossed the travel belt aside with a contemptuous obscenity. Rain splattered the bushes, drops gleaming in his hair. "Nothing in that but greenbacks. How the fuck did this guy get any cash?"

"Where there's a will..." Swann crouched easily, going through the one-handed man's ditty bag. A few civilian rags; a battered black Patriot uniform hat with red camp piping; a similarly battered old paperback of *4 Turning*, that bible for fucking Firsters and white supremacists everywhere. Syringes, two in steri-packs that held the blue-and-orange logo of the Fisherman's Needle Exchange Program. There was that brick of whatever-it-was, probably uncut. The asshole was a novice junkie, taking a hit off *that*. How a one-handed fuck had cooked it down and injected it—well, where there was a will, there was a fucking way. "Chuck, anything over there?"

The Dogg, wincing as his leg complained, peered out from between two overgrown bushes. Droplets were caught in his hair too, and he looked thoroughly unrepentant. "Nothin' but a wall and some poison ivy. Sheeeeyit."

"Yeah, well, I'm glad you didn't fucking shoot it."

"I said I was sorry."

Swann refrained from pointing out that while Chuck might have *said* it, he certainly hadn't *meant* it. That would have been unhelpful in the extreme, and if not for Chuck, they'd probably still be arguing with that fat fuck at the gates. Even Henny's patience might not have stretched far enough to deal with that petty-ass Napoleon. "God save us all from rent-a-cops," Swann muttered. The ident in the bag matched up with their quarry, Eugene Robertson or Thomas or whatever the fuck. The thin white lines behind the blond man's ears said plastic surgery. "Pana?"

"Yessir?" Her braids knocked askew and full of leaves, his second-in-command turned her head slightly.

"How's the Spook?"

Spooky, white-cheeked and trembling, hunched next to Zampana. Her sidearm had skittered off into the bushes; Chuck was keeping an eye peeled for it. Finding the two women rolling around fighting over the gun had been a kind of exotic moment, of the sort Swann thought the surrender had left behind them all.

"She's okay." Pana wiped at Spooky's face, a strangely maternal movement. "Guess it was kind of a shock seeing this guy."

"Oh?"

"Knew him from Gloria."

"Shit. Really?" Chuck's head popped up. "Found it," he continued, holding Spooky's gun aloft. "Should I keep this?"

"Spooky." Pana peered into the younger woman's face. "Hey, Chuck's gonna keep your iron for a bit, okay? Just to be safe."

"My sister." The words were raw. Spooky leaned back on her heels. "Lara. *Lara.* I knew I was blown, I went to hide, told *her* to meet the raiders and get out of town. I *told* her to pretend to be me." A dry, barking sob caught in her throat. "She didn't want to. Didn't want to. They caught her. They hung her." She shuddered again, spine arching, her head tipping back. Rain pattered down, stinging-hard, and the thunder grated along, a little closer this time.

The storm was moving in.

"They hung her up. Like laundry." Another sob. *"It was my fault. It was myyyyyyy faaaaaaaaault!"* The words ratcheted up into a scream, and Zampana put her arms around the girl, held her tight as she thrashed.

Chuck stowed Spooky's gun and worked his slow painful way through the bushes, crouched next to them with a grunt, and circled his arms, too.

"Jesus." Swann's throat was dry.

Henny watched this, his eyebrows drawn together and his mouth turned down. He stopped poking through the dead man's bag, and just crouched, his eyes strangely dark, the rain beginning to slick his hair down. When he caught Swann's gaze on him, he shook his head a little. "There's nothing here." He swallowed, his Adam's apple bobbing. "We'll go back to Montana, check the grave."

"One thing at a time," Swann told him, but Henny was already unfolding.

The Fed walked deliberately across the postage-stamp clearing, crouched, and put his arms over Chuck's. Spooky's sobs were an animal's in distress; she shook like a city under bombardment.

Swann straightened. The trapped blood from his legs rushed to his head, turning the world into a wavering underwater facsimile for a few seconds.

When it firmed up, sliding back into the groove of constant pain that was what most living turned out to be, he found himself looking at a huddled family on the floor of a clearing in a cemetery's forgotten corner, holding one of their own and soothing with *Shhh* and *It's all right* and *Let it out*.

That was the first moment Phil Swann felt like someday, somehow, the war might, just might...end.

CHAPTER EIGHTY-SIX

GROUP UP

The airfield had three hangars and a storage warehouse; it was the latter they met at while lightning stabbed the sky and the rain intensified.

"Chetolyne for the gleeson dips," Ngombe said, pointing, her cheeks gleaming with the humidity. "Right in there. Why?"

"Find something to get a drum of it open with, will you?" Swann swung his battered, shapeless hat with its drenched black feather, shooing away invisible flies. He rubbed at his stubbled head, and turned back to Simmons, Henny, Chuck, and Sal. "They was twins."

"Jesus." Simmons had turned pale. "No wonder she's fucked-up."

"Lara, Hannah, I'm not even sure *she* knows which one she is," Swann continued. "Fucking trauma. But I do know a couple things." He gazed steadily at Henny, who held a sheaf of loose papers.

"Well, fucking enlighten me, man." Simmons's shoulders drew up near his ears every time a flash painted the wet pavement outside. Artillery and cannos he could live with, but lightning made him nervous.

"You know we aren't gonna find the data in the doctor's grave." Henny flipped through the useless papers—reports filed, flimsies, plus the scraps and ident blanks the Patriot motherfucker had been carrying. "You know they're going to debrief me hard."

"Is that what you call it?" Chuck's leg was unhappy and he refused to go back to the sled for his crutch, so he made a face each time he shifted his weight.

Zampana hustled through the open bay door, a scrap of parachute silk held overhead to block the rain. Spooky ambled behind her, soaked clear through but not seeming to mind much. She paused, seeing them all gathered, and forced herself forward, stepping carefully in Pana's damp prints on the concrete floor.

"What you gonna say when they do?" Simmons studied the Fed.

So did Sal, whose left hand dropped, resting against his lower back. Once, in Kansas, he'd stood like that, and when the knife he kept tucked behind flickered out it had saved Swann's life.

Was that why Sal stayed? Who knew?

Henny sighed. "The truth." He spread his hands, a quick, placating movement. "That the doctor didn't *have* the data—he was looking to doublecross the Russians *or* the Chinese, whoever he could get to pay, but only if he could get to Alaska fast enough. That Spooky there is nuts from trauma, and she didn't do anything weirder than eat spiders the whole time I was with you. That your close rate's phenomenal because of your direct method of problem-solving."

"Sir?" Ngombe poked her head around a partition. "I got one open, sir. We dipping a cell, or what?"

"Not quite." Swann beckoned. "Come on, you assholes. Group up, but don't breathe the fumes."

The chetolyne drums stood, painted black, the code for *caustic as fuck and flammable too, ya numbnuts* stenciled on top, bottom, and twice on the body in glo-paint. Ngombe had pried the lid of one free, and the tar-black goop inside shimmered, oil-slick colors painted on its surface as it reacted with oxygen.

Swann looked steadily at Zampana, who dug in her trouser pocket. She fished out the slim, finger-long jumpdrive, turned it back and forth, and glanced at her Captain.

He pointed his chin at the Fed.

Pana handed Henny the drive. He freed his left hand and cupped it awkwardly, like he suspected it was trapped.

Maybe it was, but not physically. Sometimes, afterward, Swann wondered who would have made a move if Henny had turned around to walk away. The drum could just as easily get rid of bone, magchip, flesh. Just like the shimmering, caustic bays at Gloria.

But Henny didn't turn. Instead, Spooky shuffled next to him and held out her hand.

He dropped the drive into her palm, and a slight movement went through Swann's Riders.

Spooky held her fist over the chetolyne drum. Ngombe, visibly full of questions, kept her mouth shut and her hands in her pockets.

"Lara," Spooky whispered, and opened her fingers.

The drive's plastic casing began to hiss and bubble. Noxious steam rose, and everyone except Spooky stepped back. Spook watched as the fluid scorched and ate through metal as well, swallowing gigabytes of suffering.

When the bubbling and steaming stopped, Ngombe hefted the drum lid back on, and they took turns hammering it shut. The sound was lost in the thunder, and by the time the rain slacked and the lid was safe and tight, Henny was looking relieved and Sal had brought his left hand out again.

Swann folded his arms, fixing them all with his best head-motherfucker-in-charge look. "I ain't gonna ask if you're with me," he began.

Simmons snort-chuckled, a rich, very amused noise bouncing off the drums and sheet metal ceiling, threaded through with the last thunder roll from what was, after all, only a regular, normal summer storm from the mountain slopes.

"Shit," the Reaper said. "To the end of the line, Captain." He glanced at Spooky.

"To the end of the line," she repeated numbly. Her throat worked as she swallowed, and if her dark eyes weren't quite sane, well, they could figure that out later. *Without* stuffing her in another camp, no matter who was running it.

"Amen to that," Pana added, and crossed herself.

"Y'all are weird," Ngombe weighed in. "But interesting."

Sal just shook his head. He didn't have to say it. Not again.

Chuck Dogg winced again as he eased his sore leg. "Well, what motherfucker we huntin' next, Captain?"

It was on the tip of Swann's tongue to say *I'm retiring*. Spooky's grave, wounded gaze dropped to her feet, and she swayed a little. Something in Swann's chest tightened into a good hard knot.

It wasn't painful. Instead, it felt…steady, for once.

It was Henny who answered. "There's no shortage." He rolled up the papers into a cylinder. Tighter, tighter. "But for right now, maybe we should get something to eat before we get back on the sled."

"Oh *fuck*," Simmons groaned, with feeling, and a bitter little smile creased Swann's face.

ACKNOWLEDGMENTS

This book has had an extremely difficult birth. Thanks are due to Devi Pillai and Miriam Kriss, who fought hard and prevailed; Lindsey Hall and Tim Hely Hutchinson, who bridged several gaps; Sarah Guan, who shepherded a weary writer through the home stretch; and Mel Sterling, best of all writing partners.

Many thanks are also due to the men and women in uniform who generously gave of their time and expertise to a pesky writer with floods of outlandish questions, especially Jeff Davis. Any errors are mine alone.

My children were, as always, unstinting in their support even when my temper frayed from the heat of creation, and it is partly in the hope of a better world for them that I wrote this particular tale.

Last but not least, as usual, thank you, dear Readers. I offer my stories with both hands, and you are kind enough to receive them likewise. Come in, sit down, and let me once again tell you a tale…

extras

orbit

meet the author

Photo credit: Daron Gildrow

LILITH SAINTCROW was born in New Mexico, bounced around the world as an Air Force brat, and fell in love with writing when she was ten years old. She currently lives in Vancouver, Washington.

if you enjoyed

AFTERWAR

look out for

84K

by

Claire North

The penalty for Dani Cumali's murder: £84,000.

Theo works in the Criminal Audit Office. He assesses each crime that crosses his desk and makes sure the correct debt to society is paid in full.

These days, there's no need to go to prison—provided that you can afford to pay the penalty for the crime you've committed. If you're rich enough, you can get away with murder.

But Dani's murder is different. When Theo finds her lifeless body, with a hired killer standing over her and calmly calling the police to confess, he can't let her death become just an entry on a balance sheet.

Someone is responsible. And Theo is going to find them and make them pay.

Chapter 1

At the beginning and ending of all things...

She had not seen the man called Theo in the cards, nor did they prophesy the meaning of her actions. When she called the ambulance they said they would come soon, and half an hour later she was still waiting by the water.

And when she called again they had no record of her call, and gave her the number of the complaints department.

The sun was down and the street lights distant, their backs turned to the towpath. On the other side of the water: an industrial estate where once patty-line men had loaded lorries with bikinis and bras, pillows and sofa throws, percale fitted sheets, gold-plated anklets and next season's striped trend-setting onesies for the discerning customer. Once, the men who laboured there had worn tags around their ankles to ensure that they didn't walk too slow, or spend too much time taking a piss. If they did, there were worse places they could be sent. There was always somewhere worse.

Now there was black spew up the walls, and the smell of melted plastic lingering on the winter air.

A few white lamps on the loading concourse still shone, their glow slithering across the high barbed-wire fences down to the canal. The light made the frost on the bank sparkle like witches' eyes, before being swallowed whole by the blackness of the water.

Neila thought of calling out for help, to anyone in the night, but didn't have the courage and didn't think anyone would answer. People had their own problems to deal with, things being as they were. Instead she wrapped the man up as best she could in old towels she wouldn't miss, hiding her nice, fluffy towels under the bed. She felt a bit guilty about that, and alleviated her doubts by making him hot tea, which he could barely sip. Not knowing what else to do, she sat beside the man on the thin, mud-sunk grass by the gate of the lock and dialled 999 again, and got someone new who said:

"Oh my oh yes now of course yes bleeding by the canal do you have an address for that—no an address—how about a postcode, no I'm not seeing you on my map do you have premium or stand-ard service support for an extra £4.99 a month you can upgrade to instant recovery and full rehabilitative therapies for the—oh you're not insured…"

The call ended there. Maybe a timer cut them off. Maybe there wasn't much signal at the moment. A pair of ducks waddled uneas-ily over crêpe-thin ice, now slipping into the water below, now lurching back up onto the transparent surface above, now flapping at the sound of an eager seagull looking for a snack, now quiet again beneath the thickening blue-brown sky, paddling in listless circles.

at the end and the beginning Neila spins in circles too

The man mumbled, through lips turned blue, "You've been very kind very kind I'm fine I'm sure I'll be fine it's just I'm fine…"

He'd tried saying this before, and fainted, only for a few sec-onds, then woke and picked up where he'd left off, and she hadn't had the heart to tell him that he'd passed out while trying to be so stoical, so she let him talk until he stopped, and they stayed there, waiting, and no one came.

She decided to leave him.

At the precise moment she reached that decision, like a truck driving into a concrete wall, she knew that she wouldn't. The uni-verse crumpled and blew apart, and at the centre of it she exclaimed, "This is fucking ridiculous." She creaked to her feet, pulling him by a limp limb. "Get your backside inside the fucking boat."

She had to help him walk, and he nearly hit his head on the low door at the stern of the narrowboat as she guided him in, and he was unconscious, bleeding out on her white faux-leather couch, before she had got her boots off.

Chapter 2

Time goes a little peculiar
                    when you're not feeling so
        so sometimes you wake and you remember that you will be an old,
old man and that the one you love will die and you can't work out
                    if they die
                              or you first
                    which would be more scary? Who will be
strongest without love, alone, loveless, devoid? What is worse—for
you to lose the one you love or for the one you love to be destroyed
by losing you?

The man on the couch is vaguely aware, when he's aware of
much of anything at all, that he's hit his head and that's making
things a little...

Neila wrung out blood-red water from her third-favourite
tea towel into the mop bucket at her feet, and the bleeding still
wouldn't stop, and there was silence on the canal, and silence on
the water.

In the early years when she had first started sailing, Neila had
thought she'd love the quiet, and for a week after buying the *Hec-tor* she hadn't slept, in terror at the roar of whispers over still water.
The creaking, the lapping of liquid, the insect-hiss of thin ice pop-ping before the bow of a passing boat, the roar of a generator, the
chug chug chug of the engine, the beating of wings, birds not really
built for flight hounding each other half in sky, half on land for
food, or sex, or maybe just something to do.

When exhaustion kicked in, she'd slept like a log, and now she
understood the silence of the canal wasn't silence at all. If anything,
it was a racket, annoying in its persistence.

Not tonight. Tonight the silence made her nervous, made her think too much. She'd come to the canal to get away from thinking. Alone, once you'd thought everything there was to think, there was only being quiet left.

She turned on the radio, and listened to Pepsi Liverpool vs CheapFlightsForU Manchester, even though she didn't really like football.

Chapter 3

At the beginning of all things...

The man lies on the couch, and dreams and memories blur in a fitful crimson smear of paint.

Maybe it hadn't been the beginning, but in his dreams it seems that there must have been a point where it all started, where everything changed. Back when he had a job, back when "job" seemed like the most important thing ever, back in the Criminal Audit Office, before the winter and the snow and the blood, at the beginning there had been...

—it seemed ludicrously banal now, but it was perhaps the place where it all went to piss—

...a training weekend.

The weekend was voluntary.

If you did not attend you would be docked one week's pay and a note put on your file—"BBA." No one knew what BBA stood for, but the last woman to have these fated letters added had been given a job at a morgue, showing family members the corpses of their loved ones.

Besides, everyone knew that team players were happy volunteers.

The Teamwork Bonding Experience cost £172, payable at signup. On the first day he was told to put a cork in his mouth, stand in front of his colleagues and explain his Beliefs and Values.

extras

"Come on, Mr Miller!" exclaimed the Management Strength Inspiration Course Leader. "Enunciate!"

The man called Theo Miller hesitated, hoping the burning in his face could be mistaken for the effort of not spitting out the dry brown bung, bit a little deeper into the cork, then mumbled: "I belef fat ul pepl arg detherfin of jusfic an…"

"Project! Pro-*ject*. Use your whole mouth, use your breath to lift you!"

At night they slept in dormitories on creaking metal beds, and were woken at 5 a.m. for a group run. He enjoyed that part. He stood on top of a hill and watched an eyelash of light peek above the horizon, growing hotter, bending the sky, liked the way the shadows of the trees broke out long and thin across the land, the visible light and visible darkness in the air as fog burned away. The walls of London were too high for him to see this sight, and the places in the country where sometimes he'd gone as a child had fallen to scroungers, and the trains didn't go there any more. For a moment he thought of the sea below the cliffs, and the memory filled his lungs with salty air—then someone told him to stop dawdling, Mr Miller!

So he ran on, and pretended to be out of breath and struggling at the back, where most of the senior staff were, even though he felt like he could have run forever. It didn't do to stand out.

Management joined them at 10 a.m. Management were staying up the road at a golfing resort, but wanted to demonstrate leadership and muck in with the troops. Edward Witt, 37, fresh from Company central office—personal motto "I achieve for me"—roared across the waving long grass, "Come on! Put some welly into it!"

Theo Miller did not smile, did not blink, but concentrated harder on the painted picture of the wooden man before him, drew the axe back over his shoulder and threw it with all his might. He was aiming for the head, but by chance managed to hit it in the nuts.

"Keep going, guys!" barked Edward, bouncing impatiently on the edge of the field as the Fiscal Efficiency Team ran up and down, one statistician suspended by ankles and armpits between two others. "Don't let each other down!"

Theo wasn't sure what all of this had to do with his job. He didn't learn anything about the law, or finance, or governmental good practice. The only colleagues he felt any closer to were the ones he usually hung out with anyway, the hangdog dredges of the Criminal Audit Office who sometimes drank cheap wine on the seventh floor when the lights were out, and didn't go to the pub because they couldn't stand the noise.

If anything, the weekend only served to make office cliques tighter, as friends curled in for mutual support against the horror of the experience, shooting suspicious glances across the muddy field to ensure that everyone was suffering equally, losing all together. Edward Witt prowled up and down, encouraging competition, competition, get ahead, and one or two tried gamely, and Theo was always the third man eliminated in a contest, and penultimate man picked for a side.

It wasn't that he was inept, or even disliked. There wasn't enough personality in Theo Miller for people to love or hate. A psychic had once attempted to read his aura, and after a period of frowning so intense she started groaning with the effort of her grimace, announced that it was puce. Like everyone else from the mystic to the mundane, she too had failed to spot that his life was a lie, or that the real Theo Miller was fifteen years dead, buried in an unmarked grave. So much for the interconnected mysteries of the universe, Theo thought.

So much for all that.

At the end of the weekend they got into a coach.

The coach sat in traffic, covering twelve miles in an hour and twenty minutes, and Theo dozed. One time he saw a woman standing on the hard shoulder, waving frantically at the passing cars for help, but no one stopped, and tears rolled down her face. People didn't like to stop on this stretch of the M3. The security fence kept out most of the screamers, the scroungers and the children from the surrounding enclaves, but Company Police signs reminded all that YOUR SAFETY IS YOUR RESPONSIBILITY, and no one doubted it for a moment. You heard rumours of tax dodgers breaking in through the fence and rushing down into the lanes when the traffic got too slow to crack open boots and steal anything they could, until speed picked up again and they scuttled to safety or were mown down where they stood.

After four hours of snoozing to a soundtrack of inspirational speeches by Simon Fardell, Company ExO, the coach dropped them off at the office in Victoria. The pavements were too narrow for the tired, baggage-slung commuters waiting for their buses, leaves tumbling from the last of the shedding plane trees.

Though it was late, and they were tired and muddy and sore, Edward treated them to a sandwich dinner, held in the semisacred and barely used Large Media Suite, access usually limited to executive grade 2A and above. As they ate thin slices of cucumber between wet pieces of white bread, lights were dimmed, and Edward presented his PowerPoint of Vital Lessons Learned and Where We Go From Here, including a comic montage from the weekend of people falling into mud, dropping their axes and spraining their ankles to lighten the moment and boost team morale.

And when he was done the lights came up
and there were little pink pots of Angel Delight with a single half-strawberry on top and there
was Dani Cumali.

On the canal the man called Theo groans in his sleep and holds the blanket tight, and Neila sits with her head in her hands and wonders what the fuck she's even done

And in his dreams
　　　　　and in his memories
Dani is watching him, and that's where it all went wrong.

In the past
　　　　　These things are a little blurry but he thinks, yes,

in the past, but not that past, the more recent past, the past had already happened, the less important yet more urgent bit of the past that is

(Neila wonders if she should try and give him a blood transfusion, but where the fuck do you even start, times being what they are?)

Dani Cumali stood at the edge of the Large Media Suite in the Criminal Audit Office, and stared at Theo Miller, and that was where the world changed.

Her black hair was cut to a pudding bowl around her ears, her skin devoid of make-up, lines around her mouth, grey and thin, lines between her eyebrows, a cobweb face. Her nails were scrubbed down to thin ridges, she wore the navy blue one-piece of the catering company

and she looked at him

and he looked at her

and they knew each other immediately and without a word.

On the screen was a picture of that time during the weekend when he'd been punched in the face during the self-defence training session and his nose had bled everywhere and wasn't that hilarious our Theo Miller give him a hand

everyone clapped

and Dani saw and knew the truth.

And she knew that she could destroy him, bring down the house of lies, fraud and deceit that he had built around himself, around his name that was a lie, around teamwork bonding experiences and work reports and progress assessments and pension plans and rental deposits and

and the whole lie of his whole fucking life.

She could tear it down with a single word.

And in her eyes was the fire of the righteous and the sword.

In the beginning.

Chapter 4

The man whose name was sometimes Theo Miller had been twenty-two years old when they abolished human rights. The government insisted it was necessary to counter terrorism and bring stable leadership to the country. He'd voted for the opposition and felt very proud of himself, partially because he had a sense that this was the intangible *right* way of things, but mostly because it was the first time his new name had been tested at the polling station, and held up to scrutiny.

The opposition didn't have any funding, of course, and everyone knew that the Company was backing the winning team. But any fleeting disappointment he may have felt when they crumbled to a crushing defeat and the prime minister declared, "Too long our enemies have hidden behind human rights as if they were extended to all!" was lightened by the fact that his identity had held. He had voted as Theo Miller, and it hadn't made a difference, and no one had called his bluff.

He'd still somehow felt it would work out all right in the end.

When they shut down the newspapers for printing stories of corruption and dirty deals, he'd signed the petitions.

When they'd closed the universities for spreading warnings of impending social and economic calamity, he'd thought about attending the rallies, but then decided against it because work would probably frown on these things, and there were people there who took your photo and posted your face online—saboteurs and enemies of the people—and besides, it rained a lot that month and he just needed a morning off.

By then, of course, it was a little too late for petitions. Company men would run for parliament, Company newspapers would trumpet their excellence to the sky. Company TV stations would broadcast their election promises and say how wonderful they were. They would inevitably win, serve their seven years in office and then return to the banking or insurance branches happy to have completed their civic duty, and that was that. It was for the best, the adverts said. This was how democracy worked: corporate and public interests working together at last, for the greater good.

When it became legally compulsory to carry ID, £300 for the certified ID card, £500 fine if caught without it, he knew he was observing an injustice that sent thousands of innocent people to the patty line, too skint to buy, too skint to pay for being too skint to buy. When it became impossible to vote without the ID, he knew he lived in a tyranny, but by then he wasn't sure what there was left to do in protest. He'd be okay. If he kept his head down. He'd be fine.

He couldn't put his finger precisely on when parliament rebranded itself "The People's Engagement Forum," but he remembered thinking the logo was very well done.

Chapter 5

In the Criminal Audit Office, Dani Cumali clears away the remnants of a cucumber sandwich.

In the ancestral home of his family, Philip Arnslade stares at his mother's dribbling form and blurts, "Well so long as she's happy!"

On the canal, Neila is pleased to discover that she's not actually squeamish about head wounds at all.

By the sea, a man who may or may not be a father rages at the ocean.

extras

In the past the man called Theo cycles home from a team bonding experience, and is terrified of the face he has just seen. He didn't try to talk to Dani. Didn't meet her eye again after that initial moment of shock. Fled without a word, chin down, expression fixed in stone. Half ran to his bicycle and pedalled away without bothering to tuck his trousers into his socks.

The queues at the Vauxhall Bridge toll weren't as bad as he'd feared, and the walls of Battersea Power Station were a brilliant cascade of colour bouncing back off the clouds promoting the latest reality TV escapade, huge painted faces pouting brilliant crimson lips into the dark.

He went the long way round, past the giant glass towers of the river, then south, towards houses growing lower and cracked, overgrown front gardens, laundrettes with beige linoleum floors, churches in sloped-roof sheds proclaiming a new Jesus of fire and redemption, a criss-cross of silent railway lines and budget gyms above kebab shops for the men with vast shoulders encasing tiny pop-up heads.

He circled several times before pulling up at the stiff black gate in the crumbling red-brick wall. He couldn't remember what Mrs Italiaander, landlady folded in fuchsia, had said to him when he came through the door—she'd said something and he'd even replied, they'd maybe even had a whole conversation—but the memory of it slipped away in a moment.

He sat on the end of his bed and looked around the room, and saw as if for the first time the paucity of character it contained.

A wooden figurine of a woman dancing.

A painting of light across a misty sea.

A couple of 1950s films where everyone knew what to say and exactly how to say it.

A fern that refused to die.

With Dani Cumali's face overlaying his vision, these things suddenly seemed trivial, pathetic. The revelation jerked him almost to laughter, as the man somewhere beneath Theo Miller, who still faintly remembered the real name he'd been born with, and the hopes he'd had as a child, stared at the farcical illusion of Theo Miller he'd created and realised that in all his efforts to be anonymous he had in fact ceased to be a person whatsoever. The laughter rolled through him for half a minute, then stopped as abruptly as it had begun, and he stared again at nothing.

He sat in muddy clothes on the end of his bed, hands in his lap, and waited to be arrested. In the room next door, Marvin, Mrs Italiaander's teenage son, wannabe rock star, wannabe movie star, wannabe private detective wannabe martial artist wannabe somebody in a nobody world, played drum and bass far too loud and wondered if his mum had known all along that he'd stolen that fifty from her purse.

Downstairs, Nikesh, the other flatmate, who did something for the Company, something in insurance or actuarial or—he was never very good at explaining—cooked chicken so spicy it could burn the top off your mouth and listened to radio with the volume turned right down, too low to really hear, but it was the sound of the voices that Nikesh enjoyed, more than the words they spoke.

After a while—after the first twenty minutes of not being arrested—Theo lay back on his double bed, nearly always slept in by one, and stared at the ceiling. His room was five metres by six metres, luxurious by lodging standards. Theo had lived in it for nearly three years. He'd been renting in Streatham before, but his flatmate had got a job in something that paid more, been given a resident's permit to Zone 1 and moved in with his girlfriend. Theo's civil service salary didn't stretch to a mortgage, not with prices being what they were. Not with times being so...

...besides, he didn't have the papers to live in Kensington or Chiswick or anywhere like that, let alone the cash, so Tulse Hill it had been, two lodgers, a mother and a child pushed into a house built for three. Mrs Italiaander had never raised Theo's rent. She liked the way he cleaned the oven once a month and the new shower rail he'd installed. He was a nice, quiet tenant, and that was a rare thing indeed.

It struck Theo as likely that in three years' time he would

probably be in this same bed, on these same sheets, staring at the same crack running to the ceiling rose. This made him feel

...nothing.

He was masterful in feeling nothing. It was what he did best. He had cultivated the art over nearly fifteen years.

He checked his bank balance for the fifth time in the hope it was something better.

Wondered why the cops hadn't come for him yet.

Realised he had no idea what on earth he was doing with his life, or what the hell he was meant to do now.

Having no idea what to do with himself, he did as he always did and on Monday morning went to work.

if you enjoyed
AFTERWAR

look out for

CORMORANT RUN

by

Lilith Saintcrow

It could have been aliens, it could have been a trans-dimensional rift—nobody knows for sure. What's known is that there was an Event, the Rifts opened up, and everyone caught inside died.

Since the Event, certain people have gone into the drift...and come back, bearing priceless technology that's almost magical in its advancement. When Ashe—the best Rifter of her generation—dies, the authorities offer her student, Svinga, a choice: go in and bring out the thing that killed her, or rot in jail.

But Svin, of course, has other plans...

How far would you go and what would you risk to win the ultimate prize?

I
INTERVIEW
⊰╫⊱

INTERVIEWER: *We are here today with Yevgeny Strugovsky, the acclaimed Rift scientist, who has just received a Nobel Prize for his work in unlocking several Rift technologies. His work has proved a foundation for most of what we know about the Rift's treasures. Thank you so much for joining us today, Doctor.*

STRUGOVSKY: *Thank you, yes. Yes.*

INTERVIEWER: *You must be asked this quite a bit, but it's a good place to start: What do you think caused the Rifts? There are several different theories, including, as it were, aliens. [Laughs]*

STRUGOVSKY: *We have no way of knowing, of course. It would be irresponsible to conjecture.*

INTERVIEWER: *And yet—*

STRUGOVSKY: *All we can say for certain is that one night, eighty-six years ago, there were strange lights in the skies of many countries. Aurora borealis, perhaps. Then, the Event, at a very specific time.*

extras

INTERVIEWER: *Yes, the famous Minute of Silence. Four thirty-seven in the afternoon, UTC+2. The Kieslowski Recording—*

STRUGOVSKY: *Yes, yes. The point is, we cannot even begin to know what triggered the Event until we have ascertained what, precisely, the Rifts are.* Rift *is somewhat of a mis-nomer.* Bubble *is also a bad term;* Zone *would be more precise, but still not quite what we're looking for.*

INTERVIEWER: Rift *is the accepted term, though.*

STRUGOVSKY: *[Coughs] Yes, indeed. The most current the-ory is that these...places, these Rifts, are actually tears in a fabric we cannot adequately measure. It is not Einstein's spacetime, it is not Hawking's and Velikov's layer cake, it is not the Ptolemaic bubbles of earth and air. When we know what fabric is being so roughly torn, we may begin to reclaim those parts of the Earth's surface.*

INTERVIEWER: *Do you believe in reclamation, then? The Yarkers protest that it's against God's will.*

STRUGOVSKY: *Their religion does not interest me. The human race is staring directly into the face of the infinite on the sur-face of our little planet. The frequencies and patterns of the Riftwalls—seemingly random, but we do not have enough data yet—have blinded us to the amazing fact that the energy for them must come from somewhere. The artifacts brought back—*

INTERVIEWER: *—illegally.*

STRUGOVSKY: *Legally, illegally, they are there. And they share this same quality, of clean, near-infinite energy. I say near-infinite because we have not yet managed to dis-cern the half-life of these objects.*

INTERVIEWER: *Can we say "clean" energy, though? The incidences of mutations near Rift borders, the possibility of some radiation we have no means of measuring yet...*

STRUGOVSKY: *Ah, will there be those dying like Madame Curie, of invisible rays in the service of Science? It is perhaps worth the cost. Imagine a world where this energy is free, and we have reclaimed the cities that lay inside the Rifts. The implications for our lives, for the planet, even for travel to other parts of the solar system, now that we perhaps have the fuel to do so, these are what interest me.*

INTERVIEWER: *I see. Can you talk for a moment about the presence of rifters? Most of the data we have has come from those who can enter and leave these zones, these tears in the fabric?*

STRUGOVSKY: *They are mercenaries. It is a sad comment upon humanity that profit is pursued more vigorously than science.*

INTERVIEWER: *But there are some commonalities among them, as your fellow scientist Targatsky has shown.*

STRUGOVSKY: *He is a* psychologist, *not a scientist.*

INTERVIEWER: *Still—*

STRUGOVSKY: *It is the scientists who will solve the Rifts. They must be protected from the mercenaries and the crowds of... [Burst of static]*

2
NURSERY RHYME

⊃╫⊂

How many years ago did they show?
Threescore and ten.
How many they come back aroun'?
Never see them again.
One, two three, four five six,
We all go riftin',
Pick up the sticks!

3
EATEN THE BODIES
⊰╫⊱

First came the screaming, drowning out blatting alarms and the ear-shattering repetition of the recorded containment protocol. The long piercing shriek cut right through concrete, glass, stone, buffers, and skulls. Most of the on-duty rifters instinctively hit the ground, one or two ended up with nosebleeds, and one—Legs Martell, absolutely sober for once—going through containment passed out and almost drowned in the showers. A couple of scientists got a headache, but whether it was from the noise or the rest of the afternoon, nobody could say.

The wedge-shaped leav* should have come over the border and inched slowly to a graceful halt right inside the white detox lines, hovering at the regulation three feet above pavement. It should have then been dusted with chemicals, nootslime,† and high UV to make sure any Rift radiation or poisonous goo was

---
* Antigrav replacement for a sled, forklift, or truck. Larger ones can be used as helicopters.

† A neutral semiliquid (reverse engineered from glaslime) that soaks up any stray Rift energies or radiation.

neutralized. Instead, it zagged drunkenly over the blur,* spewing multicolored flame and spinning as two live undercells tried to cope with one gyro melted and the third cell pouring toxic smoke. The dumb fucks on tower duty even unloaded their rifles at it, probably thinking it was the Return,† the aliens who left the Rift-bubbles all over the surface deciding to revisit and pick up their dropped toys, with the tower guards first in line to be grabbed for experimentation or whatever. The terrified fusillade popped the leav's canopy and gave the fire inside a breath of fresh air.

The resultant explosion shattered every window facing the containment bay. Klaxons were added to alarms and recorded exhortations to *wash twice, dust down, wash again.* Someone got the yahoos in the towers to quit shooting, but by then it was too late. Any evidence of what had happened inside the blur-wall was well and truly shot to shit, and burned for good measure.

Wreckage that had once been a good solid piece of antigrav equipment drifted on its two remaining cells, turning in majestic, lazy circles and burning merrily. The emergency response team had been playing Three High‡ instead of suiting up as soon as something rippled in the blur and the watching rifters hit the alert, so it took them a good ten minutes to get their lazy asses out there. They foamed the whole thing, and someone got the bright idea of setting out a triangle of dampers. When they were switched on, their flat surfaces coruscating

* The shimmering, sometimes almost-translucent border of a Rift.
† Sooner or later, the aliens will come back.
‡ A card game.

with peculiar static-popping blue stutterlight, the leav thudded down, cracking concrete. It was too heavy, as if it had dragged a squeezer*—what the scientists called a localized gravitational anomaly, isn't that a mouthful—out on its back.

There are squeezers and shimmers,† and the pointy-headed wonders call them the same damn thing, when any idiot could guess you'd need to know which was *too much* and which was *too little*. Didn't matter. They kill you just the same. Except there are stories of a rifter surviving a shimmer. You never know.

Anyway, once the foam dripped away, the entire warped chassis of the leav was there, and three shapes glimmered through the smoke. One of them had to be Bosch from the physics department, because one of *that* corpse's legs was two and a half inches shorter than the other. Another one's pelvis was horribly mangled, but it could have been a woman's.

The obvious conclusion was that it was Ashe and the two scientists, with their accompanying sardies‡—who would have been in the secondary, much smaller leav—dead somewhere in QR-715. The gleaming inside the shattered leav was skeletons, turned into some sort of alloy. It took two weeks of patient work by teams in magsuits to free them from the tangle, and they were carted away to the depths of the Institute. Someone did a hush-hush paper on them—the bones were alloy, where the ligaments were all high-carbon flex with an odd crystalline pattern all over. That was the heaviness—the alloy was impervious to diamond or laserik, and incredibly dense. Whatever

---

* A heavier-than-Earth localized gravitational anomaly.
† A lighter-than-Earth localized gravitational anomaly.
‡ Slang, possibly deriving from "sardine" or "Sardaukar."

had crushed the pelvis of the third skeleton had to have been massive, unless it had been done before the transformation.

By then, though, the rifters had already held a wake at the Tumbledown. Anyone who wasn't a rifter got thrown out after the first round, and the next morning saw not a few still-unconscious freaks on the tables or under them, and even more reeling home. Sabby the Pooka got carted to the butcherblock* for alcohol poisoning. Might as well have medicated him for grief, too, since he and Cabra'd been running with the Rat ever since she rolled into town. There was nothing to bury, science had eaten the bodies, and besides, it's what she would have wanted.

That's how Ashe Rajtnik, Ashe the Rat, who held herself to be the best rifter in the world and was certainly one of the luckiest, died. After that, the higher-ups sent a commission. They discharged all the on-duty rifters, and more orders came down: Nothing went into the Rift, anything that came out was to be shot and contained. Afterward, Kopelund once told Morov he'd almost been canned, too, since he'd played loose with the regs to send in even a small research team, not to mention one with a couple leavs.

And yet, a year later, the motherfucker in charge of the complex perched at the edge of the biggest Rift in the world was looking for someone else to go in after the Cormorant.

---

* Free hospital. Generally avoided except by the very poor or very desperate.